VENTURE SCIENCE FICTION SERIES

We All Died at Breakaway Station by Richard C. Meredith
Come, Hunt an Earthman by Philip E. High
Hammer's Slammers by David Drake
Interstellar Empire by John Brunner
The Starwolf Trilogy by Edmond Hamilton
Starhunt by David Gerrold
Sold — For a Spaceship by Philip E. High
Run, Come See Jerusalem! by Richard C. Meredith
Cross the Stars by David Drake
Chronicles of the Star Kings by Edmond Hamilton
The Blackcollar by Timothy Zahn
Space Skimmer by David Gerrold
Speaking of Dinosaurs by Philip E. High
The Timeliner Trilogy by Richard C. Meredith

Series editors, Rog Peyton and Rod Milner

VENTURE
SCIENCE FICTION

INTERSTELLAR EMPIRE

John Brunner

ARROW BOOKS
VENTURE SF

Arrow Books Limited
62-65 Chandos Place, London WC2N 4NW

An imprint of Century Hutchinson Limited

London Melbourne Sydney Auckland
Johannesburg and agencies throughout
the world

First published in Great Britain by
Hamlyn Paperbacks 1985
Arrow edition 1987

Printed and bound in Great Britain by
Anchor Brendon Limited, Tiptree, Essex

ISBN 0 09 938870 7

Contents

ON STANDING ON ONE'S OWN FEET   7

THE ALTAR ON ASCONEL   13

THE MAN FROM THE BIG DARK   141

THE WANTON OF ARGUS   187

ON STANDING ON
ONE'S OWN FEET

Speaking as one who misguidedly thought that writing swords-and-spaceships stories was easy (it used to be, but then I started asking awkward questions of myself), I read both Sprague de Camp's "Range" and Poul Anderson's comment thereon with considerable interest [*Amra* v.2 #33, pp. 4-9]. I got to the point where the latter was accusing the former of modesty in omitting the Krishna-type situation as a legitimate means of mating these ingredients, and realized Poul was doing the same in his turn. Which started me thinking . . . which started me writing this.

There are two more ways, not examined in detail in the *Amra* discussion, in which this paradoxical situation can arise. First, and right under our noses, is the one implied by the horse-doesn't-need-United-Steel argument in respect of modes of transportation. We've had it in scores of After-the-Bomb stories. Modern technology requires an interlocking structure of cohesive and cooperative enterprise which in a catastrophic milieu would vanish and might not reappear in its original form.

I haven't had time to go into this in detail, although I realize on looking back that I've used it as an enormously valuable gimmick in several stories—for instance, in the sequences set on the lost refugee planet in *The Repairmen of Cyclops*. One can select out from a body of techniques a certain rather limited group which are within the competence of a single man or a small team—for example, the Afghan rifles—and provided one condition is met those techniques can then survive as folk knowledge. (Boiling water to eliminate disease germs is the obvious case in *Repairmen*; it's detached from the systematic medicine underlying it and has become a rite diligently performed but without significance for the performer.)

The condition which must be met is this: among the isolated team or community continuing the technique must be at

9

least one cobbler. I mean by that someone who will make do—who can cut through the fog of traditional methods which surrounds most modern technology and see that even if such-and-such isn't available, so-and-so will do the job. What do those Afghans put in their rifles? Cordite? Maybe— if they have a source of supply from a factory. But for all their handcrafting skill, I don't see them processing nitroglycerine over a cooking fire. More likely, they're packing their cartridges with a rather inefficient black powder.

In your post-nuclear-holocaust situation, to give a parallel instance, you'll be able to keep cars and jeeps moving provided you have somebody around who can bake the gas out of wood, or compress the methane boiled off by stable-dung, and plumb a gas-supply into the induction manifold using scrap tubing and insulating tape. Otherwise you'll be feebly coaxing horses off the local racetrack and finding they're no damned good for hauling wagons. (How many people do you know who have the Horseman's Grip and Word? I know exactly one. I know what the secret of it is . . . but where in hell do I get my hands on a piece of foal's caul?)

So: Situation One aforementioned is a catastrophic one, during which for a comparatively brief time a maximal range of incongruities coexist, and a guy with a sword may easily get the better of a guy with a gun simply because the former is an outdoorsy type who last saw his conscience in 1949 and the latter a plump-assed chair-polisher . . . like me.

Let's consider Situation Two now; it's far more stable and leads to many more promising consequences. For my investigations into this area, I can thank Poul—hence my comment about his own excess of modesty. He had a delightful scene in a *Planet* yarn years back, where a sword-swinging spaceman argued that the stars couldn't be light-years apart because he could get from one to the other in a week or two. He'd set up a borderline case of the item under consideration: what one might call an inheritance situation. And the reason why this hasn't been examined more closely in the previous articles in *Amra* is probably because on Earth it's occurred only rarely and over a small area for a short space of time.

To the quick of the ulcer: a society (community, whatever) busy using up someone else's resources and not its own is a perfect setting in which to combine the most contrasting gadgetry. In the story just referred to, and in heaven knows how many more of that sort, the inheritors are the derelict descendants of a star-spanning galactic empire.

Hmmmm . . .

When I was seventeen, I wrote a story which used exactly this background: it was called *The Wanton of Argus* (not by me) and ran in *Two Complete Science Adventure Books*. Recently it was reprinted as *The Space-Time Juggler*. I threw the lot in—every cliché I could think of, from wicked princesses to giant black slaves. So OK, I got paid for it. But when I came back to the setting I'd used, wondering if it would yield another story or two, I began to see some holes in the argument behind the background.

For instance, it takes the resources of a major industrial power to crash a can of instruments on the moon, or to operate an eighty-thousand-ton ocean liner or a fleet of jet aircraft. Unless something incredible happens, and I don't mean a faster-than-light drive, it's going to take the resources of an industrialized planet to maintain a spacefleet. A galactic empire will contain so many planets so highly industrialized and so densely populated that some part of it will survive any major crash and probably make the whole shebang into a galaxy-sized parallel with present-day Earth.

Not good enough. How do we get the local planetary populations down to peasant-agriculture numbers? How do we reduce the odds against knowledge of a fifty-percent-plus area of contemporary (star-flying) technology disappearing altogether over an entire chunk of the galaxy?

I was grappling with this when I wrote *The Man from the Big Dark*. That was OK as far as it went; I got it clear in my mind that the ships were surviving because they were built to last, while planet-bound engineering was mainly the product of the inhabitants, isolated on the fringes of the galaxy, and probably a century or two behind the state of the art at the Hub when the empire collapsed (which brings me approximately level with Asimov in his Foundation stories, though he was using the argument to a different end).

And then I got it, belatedly because as I said the Earthside parallels are extremely rare. I can only think of such instances as people mining ancient monuments for building-stone, and lacking either the patience or the skill to square a true block themselves when the store runs dry.

Suppose the early explorers of the galaxy find caches of starships belonging to a vanished race, in such enormous quantities that they can spread across the stars like seed from a puffball. Good: this provides all the necessary incongruities. You can go as far and fast as you like; you don't take a cross-section of Earthside technology in every ship; and when you get where you're going you start with local resources only. Maybe you don't make a very good job of it. In that case, when some next-door system gets into an expansionist mood you rather welcome being taken over and garrisoned by legionaries who bring advanced medicine (we *should* have invited Mrs. Jones who knows first aid!)—and maybe you do well enough to launch out in the conquest game yourself.

But at no point does human knowledge of the borrowed technology catch up with the application of it. This is no surprise, though—out of the next hundred people you see drive past you, how many do *you* think could change a spark plug or grind a valve? In certain previously advanced areas of the galaxy understanding will be achieved; maybe humans get to the theory underlying the stardrive . . . but where from there? To build the tools to build the machines to apply the theory, and that may take generations.

Then you find you need some Sirian technetium to finish the job, and the Sirian system was closed out last Wednesday by the invaders from Algol and you'd better abandon planet because this is their next stop. . . .

And so on. It leads with satisfying frequency to the picture of Our Hero's ancestors standing in the shade of their gigantic starship sharpening bits of stick and toasting them in the campfire to prod their supper with.

It also led to a thing called *The Altar on Asconel*, and probably more later now I have the background sorted out.

THE ALTAR
ON ASCONEL

I

At last, after almost ten years, the moment had come. He
felt himself ready for the task he had undertaken.

Spartak of Asconel closed the latest of hundreds of books
which he had consulted, drew a deep breath, and gazed
around his cell. Other books were piled high on every shelf;
beside them were tape, crystal, and disk recordings, reels of
microfilm, manuscripts—the winnowings of a decade-long
search through the unparalleled store of knowledge here on
Annanworld.

The switch from student to teacher was as easy as picking
up the microphone of his own recorder and uttering the first
words. Yet it was somehow not easy at all. In one instant he
would change the pattern of his life—not obviously, as when
he left Asconel forever, but subjectively. The realization
brought with it a curious floating sensation, as though he
were suspended in space between two planets.

Abruptly he was impatient with his own reluctance. His
hand closed on the microphone as though seizing a noxious
plant that must be gripped firmly to prevent it stinging, and
he began to speak in a measured voice, not diffident or hesi-
tant, but nonetheless unassured, as if it were a long time since
he last made a dogmatic assertion of the truth.

And that was so. Life on Annanworld centered on a single basic assumption: that mankind knew a great deal, but understood virtually nothing.

"The fall of the Empire," he commenced, and heard in imagination the crashing of worlds like bowling balls being hurled down a skittle alley, "is for most people shrouded in a mystery only less deep than the obscurity attending its foundation, and that although the former event is closer to us in time than the latter by some ten thousand years. The reason in both cases is the same, and so simple that it generally has to be pointed out before it is noticed. It is as difficult to maintain detailed records during a landslide as it is during an explosion.

"The erosive effect of ten millennia has stripped the deceitful flesh from the story of the Imperial rise; today we are fortunate enough to have only the skeleton arrayed before us. We know that we were borrowers; we know that we inherited the abandoned property—most significantly, the interstellar ships—of a people who matured and died in the galactic Hub while we were struggling outward from our legendary planet of origin. We know that this chance bequest allowed our race to spread among millions of stars like an epidemic disease. We know that our reckless habit of spending our resources as though their store were infinite was sustained for the entire lifetime of the Argian Empire by the billion-vessel spacefleet of our mysterious benefactors. Details beyond this bare outline, however, can now almost certainly never be reclaimed. It is as though one were to blink and find a century had passed. Blink now, and man is creeping along the galactic rim, in those areas which were later to be regarded as the home of mutants and pirates—but which, significantly, were and remain the only areas where interstellar ships have been built by human beings. Blink again, and Argus is already a wealthy world, imposing economic domination on its neighbors like Phaidona. Blink once more, and the Empire's writ runs all the way to the Marches of Klareth, and the threshold of the Big Dark."

Now he was warming to his tale, the greatest in the checkered span of human history. His hooded eyes saw other sights than the plain stone walls of the tiny room; the note of uncertainty was fading from his voice. He was scarcely aware of the opening of his door, and did not turn to look at the gray-clad novice who appeared in the entrance.

"So total was the absorption of our borrowings into the

pattern of human development," he continued, "that tens—perhaps hundreds—of billions of people were born and died without being able to conceive an alternative to the structure of the Empire. Yet ... something strained past its limit. Something was overburdened, and broke. And the Empire fell."

The novice, impatient perhaps, moved from one foot to the other; the disturbance caught a fragment of Spartak's attention, and he bowed his bearded head in a brief nod of acknowledgment, though without breaking the flow of his discourse.

"The collapse left more worlds than we can count suspended as it were, in a void between a glorious past and a future so bleak it has been nicknamed, already, the Long Night. Most relapsed toward barbarism; having been dependent for millennia on the tightly knit network of galactic trade they could not support their own populations. Others, somewhat more fortunate, contrived to hold on to a portion of what they had formerly enjoyed, but at the expense of extreme privation and a near-total denial of individual liberty. An example in this category was Mercator, which conquered and then bled two nearby worlds to preserve itself. Again, there were worlds—including Argus itself, the galactic capital—where the dissolution proceeded slowly enough for adjustments to be made without undue violence."

A draft from the still open door stirred some notes before him, and reminded him that the novice was waiting for a chance to speak to him. He began to hurry, wishing to get the whole of his initial argument on record before interrupting himself.

"The purpose of this present work, however, is to make a contribution toward the documentation of the first truly human expansion through the galaxy—one, that is, which does not depend on the leavings of another species. It may never take place; we may have squandered our energies too swiftly, and already be going into a permanent decline. On the optimistic assumption that the present trend is to be reversed, the seeds of such a regeneration may most likely be found on worlds sufficiently far from the cataclysmic effect of Argus's decay to have maintained their society under the guidance of benevolent rulers, like Loudor, Klareth, and the subject of this study: my home world of Asconel."

He put aside the microphone, and the hum of the recorder

died. Shifting his lanky body in its coarse brown robe to face
the intruder, he looked questioningly at him.

"I'm sorry, Brother Spartak," the novice said. "Brother
Ulwyn sent me with a message from the gatehouse. There is
a man demanding to see you who claims to be your brother."

Spartak repressed an exclamation of astonishment and put
his hand to his crisp brown beard. He said, "Ah—well, it's
not impossible. I have brothers, though I never expected to
see one of them on Annanworld. . . . What's his name?"

The novice looked unhappy, and shuffled his sandal-clad
feet on the stone flags. He said, "I'm afraid Brother Ulwyn
didn't tell me."

"What does he look like? Did you see him?"

"I caught a glimpse of him through the bars of the gate.
He's—well, not as tall as you are, and he has red hair. And
there's a long scar down his right cheek, which looks like a
sword-cut." The novice added the final detail eagerly.

"That's not very helpful—all three of my brothers have red
hair and all are shorter than I am, and last time I saw them
none had a sword-scar!"

"He bears no resemblance to you that I could tell," the
novice suggested after a pause.

"That's no help either," Spartak grunted. "I call them my
brothers, but in fact we're half-brothers only. Well, it can
hardly be Hodat, who rules on Asconel, so it must be either
Vix or Tiorin. Does he—? But why am I asking these ridiculous questions? All you have to do is send him in!"

"Unfortunately—" The novice swallowed in enormous embarrassment. "Unfortunately Brother Ulwyn cannot admit
him. He carries a gun, and will not part with it."

In spite of himself, and his oath of allegiance to the principles of his nonviolent order, Spartak felt he was beginning to
grin. "It sounds like Vix," he said gravely. "Tell me, has he
already threatened to burn his way in if the gate isn't
opened?"

"I—I imagine so, from Brother Ulwyn's agitation," the
novice confirmed, and ventured a shy smile.

"That'll be Vix," Spartak murmured, and got to his feet.
"Ten years haven't changed him very much, that's obvious.
Well, I'll go with you and find out what he wants."

They passed through twilit passages, cool for all the baking
heat of noon outdoors, and walked the length of the gravel
paths between the crisp green lawns, the low trees and beds

of carefully tended flowers. Here and there, groups of gray-clad novices—among them an occasional off-world student in gaudier clothing—gathered about their brown-robed tutors, discussing knotty points of human history. Spartak caught random phrases as he passed, but only a few, for without realizing he had quickened his stride till the novice was scuttling to keep up. After all, the appearance of a brother he hadn't seen in a decade—even a half-brother—was event.

At the threshold of the gatehouse Brother Ulwyn came to meet them. That was en event, too; the gatekeeper was stout, elderly, and usually imperturbable. Now his round face was sweat-shiny and his voice wheezed with agitation.

"That—that *ruffian!*" he exploded. "He carries arms all about him! He offered violence to me—to *me*! And on Annanworld! You must calm him, Spartak, and persuade him to enter—already there's a jeering crowd from the village beyond the gate, and more are gathering all the time."

"Let me through, and I'll talk with him," Spartak said.

"But calm him, and bring him in," Brother Ulwyn stressed, reaching for the bunch of keys that swung at his girdle. "Do you know, I think if the peephole had been larger he'd have dragged me through it?"

Moments later Spartak emerged onto the dusty roadway that led up from the village in the valley a short walk distant. As Ulwyn had said, a crowd had gathered on the other side of the road, grinning and chattering. A few paces away from them, sitting on a milestone and looking thunderously angry, was Vix, the sword-scar about which the novice had spoken milk-white on his rage-red cheek. It was small wonder that Ulwyn had been agitated; across his back Vix wore an energy gun which would probably have been capable of razing the gatehouse with a single bolt.

Spartak threw his hood back on his shoulders. Vix stood up. He spoke his brother's name in a strange, uncertain voice: "Spartak—?"

"Yes, it's I. Though the beard is new to my face since last we met."

All the fury, and with it all the spirit, seemed to drain out of Vix in an instant. "So it's true," he said wearily, and spat in the dust before turning with a shrug to ease the weight of his gun and starting along the road toward the village.

II

Puzzled, the gaping country folk fell silent, apart from one who laughed. But he too was silent the moment after Vix had scythed him with a murderous glare.

"Vix!" Spartak cried, and lost the self-control which ten years on Annanworld had ingrained in him. He caught up his robe and closed the distance between himself and his half-brother in a dozen loping strides, the loose soles of his sandals slapping up little clouds of yellow dust. "Was that why you came to seek me out?"

Vix spun to face him and set his hands squarely on his hips. He had to throw back his head to look directly into the younger man's eyes; he was head and shoulders shorter of the two, but made up in muscles like steel springs for his lack of inches.

"I couldn't believe I'd been told the truth about you!" he blazed. "I never thought that the son of a Warden of Asconel would skulk in his hole and make no move to right injustice! Well, now I've had it forced down my throat. I'm off to find Tiorin and see if he still speaks a language with which an honest man needn't fear to foul his mouth!"

"What are you talking about?" said Spartak in icy tones.

Vix's green eyes flashed. "Ah, so you think to save your newly bearded face, do you? What's this—you're claiming not to have heard the news? That's rich! On Annanworld, the university planet of the Empire, where all knowledge is collected and stored!"

Spartak took a deep breath, fighting the premonition that had overcome him at Vix's astounding behavior. He said, "Our business is more with the past, trying to analyze what brought about the downfall of the Empire, than with the present. I've been doing the research for a history of Asconel, but the latest news I've had is—oh—five years old at least."

"Save the sales talk for the yokels," Vix grunted, jerking his head toward the villagers grouped by the roadside. "Well—I'll believe you, because you're my own father's son. And then I'll see what counterfeit metal you hide under that cheap brown robe. Hodat is dead, and—"

"Dead?" Spartak blurted. "When? How?"

And on the instant, so swiftly that he returned to full attention in time for Vix's answer, he felt himself transported back in space and time to their last meeting: in a glade on the royal island of Gard, in Asconel's placid tropical ocean.

They had come together, the three brothers, alone: Tiorin the eldest, Vix the next, and—standing a little apart, because he had been apart from birth, being the child of his father's second wife—Spartak.

For long moments after the departure of the attendants who had accompanied them here, there was no sound except the distant plashing of the summer sea and the quiet humming of insects about their immemorial business of fertilizing the flowers. Spartak used the time to look at his half-brothers and fix them in his memory. He would miss them, despite the fact that they had never been as close to him as they were to each other.

They had the red hair of their mother and the stocky, brawny build of their father; so did Hodat, who was to be Warden of Asconel at noon today. But Spartak had the gaunt tallness of his mother's line, rooted in a past of which even she herself knew little—the late Warden had taken her a year after being left a widower, and then she was only a wandering singer and teacher who had been born twenty systems distant of an unknown father. Younger than Vix by four years, Spartak already had the scholar's stoop, the hooded thoughtful eyes of one much given to study.

Tiorin broke the uneasy silence. He had called the meeting, so the others waited on his words.

"It has all happened so suddenly," he muttered, little above a whisper. There were nods of encouragement.

Suddenly! Spartak thought. Why, only last month ... And now three orphans, himself included. He thought of his mother, gone to death with her lord in the flaming ruin of their lightning-struck skyboat, and found he was picturing visions more horrible than he could bear—a roasted face, from the lipless hole of which came screams.

"I'm sure none of us ever made plans for this day," Tiorin resumed. "Nor Hodat either—except that he knew he was to take the Warden's chair eventually. So this is a matter we've never discussed between us. Now we must face it. Spartak?"

Startled at having his name thus uttered, Spartak raised his bent head.

"You've learned a deal about the fall of the old Empire," Tiorin said. "You know what's happened in many places—

too many—since the prop of Imperial support was withdrawn."

"You mean—" Spartak was groping. "You mean when there was a quarrel over the succession to power? Why, yes!" *So this is what it's all about,* he added silently to himself.

"Now just a moment!" Vix took a pace forward. "Is there supposed to be some notion going around of usurping Hodat's chair?"

Tiorin, who had matured a little past Vix's suspicious touchiness, raised a pacifying hand. "You jump ahead of me, Vix. We've known since childhood that Hodat would one day succeed to the Warden's chair, and I don't think any of us would envy him this task. We've seen from the inside what it's going to be like—an infinity of hard work, a paucity of reward and comfort. But what I'm afraid of is something more subtle than the possibility you mentioned."

He found himself a seat on a chair carved from the living trunk of a tree, and relaxed into it, his hair very bright against the dull brown bole.

"I don't pretend to Spartak's knowledge of what's gone on elsewhere," he continued. "But I've heard stories that frighten me . . . It doesn't have to be the doing of a rival heir which oversets a smooth succession. It might be an independent faction taking someone's name in vain. Vix, you've generaled an army to put down insurrections in the northern islands, and you're pretty well regarded over there."

"I should think so," Vix agreed without a trace of modesty, letting his hand fall to the butt of his sidearm.

"Now suppose in five years, or ten, some discontent arises there, and the rumor goes about that you'll seize power and deliver them from some harsh decree of the Warden—may you not find yourself called to put down a revolt of which you're the patron without your knowledge?"

Spartak felt a stir of admiration at the way Tiorin was broaching this subject to the touchy Vix; he himself could never have found such tact, being unused to the devious paths of diplomacy.

"It could well happen," Vix conceded grudgingly.

"We have nine hundred million people on this planet," Tiorin stressed. "It could happen far too easily! It could happen to me, likewise—I've never disciplined myself as Hodat had to, for I've always assumed he'd live and inherit, and consequently I've been . . . let's say more popular than he was. I've had a lot more fun as a result. But I'd hate to think that anyone could visualize me as a more easygoing Warden, and try to rebel against Hodat in the hope of having me take over. Even you, Spartak, might find yourself in a similar plight."

"Me? How?" Spartak raised his eyes in disbelief.

"I mean no disrespect," Tiorin emphasized. "But your reputation isn't so—so fiery as ours. An ambitious party wishing to become a power behind the Warden's chair might think of you as pliable, a potential puppet. Knowing you as I do, I believe they'd be mistaken. *But . . . !*"

Vix clapped his half-brother on the shoulder with bearlike clumsiness; the blow stung, but Spartak, from long habit, smiled under it. "I'll grant that," Vix declared. "I used to think he was just a milksop, but I've come to have some respect for brains since I've had a man's problems to contend with. He doesn't fool easily, this boy here!"

At age twenty-two, it was Vix's use of the term "boy" which made Spartak wince, rather than the bang on his shoulder. He said, to cover his annoyance, "Well, Tiorin? What lies behind this smoke screen of veribiage?"

"I think we should all leave Asconel," Tiorin said.

Once more there was silence. During it, Spartak thought with an aching heart of a lifetime with this green, hospitable world, its orderly cities, its prosperous commerce, its high reputation among less fortunate neighbor systems, its bleak majestic mountains, and its soft tropical sea. . . . He almost cried aloud: *Not to see Gard again, not to stand and watch the sun go down behind the Dragon's Fangs, not to eat island-caught fish and bread from the plains of Yul—!*

And then he thought of his mother, a wandering singer and teacher who had seen and perhaps loved twenty worlds before she saw and loved the man to whom she bore her son.

He said, in a voice that surprised him by its steadiness, "I think you're right, Tiorin. And I'll go. I've often wanted to visit Annanworld—wished I could have been sent there to school as used to be done in the old days of the Empire. I think I could almost be happy there, among the stored-up knowledge of the galaxy."

"I can believe that," Tiorin said with a wry smile. "And it makes me envy you. For myself, I propose to travel, merely. It will take a long time to blot out Asconel in my heart. And you, Vix?"

They both turned and looked at him. Spartak half expected him to bluster that he would not leave his home—that to be

asked to go was tantamount to accusing him of plotting a
revolution against Hodat. But though some such outburst apparently trembled on the tip of his tongue, it never emerged.

"Well, indeed, what is there to keep me?" he began in a
high angry voice, as though rebuking himself. "It's going to
be a quiet dull place under sober Hodat, isn't it? There's no
more discontent in the north that can't be snuffed out by a
squad of men under a drunken sergeant, and if I pick fights
in the street to pass the time the city guard will haul me in
and my brother—my own brother—will talk to me like a father! And I've had most of the women I ever wanted here,
and tasted all the best vintages, and hunted the few remaining
game animals so successfully we're reduced to mere cubs and
ancient cripples! Yes, I'll go, and with good will, to some
place where they fancy a fighting man—take service, maybe,
with the army of Mercator or go hunting pirates in the Big
Dark. Yes, I'll go."

But he looked desperately unhappy as he stared straight
ahead of him, not seeing the green foliage of the trees.

And all the memory of that final meeting was vivid in one
single second when Spartak hung on Vix's answer ten years
afterward, there beside the stone gatehouse of his Order on
Annanworld.

"Hodat is dead. Murdered," the redhead stressed. "And a
usurper has made himself Warden. And he has brought a
foul cult from no one knows where, and his evil priests lord
it over the citizens of Asconel!"

"But—when? How?" Spartak clutched at the other's arm, a
torrent of questions rising in his mind.

"The news was already stale when it reached me on Batyra
Dap. My first thought was to raise forces and liberate the
planet, but it costs hard cash to hire an army, and I've—not
been so lucky as I hoped." A grim sardonic twist drew up
half his mouth; the sword-slash seemed to have paralyzed the
other side of his lips. "And anyway, by this time Bucyon—
that's his name, mark it well—has by all reports made a
cringing pack of dogs of our once-proud people. I thought
you'd have left Annanworld as I left Batyra Dap, hot on the
news; instead, I've found you here."

"You must tell me—" Abruptly aware of where they stood
on the hot dry road, Spartak broke off. "No, come inside and
take refreshment and tell me there."

"They won't let me in," Vix grunted.

"Not you—the weapons you wear. We're an order sworn to absolute nonviolence; no knife, sword, or gun is permitted inside the gate. But you may safely leave your weapons with Brother Ulwyn, and collect them on departure."

"Much help you'll be," Vix sighed. "To think I came so far, and find you bound by an oath to abjure violence, when that's what it'll take to set our home world free. Still, I'll come with you and tell the tale, and see if the horrors in it stir some spark of love for Asconel after all this time."

III

"A fine comfortable backwater you picked yourself!" Vix exploded. He was in a padded chair in the anteroom of the refectory; the order to which Spartak had pledged himself had a tradition of hospitality to travelers, and it had only taken a word about Vix's journey to the chief steward to produce a meal of cold meats, bread, and fruit such as the Warden himself on Asconel would have been proud to present. Also there was wine aplenty, though not stronger drink nor any of the Imperial euphorics like ancinard. The rules of the foundation decreed a clear head.

"Now I begin to see," the redhead added around the leg of katalabs on which he was chewing, "why you decided to come here rather than be a wanderer like Tiorin and me!"

It was going to take a long time to dispel the hostility Vix had conceived toward him, Spartak realized. And that wasn't so surprising if one reflected on it. After all, at their last meeting at home, Vix had confessed that he had regarded Spartak as a mere milksop, not recognizing until he came of age that the difference in their temperaments which he mistook for cowardice was the mask covering a considerable degree of intelligence. Overlay this lasting childhood impression with the setbacks and disappointments leading up to this encounter on distant Annanworld, and you got an inevitable antagonism.

Determined not to feed it, Spartak said mildly, "Annanword has been as little touched by the disasters associated with the downfall of Argus as was Asconel—less, perhaps. I don't know why it was originally decided to make the main center of galactic learning an isolated world like this—maybe the idea was that it should be free from the hustle and bustle of Imperial affairs—but it certainly paid off in the long run."

"Don't tell me," Vix muttered. "I can see, and taste, all that!" He drained his wine mug and offered it for replenishment to the gray-robed novice waiting on them.

"By the stars, I haven't had a meal like this in five years! And to think I was fool enough to pick a fighting order for myself!"

Startled, Spartak blinked at him. "You joined an order too?"

Mouth full, Vix nodded. "I took service with one of the rump forces left over from the Imperial collapse, full of bigheaded ideas about reimposing galactic rule on the rebellious worlds. But it's all comet-dust. I've slept on the bare ground as often as not, drunk dirty water till the medics had to stick me full of needles and bathe me in rays, collected this scar and others which I can't show in polite company. . . . Ah, but it hasn't all been so bad. I've enjoyed myself in my own fashion, for if I hadn't I'd have dug myself a piece of mud somewhere and planted corn."

He swallowed the last of his food, leaned back in his chair, and burped enormously. Wiping his mouth with the back of his hand, he stared at Spartak.

"You're waiting there very calm and smug, aren't you?" he accused. "I thought you'd ply me with questions all the time I was eating!"

"I was sure you'd tell me in your own good time," Spartak answered peaceably. He was going to have to tread very carefully in his dealings with this irascible older brother, that was plain. "In any case, the shock of hearing Hodat was dead seems to have—" He made a vague gesture. "Chilled my mind, so to speak. I can hardly credit it."

"Ah, you always were a corked bottle. Ashamed to show your feelings in front of anyone else. If you have any feelings, that is." With the solid food in his guts, Vix was reverting to his normal manner.

"I'd like to hear the full story now," Spartak suggested.

"From me you won't get the full story," Vix countered. "I guess no one knows it except those devils on Asconel—Bucyon, and the witch Lydis, and maybe that monster Shry!" He shot a keen look at Spartak. "You flinched when I said 'witch,' and 'devil' too—don't you hold with such terms?"

Spartak looked at the table before him, choosing his words carefully. "There are certainly records of mutations developing possessed of what are generally called supernormal talents," he granted. "Indeed, it was part of Imperial policy for some millennnia to maintain the stability of the status quo by locating such mutations and—if they hadn't already been put to death by supersititious peasants or townsfolk— transporting them to the lonely Rim worlds. There are said to be whole planets populated by such mutations now. But words like, 'witch' have—ah—unfortunate connotations."

"I'll tell you something, *kid brother.* You're talking like your dust-dry books, not like a human being!" Vix gulped another mouthful of wine. "Maybe you've cooped up here so long you've forgotten how to make regular conversation!"

The jab went home. Spartak flushed. "I'm sorry. It's true I've spent more time reading than talking these past several years. But it's been in a good cause," he added defensively, thinking to penetrate the other's hostility. "I'm working on a history of Asconel."

"Faugh! I'm not concerned with the dead past. I'm worried about the future. Don't your books tell you that that's under our control, while the past is what we find it and we can't set it to rights?" Another gulp of wine, and once more the mug was held out for refilling. "Besides, I don't much hold with working at a distance. Asconel is its own history."

"I—" On the verge of a hot objection, Spartak checked. "I'll tell you something, too," he continued after a moment's pause. "That's a far more philosophical remark than I ever expected to hear from your lips!"

"By the nine moons of Argus, if you can't learn something in ten years' traveling, you might as well be dead." Vix put his hand to his waist, as though uncomfortable at the absence of his sidearms. "And I'm not dead. Well, let's not bicker among ourselves. I'll tell you what I can, if you'll agree not to argue about my calling Lydis a witch."

You challenged me on the term. . . . But Spartak bit back the retort. He was now absorbing the important points of what Vix had told him: Hodat dead, a usurper ruling Asconel, some cult with an arrogant priesthood dominating the citizens. All this added up to a frightening whole. He nodded for Vix to go on.

"The reason they call Lydis a witch seems plain enough fo me," the redhead asserted. "Don't you recall Hodat as the most levelheaded of us? Don't you recall what plans he'd made, of his own accord, for his eventual marriage and fatherhood?"

"Surely," Spartak agreed. "He had in mind to make a

formal alliance with some other world which had recovered
well from the Imperial collapse."

"Right. What could have made him settle for a woman
whose very home planet wasn't known?" Vix thundered. "If
that wasn't witchcraft, I'm a— No, I get ahead of myself.
Listen.

"This woman Lydis appeared one day, off a ship from no
one knows where. Somehow, she got herself to the attention
of Hodat, and once they'd met, things went out of control.
He said, so the story runs, that this woman knew his inner-
most thoughts—that she was like a part of himself. Before
anyone knew what had happened, she was being talked of as
his wife-to-be.

"True, for a while things went well enough, I'm told. The
witch Lydis was said to be beautiful, which is a good start for
any woman, although she never appeared in public expect in
a long black gown with a veil over her hair. Like Tiorin foresaw, there was a plot to depose Hodat because of some
decree or other, and allegedly she warned him of it, having
seen into the minds of those who planned it."

"A telepathic mutant," Spartak muttered. "There are said
to be some such. . . . I'm sorry. Continue."

"So far so good. Then the priests of Belizuek started to
come in. It had always been Imperial policy that if anyone
was fool enough to want to spend time talking to idols or the
empty air they should be allowed to get on with it, so under
the guise of religious freedom they were permitted to land.
Hodat started listening to them a great deal. I ought to say
this was some cult to which Lydis herself adhered, by the
way—said it was from her home world of Brinze.

"People started to get worried when the rumor got around
that Hodat was considering adopting this belief himself; when
the word was passed that he might impose it on the whole of
Asconel, people got really alarmed." Vix broke off, noting an
expression of dismay on Spartak's long, bearded face. "Hm!
Taking notice now, aren't you?"

"But— Oh, never mind," Spartak snapped. "Go on!"

"The first and worst of the priests was a man called Shry,
a cripple of some sort in a black gown. By then, Hodat was
completely obsessed with Lydis, and Shry had Lydis's ear. A
new tax was imposed to finance a foundation of Belizuek
teaching and build a temple, and that was just the thin end of
the wedge.

"They say Grydnik was the first person to grow anxious. Remember him?"

"Ah—Port Controller of the main spaceport," Spartak rapped.

"Correct. I knew him well at one time. He started to wonder where these hordes were coming from—there seemed to be a never-ending supply of priests and acolytes and whatever. He checked on this place Brinze in all the Imperial records. There is no Imperial record of any such planet." Vix slapped the table with a look of triumph.

"That doesn't necessarily mean anything. The Empire never embraced the whole of the galaxy, though people generally assume it did. It could be a Rim world, some distance from the Hub." But Spartak felt sweat crawling on his skin.

"And what benefit to Asconel is likely to come from a Rim world probably peopled by pirates and mutants?" countered Vix. "But wait a while longer. I haven't told you the half of it." His face darkened.

"The tax was followed by the extension of special privileges to the priests, the foundation of temples in all the big cities—this thing one year, that the next. And then . . .

"I guess it was the sacrifices which sparked the last resistance in Hodat. Bemused though he was by the witch, he yet had enough love for Asconel and its people to refuse that horrible last step."

"Sacrifices?" Spartak heard his own voice utter the word an infinitely long distance away. "Not—human sacrifices?"

"Human," Vix echoed, and the word seemed to curdle the air of the room. "And it was then, while Hodat yet refused, that Bucyon came from space with a fleet the equal of the one I used to fight with over by Batyra Dap— ex-Imperial ships.

"They took over. They killed Hodat. And Bucyon sits in the Warden's chair with Lydis at his side—she having been the bait dangled ahead of Hodat to lead him to disaster. And Asconel is a ruin of all our father's hopes."

"Is there no resistance to the usurper?" Spartak whispered.

"Some, some. I hear that Tigrid Zen—remember him?—is either in exile or in hiding on one of the outer planets of the home system, trying to find an opening in the net Bucyon has cast around Asconel. But at last hearing, the devils had proved too clever, and there's no spirit in the people to support an uprising."

Spartak get blindly to his feet. He said, "I—I must go and

speak to Father Erton, and tell him I'm called away. And
then I'll fetch my belongings and come with you."

"Well!" Vix studied him. "That's more like the response I'd
hoped for, late though it is. But I warn you, I can't tote all
your beloved books and such around the galaxy! I've grown
used to traveling light in these past ten years."

"My books are in my head," Spartak said quietly, and
went out.

IV

Out in the corridor, Spartak barely paused as he snapped
his fingers at a passing novice. It was the same one, by coin-
cidence, that Brother Ulwyn had sent with the panicky
message about Vix's arrival; he was having a bad day's general duties. Sighting, but obedient enough, he came trailing
Spartak and listening to the curt instructions: *Inform Father
Erton I wish to see him, collect my belongings and pack them
in my cases, have the kitchener prepare two travel packs of
food. . . .*

Their paths diverged just after the last order had been issued, the novice turning right toward the block of cells in
which Spartak had lived since being accepted into the order,
Spartak himself continuing straight ahead toward the library.

He entered the enormous hall with sufficient lack of the
proper ceremony to draw a reproving glare from the Head
Librarian, Brother Carl, in his high pulpit overlooking the entire array of more than five hundred low-walled cubicles. But
he barely noticed that; he was concerned only to spot a vacant cubicle on the master plan-board and make his way to it
as quickly as possible.

There was a place unoccupied at Aisle II, Rank Five. He
almost broke into a run as he approached it. Without bother-
ing to close the door behind him he dropped into the single
chair and punched a rapid succession of buttons on the panel
which formed the only other feature of the tiny booth. One
finger poised to stab the *Presentation* button, he hesitated;
then he decided it was best to have a permanent record, and
run the risk of the knowledgeable library computers swamp-
ing him with a flood of literature. He punched for a print-
out instead of spoken or screened data.

Then he took a deep breath. "Brinze," he said. "Planet, presumed habitable, location unknown."

He waited in a mood of grim expectancy. It was all very well for Port Controller Grydnik, out on Asconel—which was, after all, rather an isolated world—to state that Brinze didn't exist because there was no Imperial record of it. But the records on Annanworld weren't so parochial.

The library disgorged a small plain card, no larger than the palm of Spartak's hand, from the slot at the base of the panel. Dismayed, he picked it up and read it. It ran:

"*Brinze*, planet presumed habitable, location unknown. No data. Request verify basis for question."

He tore the card across and threw it away. "Belizuek," he said. "Religious cult or feature of cult."

The answering card was slightly larger, but not much. On it were the words: "*Belizuek*, title and object of veneration of religious cult introduced to former Imperial space at *Asconel* (q.v.) approximately four years ago. No data on origins. No data on ritual. Unconfirmed reports of human sacrifice posted as *Improbable*."

"Bucyon," Spartak said. "Personal name. Lydis, personal name." Deliberately he refrained from cross-referencing to Asconel. The fact that the library contained information even as meager as what it had given him on this mysterious Belizuek cult had taken him aback; he had imagined that in his ten-year research for his projected history of his home planet he had exhausted every single reference in the entire store.

"*Bucyon*," the third card said, "present Warden of Asconel. *Lydis*, present consort of Bucyon. Unconfirmed reports of usurpation by violence posted as—"

He didn't bother to see under what delicate category the memory of the library had entered those reports. He crumpled the card and tossed it aside in fury.

"I'm an idiot," he growled. "All kinds of an idiot!"

This material the library was supplying to him was nothing more than the siftings of the story Vix himself had just told in the refectory anteroom. Brother Ulwyn, in the gatehouse, must have informed the library as a matter of routine that a visitor from Asconel by way of who-knows-where had arrived, and the library, finding it lacked recent news of that planet, had automatically eavesdropped on this much-traveled stranger. Techniques like these—some of them scarely ever used—had been partially responsible for making Annanworld into the most notable of all the Empire's information centers.

For some minutes after that, he just sat. He had hoped to present a whole stack of data about Brinze and Belizuek to Vix, as some sort of justification for having hidden away in this placid backwater—Vix's gibe was half-true, he had to admit. And it turned out there was nothing in the library but the same rumors, now rendered third-hand.

Wearily, he wondered whether his ostensible reason for compiling a history of Asconel was sound. Was there going to be a renaissance of galactic civilization, based this time on human achievement instead of a borrowed technique of starflight? Or was he simply whistling against the dark? Once, news had come from a million worlds within the year, so swift and reliable was the Imperial communications net. How much had changed! He had told himself Asconel was among the few worlds where anything significant was likely to happen—yet prior to Vix's arrival, his last news had come to him two years ago, and was already three years stale, so that the vaunted library was forced to gobble crumbs of unverified data to bring its stock up to date. . . .

The door of the cubicle was pushed aside, and a startled off-world student was there, carrying a recorder. "Oh! Excuse me, Brother, but this cubicle was shown vacant on—"

"That's all right," Spartak said, rising with limbs that seemed to have stiffened from the passage of a lifetime. "I forgot to shut the door and close the circuit. But I've done what I came to do, anyway."

"You'll forgive me," Father Erton said in his wheezy, ancient voice. He was very old; rumor placed him at well past the century mark. "I should perhaps not say this. We are a center for study and distribution of information, and it's only a courtesy obligation that we place on those who make such extensive use of our facilities as you have done, to recompense us with some original work before leaving." But he loaded the words with a glare, and Spartak, who had always regarded the master of his order with great respect, felt impelled to excuse himself against the implied charge.

"I have no intention of departing permanently, Father," he said. "It is simply that this news—"

"Moreover," Father Erton continued, totally ignoring the interruption, "Brother Ulwyn gives us most unfavorable reports of this half-brother of yours who comes to drag you away. Says he is violent in the extreme. Heavily armed. Scarred from fighting!"

"But Asconel is one of the few—"

"You may have no intention of departing permanently," Father Erton proceeded, as though his ears and mouth were keeping different time-scales, the gap between them amounting to several seconds, "but someone else—for example, the alleged usurper on Asconel—may take no notice of what you plan, and your chance to return will be . . . *pffft!*"

"I'm sorry, my mind is made—"

"And it would be a shame to waste a mind of your caliber on some desperate single-handed attempt to stand against the general tide of galactic decadence. I grant you, Asconel was a great name in Imperial days—but so was Delcadoré, so was Praxulum, so was Norge!"

"Delcadoré still functions as one of the Imperial—"

"Most crucial of all is my final point. If you leave here and while absent infringe the vow you took to renounce all forms of violence, you cannot be readmitted." Father Erton leaned back with an effort and stared at Spartak.

"I am not by temperament a violent person," Spartak forced out, acutely conscious that Father Erton's refusal to listen to a word he had to say had made him long to employ a great deal of violence on his sparse gray pate. "My intention is merely to—"

"Your intention is to throw away ten years of valuable study on a heroic gesture. You may well not return alive, and even if you do you stand the same chance of turning back the calendar as I would have of combating a tidal wave. I understand your attachment to Asconel—why, I myself, after seventy years, still occasionally find myself nostalgic for my own birth-world! And that the appeal comes from your half-brother makes it even more understandable that you should be tempted. Nonetheless, I urge prudence, a night's sleep before your final decision, and—best of all—a reconsideration."

Spartak got to his feet, a cold rage filling his breast. "Now listen to me," he said between his teeth. "You know what's going to happen here? One of these days someone who doesn't give a yard of a comet's tail for some hypothetical Second Galactic Empire is going to remember Annanworld, and he'll whistle up a few score jollyboys with armed starships and knock this pretty study down around your ears. Then he'll pick over the survivors and choose out the girls for raping and some of the novices for general drudgery, and loot the wreckage for enough to last him out a lifetime of luxury. And if this doesn't happen, it's going to be because a few places like Asconel and Loudor and Delcadoré held to the old-fashioned ways, stood up for justice and order and the rule of law, and did their best to keep the pirates and the slavers and the privateers from off your neck!"

Father Erton gazed up at him unblinkingly. He said, "It's taken you ten years, has it, to come around to this way of thinking?"

"No. More like ten minutes. I suddenly started to wonder where our resurgent Galactic Empire is coming from if our Asconels are allowed to go down into barbarism."

"And this was sparked by talking to your brother?"

"Yes."

"You should perhaps have questioned him more closely," Father Erton said. His old neck was getting stiff with gazing up at Spartak far above; he let his eyes drop to the desk at which he sat. "According to what he told Brother Ulwyn when he was trying to threaten his way past the gate, he's been serving with the Order of Argus, which was the rump of the old Imperial Tenth Fleet. They hired out to Mercator for its conquest of those two neighbor worlds it now rules; they sacked three cities on Poowadya in search of —ah—*provisions*, I believe they said; they exterminated the remains of the former Twenty-Seventh Imperial Fleet because the latter had the same aims and objectives as themselves and was making slightly better progress. . . . Rather a poor record, on the whole, for one who wants to save Asconel as a nucleus of a resurgent civilization!"

"I doubt if Vix cares one way or the other, just so long as Asconel is decently governed and prospers by modern standards. I was giving you my reasons, not his."

"Then go." Father Erton sighed. "But remember! If you commit yourself to violence, save the expense of coming back!"

Vix was waiting at the gate, with the novice who had brought Spartak's belongings, Brother Ulwyn hovering nervously in the background. There were three large bags piled on the path.

He hailed Spartak accusingly as the younger man came into view, face dark as a storm cloud. "Hey! I warned you, I travel light! If you expect me to carry this lot for you—"

Spartak shook his head. He had never been strong as a child, and doubtless Vix still thought of him as a weakling; now, though, was hardly the time to explain about the scientific dietary used on Annanworld, which enabeled each individual to realize the maximum strength of his muscles by providing the optimum available energy from his food. He merely gathered the three big bags and slung them together over his shoulder.

"Let's go," he muttered.

Vix gave him a puzzled look. "Listen, if you have any doubts about what you're letting yourself in for, stay put! I'd rather not be trammeled with a reluctant passenger—"

"Don't worry," Spartak cut in wearily. "I'm having second thoughts about staying here these past ten years, not about leaving. Are we going, or not?"

"Why—why, of course. At once!" And the astonished Vix swung around to claim his weapons from the perspiring Brother Ulwyn.

V

They went a considerable distance in silence, with no one else in sight except some children playing on a hilltop. The group of villagers who had been in evidence earlier must have followed Vix up the hill out of mere curiosity.

Spartak was engaged with his own bitter thoughts, and was anyway used to long hours of private study and contemplation, but it occurred to him when almost halfway to the village that it was unlike Vix to hold his tongue so long. He was in the act of turning his head when the older man erupted.

"And this is supposed to be the great place for knowledge and science and everything! Here we are, going on foot in blistering sunshine, dust kicking up fit to make you choke— not a skyboat to be had in that primitive town there!"

"It was—uh—a deliberate policy." Spartak sighed. "You might not think it, but it's possible to get from any point on Annanworld to anywhere else with one full day, elapsed time. And there are spaceports at the corners of an imaginary dodecahedron, providing twelve equally spaced points from which you can go off-world. That was deemed to be fast enough for a planet whose chief concern is the accumulation of knowledge."

"Yes, but—" Vix shrugged. "Galaxy, what am I doing raising complaints? I got started late enough on this whole business; the fact that I have to walk to the nearest transport terminus is just an extra irritation. I have this feeling that I ought to be doing everything at maximum speed."

Spartak didn't answer, and they trudged some half-mile or so farther before he did speak again.

"How—uh—how did you come here? By the regular spacelines?"

"Blazes, no. In this corner of the galaxy, shipping schedules are down to monthly, sometimes bimonthly frequencies. I should sit on my butt while they get around to organizing a crew and lifting their creaky old tubs? No, I have my own ship now."

"Your own ship?" Spartak echoed in surprise. "You've done well. I've not heard of a privately owned starship before."

"Don't picture any ship of the line," Vix grunted. "I have an Imperial scout, probably one of the original ships they tell me we found when we came out into space the very first time. I've never dared compute how old she must be."

"Twenty thousand years," Spartak said positively.

"Twenty—?" It was Vix's turn to be astonished. "Oh, never!"

"If it's one of the original Imperial vessels, it must be. According to what events you take as marking the establishment and the collapse of the Empire, it lasted something between eight and a half and nine and a half thousand years. By the time we came out to collect them, the various artifacts our predecessors left behind were already at least as old as the whole lifespan of the Empire."

"This is something I've never got straight in my mind," Vix said slowly. He seemed to be groping for some subject of conversation which would be sufficiently neutral to let him get to know this stranger-brother of his, who had adopted a way of life so alien to his temperament and yet now had to be his companion and confidant. "I guess you must have put in a deal of study on it—hmm?"

"I did when I first came to Annanworld," Spartak agreed. "I had this overambitious idea that I was going to find out how the Empire originally arose. But the records simply don't exist; no one had much time for documentation when we first stormed through the galaxy, and later on, what little had been recorded was either destroyed or simply rotted away. We've never had the skills required to build something to last ten thousand years. Even an Empire!"

"But—well, at least you can tell me how it is we're still flying ships supposed to be as old as you just said."

"We've made some intelligent guesses. The best and most likely is that at some time later in their own history the people who left the ships behind lost interest in physical activity, and built sufficient ships and some few other items to last out their—well, maybe their lifespan. Or else they went to another galaxy because they'd studied this one from rim to rim and exhausted it and themselves. But they'd built well, and it took us ten thousand years to use up what they left behind."

"It's not used up yet, not by a long way," Vix countered.

"Yes, but what time couldn't do to those ships, we've done deliberately. It costs to buy a ship, but it doesn't cost anything to run one, for they're self-fueling and almost indestructible. The Argian fleet numbered one hundred million vessels at the height of Imperial power, and there must have been almost one thousand times as many as that in service throughout the galaxy. Yet now—as you just said—there are so few ships you may wait a month for passage on what used to be a flourishing Imperial starlane."

"We're building some ships of our own, though—"

"Where? Not in Imperial space, Vix. Out on the Rim, where the Imperial writ never ran. I sometimes think I'd like to go out there, to see what human endeavor can do by itself, without accidental help from a vanished race."

"A long trip without much prospect of reward," Vix said. "Me, I'll stick around the Hub. Numbers like a hundred million can't mean much to a man unless he's prepared to think of planets as grains of dust and human beings as less than bacteria. And no one raised on a world as sweet as Asconel could do that."

Spartak shifted his heavy load to the opposite shoulder. He was a little relieved at what Vix had just said. In the years since they last met, this fiery older brother of his had clearly matured as Tiorin had done, and there was a good chance, he reasoned, of their becoming friends at last.

"Want me to take over one of those bags?" Vix offered now, forgetting his downright refusal to help in carrying them.

"Hmm? Oh—no thanks. They're not as heavy as they look. If I do get tired, I'll tell you."

But Vix hadn't lost all his former touchiness; at the declin-

ing of his help, he put on a scowl and left it there for the
next several minutes.

"How did you—how did you come by your ship?" Spartak
asked eventually, after casting around for some way of keeping the talk moving.

"Took it as my pay after we put down the rebellion of the
old Twenty-Seventh Fleet."

Spartak remembered Father Erton's accusation against the
fighting order to which Vix had pledged himself; he swallowed dryness and was glad when the other left the subject
where it lay.

"That's not all I've picked up, by any means, though most
of what I've had I've spent as fast as I got it. Matter of fact,
I guess there may be some problems if you've fallen into the
ways of these sexless monks you've kept so much company
with."

"You have a girl with you?" Spartak suggested.

"That's right."

"A slave?"

"I don't like the tone of your voice," Vix said sharply. "I
don't pay her regular wages, if that's what you mean, but I
keep her, feed her, clothe her—and she does the chores for
me that a woman usually does for a man. But there are other
reasons why a girl keeps company with a man without being
enslaved. Have you forgotten, cooped up in your hermitage
here?"

"Have you been together long?" Spartak inquired peaceably. He was tempted to correct Vix's mistaken idea of the life
led by his order, but after the row with Father Erton he felt
he no longer held a brief to defend it.

"About five years altogether." Vix brightened a little; they
were in full sight of the transport terminus in the village.
"Ah! From here we can get to the spaceport in under the
hour."

"There she is," he exclaimed, throwing up a proud arm to
point. "The smallest vessel in sight, but mine. Go over and
stow your bags. I have to pay port dues and get clearance—
they still observe all sorts of old-fashioned rules and regulations here."

"Ah—this girl of yours," Spartak ventured. "What's her
name, for when I meet her?"

"Vineta. Don't worry—she knows it's you coming back
with me if anyone off this world does."

Spartak shrugged and made off across the hard gray surface of the port. A great deal must have changed in the last few years, he reflected, for his brother to have secured a ship of his own. Governments of planets, great trading enterprises, and other corporate organizations had owned ships under the Empire; if these bodies were letting go of the items most indispensable to the continuance of galactic trade and communication, decay must have spread far and fast.

There was one exception to the list of ship owners he'd mentally made: pirates sometimes claimed to own their ships absolutely. But he preferred not to linger on that idea.

He came close to the ship now. The access ladder was down; awkwardly he clambered to the top, his bags swinging. He rapped on the door of the lock, thinking: *Twenty thousand years! It is incredible!*

When no one opened to him, he tested the manual lock release. It opened the door for him.

He frowned. It was unlike Vix to risk leaving the ship thus. But if he'd done it, perhaps it was to comply with some regulation such as he'd mentioned—or else this girl of his felt safe on her own. He climbed inside and called aloud. "Ah—Vineta? Are you there?"

But there was no one in any of the accessible compartments of the vessel: control cabin, living quarters, sleeping quarters, even the sanitary facilities were all empty.

He was standing, puzzled, in the control room when Vix came stamping aboard, and forestalled the redhead's questions with a curt sentence.

"She wasn't here when I arrived."

"What? Vineta! *Vineta!*"

The harsh sound reverberated in the hollow hull. No answer came. Vix set to searching, as Spartak had just done, and came back moments later with his face a mask of fury.

"Gone!" he roared. "After all I've done for her, to walk out like this—take to her heels without even clearing out her gear! The little baggage! The little radiation-spawned sweet-tongued—"

"Vix," Spartak said very softly, "are you altogether surprised?"

"What do you mean by that?" the redhead blasted.

"I remember from—from back home. The way you used to treat your women sooner or later turned them against you. And the life you've been leading isn't the sort which would make you any more gentle."

"So you think she just waited till my back was turned and ran for it?"

"Not exactly. But Annanworld had quite a reputation. Isn't it possible that she decided she was tired of a roving life? She'll never have been to Asconel, probably never stopped on any single world with you for more than a short stay——"

"What are you talking like this for? You never even saw the girl!" Vix wiped away sweat that had started on his forehead. "Ach! Go stow your gear in the lower cabin—that was hers, and some of her things are still there. I'm going to ask the port authorities what became of her, and fetch her back by her hair if I have to!"

He gave his half-brother a final withering glare. "Well, move. Or would you rather I left her behind, because it might embarrass you to have my mistress here in such a confined space? Is that why you're trying to talk me into thinking it's my fault? If she was going to run off she could have done it on a dozen other worlds without waiting for this precious favorite of yours!"

Spartak said nothing, but picked up his bags and made his way to the lower cabin as directed.

VI

A frown of self-directed anger pulled his brows into deep furrows over his nose, Spartak glanced around the lower cabin, barely taking in the pathetic few belongings which bore witness to the occupancy of it by the girl Vineta. He had not meant to spark an argument with Vix; it was simply that ten years on Annanworld had accustomed him to going straight to the point in the interests of exposing the truth, and he had largely forgotten how to use tact. He had been shorn of most of his false conceptions of himself, and was glad to have lost them. But it made no odds that Vix had almost certainly treated his girl the same as he always treated women—even beating her occasionally. To have told him that she had probably grown tired of him and run off was a stupid error.

Sighing, he cleared away the miscellaneous junk disposed on the shelves and in the drawers. Without his at first realizing, they made a picture to him: a kind of implied portrait of their owner. This curiously shaped seashell, from some planet where the Mollusca had a copper-based metabolism to judge by the bluish sheen of the lining; this necklet of rock crystal, pink and blue and yellow; this solido of two smiling elderly folk—her parents, possibly?

It wasn't until he came to tall closets in the far corner and found half a dozen costumes hanging there, together with a small stringed instrument which he did not recognize, that he checked and started to think seriously about the conclusions he ought to draw. Even then he went ahead with what he had originally intended—changing clothes, putting aside the brown robe of his order in favor of garments not worn since his arrival on Annanworld, but still a fair fit to his body, whose leanness had remained constant since his late adolescence.

There was a reminder in that stringed instrument of his own mother, who had been a wandering singer and teacher. It was the means of getting a living. Surely that, and the clothing, would not have been left behind, no matter how eager she was to escape Vix and lose herself on Annanworld? And it was still less likely that she should have abandoned small souvenir items, like the solido, which were no burden to carry and presumably held emotional significance for her.

Maybe she went aground to buy something, he told himself at last, marveling how sluggish his mind had been made by the annoyance his disagreement with Vix had caused. *I must tell Vix not to do anything rash*—

In that instant, when he stood with one leg in his old but serviceable breeches of Vellian silk, the ship's gravity went on, and within seconds he felt the surging of the drive. This was not the slickly smooth operation of a large liner, elaborately maintained for the passengers' comfort—like the only other vessels in which he had ever flown space. It was the jarring violence of a scoutship stripped for action, without frills, and seemed to vibrate all the way into his belly, triggering a reflex nausea.

He resisted it in near-panic, thinking what foul company Vix would be if he worked out for himself, many systems distant, what Spartak had just deduced from the clothing still in the cabin.

He struggled out into the corridor, and as he turned from sliding shut the cabin door he caught a glimpse of movement at the foot of the companionway leading up to the control room. It was too brief, and the drive-induced nausea was now too strong, for him to get a clear view of the person who had

gone by, but the obvious deduction was that Vineta was
aboard after all.

He had no time to work out where she might have been
hiding; he was completely unfamiliar with this design of ship,
and if Vix hadn't found her she must have concealed herself
very thoroughly. Or else Vix himself wasn't yet aware of all
the nooks and crannies in his prized new possession. . . .

No, rational thought was beyond him at the moment. Wait
till the drive settled down to free-space operation—that
would be soon enough to solve the riddle.

He was on the point of returning to his cabin when he
heard the cry.

"Spa-ar-tak!"

And the drive went off.

The shock was like a dash of cold water, clearing the fog
from his brain. With reflex speed he made for the companionway, scrambling up it with the agility of a Sirian ape.

The shock was renewed as soon as he saw what was happening in the control room. It was no girl that he had
glimpsed passing this way. It was a man, huge and bulky as a
Thanis bull, his hair wild, his body cased in crude leather
harness and his feet in steel-tipped boots, who now was wres-
tling chest-to-chest with the tough but far smaller Vix, over-
bearing the redhead in a crushing embrace.

Vix tried to butt him on the nose, failed as the attacker
jerked his head back, lost his balance to one of the steel-
tipped boots as it cracked against his ankle, and went slamming down to the floor. He had had no time to draw his
sidearms, obviously—perhaps he'd mistaken the sound of the
stranger's approach for Spartak's—but he'd done well in the
first instance, for a short sword lay at the foot of the control
board: his assailant's, logically, which he had somehow contrived to dash from his grip.

Horrified, Spartak saw the two antagonists crash to their
full length, saw the stranger break Vix's grasp on his right
wrist and force his hand closer and closer to the redhead's
throat. Wild pleading showed in the green eyes, but there was
no breath available for him to call for aid again.

To renounce his oath so soon? To pick up the sword from
the floor and drive it into the stranger's back? It could be
done, but—

And then he remembered, as clearly as if he were hearing
it in present time, the voice of one of his earliest tutors on
Annanworld. "Always bear in mind that the need for vio-

lence is an illusion. If it seems that violence is unavoidable, what this means is that you've left the problem too late before starting to tackle it."

Spartak dodged the struggling men and made for the control board. As he scanned the totally unfamiliar switches, he heard a sobbing cry from Vix—"Spartak, Spartak, he's going to strangle me!"

Time seemed to plod by for him, while racing at top speed for his brother. But at last he thought he had it. He put one hand on the back of the pilot chair, and with the other slammed a switch over past its neutral point to the opposite extreme of its traverse.

Instantly he went heels over head. But he was prepared for this; in effect, he fell to the ceiling like a gymnast turning a somersault, and landed on his feet with a jar that shook him clear to the hips. The universe rolled insanely around him, and through a swirling mist of giddiness he saw that what he had intended had indeed come about. Locked in their muscle-straining embrace, Vix and the unknown man had crashed ten feet to the ceiling as the gravity reversed, and now Vix was on top—and breaking free! For the force of the upside-down fall had completely stunned the stranger.

Spartak reached out, clutching Vix by the loose baldric on which he normally slung his energy gun, and reversed the gravity once more, restoring its normal direction. The attacker slammed to the floor again while he and Vix fell rather less awkwardly; this time, he moved the switch with careful slowness, not exceeding a quarter-gravity till he felt his soles touch the floor.

And then he said, "Who is he?"

"I—I—" Vix put his hands to his temples and pressed, breathing in enormous sobbing gasps. "What did you *do*?"

"I put the gravity over to full negative."

"But—" Vix began to recover. "But—how? Do you know these ships, then?"

"No, I've never seen one before. But it followed logically. There's always an automatic gravity compensator on a starship, for high-G maneuvering in normal space, and it seemed reasonable to expect a manual over-ride on a vessel like this which might get damaged during combat."

"You mean you just took a chance on it, while he was throttling the life out of me?" Vix exploded.

Clearly the redhead had suffered one of the worst frights of his life. Spartak hesitated.

"Why didn't you just pick up his sword and run him through with it?" Vix blasted on.

"Ah—well, if I'd done that," Spartak countered in the calmest tone he could manage, "he wouldn't have been able to tell us who he is and why he set on you. As it is, here he's no more than stunned, and you're alive to ask him the right questions."

"I guess so," Vix agreed sullenly, and gave the dazed attacker a prod in the ribs with his foot. "I look forward to beating some answers out of him, at that. Here, I'll put some lashings on him before he wakes up."

He started to a corner chest in search of ropes.

"I don't think you'll have to beat the information out," Spartak ventured. "I have some stuff with me which will probably make him talk a lot faster than that."

"Such as what?" Vix found a length of braided leather and a short flexible chain, and started to bind the man's limbs.

"I—uh—brought some medical things I thought might come in handy," Spartak said, swallowing hard. Ever since his childhood, fighting and violence had physically upset him, and the glee in Vix's voice as he proposed torturing the man to make him talk had picked up the backwash of the nausea from the drive and redoubled it. "I'll go fetch it right away!"

But first, he told himself, he'd better take a dose of something to calm his own stomach.

He was at the door of the lower cabin, fumbling to open the sliding panel, when he felt the knocking beneath his feet.

Astonished, he stared down at the flooring of featureless metal plates. The knocking came again, more vigorously, and his eyes suddenly spotted a small cluster of bright new scratches at one end of the plate on which he stood.

"By the moons of Argus!" he exploded, and dropped to his knees to lever up the plate and push it aside.

In the compartment beneath him lay the missing Vineta, a crude cloth gag in her mouth, her clothing torn and a huge bruise discoloring the soft olive skin of her right cheek. She was small and slender, but ever so her assailant had had to cram her by main force into the tiny space under the floor.

Frantically he lifted her out and set her on her feet; she stood for a second holding on to him, shaking out her space-black hair, then seemed to recover a little and let go of his arm. He made to remove the gag, but she shook her head and tore it out herself.

"Are you Vix's brother?" she whispered. Her voice was pitifully hoarse.

"Yes—yes, I'm Spartak."

"Is he—?"

"He's all right. He's up in the control room tying up the man who attacked him—and you too, presumably. How did it happen?"

"He had a message sent from the port controller to say he was some sort of official." Vineta swallowed painfully. "And Vix had told me that on Annanworld they had lots of regulations left over from Imperial days, which we'd have to comply with or be delayed in leaving ... so I let him come aboard."

She passed a weary hand over her forehead and then touched the bruise on her cheek, wincing. "Thank you for letting me out," she whispered. "I was so afraid. . . ."

And she turned to hurry in search of Vix.

Spartak watched her go. The rips in her costume exposed much more of her tight, firm body than he cared to see, and a completely irrational envy overcame him against his will, at the thought of the endless succession of beautiful women Vix had enjoyed and abandoned. Contrary to the assumption Vix had made, his order on Annanworld didn't demand celibacy, and even Father Erton had kept up an association with a woman in the same specialization as himself, which had endured for almost thirty years. But his own two or three attempts to form such a relationship had foundered on his shyness and his reluctance to detach himself from his studies.

Now, without warning, he found he was wistful, as if he had left some very important part out of his life.

VII

The last thing he expected to find when he returned to the control room clutching his large black medical case was a full-blown shouting match. But he heard it even before he came in. Vix was bellowing at the girl.

"You realize he could have killed me? You just let him in—opened the lock for him and let him in! You didn't keep a gun on him, or anything sensible like that—oh no, you wouldn't have thought of it!"

"But you told me yourself we had to . . . !" The answer dissolved on a high note which foreshadowed tears.

"What conceivable reason could the controller have to send someone aboard before I got back?" Vix thundered. "I ought to take the hide off you!"

Spartak pushed the door aside, and Vineta ran into him blindly, making headlong for the privacy of the lower cabin. He caught her with his free hand, and spoke sharply to Vix.

"You ought to be ashamed of yourself! Just because you've been scared white, that's no reason to take it out on her. She's had a worse shock than you have—look at that bruise on her! And you know where I found her? Folded up like an embryo in a tiny hole under the floor of the lower corridor! Here," he added in a gentler tone to the girl, looking for a place to set down his medical case. "I'll put something on the bruise and give you a pill to calm your nerves."

She accepted his ministrations dumbly, swallowed the pill as directed, and whispered, "Can I go now?"

"Lie down for a while—you'll be all right." Spartak gave her a comforting pat on the shoulder and stood aside for her to leave.

"I'm—sorry," Vix said with an effort as the door slid to. "You're right, I oughtn't to talk to her that way."

"It's better to think of points like that in advance and not afterward," Spartak answered curtly, and crossed the floor to drop to his knees beside the bound man. "Hmm! How long has he been awake?"

"Awake?" Vix echoed in astonishment. "I thought he was still knocked out."

"Hold it," Spartak rapped, foreseeing that Vix's next impulse would be to kick the man into talking. "Let's see what I can do to loosen his tongue before you—" He reached behind him for an injector and a small vial of grayish liquid.

"What are you going to give him?" Vix demanded.

"It's one of the old Imperial drugs—not really meant as a truth drug, but supposed to bring forgotten experiences back to consciousness during psychotherapy." With deft fingers he loaded the injector.

"Why did you think *that*, of all, drugs, might come in handy?" Vix grunted. "Think I might be precessing with my gyros, maybe?"

"You do take everything personally, don't you?" Spartak sighed. "As a matter of fact, I thought it might help us to find out how this Belizuek cult gets the hold it's supposed to have over apparently rational people like Hodat. There," he added, shooting the dose into the bound man's wrist veins.

"How long does it take to work?"

"A few seconds. . . . Open your eyes, you!"

The bound man complied after an obvious struggle to go on feigning unconsciousness.

"Who are you? Where are you from?" Spartak asked.

"I'm—" Another, equally unsuccessful struggle to still his tongue, and a yielding. "I'm Korisu, and I come from Asconel."

"From—!" Vix took a pace forward in amazed horror.

"What was your mission and who ordered you to do it?"

His eyes fixed open and seeming glazed, the man whispered, "I was sent by Bucyon to track down Vix and kill him."

"Why?" thundered Vix.

"Because he'd heard that you planned to raise an army and depose him, and wipe out Belizuek on Asconel."

"I'm Spartak, Vix's half-brother," Spartak said softly. "Does my name mean anything to you?"

"Y-yes. After I'd found and killed Vix, since I was on Annanworld anyway, I was to locate you and eliminate you as well."

"Has someone been sent after Tiorin?" Vix demanded.

"I—I don't know for sure. I think so. But nobody knew where he was when I left home. There was a rumor that he had gone toward the Hub, to travel in what's left of the Empire. Someone mentioned Delcadoré."

"Then that's where we'll go!" Vix declared, and strode toward the control board.

"Just a moment," Spartak said. "There are some other things I want to set straight. You, Korisu—are you a follower of Belizuek?"

"Of course I am. Everyone on Asconel is nowadays."

Vix uttered a filthy string of oaths.

"What is Belizuek?"

"He is all-seeing and all-powerful. He reads the inmost thoughts of men and no one can stand against him. He's a superior being and men ought to recognize that and serve him."

"Is he a telepathic mutation from human stock?"

"I've never seen him. But the priests say he's different. Superior. Deserving of our worship."

Spartak wiped sweat from his face. "I'm told he demands human sacrifices. Is that true?"

"No, of course not!" Shocked, the bound man tried to sit up, and failed. "The priests say it's blasphemy to call it sacrifice. It's a free-will offering, and it's an honor to serve Belizuek in that way just as in any other."

Spartak's jaw set in a grim line. If in such a short time Bucyon and his consort Lydis had managed to persuade all—or even a substantial part—of the citizens of Asconel that this transcendent rubbish was the revealed and mystic truth, their mission wasn't going to be confined to so simple a task as deposing the usurper and restoring the rightful Warden.

"Where does Belizuek come from?"

"The priests say he's existed since the beginning of the galaxy."

"Then where is Brinze?"

"That's where Shry and Bucyon and Lydis and some of the others come from. But I don't know where it lies."

"Delcadoré," Vix muttered to himself, over at the control board. "I hadn't meant to go so close to the Hub—there are still idiots around there with dreams of Imperial glory, and it's risky. But if that's where Tiorin is said to be ..." He glanced over his shoulder. "I have a course set up now. Anything more you want from him?"

"Not right now." Spartak straightened. "What shall we do with him?"

"Put him where he put Vineta, why not?"

"No, that's too small—literally and absolutely. In a closet we can lock, that would do."

"There's an empty one next to the head," Vix grunted. "I'll help you lug him down there."

Still weary from the mental strain as well as from the physical effort of hauling the reluctant Korisu to his prison, Spartak stole into the lower cabin. Vineta had stretched out on the left bunk, and was sleeping with deep and regular breathing. Near her pillow she had ranged the little objects to which she plainly attached a great deal of value: the shell, the solido, the cheap jewelry. . . .

Spartak put his medical case away and crept out again.

"You again, Spartak?" Vix called as he reentered the control cabin. "Say—uh—I ought to thank you. I guess I was too shaken up to remember. It was very smart, the way you stopped the fight. And it was just as well we tackled him your way and not mine. Apart from anything else, I imagine you're now convinced that I wasn't spinning you a wild fantasy about what's happened on Asconel!"

Spartak shook his head distractedly. "It's incredible," he muttered. "The speed and completeness of the process, to have produced a fanatic like Korisu in so short a time—it almost persuades me that you were right about witchcraft."

Vix hesitated. Then he put out his hand. "Brother, I was of two minds whether to go to Annanworld and seek you out. I wondered if I might not burden myself. But ten years is a slice out of any man's life, and love for a world like Asconel is a bond to bring men together."

Spartak put his hand into the other's grasp.

But the full measure of Korisu's fanaticism did not emerge until much later—until the time when they went to feed him in his cramped prison and found that he had contrived to strangle himself, against all probability, with the braided leather Vix had used to bind his arms. . . .

The shadow of that incredible death still lay over them when they gathered in the control room to watch the planet Delcadoré grow beyond the main ports. To break the intolerable silence between them, Vineta—recovered almost completely from her treatment at the hands of Korisu—spoke up.

Vix, occupied with the controls, tossed an answering grunt over his shoulder. "Ask Spartak—he has the head full of knowledge. I've not followed the progress of events down here toward the Hub. Still too rigid and organized for my taste."

The girl glanced at Spartak rather shyly—they had hardly yet got to know one another during this brief trip, and she had spent most of her time out of the way of both brothers, although Spartak had seen enough to convince him that Vix still at heart regarded women as expendable; currently, he just did not have the time to get himself another if he lost Vineta, and was doing his clumsy best to keep on her right side.

"Well," Spartak commenced, "this was formerly one of the main garrison systems for the Imperial fleet, and when the Empire began to lose its outer reaches this was one of the—the foci, so to speak, on which retrenchments were made. I think it's now effectively a frontier system. The Empire hasn't vanished, of course, but only shrunk to a fraction of its former size."

"That's what's worrying me," Vix interjected. "I've tangled with certain bone-headed parties who seen to imagine the Empire still flourishes. For my part, I think it's now a farce, and will only prove a handicap to some new and more stable foundation."

Spartak nodded in surprised agreement.

At that moment a light sprang up on the communicator panel, and Vix reached over to activate the circuit. A voice boomed out with a ring of crude authority. "Identify yourself and your ship!"

"See what I mean?" Vix muttered wryly, and added more loudly, for the benefit of the distant challenger, "Vix of Asconel piloting my own vessel, on private business and landing on Delcadoré."

"Asconel, hmm?" The voice was as clear as if it came from the next room, even when at lower volume it continued, "Where in all of space is that?"

Other voices, much fainter but quite distinct, chimed in. "Asconel—isn't that where . . . ? Well, it's off toward the Rim anyway, so I guess it'll do. Anything to shift this problem off *my* back. . . . Yes, we'll settle for this one—we don't want to wait till the galaxy freezes just to find a ship bound for the Big Dark or somewhere *really* distant."

Vix and Spartak exchanged appalled glances, and the first voice roared out again.

"Vix of Asconel, you're under Imperial requisition. Do you hear and understand? Your ship is under Imperial requisition. Do not attempt to evade this order, or it will be the worse for you!"

"What does this all mean?" Vineta whispered.

"Right now, that's what it means!" Vix replied in white-lipped fury, and gestured toward the viewport which moments ago had held only Delcadoré, its larger moon, and the stars beyond.

Now, like a monstrous fish swimming leisurely to intercept smaller prey, there loomed the gigantic shape of an Imperial ship of the line, the ancient Argian symbols blazoned at prow and stern, for all the galaxy as though Argus could still issue orders to a million planets, and prepared to back this false contention with the all too real support of firepower equal to the output of a minor sun.

VIII

Fighting and running were out of the question. When the order was given to make a landing on Delcadoré under the escort of the Imperial battleship, Vix—punctuating his pilot work with oaths that seemed to grow fouler by the second—furiously complied, while Spartak tried to console him with the suggestion that at least so far they weren't being told to do anything but what they had intended all along.

Meanwhile, Vineta stood close against him, her large dark eyes fixed as though hypnotized on the hull of the escorting ship, her whole body trembling with the unexpressed terror she felt at the nameless threat the "Imperial requisition" implied.

Spartak's heart lifted, though only briefly, when he saw what forces the Empire could still command—there might be a thousand vessels, he guessed, docked here at what huge illuminated signs still declared to be the Headquarters Port of the Third Imperial Fleet. Then he took a second look at those monstrous hulls, ranged like a forest of branchless metal trees across the concrete plain, and realized he had failed to make an obvious deduction. The Empire, by all accounts, was struggling against decay and rebellion all through the galaxy—why then were so many ships out of the sky at one place and one time? And he began to spot the clues which accounted for their presence: gashed hulls from distant battles, plating removed by the hundreds of square feet to expose the vital equipment within which was being cannibalized to maintain those ships still capable of flight.

Maybe somewhere out near the Rim there was a world where ships stood like this in vast numbers, but not antiques used to the limit by reckless commanders—new ships, human-made, ready to bring inward to the Hub those who for ten millennia had been harried away from the Argian domains and had bided their time on the threshold of intergalactic emptiness, waiting for the inevitable collapse.

If there were much a world, he thought, it would be worth hunting for. The shadow of an idea crossed his mind, and was dispelled immediately by the arrival alongside their own vessel of officials from the port controller's staff.

Vix vented his anger on them in a single blast of abuse and

complaint. They ignored him as they might have ignored a
breath of wind. Spartak, urging Vix aside, attempted to tackle
them on a more rational basis, inquiring the authority for
"Imperial requisition" and contesting the legality of giving orders to non-Imperial citizens.

The officials sighed and produced guns. It seemed that this
had become the standard substitute for argument on Delcadoré.

All three of them were taken—for Vineta refused to stay
alone aboard the ship after her experience on Annanworld—
to wait in a large, light anteroom outside the office of the
port controller. There was no one else there apart from a
man of early middle age, who to their horror lacked both a
leg and an arm. They could not refrain from staring at him;
on a world returning to barbarism after the withdrawal of
Imperial support, such a sight might have been expected, but
Delcadoré was supposed to be an outpost of the still viable
Argian civilization.

The man cracked a bitter smile as he saw their eyes covert-
ly turning on his injuries.

"I'm not pretty any longer, am I?" he rasped. "Well, not to
wonder at that! If you'd been picked out of an airless wreck
the way I was, you'd have . . ." A fit of coughing interrupted
his angry words, and racked his body for a good minute before he could answer Spartak's tense questions.

"Oh, sure they'll fix me up sooner or later. But that can wait,
they tell me. I'm the only survivor from my whole team, and
all they want to know is where they went wrong. I'm going to
tell 'em, too! Without mincing my words!"

"What happened?" Vix snapped.

"Fools—gas-brained fools! I could have told them. . . ." The
man's eyes were unfocused, staring through the wall at a far-
away disaster. "Hiring pirates, that's what they've hit on as
their latest brain wave! A whole Imperial fleet revolts under a
commander who thinks he can do better than the mud-heads
we have in charge at the moment—and who's to say he
couldn't? Sometimes I think *I* could! And what do they do to
combat this? They hire a ramshackle bunch of pirate ships,
thinking to keep them from pillaging some Imperial planet
this way, send out a command echelon to give the orders —
that's where I got involved—and sit back and pour some
more ancinard. And what happens? Exactly what any school-
child would have said: you can't give pirates orders, so they
break and run, and the Imperial-trained rebels pick them off

like scooting watersliders, and then the Imperials-that-were loot the very planet the pirates were aiming for, to make up for the inconvenience and minor losses they suffered!"

"Which fleet?" Vix demanded.

"The Eighteenth." The injured man stared at him. "What other did you think it was?"

"What do you mean, 'what other'?" Vix countered. "The Twenty-Seventh is wiped out, as I well know—but it could have been the Tenth, or the Fortieth, or the Forty-Second, or—" He broke off, the other man's eyes burning at him.

"Are you sure?" the cripple whispered, after glancing around to make sure there was no one else in earshot.

"Of course. I've just come from Annanworld, before that I was at Batyra Dap, and before that Poowadya, and before that—"

"All these fleets are still operating? In revolt, but still operating?"

"At the last hearing, yes. Bar the Twenty-Seventh, as I mentioned."

"The liars," the cripple whispered. "The dirty, double-tongued, deceiving, damnable—"

"Vix of Asconel!" a speaker cried from the wall. "Go to the door which will open on your right. Bring your companions with you."

Puzzled at the cripple's reaction, Spartak lingered to put a final question to him, and got the answer he had half expected but was barely able to credit. If a high-ranking officer of the crack Third Imperial Fleet had been lied to about the fate of so many other fleets, lying must have become the general policy of the rump Empire. How long could it stand on falsehood? He had envisaged another century or so before its prestige diminished to the point at which rebels and outlaws were tempted clear down to the Hub—ultimately perhaps to Argus itself. But if they were already so desperate at the reduction of their loyalist forces that they were hiring pirates as mercenaries, the word would travel fast, and the next time the Empire would find pirates and rebels combined against it; there would be an end to futile shifts like trying to make the two enemies destroy each other.

Gloomy beyond description, he found he had followed Vix and Vineta into the adjacent office, and there confronted a podgy, gray-haired woman in a uniform encrusted with meaningless decorations and ostentatious badges of rank.

"Sit down," she said tonelessly. "Which of you is Vix, the alleged owner of the ship we've requisitioned?"

"Alleged!" Vix purpled again. "I have clear title—"

"I'm not arguing." The woman sighed. "If you want to go into legalisms, starships are by definition Imperial property and only leased to corporations, trading companies, or—save the mark—individuals." Her mouth twisted as though in disgust. "But where would it get me to rely on a thin argument like that? I imagine you're competent to handle the ship, and if I wanted to commandeer it I'd have to pick someone equally skillful, and that's not easy because next thing you know he'd be headed for the great black yonder. . . ."

Spartak found himself suddenly pitying the woman, for she had defined herself instantly by what she had said: a weary official trying to keep things going while chaos battered at the structure of law, order, and principle by which she had to be guided. He signaled Vix to be quiet, and leaned forward.

"May we know your authority?"

The woman blinked heavy lids at him. "Frankly, I'm not sure which capacity I'm acting in right now—I have so many jobs I sometimes lose track. I sit in this room as assistant immigration supervisor, Delcadoré West/North Sector. I have the requisition on your ship as Acting Transport Director, Imperial space, Delcadoré volume. And I'm under orders from the Planetary Government, Department of Public Order, and legally empowered to represent them."

"We have business here," Spartak said. "If we could know what you want our ship for, we could perhaps—"

"To the Big Dark with your business," the woman said. "I have a solution to one fiddling little problem out of about ten thousand waiting for me to deal with, and I'm not disposed to compromise."

"Now you listen to me!" Vix burst out. "First off, my ship is mine and I'm not handing it over to anyone who still has delusions of glory about the Empire! Second, my business here is important not only to me but to my home planet, and I'm not going to be cheated out of it. And third—"

"Oh, shut up," the woman said. "Third is probably going to be something about not being an Imperial citizen. You're an Imperial citizen if you were born an on any planet which was ever part of the Empire, and Asconel was—your Warden still holds his fief from Argus, and his space fleet too."

"The blazes he does! The present Warden's a usurper, and

he brought his fleet with him from some world called Brinze which the Imperial records don't show!"

"I wouldn't know." The woman shrugged. "Don't think I have time to keep up with what's happening on backwater planets like that, do you? What's left of the Empire generates enough problems to keep my attention fully occupied. So swallow this, and digest it at leisure.

"We have a girl here who can apparently read minds—a mutant, obviously. We could have let her be stoned to death, I guess; things are nearly that bad already, even on Delcadoré. But when we can we cling to the Imperial rules, because they're better than anything else we have, and the Imperial rules say we keep the status quo by putting her out of the way on some habitable planet off toward the Rim.

"In the old days we could have assigned her passage on regular liner routes, under Imperial guard and protection to make sure some superstitious knothead didn't assassinate her before she reached where she was sent. According to my best information—which I'll share with you since you're from way out anyway—there isn't a single commercial routing left which would get her to a Rim system in less than a year. Coordination has gone to hell, schedules aren't reliable, and pirates are picking off so much traffic the lines are closing down or flying only in armed convoy.

"So you'll have to do. I'm having this girl brought here from wherever the blazes she's been kept, and the moment she arrives you're going to take off and head for—what's the name of that place?" She pushed a stud on the arm of her chair and consulted a small screen set at an angle beside her. "Ah, yes—Nylock. I picked it because it's comparatively close: a straight-line route from here to the Rim."

Vix was half out of his chair with rage. "You can't do this!" he thundered.

"Be grateful," the woman said stonily. "I could have sent you anywhere—out the far side of the Big Dark, come to that! How do you fancy your chances with the pirates in that volume, hey? Used to take three Imperial battleships to get across there safely!"

Spartak, controlling himself better than Vix but nonetheless white-hot inside, forced out, "What right have you to make the requisition anyway?"

"Argian decree," the woman said. "If you want the number and text I'll get it for you, but it runs to seventy figures and two full recording crystals, and seeing it won't make a grain of difference. I don't care for your business on Delca-doré, I don't care for your complaints and objections—all I care about is getting shut of one irritating problem."

She stabbed another stud on her chair-arm, and the doors of the room slid back.

"And don't think, either, that there's an easy way to avoid doing as you're told—dumping the girl in space when you get out of our jurisdiction, for instance, and trying to sneak back here. You'll be welcome to conduct your business when you've finished ours. And to make sure you do—"

Soft footfalls sounded behind Spartak's chair, and he half turned to see menacing uniformed figures there.

"We condition you," the woman said. "You won't be able to be comfortable or happy or sexually potent or even sleep properly from now on unless you're directing all your efforts to the completion of the mission on which you're sent."

IX

The efficiency of the conditioning process was flawless: impersonal as a mechanical repair, thorough as the work of a first-rate surgeon. Spartak, who knew something of this and related psychological techniques from his wide researches on Annanworld, had hoped to offer at least token resistance to the drugs and hypnotic instructions employed on him. But it was useless. As though a shutter had snapped down over his brain, he blanked out, and on reawakening he found he could recall nothing of what had happened except at the two extreme levels of his awareness. Consciously he knew he had been conditioned; subconsciously he was disturbed, as it were by an itch, that was already intense and would grow to be unbearable if he did not at once comply with the Imperial order.

He was appalled beyond measure. If this experience was anything to go by—and he felt it was, for the odds against a random sample in a society organized on a multi-billion population basis like the Empire being anomalous were tremendously high—it appeared that the chief tools of the Imperial power had been reduced to lies, propaganda, and the threat of obliteration.

Small comfort, in view of that, to know that the galaxy

now held forces too strong to be impressed by the last of those three instruments!

And perhaps worst of all was the fact that they were so confident of the reliability of the conditioning that they permitted him, Vix, and Vineta to return to the ship without escort, knowing that until the telepathic girl was delivered to them they would sit and wait, and once she arrived they would helplessly depart for Nylock, the only place in the galaxy where they could be sure of release from the imprinted command.

"Is there nothing we can do?" Vix pleaded for the tenth time. His courage in regular combat, his habitual assertive self-confidence availed him not at all when faced by a weapon as subtle as this conditioning. It had perhaps been an inspiration on the part of the gray-haired woman to cite sexual impotence as one of the consequences of failing to comply with her decree; in any case, Spartak was reminded of a theory he had once formed about this red-haired half-brother of his. Vix's insatiable demand for women was a way of compensating for the fact that he was youngest of three brothers, much alike—he needed women's attention to reassure him about his own individuality.

For a long moment Spartak didn't reply. All he would have said would have amounted to the same as he had already repeated over and over. He knew of nothing that could be done without psychological assistance as skilled as what the Empire could draw on, and it couldn't be obtained without putting the ship into space for some other, friendlier world—and once in space, the compulsion would be far too strong to withstand.

The pause gave Vix a chance to think of something else: Vineta was weeping silently in the corner of the control room, her face pale and drained of hope. Vix rounded on her.

"Stop that sniveling, woman!" he blazed. "I can't do anything about what's happened—can I? Control yourself and stop crying as if I'd been beating you!"

"Vix!" Spartak snapped. "You ought to stop taking your frustration out on the poor girl! It can't make much difference to her where you drag her away to—Nylock and Asconel are both meaningless names to her. If she's in tears it's for your sake, not her own."

The cloud of gloom lifted momentarily from Vineta's perfectly shaped features, and she found the energy for a sad

smile of gratitude at the intervention. Beside himself, Vix retorted, "I suppose you're glad of this, are you? Glad we're
being sent to some back-of-beyond planet instead of to Asconel where we belong! There's fighting there—or will be—
and you have no stomach for it!"

Spartak clung grimly to the shreds of his own temper. The
abstract principles inculcated in him on Annanworld, though,
were very hard to apply under present circumstances.

"How long did you spend burrowing in your piles of stale
knowledge?" Vix sneered. "Ten years, isn't it? And does nothing you learned in all that time tell you how we—?"

He was interrupted by a bang on the outer door of the
lock. Hardly stopping to draw breath, he charged away on a
new line of complaint: "Now our time's up—they've brought
this telepathic mutant along and the moment she's aboard
we've lost our last chance to figure out a way of staying on
Delcadoré and tracking down Tiorin!"

The idea struck Spartak that having a mind reader close to
him frightened Vix as much as being sent far away from Asconel. Superstition, merely—or the fear of having some secret
misdeed revealed? For himself, he knew he would welcome
thin consolation in this opportunity to find out the truth behind all the rumors which he had heard. The policy of depor-
tation which the Empire had instituted to insure itself against
wild factors in the peoples it ruled by imposing statistical av-
erages on them had worked well, but it had also fed the
imaginations of the ignorant.

He got to his feet. Somehow he wasn't so sure as Vix that
the mutant girl was waiting at the entrance. He would have
expected a call from the port controller and perhaps some
triggering command to reinforce the conditioning of their
minds, not a simple knock without advance warning.

He unlocked the panel and slid it aside.

The person who met his gaze was a little man, apparently
very nervous, with protruding teeth and wide startled eyes.
He held tight to the guardrail around the narrow platform, as
though he were afraid of losing his balance and crashing to
the ground.

He said in a squeaky, eager voice, "Is this the ship from
Asconel?"

Spartak nodded, and the nervous man was infinitely relieved, even going so far as to take one hand from the rail he
clutched.

"Please! May I come inside and discuss a proposition with you?"

Spartak hesitated, then stepped back and gestured that the other should pass him. Vix, from within the control room, called out fiercely to know what was going on.

But the nervous man would not say anything further until he was safely in the control room himself. Then he drew himself up importantly.

"My name is not of any consequence," he commenced. "It is in fact Rochard, but I am representing a—uh—a third party who is very desirous of securing passage to your planet. For some time he has had his agents making inquiries at all the spaceports on Delcadoré, asking about ships from Asconel and nearby systems, offering a generous fee for a flight there. Yours is the first such ship to come to my notice since I was requested to assist him."

Vix and Spartak exchanged astonished glances. Then the redhead pursed his lips as if to spit.

"Can't help him," he snarled.

Rochard put his hand suggestively into his belt-pouch, and there was the mellow jingling noise of solid Imperial coin. He said, "I'm instructed to make a very liberal payment in advance, and then my—uh—principal will guarantee double the old commercial rate for the distance. You'd be well advised to—"

"It's nothing to do with money," Vix broke in. His shoulders bowed, and he turned half way from Rochard. "Go look for some other vessel. If I could, I'd cheerfully take him to Asconel and not ask one circle for the flight—that miserable world needs outsiders to visit it and view its present plight! But it's out of the question."

Bewildered, Rochard renewed his original offer, his wide alarmed eyes seeking a clue to the refusal. Abruptly Vix whirled and clamped a hand on his wrist.

"Out! Or I'll throw you out. You can't take no for an answer, can you? I guess you're losing a fat bonus for finding us, hey? Well, have your argument with the woman who sits in the port control building yonder!" He added a vivid and obscene description of her.

"Just a second," Spartak whispered. His mind had been buzzing ever since Rochard's entrance with a wild, fantastic notion. Even now he was reluctant to utter it, but he felt he must.

"This 'principal' of yours—he isn't by some miracle a man called Tiorin of Asconel?"

Rochard started. "Why, you know him!" he blurted. "How do you know him? I was forbidden to name him to anyone."

"Don't you see a resemblance between him and this man who holds your arm?" Spartak rapped out. The success of his million-to-one probe had shaken him, physically, so that he was now trembling with excitement. As for Vix, he was so started he had completely forgotten to release his hold on Rochard.

"Why—I guess so. But there are many worlds where one genetic strain has dominated others and produced a general likeness between many people."

"This is no accidental resemblance. You're looking at his full brother Vix. And I'm Spartak, his half-brother."

"Amazing!" Rochard breathed. "Why, for this he'll pay me double—tremble—ten times what he promised! Please let me go," he added cringingly to Vix. "I must carry the news to him at once."

"It still won't help much," Spartak grunted, silencing a threatened interruption from Vix with a lift of his eyebrows. "We've been put under Imperial requisition, and conditioned to take a mutant girl to some place called Nylock. You must be well in touch with what goes on around here—what can we do to get out from under this?"

Rochard's face fell. He said, "Oh, no. . . ." The two words were like the sighing of wind through bushes in a cemetery.

"Is there someone we can bribe to have the conditioning reversed?" Spartak urged. "Is there anyone we could go to for counter-conditioning?"

"How about Tiorin himself?" Vix snapped. "What's his situation here? How's he fixed for contacts, government influence, things like that?"

Rochard spoke so rapidly he was almost babbling, his gaze apparently riveted on the imaginary spectacle of a fat reward disappearing into space. "Your brother is in no position to help you either! He's not meant to be on Delcadoré at all. You see, some short time ago there came a man from—I think—his own world, yours too of course, an assassin, from whom he barely escaped. Since then he's been in hiding, and only some few trusted agents have been told he's still here; for the sake of any more would-be killers, the news was passed that he had left for Argus to raise aid against the new rulers of Asconel."

"Do you know where he is? Can you contact him quickly?" Spartak demanded.

"Why, within minutes if he's at the usual place. But it may take a while to bring him to you. If you're under Imperial requisition you can't leave the ship, and any attempt you make to communicate with people on the planet will be automatically jammed."

"Get hold of him at once anyway," Spartak ordered. "It's our only chance."

Frantically Rochard dashed for the door.

Spartak turned to Vix, wiping sweat from his face. He said, "It might have taken weeks to track him down here—he might have fooled us, along with Bucyon's assassins, and we'd have gone on a ridiculous chase to Argus looking for him. Even if we have to go home via Nylock, we may prove to have wasted amazingly little time."

"If we get back from Nylock," Vix said. "If we get him aboard in time to make the trip with us, and the girl isn't brought here before he arrives. If. If. *If!*"

"I should have given Rochard a message to cover that risk," Spartak whispered. "Told Tiorin to wait for us, and we'd be back to locate him right here."

"You were not expecting to find your brother on this world at all," Vineta suggested unexpectedly. "You were prepared to find he had left for somewhere else."

Spartak nodded absently.

"Then you are in luck," she said with a shrug. "Try to look on that side of it. I will go fix refreshments against your brother's arrival."

She slipped silently from the cabin, and the two men settled down and tried to abide by her extremely sensible advice.

X

It seemed that a slow eternity passed before they again heard a bang on the outer door. Vix leaped to his feet.

"That *must* be the girl being brought!" he declared. "And we *still* haven't heard from Tiorin!"

"I don't think so," Spartak countered, and now voiced the thought which had occurred to him earlier: that the port authorities would certainly advise them of the girl's arrival by communicator. He went to open the lock, and found Rochard had returned.

"I wouldn't have been so long," the nervous man exclaimed, "but I thought it safer to try to reach you by communicator rather than come back. Only once you're under Imperial requisition even the palms I can normally grease seem to be put back in their pockets ... To the point, since I did have to come here again: your brother is on his way, and if you can delay your departure one more hour he'll join you. Uh—I can't help wondering," he finished in a fawning tone, "whether I may not have done you, too, some small service ... ?"

Spartak had been isolated in the environment of his order on Annanworld for so long that at first he did not get the point of this delicate probe for a gratuity. When he did, he found he was ignorant of the current purchasing power of Imperial money. He fumbled a twenty-circle piece from his pouch, and that seemed to satisfy Rochard; at any rate, he gave a mechanical smile and scampered down the ladder again.

"I wonder who he is," Spartak murmured to Vix when he had relayed Rochard's news.

"Him?" Vix shrugged. "He's of a type which I've seen spring up on a dozen worlds—carrion worms infesting the gangrened body of the old Empire. Probably he's regretting this instant that we're not doing anything which would entitle him to a reward if he informed on us to the port authorities. That's how people like him make a living: buying and selling information for use in blackmail, law evasion, and petty crime in general."

"I thought he was a frightened fool when I first saw him," Spartak admitted. "But he must be pretty astute."

"Astute? Him? He didn't even try to find out if we were from Bucyon, like the assassin he told us about who came after Tiorin. He might have sold out his best employer and seen his throat cut without reward to himself."

Spartak was briefly silent. Then he mentioned his unfamiliarity with the purchasing power of money nowadays, and added ruefully, "I think I've been too long away from real life, Vix!"

"I could have been put away from it permanently, but for quick thinking on your part," Vix retorted in a gruff tone. "At least we know we need only delay another hour now. I hope they're having trouble locating this mutant girl."

But barely half the hoped-for period had gone by when the communicator barked at them.

"Vix of Asconel, come to the port control building. Your passenager under requisition is here."

Vix and Spartak exchanged glances that promised determination to resist, and sat tight, their mouths clamped shut on the temptation to answer and comply.

After a second peremptory order, however, there was a noise from below, and Vix jumped up.

"Vineta!" he exclaimed. "The conditioning is on her too, isn't it?"

Spartak nodded. "Is she trying to get out of the lock?"

"No, it doesn't sound like it." Vix went to the door to peer out. "No, she's coming here!"

The girl's face was pearled with sweat, and her teeth were chattering. "Vix, you must shut me in the cabin!" she forced out. "Or else I cannot stay against the orders I can hear!"

"Hear?" Vix rapped out.

She nodded. "Like a little voice in my own head, whispering all the time."

"It's a good idea to lock her in," Spartak confirmed. "I wish there was some way we could lock all of us in—is there?"

"Not that I know of," Vix grunted. "Sooner or later, even if we closed everything fast, we'd be driven to operating the emergency escape hatches, which can't possibly be locked."

He did as Vineta had asked, and on his return put a question to Spartak. "Little voices inside the head—is that how it feels to you?"

Spartak shook his head. He answered loudly as another command came over the communicator, trying to drown out the words with his own. "It affects different people different ways, I'm told. It gives me a helpless tightness in the guts, makes my mouth dry, and I think eventually it will blur my vision."

"How long before it gets unbearable?"

"I don't know. How strong are we?"

But the authorities' patience was shorter than their endurance. With ten minutes still to go before the promised time of Tiorin's arrival, there came a thunderous banging on the lock door, entirely different from Rochard's timid knock.

"Tiorin?" whispered Vix, whose neck was now corded with

tension as he struggled against the invisible compulsion to leave the ship and fetch their unwanted passenger.

"I guess it could be," Spartak replied with difficulty. "I'd better go see. I think I know more about what's been done to us than you do—I stand a marginally better chance of arguing for a while longer if it's not Tiorin down there."

"Go ahead," Vix consented, and his face twisted with self-contempt at his own frailty.

It was not Tiorin. It was the pudgy woman with gray hair, accompanied by a squad of uniformed guards and the mutant girl—presumably—laid out on a stretcher on the back of the groundcar in which they had all ridden over to the ship.

"You there!" she roared at Spartak's appearance. "If you fight our conditioning much longer, you won't be in a state to fly space! If that's how you think you're going to evade my orders, I tell you straight you won't get away with it! I'll condition one of my own pilots and drag you out to jail, and Delcadoré will be the only planet you see for the rest of your lives!"

A cloud of formless terror due to the conditioning enveloped Spartak's brain. He was unable to speak. Ignoring him, the woman turned to the guards with her.

"Get that girl off the car and put her aboard!"

Slowly, the terror retreated as Spartak called on every trick of self-discipline taught him on Annanworld. He found his voice again, could see clearly as the guards awkwardly sought to get the stretcher up the ladder to the lock at which he stood.

A shocking possibility crossed his mind, and everything else, conditioning included, fled from his awareness. He leaned forward on the rail, peering down at the girl. From her face, and the slightness of the body under the blanket in which she was wrapped, he deduced that she was scarcely more than a child—fifteen or sixteen, perhaps.

But that wasn't what transfixed him. He had assumed her to be unconscious, perhaps injured by the peasants or whoever had tried to stone her to death—the gray-haired woman had mentioned something about that. However, he had seen without a shadow of doubt that her eyes were open.

"What's wrong with that girl?" he called.

The guards, busy trying to get her up the ladder, didn't answer. The woman on the car merely scowled.

Behind him in the lock, Vix appeared, clutching his gun but somehow unable to find the trigger, so that his hands wandered absurdly over the stock and barrel, like jointed insects with minds of their own.

"Is she sick, or hurt?" he inquired feverishly.

"I don't think so," Spartak rapped out.

"Get back!" One of the guards manhandling the stretcher shouted up to them. Despite himself, Vix obeyed instantly. Spartak heard him cursing under his breath.

The stretcher grated over the edge of the platform and was slammed flat. Blue eyes in a face which would normally have been ruddy and healthy, but had turned sallow, stared at the sky, not even turning to see into whose care she had been committed.

"Catatone!" Spartak thundered, and rage so great that it overcame the force of the conditioning stormed into his limbs.

"What did you say?" Vix cried.

"She's under catatone! It's a paralyzant—they first got it from the poison of the Loudor ichneumon." He stamped to the guardrail and stared down at the gray-haired woman.

"Correct!" she applauded mockingly.

Vix plucked at his arm. "Isn't it as well?" he whispered. "After all, to have her—"

Spartak brushed aside the other's hand. "It's the cruelest thing in the galaxy!" he blazed. "Because it *only* paralyzes! It doesn't dull pain! How'd you like to be unable even to moisten your eyes by blinking—or move to relieve a cramped leg—or control your bowels?"

He heard Vix draw his breath in sharply, and from the corner of his eye saw that the redhead was staring with dismay at the girl's taut body.

"And don't you know why they did it?" Spartak raged on. "Because there's so much lying and deceit going on in this once-proud Empire they're afraid a mind reader could tell a few unpleasant truths to the people they're duping—like the man we met earlier, shy of his arm and his leg!"

He saw as clearly as through a telescope, that his taunt had made the gray-haired woman wince. Without conscious intent, he shot out his arm and seized the energy gun from Vix's fumbling grasp. Trying desperately to stretch this moment of not-thinking to its utmost, he levelled the weapon and found the trigger.

"Where's the antidote?" he shouted. "Get me the antidote or I'll burn you where you sit!"

There was a dreadful silence. Incredulous, the guards

turned at the foot of the ladder and stared up at him. He was shaking with the effort of keeping the gun sighted on the gray-haired woman, but somehow finding the resources to go on.

"We—we haven't got it!" the woman quavered.

"Then get it!" Spartak told her. "No, not you—you're my hostage. Send one of these bullyboys for it. And tell him to run both ways!"

Vix put his hands on the guardrail, clamping them till the knuckles were white. Seeming to draw strength from his brother's example, he cried, "And tell that man below not to pull any tricks—I saw him move for his sidearm!"

The guard who had tried to get at his gun jerked his hand back from his waist, holding it out at his side.

"Hurry!" Spartak rasped. "Your conditioning is good. I might decide I have to give in—but I'll burn you first!"

The woman shrieked terrified orders, and the guards broke as one to dash back to the port control building and fetch what was required.

The time that passed now was hardly human-scaled, inside Spartak's over strained mind. It was time slow enough to suit the growth of galaxies, the cooling of suns. Yet there was nothing in all of space except a frightened fat woman on a ridiculous little groundcar, trembling as the gun stayed aligned with her head.

Could he endure? His guts were chilled with nausea; his vision was swimming and there were random, insane noises in his ears. The metal of the gun seemed alternately burning hot and freezing cold, and often he had the illusion that—like Vix—he was not gripping the trigger, but fumbling in front of and behind it.

"There he comes!" Vix said. He pointed, but Spartak dared not look away from the sole focus of his attention.

"Let him bring it up," he breathed. "Put it alongside the girl's head."

"Bring what up?" Vix glanced at him in wonder and not a little admiration. "Oh! Not the guard coming back—but Tiorin! I can see his red hair plainly!"

"I don't care about Tiorin," Spartak said. A vague puzzlement flashed across his mind: he did care really, didn't he? Only somehow it was less important than the main purpose, the bringing of the antidote for catatone. . . .

"Spartak, listen to me," Vix was saying out of infinite distance. "Spartak, Tiorin is here—he's come up to the lock and brought the antidote with him. I told the guard to give it to him and here he is and he's brought it. You can put down the gun and we can leave."

Spartak's temporary universe, containing only himself, the gun and its target, crumbled, and utter darkness overwhelmed him.

XI

Two blurred faces topped with red hair swam in Spartak's unfocused vision. He struggled to bring the images into register with one another. The effort made his eyes hurt. He gave up, and only then discovered that there were two faces in reality, not merely in his imagination. One of them belonged to Vix. But the other—

Of course. Tiorin! Memory came flooding back, and he was able to force himself up on his elbows. He was lying on one of the bunks in the upper cabin, and both his brothers were leaning over him with expressions of concern.

"Spartak?" Tiorin said doubtfully. "How do you feel?"

Thoughtfully Spartak took stock of his body and still more of his bruised mind. He said eventually, "Bad. But I'll survive."

"By the moons of Argus, it's a miracle," Vix declared. "I shall never know till my dying day how you managed to keep that gun on its target. I had something like that in mind, but I couldn't control my hands under the conditioning."

"They're alleged to know a good many things on Annanworld which have been forgotten elsewhere in the galaxy," Tiorin said. "Where's that jug of broth your girl brought? Oh, there. Give some of it to Spartak—it'll help to restore his strength."

Vix carefully set the spout of the jug to Spartak's lips, his other arm serving as a prop behind the younger man's shoulders. Spartak sipped and sipped again; the broth was hot and spicy, and he thought he detected the faint flavor of some energy concentrate under the masking tastes.

Meantime, he had a chance to look at Tiorin, whom he had not seen since the day of Hodat's accession to the Warden's chair.

His second brother had aged noticeably. He would in fact

be—Spartak calculated rapidly—forty-one, which in the heyday of galactic civilization had been late youth, not early middle age. But the extreme wealth of the Empire was needed to support freely available geriatric treatment; now, and for the foreseeable future, only those fortunate enough to inhabit secure planets like Annanworld would enjoy the old benefits. He had a passing vision of peasants grubbing on decadent worlds, mating in their teens, the women worn out by childbirth at age thirty. It was not a pleasant idea, and Spartak spoke hastily to distract his mind.

"Tiorin, it's incredible that we should have located you!"

"Not really." Even Tiorin's voice had changed from what Spartak recalled: grown deeper and become colored with a sort of drawl to suggest that he weighted every single word. "I've been explaining to Vix how it happened. Right now, he tells me, you're feeling very annoyed at the pretensions of the rump of the Empire, but it saved my life by still possessing some of the old advantages—an efficient law force, swift communications. . . . It was no secret that I was second son to the former Warden of Asconel, you see. I'd found it helpful to draw on the small prestige this conferred. And when Bucyon's assassin arrived, and started asking rather too freely where he could find me, some inspired official grew alarmed. He sent a warning to me, and we laid a trap for the would-be killer; it was from him that I learned about this hellish cult Bucyon has imported, and also of course about the death of our brother Hodat."

A shadow crossed his prematurely lined face.

"Accordingly, I had it noised about that I'd gone to beg Imperial aid in the deposition of the usurper at the court of Argus."

"I still don't see why you didn't," Vix muttered.

"You of all people should know," Tiorin retorted. "Holding what it has is beyond the Empire's power now—whole fleets are rebelling and setting up on their own. . . . What chance would I have had of securing aid except on terms that would be ruinoius to Asconel? Do you know what price the old Twenty-Seventh Fleet set for their return to Imperial jurisdiction? You, Spartak?" On receiving headshakes, he concluded, "The free right to sack the planet Norge!"

Spartak, shocked beyond measure, pushed aside the empty jug of broth. "But Norge was one of the last Imperial outposts beyond Delcadoré!"

"Still is. The price was refused. But the point is: the price was set. I'd have had to promise something similar in respect of Asconel, and I wouldn't have had the heart." Tiorin scowled. "No, it seemed to me that my only hope was to exploit my inborn capital as Hodat's legal heir; that's why I hired agents to inform me of the arrival of any ship from Asconel. I was afraid the most likely occupants of such a ship would be more assassins, out to complete the job I'd once frustrated, but by good luck yours was the first vessel to reach Delcadoré since I learned the news."

"You're relying on your appeal to the citizens to make them rise up in support of you against Bucyon?" Spartak suggested.

"So are you, I gather," Tiorin countered.

Spartak shook his head heavily. He said, "I talked with Korisu, the man Bucyon sent to murder Vix—and of course myself as well if possible. My judgment is that if Bucyon has contrived to turn a once-loyal citizen of Asconel into a fanatic supporter of his regime and his cult, it's going to take more than simply fomenting a counterrevolution to set our planet free."

There was a depressed pause. Vix broke it with his habitual intolerance of extended silence. "We're going to have all the time in the galaxy to work out our plans," he grunted. "Once you dropped that gun and keeled over, Spartak, the conditioning took hold on me, and I had—*had*—to get to the controls and set our course for this planet Nylock. And we're well on the way there now."

"The girl!" Spartak said, and swung his feet to the floor. "Did you give her the antidote?"

"We thought we'd better not," Tiorin admitted. "Obviously you knew something about medicine in general and catatone in particular, and I'm afraid I've learned little about anything in the years we've been apart. I've gone on indulging myself."

"Wise of you, I guess, but . . ." Spartak stood up, swaying, and had to close his eyes briefly as empathic agony stabbed him at the thought of the torment the mutant girl was undergoing. "Where is she?"

"I told Vineta to make her comfortable in the other cabin," Vix muttered.

Spartak hesitated. Then he spoke his mind, as his training on Annanworld had accustomed him to do. "Listen, Vix! It's painfully obvious that you hate the idea of having a mind reader aboard. I guess you'd rather leave her the way the Empire liked to have her—incapable of speech, so she can't give away any secrets she picks up. But mutant or not she's a human being, and sheer chance decreed that she should be gifted with abnormal talents rather than you or I or Tiorin. If she's survived into her teens, she's bound to have learned discretion and foresight. She won't reveal the things you want to keep private."

"I hope not." Vix shrugged. But he seemed ashamed of himself, and turned away without further comment.

"Here's the vial of antidote," Tiorin said, fumbling in his belt-pouch. "I hope it's the real stuff, not some fake they palmed off on us to make us leave the planet."

"We'll soon find out," Spartak answered grimly.

Vineta looked up, startled, as he entered the lower cabin, then gave him one of her quick shy smiles. He nodded in response before dropping to his knees alongside the mutant girl and reaching for his medical case.

"She doesn't move at all!" Vineta exclaimed. "She is alive, isn't she? But how does she breathe?"

It was an astute question. Not for the first time Spartak found himself suspecting that this self-effacing girl was the exact opposite of Vix: where he talked much and thought rather too little, she probably thought a great deal despite speaking very seldom.

"You haven't looked under this covering?" he suggested.

Vineta nodded. "She's clothed in some thick garment—I couldn't see how it fastened, so I left it."

Spartak drew the blanket aside. The girl's body was revealed completely enclosed in a suit that glistened as if wet. A bulging hump showed across her bosom; another made her belly rise as though she were pregnant.

"Yes, I've seen that technique before," he said—more to himself than Vineta. "Turn her head on the side, please. I shall have to put the antidote into the neck arteries; if I take the suit off she'll suffocate before I save her."

If Tiorin's ghastly suspicion is correct, she'll die anyway. . . . But he drove down that thought and administered the antidote with deft fingers.

Seconds dragged away like hours—and she moved. Spartak realized he had been holding his breath; he exhaled gustily. "Now we must get the suit off, quickly. See, it fastens on the shoulders and at the hips. Open that side."

With a sucking noise the wet-looking material let go. The skin revealed was pallid and unhealthy, somewhat swollen with accumulated fluids and here and there wrinkled up into ugly white ridges.

"That's how she breathed—see?" he explained, as the mound on her bosom was exposed, and proved to be a machine in a metal casing. "That drives air in and out and acts as a pacemaker for her heart. And this"—the similar device on her belly—"takes care of bodily wastes, but not very well."

Now the mutant girl had sufficiently recovered for an expression to come to her face, and at the sight of it Vineta could not stifle an exclamation of horror. It was the worst look of pain Spartak had ever seen.

"Can you do massage?" he demanded, stacking the prosthetic machines on a handy shelf. "Space knows how long she's been kept from moving—the return of normal sensation will be pure torture!"

Vineta's hands flew to the pale stiff limbs and began to rub.

"Thank you." The words came on breath alone, barely audible. "Thank you. You can stop now. The pain's gone."

Spartak sat back, exhausted, and stared at the girl. "Are you sure?"

"Quite sure." A small tongue slipped out to moisten her lips, which were chapped. "You are Spartak, yes? And you are Vineta?"

Spartak's eyebrows drew together. So far as he could recall, he hadn't addressed Vineta by name, nor been addressed, since entering the cabin. He said, "Did you read our names from our minds?"

A smile came and went on the mutant girl's face. She said, a trifle louder as her vocal cords came under control, "Yes. And it feels very good. I have felt so much fear in people who knew what I am, but in your mind I feel—what to call it? Curiosity, I think. And in hers, much kindness. I am so glad to be here."

"Then you also know what's going to happen to you?" Spartak suggested.

"Yes. And I see why you ask. Frankly, I don't care where I go so long as it's away from—from the past." The small sharp-featured face clouded.

"I'll let you rest now," Spartak said. "Vineta, perhaps you should bring her some of that broth you made for me—it seems to have brought about my recovery from shock very quickly." A thought struck him, and went unvoiced by deliberate decision as his eyes returned to the mutant girl.

She gave a thin chuckle. "My name's Eunora," she said. "You have a clear mind, Spartak—it's like looking into a deep transparent pool of pure water, and I can see all the way to the rocks at the bottom except in one place. And that's where you've been conditioned to take me to Nylock."

"I imagine," Spartak said with difficulty, "that you can make allowances for my brothers. I don't think they feel as I do about—about people like you."

"No, I can sense them—just barely." Eunora shut her eyes and seemed to be listening to distant noises. "They are both full of resentment; the conditioning lies on all their thoughts like dense fog, and one of them can't help thinking that I'm responsible for the delay in your mission."

After that, silence. Spartak caught Vineta's eye and nodded her out of the cabin. Then he went, heavy-hearted, to rejoin his brothers.

XII

The two others had gone up to the control room again. As he approached the door, he heard Vix's voice raised.

"Well, I know Spartak's views on this, because he told me."

"And they are—?" Tiorin prompted.

"That we might have spent months hunting you, maybe going clear to Argus on the false trail you laid, so we should be glad our only delay is this little side trip to Nylock."

"Suitably philosophical, I guess," Tiorin replied as Spartak paused outside the door, "for someone who took vows to an order on Annanworld. It's a hotbed of philosophy, I'm told. For my part, I agree with you—if luck runs your way you ought to grab its tail and hang on tight! Is there no means whereby we could get around the conditioning imposed on you? I'm not conditioned—could you give me a course of instruction and let me fly the ship to Asconel?"

"No, for two reasons." Spartak slid the door aside and stepped into their view. "First, conditioning of this order of efficiency turns your own mind against your wishes—if Vix were to try to teach you how to pilot the ship, he'd so instruct you as to insure that you set course for where we're commanded to go. Or, if by some miracle he avoided that trap, he and I and probably Vineta would conspire to take the controls away from you again. And secondly, even if you did succeed in getting us to Asconel, we'd arrive there in the sort of state I was in when they finally brought the antidote for Eunora. Only worse. The strain might literally kill us; I'd certainly expect us to be incurably insane."

"The girl!" Reminded of his other omnipresent anxiety, Vix tensed. "Did you—uh—cure her?"

"And what was the name you used?" Tiortin added.

"Eunora." Spartak combed at his beard with agitated fingers. "I guess you could say she's cured—she's released from the paralysis, at least. But I'm astonished at how normal and levelheaded she seems. It's not what you'd expect from someone of her age—still very young—treated in such an abominable fashion." He paused and frowned. "Oh—maybe I'm being overly suspicious. Maybe she's just so glad to get free of the Imperials and the people who were apt to stone her. . . ."

"Is that what they were going to do?" Tiorin exclaimed.

"So we were told by that fat old fool at the spaceport on Delcadoré," Vix confirmed. "Well, we have to make the most of our chances such as they are. Spartak, when you came in we were discussing how to tackle the problem. Tiorin has unconfirmed reports of a center of resistance established by Tigrid Zen on Gwo."

"How old are these reports?" Spartak asked sourly. "Gwo is too close and too obvious for Bucyon to overlook it." He had been taken to Gwo once, and never forgotten the impression it made on him; marginally habitable, it served Asconel and five or six neighboring systems as a source of raw materials, the far greater distance for transport as compared with asteroids in their own systems being counterbalanced by the extra convenience of working with breatheable atmosphere. It was a bleak, oppressive world, its vegetation drab olive and gray, its climate wet and windy, its oceans perpetually tossed by storms.

The point apparently hadn't occurred to Vix. He glanced at Tiorin. "Is this something you had from Bucyon's assassin?"

Tiorin nodded. "But I did confirm the story by checking with the crews of ships that had recently passed within— well—earshot, so to speak, of Asconel. There's a spaceman's slang term for that; what is it?"

"Rumor-range," Spartak answered shortly. "Four kinds of news: standing there, landing there, rumor-range, and rubbish."

Vix gave a humorless chuckle. "I'm surprised at you knowing that, not even having been a spaceman yourself."

Spartak made a gesture of dismissal, dropping into a seat. "Speaking of Bucyon's assassin reminded me. Your tracks may be fairly well covered on Delcadoré, Tiorin—though after meeting Rochard, I'm not so sure of that. Ours certainly are not; the most casual inquiry on Annanworld would give a lead to Vix and me. And Bucyon is hardly likely to rest content with the tripple frustration of his attempts at wiping us out. Indeed, I'm amazed he relied on lone agents—in his position, I'd stop at nothing to get rid of all of us."

Tiorin nodded, his face grave. "The impression I had from the interrogation of the man sent to kill me was that fanatics deluded by the cult of Belizuek acquire the illusion of being invincible, capable of undertaking any mission single-handed. But I grant that this isn't an impression apt to survive a succession of setbacks like the ones luck has brought us up to now."

"Fanatics are tricky to handle," Spartak muttered. "If you catch them on their blind side—say by doing something they define as impossible—you can cope with them easily. If you stand in their way as we must stand in Bucyon's ... Or do we?"

"What do you mean?" Vix snapped. Then a light seemed to dawn on him. "Oh! Do you mean that this errand to dump the mutant girl is something of Bucyon's doing?"

"A means of getting us out of the way? I doubt it. Even Bucyon could hardly organize a chain of coincidences like that. No, what I mean is this: if he's managed to inspire dupes like Korisu and the man sent to kill Tiorin, if he's reduced the citizens to a state of blind adoration, he may feel secure without disposing of us. He may wait for us to come home, frantic with rage, and then pick us off at his own convenience."

Vix's face darkened. "By the moons of Argus, I'd like to test that idea! I'd like to set course now for Asconel and pitch Bucyon and his woman Lydis from the top of the Dragon's Fangs—*ach*!"

The last sound was not a word, but a gasp of agony, and he doubled over. Alarmed, Spartak jolted up from his seat, but Vix waved him back.

"Second time that's happened," the redhead wheezed. "If I

so much as think about going straight to Asconel, I get a gripping in the guts, but if I speak it out loud, it's like molten metal being poured into my belly."

"It's the conditioning," Tiorin said. "It must be."

Spartak nodded. "Think about Nylock," he urged Vix. "Think about going to Asconel after we've left the mutant girl behind. It'll calm you and you'll be eased."

"Go on talking on those lines," Vix whispered. The whole of his face had paled to the whiteness of his long scar.

"Uh—yes." Spartak turned to Tiorin. "Well, the simple plan is to link up with Tigrid Zen. By the way, though: who is he? Vix assumed that I'd know him, but I don't recall the name."

"He was Vix's senior aide when they were putting down the revolt in the norther islands," Tiorin said. "A former sea-sailor who entered government service because of the rebellion."

Spartak nodded. He remembered very vaguely a man with a bushy black moustache and a roaring voice—that would be Tigrid Zen.

"But he's been closer than we have, he's had a long time—and we don't hear news of any progress toward victory." Tiorin scowled. "We have the mystique of our blood to draw support, descended as we are from the Warden who steered Asconel through the storms which followed the collapse of Argian influence in our sector of the galaxy. That might tip the scales in our favor. But after ourselves, I know no one more likely to rally resistance to Bucyon than Tigrid Zen, and if he's failed . . ." He shrugged despondently.

"We're guessing," Spartak said angrily. "What we need to do is make straight for Asconel—contact Tigrid Zen if we can, but not chasing him if he's gone hunting support in some other system. Then on Asconel, perhaps disguised, we ought to—"

He broke off. Tiorin was gazing at him queerly.

"What is it?" he demanded.

"You just said 'make straight for Asconel,'" Tiorin exclaimed. "And nothing happened to you! When Vix said the same thing, more or less, he doubled up in pain."

Blank, Spartak tried it again. "We should make straight for Asconel. I want to go straight there now. I intend to go straight there now." He jumped to his feet. "By the moons of Argus, you're right! Vix try it!" Excitedly, he rounded on the redhead.

"I—!" Vix moistened his lips and gathered his courage, fearing another blast of the torture which had overcome him moments earlier. "I want to go to Asconel. Now."

And slowly a smile replaced his look of anxiety.

"The conditioning's failed!" Tiorin exploded. "It must have been badly implanted—"

"No!" Spartak rapped. "I felt it, and believe me, I *know*. The psychologists who treated us knew their job. Either we're suffering from a delusion, implanted as a second line of defense against the breakdown of the main commands, or—No, that can't be right. We have you as a control, Tiorin; you're not conditioned, and you'd observe that. Then that leaves one single possibility, and I think I know what it is."

"Tell us!" cried Vix, almost beside himself with joy at being unexpectedly released from his invisible bonds.

"Eunora," Spartak said.

"What? The—the mind-reading girl?" Vix took half a pace back as though recoiling from a physical shock. "But—how?"

"I don't pretend to know that," Spartak said. "I'm just eliminating the things I know to be out of the question, and I find one unknown factor operating. Let's go see her and find out—"

"That won't be necessary," a soft voice said, and the panel of the door slid aside to reveal Eunora herself. Spartak had not realized till this moment how tiny she actually was; she barely came to Vix's elbow, and he was the shortest of the three men. She had borrowed one of the costumes he had seen in Vineta's closet when he boarded the ship on Annanworld, and it hung loosely on her as though she were a child dressing up in her mother's clothes.

"Eunora! Did you take the conditioning off us?" Spartak blurted out.

The girl gave a grave nod.

"Then I can't begin to tell you how grateful we are!"

"That's right!" Vix confirmed. His face was alight with enthusiasm. "Why, you may have saved a whole planet's people by saving us that trip to Nylock!"

Eunora didn't answer at once. She walked into the control room with careful, mincing steps, seeming still to be finding out how her unparalyzed legs should support her. Behind her, a trifle nervous, but looking calm enough, came Vineta, who had presumably tried to dissuade her from leaving her cabin and failed.

"I didn't know about this—this *conditioning*," the mutant

girl said at last. "It was only when I felt the pain and twisting in your mind" —nodding to Vix—" that I decided I had to find out about it. It's . . . interesting."

A nameless premonition filled the air.

"It's difficult being a mutant," the soft voice went on. "Hardly daring to use the gift—afraid all the time that it will leak out and then there'll be . . . killing. But it's grown without my noticing. I have more talents than I ever realized. I was able to work on your minds like a locksmith picking locks, locating and releasing all the implanted orders." She gave a little crazy giggle. "And when you see how it's done, it's so simple!"

Spartak's whole body had gone cold as ice. He waited numbly for her to make the point which he forsaw with terror.

"Asconel. That's where you want to go. But I don't think I like the idea much. It's an Imperial world—or was. So they don't tolerate my kind of people. Also it's going to be a place of fighting. I can see that in your mind, Vix. You want to go there and fight against these priests and this man called Bucyon, and because you're so frightened of having your mind probed you'll probably be glad if something bad happens to me. Spartak perhaps not—I don't know. But even he . . ."

She hesitated. Then she giggled again. "Well, I've found out about conditioning now. I see how it's done. I think I can probably make you do what I want. There's only one question that remains: it's such a big galaxy, so where shall I make you take me?"

She looked around her petrified audience with mocking eyes. "Go on!" she urged. "Think of the other places I might like to be taken—anywhere but Asconel or back where I came from—and then I'll get you to pilot the ship there!"

XIII

Horror-struck visions raced through Spartak's mind in three successive and distinct stages.

First, there was the appallingly vivid picture of them all condemned to serve the whim of this mentally unstable girl, slaves bound with unseen chains, compelled to take her on a colossal joyride around the wheel of stars which was the galaxy.

Second, there came a flood of memories of Asconel: its seas, its mountains, its forests and open plains, every recollection painful with yearning. He had resigned himself long ago, that day on the royal island of Gard, to a life of exile, but since Vix came to find him he had without realizing conceived an ache and a desire to go home that now permeated every fiber of his being. The agony of deprivation was almost physical in its intensity, like hunger or—more nearly—like sex.

And third, as he began to bring his whirling thoughts under control, followed the shadow of a question. Could even Eunora, who had certainly released them from the Imperial conditioning, reverse the process with her supernatural talent, imposing fresh commands in place of those she had wiped out? *Could* she? Surely a mere child would find the range and sweep of adult minds—male minds, moreover—beyond her abilities to master.

Or maybe not. Here there were so many unknown factors, he was almost afraid to believe he dared hope.

But not one said anything. He and his half-brothers simply stared at Eunora, as though her tiny face and body held an infinite fascination for them. Bit by bit, the waiting grew to be a strain on her, and the expression of mocking triumph she wore gave place to a look of uncertainty.

At last she burst out, "Do as I tell you! Do as I tell you!" But the words were tinged with hysteria.

Behind her shoulder, Spartak saw Vineta move. She came forward into the middle of the control room floor, and spoke unexpectedly in a level voice.

"I want to go to Asconel. Because that's where Vix wants to go."

"Shut up!" Eunora rounded on her, the skin around her eyes crinkling up as though she were about to cry.

Murmurs of astonishment came from Vix and Tiorin. Spartak was not less surprised then they at Vineta's intervention, but he was perhaps better equipped to see how it was possible than they were. He forced his thinking along the most promising line, remembering that Eunora was exposed to all of them at once.

Deliberately he fanned the coals of his resentment into flame, visualizing her as she had been when she was brought to the ship—corpse-stiff, kept alive only by machines, and suffering unspeakable cramps and soreness. *Is this how you repay our help?* he whispered wordlessly inside his head. And beyond that, more subtly: *Is this the life you want, for years, forever perhaps—the loneliness of power, without love, without friendship and trust?*

"Stop it!" she whimpered, and dashed at him to beat on his chest with her little absurd fists. He folded his arms and stared sternly down at her.

Once you begin it, you can never stop. And behind the thought, carefully constructed pictures of faceless people, by hundreds and then by thousands, plotting to escape from her control and drive her down to final darkness.

"Stop it!" she shrieked again.

He complied, and thought instead of Asconel, a fair world, hospitable and kindly, with himself and Vix and Tiorin and Eunora, too, enjoying its sunshine, its wine, its fields and cities.

Helpless, the girl bent over and covered her face with her hands. The threatened onslaught of tears overcame her. Impulsively, Vineta put her arm around the girl's shoulders, and she turned and buried her sobs in the long dark hair.

"What—what happened?" Vix whispered, moving as though waking from nightmare.

"I wouldn't be surprised if Vineta could tell you," Spartak answered slowly. "You've been underestimating this girl of yours, Vix! She thinks very clearly indeed."

Vineta, comforting the weeping Eunora, shook her head. "I only know what store Vix sets by going to Asconel. And I couldn't bear to think of him—and all of you—being turned into toys for *her*."

"And there you have it," Spartak grunted. "Eunora found it easy to release the conditioning the Imperial psychologists imposed on us, but to implant new commands of her own against the terrible need we all have to go home and set our people free—that's not something one untrained child can achieve!"

"But—" Vix started to object.

"Think of it this way," Spartak interrupted. "Anyone can take a ship out to space, yes? Because space is big and open, and there's a margin for error of a million miles if you need it. But landing is something different again; one aims for a spaceport perhaps no more than a mile across, and probably for a berth measured in yards rather than miles. That takes skill and long practice. Similarly, wiping out commands which the victim resents is easy for Eunora. To overcome our resistance and bend us to her will proved beyond her."

"But never mind how it was done," Tiorin snapped, wiping sweat from his furrowed brow. "The question is, how do we cope with her from now on? If she's apt to repeat that little performance—"

"Dump her in space," Vix said shortly. The naked brutality of the words jolted all of them, and especially Eunora, who spun in terror to gaze at him.

"That's disgusting, Vix!" Tiorin countered. "Nonetheless— since you're free of the compulsion to take her to Nylock, I think we should put her down on the nearest habitable planet and be glad to be rid of her."

"I . . ." Vineta let the word hang timidly in the air. Spartak gave her an encouraging nod.

"Go on, Vineta. Like I said, you're a clearer thinker than most people. I'd be interested to hear your view."

"Well . . ." Vineta licked her lips. "I've heard from Vix that this mysterious woman Lydis gained power over your late brother Hodat by appearing to read his thoughts. And what I've heard, too, about the way the people on Asconel have been changed from free independent citizens to blind fanatic dupes of the Belizuek cult sounds like the effect of some sort of conditioning. I—well, I didn't have a very happy childhood. Even though I wasn't set apart from everybody the way Eunora is, I often felt the way she did just now— desperate to get even with the universe, wanting to be as cruel to others as they had been to me. So I can't even be angry with her.

"And . . ." She hesitated. "I can't see into your minds the way she can, but I do believe that you're the nicest people I've ever had to deal with. Vix, for all that you have a temper like a star going nova, you can be very kind, and Spartak here is such a gentle person, and strong inside too. I think perhaps when she's recovered from the dreadful things they did to her on Delcadoré, Eunora will see that the same as I do. And when she does—well, isn't it going to be tremendously valuable to have someone with us who can see into people's inmost thoughts? Won't it save months of spying and guessing, trying to find out how Bucyon keeps his hold on your citizens at home?"

There was a pause. Tiorin broke it.

"I see what Spartak means about you, girl. I hadn't looked at it that way myself. But it's the first really constructive suggestion I've heard for tackling the problem we face. My one reservation is that we can't be sure about Eunora. Are we to undo the effects of years of maltreatment in a few days?"

Spartak drew a deep breath. "I'd be willing to try, if she'll cooperate."

Eunora gave a little frightened cry. "I see what's in your mind, Spartak! No! No!"

No? His sober beared face bent close to hers, he let himself think through the idea in detail, trying to maintain the same mood in which he had taken his vows to the order he joined on Annanworld: the sense of disgust inspired by the stupid violence attending the collapse of Imperial authority, the longing for rationality, calm judgment and peace which drove him to his imposed exile.

But it wasn't that, he realized later, which impressed her. It was the memory of the agony he suffered while waiting for the antidote to be brought so that he could release her from catatone paralysis.

"I don't like this," Vix muttered in the background. "I still feel we'd be better off if we got rid of her."

"Wait," Tiorin counseled. "Look now!"

With an expression of total childlike trust, she had put her tiny hand in Spartak's large one, and he was leading her without another word from the control room.

"What?" Vix demanded. "What?"

It was Vineta who answered, her eyes on the door which had closed behind Spartak. "I think she saw what he endured for her sake before we left Delcadoré, and decided that if he could do that for her, she could do as much for him."

When Spartak returned, much later, his face was stamped with incredible weariness.

"She's sleeping," he said in answer to an eager question from Tiorin. "Oh, but I've dug some foulness from that mind of hers! Like seeking jewels in a pile of dung!"

Obviously not yet convinced of the wisdom of keeping Eunora aboard, Vix demanded harshly, "What did you do?"

"Hmm?" Rubbing his eyes, Spartak spoke around a yawn. "Oh—I gave her some of the same drug I used on Korisu. I told you it was employed in psychotherapy. Before she's capable of liking us, or anyone, she's got to be cleansed of the hate she's conceived for the human race—and are you surprised at that hate? The Empire, afraid of being toppled by some superiorly gifted assailant, made it policy to deport mutants, and the common people turned that policy into fear for their own security. You'd stand up to a raving crowd, defying them with your gun, or a sword, or your bare fists if it came to that. But she's a child! How can she understand and forgive a mob of fools driven out of their minds with superstitious terror?"

Vix hesitated for a long moment. Finally he shrugged. "I don't like the idea, but—but you know a few things I don't, having spent so long with your nose buried in your books. So far, things have turned out well for us. I'll go along with you. But if she pulls another trick like the one she scared us with, I'll dump her in space as I said I would!"

"She's not less human because she's a mutant," Vineta summed up. "She's a hundred percent human—*plus*."

"Well said," Tiorin approved. "Now, though, we have a choice to make, Spartak. Vix feels we should go directly to Asconel, for fear of wasting any more time. I think it would be safer to try to contact Tigrid Zen on Gwo. Things have changed terribly on Asconel; even if we disguise ourselves, we might be betrayed by some chance ignorance."

"But will Tigrid Zen be any better informed?" Vix challenged. "If the stories we hear about Bucyon's mastery of Asconel are correct, he won't simply be able to come and go freely. He may not even have been able to land ships at home. And someone who's totally cut off can't give us much guidance."

"I'll give you one sound reason for visiting Gwo first," Spartak said. "Vineta reminded us of it, just now. Lydis is alleged to be a mind reader too. Suppose she's one of many; suppose the technique whereby Bucyon overcame all resistance so easily is a mutant trick. How do we disguise our minds against discovery?"

Vix blanched. With the memory of Eunora's powers fresh as it was, that shaft struck home in him. He admitted, "I hadn't considered that. If you're right, though, would—?"

"I don't know if Tigrid Zen could advise us," Spartak cut in, stretching his exhausted limbs. "But he could warn us. I say we make first for Gwo anyway."

"I'll set up the revised course, then," Vix muttered, and moved to the controls.

XIV

Cautious as a wild beast sniffing at bait in a suspected trap, they circled the mining world of Gwo. It was a lake-planet and not an ocean-planet; in other words, its land surface rather than its water surface was continuous. Although it had a CO_2 water ecology, it had never been permanently settled in the days when men first blasted through the galaxy; with a vast number of more Earth-like planets to choose from, they could let places such as Gwo alone.

It wasn't short of water, however. The atmosphere was sponge-saturated, and every least hillock was a watershed. The effect over aeons of time had been to turn uplands into bare, rounded rocks, and fill all the valleys with deep layers of rich sediment supporting the typical drab vegetation. It was from these sediments that the half-dozen nearby human worlds had drawn their raw materials.

Had. Spartak reflected on the chilling implications of that word as the echo of Vix's exclamation died in the still air of the control room.

"It seems to be dead. . . ."

"It can't be," Tiorin objected. "They might have had to cut back their mining, but to abandon it completely—"

"It's been ten years," Spartak broke in. "Asconel was the most stable of the planets hereabouts, and think what's happened to it now. Revolution, civil war, plague—a dozen things might have put a stop to luxuries like mining another system. Vix, do we have no clue at all to the location of Tigrid Zen's resistance hideout?"

"You'd expect it to be based on Asconel's old holdings here," Vix grunted. "Except that if it was, Bucyon could too easily locate it and wipe it out."

"Maybe he did," Tiorin muttered.

"Maybe." Vix reached toward the communicator switches. "We'll just have to risk a call, I guess."

"Hold it," Spartak rapped out.

"What else can we do?" Tiorin glanced at him. "Agreed, we may run ourselves into a Bucyon ambush, but we could spend a lifetime hunting through the mist and drizzle here."

"I have a better idea," Spartak said. "Let me bring Eunora up and ask if she can help us."

She came willingly, her hand in Spartak's like father and
daughter. He had never hoped that there would be such rapid
progress in gaining her friendship and trust, but he had over-
looked the fact that since she could see into his mind she
could examine her personality as in a mirror, using his
knowledge of psychology to afford an insight into her thinking. With incredible speed she had discovered why she nur-
tured blind hatred against ordinary people and why she had
been senselessly persecuted; then, borrowing from Spartak's
calm assessment of human inadequacy, she had seen how to
rise above mere resentment and achieve a sort of pity.

Even Vix had been impressed by the result. Now, as she
came into the cabin, he gave her a smile of welcome.

"Yes, I can tell you where you'll find your friends," she
said. "Over there!"

She pointed. "It's a long way—half around the planet. But
there are a lot of people, perhaps as many as a hundred."

"A hundred!" Tiorin was appalled. "If that's all he's managed to gather together out of the nine hundred millions on
Asconel, what are we hoping to do?"

"More," Spartak said briefly. "Vix, let's go there."

When they broke through the cover of cloud and hovered
amid ceaseless rain, the drops trickling down the viewports,
they found themselves above a heavily wooded valley. No human habitation was in evidence, and Vix jumped to one of
his typical conclusions.

"Eunora's wrong. There isn't anybody here."

"Yes, there is," the girl replied stubbornly. "Hiding!"

"Hiding where?"

"Go down lower and you'll see."

Reluctantly Vix complied. Shortly, Tiorin let out an exclamation. "Those—those aren't natural trees! Look, they're on
nets suspended above ground level."

"Identify yourselves or we'll shoot you down!"

The voice blasted from the communicator, making them
jump. In earnest of the threat, a bolt of energy sizzled up from
a concealed gun emplacement, leaving a streak of white
steam to mark its path through the dripping sky.

Tiorin leaped to the communicator. "Vix of Asconel's
ship!" he shouted. "Spartak of Asconel and Tiorin of Asconel
are aboard! We're looking for Tigrid Zen!"

A moment of blank disbelief. Then: "Would you say that

again?"—in the meekest possible tone. And lower, as if to someone beside the speaker: "Go tell the general at once!"

A gap opened in the camouflage of fake vegetation. "Come down slowly," the distant voice instructed. "We have our weapons trained on you, so don't make a careless move."

"Eunora," Spartak murmured, "can you convince them that we are who we are?"

"I'll try," the mutant girl agreed doubtfully, and closed her eyes.

Abruptly, the communicator sounded again. "All right, we're satisfied. Welcome! Welcome!"

Tiorin cocked an eyebrow at Vix, who had overheard Spartak's soft request to Eunora, and the redhead shrugged and set the ship down.

The relief of finding that there really was a nucleus of anti-Bucyon forces here was soon tempered with dismay, however. As Eunora had said, the total amounted to some hundred persons, ill-clad and half-starved, the proud possessors of two small spaceships which had formerly belonged to the Asconel navy and had been snatched from Bucyon's grip after his own fleet attacked Asconel. One ship was here; the other had been sent on a mission to try to raise help among neighboring systems—at latest report, without success, for everywhere the tale was the same, and the withdrawal of Imperial authority had left those systems with problems of their own.

Tigrid Zen himself, who came to embrace his former commander Vix with tears in his eyes, had aged twenty years in the ten since Hodat's accession. His hair was vanished from his head, and his long moustache was grizzled. His uniform was dirty and there were holes in his boots. None of his followers were in much better plight.

But he made the newcomers as welcome as he could, treating them to a meal in the mountainside cave which served as his headquarters, and from him they heard the sorry tale of Asconel's capitulation at first hand.

"It was terrible," he muttered. "At first, you see, it didn't seem too bad. This woman Lydis—granted, she followed some ridiculous cult or other, we thought, but there was some compensation in Hodat's obsession with her. Twice she enabled us to frustrate a plot against him—though now I'm not sure she didn't inspire the plots herself, to gain his confidence. Her, or this loathsome cripple Shry whom she brought in as—well, her chaplain, I guess you'd say.

"We owe it to Grydnik that we weren't completely duped." He nodded at the former port controller of the main Asconel spaceport, a shrunken man who had once been fat but since his exile on Gwo had become a body cased in the loose bag of his own skin. "He challenged the easy admission of all these people from Brinze, saying there were too many greedy priests among them and no one who could offer the hard work and technical skills we needed. But Hodat grew deaf to our pleading. First he ordered the erection of this temple, then he imposed the taxes to establish centers of Belizuek in every large town, and finally—well, I'm sure you know. He was murdered, and in the resulting confusion Bucyon's fleet came from space and overwhelmed our defenses. The priests and other immigrants from Brinze proved to be a well-trained underground movement, which paralyzed our defenses and our communications. Now we are as you see: a hopeless band of loyalists stranded in exile."

"Tell me about Bucyon," Vix said softly, "and this woman Lydis."

"Bucyon—he's a big man, with swarthy skin and a bright brown beard. They say he's a strong personality, dazzling to those who come in contact with him. But he keeps aloof." He gestured to an aide standing by. "We have pictures of him and Lydis. Bring them."

"And Shry," Spartak said. "In what way is he a cripple?"

"Hunchbacked. As though some monstrous growth covered him from neck to waist, bulging out obscenely. Ah, here are the pictures. You'll find them everywhere on Asconel now, venerated like idols by the stupid citizens!"

He slammed them down on the table. Vix, who had requested information about Bucyon and Lydis, studied them with care, lingering longest on the portrait of the woman.

"She's very beautiful," he said.

Spartak nodded. Although the picture showed her in long black robes, with a veil over her fair hair, her face was of a perfection to tempt the King of Argus.

"This I swear," Vix said between his teeth. "One day I shall enjoy that woman. I shall take her, and throw her down, and . . ." His hands curled into claws.

Tiorin broke the ensuing silence. "And what is it like on Asconel now? You have contact with people there—I hope."

"A certain amount. Bucyon has grown contemptuous of

our opposition, and we contrive to get our ship through for a landing every now and again, to land spies or put fresh heart—such as we can—into the very few who harbor loyal memories of Hodat. But as to present conditions there, why, you should ask our latest recruit Metchel." He indicated a stocky man who stood a little apart from the others present. "We brought him away at our last landing. He was scheduled to be sacrificed to Belizuek, and wasn't duped as so many are. Can you credit that?" Tigrid Zen added bitterly. "Our people, offering up their lives!"

There was a hiss of indrawn breath from the brothers.

"Conditions on Asconel. . . ." Metchel shrugged. "Well . . . look around you, and imagine this expanded to the whole planet. Everywhere despair, poverty, plowland gone to weed, fishing boats rotting at the quay, commerce reduced to the passage of tax payments in order to support the burden of the fat and greedy priesthood. But nobody cares—the entire populace is deluded into thinking that they don't matter anymore; only Belizuek and his followers count. It's true that people willingly offer up their lives in sacrifice at every temple."

"How is the sacrifice conducted?" Spartak asked.

"I don't know. No one sees but the priests, and they don't talk.

"And what's Belizuek?"

Metchel shook his head again. "The priests say 'he.' In every temple, behind a screen, there's a sanctum for him. Daily one must go and bow to him, sing a song in his praise, and hear an exhortation by the priest in charge, which usually boils down to this: that we are dirt under his feet, our only purpose is to serve him, and he has existed as long as the galaxy. Incredible as it may seem, this convinces people; they go to their miserable work and dirty homes and starvation meals and comfort themselves with what the priest said."

Metchel's face twisted, and he added violently, "I hope to go back soon. I can go to another town, perhaps, and work to overthrow Bucyon."

Gloom descended on the listeners. Painted thus, the task before them seemed impossible. Spartak put his elbows on the table and buried his head in his hands.

Beside him, Eunora plucked at his sleeve. He shook her hand away with impatience, but she insisted, and he wearily bent his head close to hear her whisper.

What she said shook him to the core.

"Metchel is lying," came her faint, clear breathy message. "He's an agent sworn to Bucyon, and when he goes back he plans to tell where this place lies so that it can be wiped out by Bucyon's fleet."

"Are you sure?" Spartak's head whirled with suspicions. *Is she trying to ingratiate herself? Are we to be deceived?*

"If you don't believe me," Eunora said in pique, "you only have to use on him the drug you used on Korisu. And I tell you it would be a waste. If I can't tell when someone's lying, who can?"

XV

Centuries of despair seemed to settle their weight on the shoulders of Tigrid Zen as he listened to the flood of hatred and abuse Metchel poured out, lying on the crude wooden bed to which they had bound him. They were in a secondary cave of the system in which he had established his hideout, the only light the yellow glow of an almost expired handlamp.

"What made you suspect he was lying?" he asked Spartak.

The bearded man hesitated. "Does it matter?" he countered finally, deciding it was better not to reveal Eunora's talent for fear there might be superstitious alarm at her presence on Gwo. "You've heard what came out when we unlocked the doors of his mind."

His eyes sifted to the medical case alongside the bed. He had spent a great deal of his most useful drug on Eunora aboard ship, on Korisu and now on Metchel. But he didn't feel it was, as Eunora maintained, a waste to have acted as he did. Granted, the mutant girl could see into the traitor's mind, but apart from wishing to establish that she was telling the truth, he had suspected there might be things in Metchel's memory Eunora could not understand well enough to describe to a third party. And he was convinced he was right.

"What are we going to do?" Vix muttered from the dim recesses of the cave. It was the third or fourth time he had asked the same question.

"I don't know." Tigrid Zen sighed. "To think that a spy for Bucyon could fool us so easily—come right here to our secret headquarters and worm his way into my confidence—oh, it makes me ashamed! I'm growing old, sirs. I'm turning into a senile fool."

Tiorin clapped him comfortingly on the back, but didn't voice any denial. Instead, he said, "What worries me is that this suggests some of your underground contacts on Asconel have been infiltrated by Bucyon's men. By what miracle does he gain this blind obedience? I'll swear that Metchel told the truth—why, haven't we heard him repeat much the same under this drug of Spartak's—when he described the shocking way poverty and ruin have overtaken our once-prosperous people. Yet he doesn't *care*. For him, Bucyon is a superman, Shry is the voice of a divine oracle, and Belizuek is a being so superior to humanity that his service excuses the worst of insults to human dignity."

"What is Belizuek?" Spartak said softly.

There was a pause. Tiorin said at length, "Go on, Spartak. You have something in mind."

"Yes." Wearily Spartak rubbed his forehead. "Vix had a vague plan originally which consisted of landing on Asconel in secret, perferably having raised forces elsewhere to aid the loyalists when they rebelled against the usurper, and rely on his—our—prestige as Hodat's legal successors to foment an uprising. But this assumed we were coping with an ordinary tyrant: a dictator such as any world might throw up from the chaos of post-Imperial decline, against whom the forces of unpopularity would already be at work. Correct, Vix?"

Vix nodded. "I had it in mind to land in the northern islands. I imagined I would still enjoy some support there."

Tigrid Zen grunted. "I had that same idea. That was my first tactic when Bucyon came. But thought it's true we've been maintaining contacts with home through our former friends in that area, I'm no longer sure whether I was right to trust them or whether Bucyon has subverted everybody and now laughs at me."

Spartak leaned forward, elbows on knees, and shot a sidelong glance at the prone figure of Metchel, now breathing heavily in a stupor induced by the drug he had been given.

"Neither Metchel, nor Korisu, nor the man who came to try to kill you, Tiorin, would have knuckled under to any ordinary dictator. Our traditions of good government, loyalty to the legal Warden, and public justice would have ensured that a mere usurping tyrant met the full force of a popular revolt—if not instantly, then within a year or two of his seizing power. Clearly, Bucyon is no ordinary tyrant. What has he to make him different from anyone else?"

"The woman Lydis?" Vix hazarded. "Allegedly she can read minds."

"That, yes." Spartak nodded. "But far more important, he has Belizuek. A figment of the imagination, a mere cult-object? I think not."

"What, then?" Tiorin snapped. "A mutant of human stock?"

"Again, I think not. Remember, we've heard from Metchel how Belizuek is present in every temple in every town on Asconel, and here under the drug he's further informed us that Belizuek is said to be present everywhere on Brinze—wherever that world may lie."

"Something—artificial, perhaps?" Tiorin suggested. "A mechanical device which subdues the hostile thoughts of the people who come within range?"

"That's a possibility I hadn't considered," Spartak conceded. "And it would explain a good deal."

"Can't we milk something further from Metchel?" Vix exclaimed, jumping to his feet. "He can't really be so ignorant about this deity he follows as he pretends!"

"But he is. I'm satisfied on that score." Spartak spread his hands. "Only the priests know what Belizuek is. Logically, since Belizuek is what we have to fight and not just a man called Bucyon, we must go to Asconel and—well, I guess kidnap a priest to interrogate him in the same way."

"And then?" Tiorin countered.

"Who knows? But until we have positive information, we're wasting our time."

"To go to Asconel would be foolhardy," Tigrid Zen said. "Sirs, until I've had a chance to determine which of our contacts Bucyon has subverted, I can offer you no help at home, name no one you could look to for shelter and protection—"

"Careful," Spartak cut in. "You're falling into a trap in which Bucyon would like to see us all caught, if I'm not mistaken. Consider: he's been in power on Asconel for some time, yet Metchel must presumably be the first traitor he's infiltrated into your loyalist underground at home—if not, he'd have located this base and wiped you out already. If Belizuek were all-powerful, the process of conversion to his cause would be sudden and complete. I think it's not; I think it affects many people—most people—quickly, but there remains a certain number who are capable of resistance. As time passes, they grow fewer and fewer." He sketched a rising curve in the air with his finger. "But I'd estimate one full generation as the time required for absolute planet-wide submission."

"It's a comforting thought, anyway," Tiorin said. "Look, though, Spartak! If Belizuek is the key factor, why should we not simply raise a few ships—possibly hire them from the fighting order with which Vix has been serving— and bombard all his temples from space?"

"What payment will you offer?" Spartak said glacially. "The right to sack Asconel for three days afterward? And if you're to take the Warden's chair, what chance do you think you'll have of ruling a people who's been blasted at random, by the million, maybe? They're happy under Bucyon, remember! If they weren't, they'd have rebelled of their own accord. And you won't simply take out the temples from space—that order of accuracy is beyond our powers. Whole towns would probably be razed by such a bombardment."

"Ground infiltration and sabotage," Vix said, half to himself. "Blow up or burn the temples."

"That still leaves the problem of reconciling the people to what we've done," Spartak pointed out. "No, I say we're wasting our breath until we know what Belizuek is and how he—it—they—dominates the citizens."

"So we go to Asconel." Vix shrugged. "Excellent. About time. Swallow your misgivings, Tigrid Zen, and tell us how good are our chances of making a landing undetected."

"Fair," the grizzled man muttered. "Among the things which Bucyon has let go to rack and ruin is the space-side detection system. He has a large fleet, now including the remnants of our own which surrendered, but it seldom flies space. My guess is it won't fly again till the time comes to spread the plague to some other miserable world."

"I know a place in the northern islands which I marked once as a good secret landing-ground," Vix offered. "I had it in mind to sneak forces around behind the rebels, but I never had to use it."

"Once landed, though, what then?" Tiorin said. "We're not likely to have been forgotten in ten years. You, Vix, least of all. Spartak, just possibly . . . yes?" to Spartak.

"We have a means of telling our friends from our enemies," Spartak said significantly. "One which Vix considers unreliable, but which I have now some confidence in since it served to unmask Metchel here."

Tigrid Zen looked from one face to another but refrained from asking any questions.

"That helps a little," granted Tiorin. "At least we can determine whom we turn to for food, shelter, information. . . . But I still say we'll be recognized."

"I thought of that back on Annanworld," Spartak murmured. "We shall have disguises our own brother Hodat would not penetrate. I've given some thought too to the problem of how we might travel. I'll have to interrogate Metchel more fully on some of the details, but we all have skills we could employ on any world struck down by poverty. I might pass as a doctor of medicine, for instance. Vineta is a musician—at least, she plays some instrument or other. Tiorin, do you still sing the songs you used to shock me with?"

Tiorin, startled, said, "Am I to be a minstrel—a clown, perhaps?"

"Please! Unbecoming to your dignity or not, we're going to have to pose as people who can convincingly travel around, unsettled in any one town, and with the iron grip Bucyon has taken on the planet there must be very few people traveling for pleasure any longer. Trudging the road in search of work and food, yes. If you compare the situation which obtained on—oh, never mind. Just take my word that I've studied the pattern of social dislocation which evolves when a formerly wealthy planet decays in a single generation to a place of poverty."

He didn't wait to hear further objections, but turned to Metchel again, reaching his hand out for his medical case.

"There's just one trouble. As soon as I'd mentioned the possibility of my posing as a doctor, I realized that the sick are probably now exhorted to offer themselves to Belizuek. So a doctor may not—"

"You're wrong," Tigrid Zen said heavily, stirring his stiff aging body as though shifting a heavy load. "That's perhaps one of the most dreadful things of all. Belizuek refuses the sick, taking only the healthy and strong. And they go to him. They offer themselves willingly. Galaxy, what can *we* offer that will withstand a force like that?"

Tiorin gave a sudden bitter laugh. "I think we're all insane," he muttered. "What are we doing? Setting out to reconquer a planet taken by a usurper who can bend its people to his will like twigs off a tree! And how are we to do it? By going home as tramps and mendicants, too poor to keep ourselves, let alone hire a spacefleet to attack Bucyon's!

And what forces have we? A hundred sick and starving wretches, huddling from the eternal rain on this forsaken ball of mud!"

Metchel, forgotten on his crude bed, moaned and whimpered. The drug must be losing its grip, Spartak realized; when he recovered and remembered that he betrayed the secret of his mission, only his bonds would keep him from following Korisu's example.

Deliberately Spartak turned his back on his brothers, opening his medical case again.

"If that's how you feel," he said over his shoulder to Tiorin, "do as you wish. Go hunt mercenary forces—blast Belizuek's temples from space! But for me . . . if I have no other resources than my own body and mind, that's what I'll use. Vix has taken a vow on himself, to cast Lydis down in the mud and enjoy her. I'll take one also: to unmask Belizuek, whatever he or it or they may be."

There was a brief silence. Then Tiorin said, "And I. I'll unseat Bucyon from the Warden's chair, or die in the attempt."

Stiffly, slowly, Tigrid Zen got down on his knees and kissed the rightful Warden's hand.

XVI

Now that the time of their homecoming was finally upon them, they were overtaken by a sense of estrangement which was irrationally reinforced by the disguises Spartak had prepared. He had some confidence in his beard and the passage of ten years to change him; nonetheless, he had altered his hair-color to blond, Tiorin's and Vix's both to jet-black, worked delicately over the line of chin and eyebrow and nose with soft inert substances injected below the skin, till the resemblance between all three of them and Hodat's brothers was reduced to a similarity of stature and gait.

That would have to suffice. Would *have* to.

But the physical illusions combined with a feeling that each was retreating into a universe of private thought where the others could not follow, and in a desperate attempt to retain their newly refound kindship even Vix—warily supervising the controls, ever alert for the signal which would indicate that Tigrid Zen was overoptimistic and Bucyon's forces indeed watched the space around Asconel for intruders—was driven to speak at random for the sake of breaking the tension.

"It's winter down there," he muttered. "I'd forgotten. That makes things difficult."

"We'll have to get some warmer clothing," Spartak agreed, "especially for Eunora, who has nothing."

"I wasn't thinking of that so much." Vix shrugged. "If there's snow on the ground, it'll be much harder to land unseen—and impossible to get away from where we do set down without leaving tracks."

Tiorin made to speak, hesitated, finally gave a bitter laugh. "I was just about to ask where we should buy our clothing and whether it would be safe to show our Imperial currency. But it suddenly struck me that if we're to trust Metchel's descriptions we'll be lucky to find anyone with clothing to sell even in a town."

"Aren't you exaggerating?" Vix said.

"I doubt if he is," Spartak put in. "The entire planet will be shockingly changed, Vix. Production, distribution, communications—all reduced to the bare minimum needed to support Belizuek's domination. Rags will have become precious, and to throw away a crust of bread will be unthinkable. Typically, it'll be safe enough to show Imperial currency, and what's more it'll buy incredible quantities of anything that's for sale, but our own money will have become effectively worthless."

"Then how can people live?" Vix demanded savagely.

Vineta spoke up from the corner of the control room in which she huddled with Eunora; being close to her own childhood, she had established a sort of shy intimacy with the mutant girl. "Vix, you've seen how it is on worlds we've traveled to with your order. They live like beasts, ready to fight for a morsel of food, neglecting everything but the sheer necessity of staying alive."

"I guess so." Vix sighed. "But I can't transfer what I've seen on worlds like Batyra Dap to my own beloved Asconel."

His fingers curled like claws, as if he had Bucyon's throat between them.

Spartak said hastily, "We're agreed at least on what we do at first, aren't we? We land as Vix recommends on the southerly tip of the island which the town of Penwyr stands on. There's a concealed site for the ship; the people stood loyal to our father while Vix was putting down the rebels; there's a temple at Penwyr, the only one on the island. And it's—well, if not easy, at any rate possible to get to Penwyr on foot, so that we run the least risk of being reported and attracting the attention of the priesthood. Once arrived, we go directly to the temple and try to find out what Belizuek is behind these screens which always hide him. If we must, we'll kidnap a priest and interrogate him back at the ship. Meantime, Eunora will tell us which of the people we meet still harbor the seeds of resistance to Belizuek and we'll sound out those we feel we can trust to guide our long-term planning."

"Can we just walk into the temple?" Tiorin asked. "I know Metchel told us everyone had to go there daily—"

"It's not quite like that," Spartak corrected. "Every morning there's a ceremony to honor Belizuek, but not all the citizens are required to do daily homage. In towns they are expected to go to the temple one day out of three; in the country, one day in six. But it seems not to be looked on as a duty; it's one of the great events in lives which have become uniformly drab and depressing. Accordingly, the temples are open all day, from dawn to dusk, so that people with particularly fervent adoration for Belizuek can go and prostrate themselves."

"What do they do at these sacrifices?" Vineta put in.

"Metchel said that every twenty or thirty days there's a special ceremony at which the volunteers are decked with flowers and walk behind the temple screen to the sound of joyful music." Spartak's face darkened. "What becomes of them, nobody knows except the priests. But they are never seen alive again."

"Are they seen dead, then?" Vix growled. "Served as the main dish at a banquet, maybe?"

Tiorin exclaimed in disgust.

"What time of day will it be when we set down?" Spartak asked.

"Around sunrise. If we make haste, we can reach Penwyr just in time for the morning ceremony at the temple." Vix scanned his control panel closely, and gave a nod. "I think Tigrid Zen was right—we can go to land without being challenged. Here's hoping!"

He put the ship into the landing trajectory.

The lock door slid aside. Beyond lay a bleak, forbidding landscape: gray rocks, contrarily shadowed with the whiteness of drifted snow, skewered with the trunks of leafless trees of which the very crowns were just catching the first rays of dawn. There was no sound except the distant noise of the sea gashing its teeth. The air was bitterly cold.

But it wasn't the sudden chill which made Spartak shiver and brought the tears stinging to his eyes. It was the sum of all his childhood memories.

Asconel! Mother of us all, that you should be brutally raped and betrayed!

His emotion choked him, and by the long silence he knew his brothers were equally overcome.

It was astonishing, therefore, that the first voice to disturb the cold morning was Eunora's. Scarcely louder than a whisper, it said: "Forgive me, all of you. If I could have seen the love you have for your home, I'd not have frightened you by threatening to make you—make you . . ."

She could not finish, but they all knew what she meant, and they gave her frosty smiles in acceptance of her apology. Vix, gathering himself quickest of the three men, crossed to her and put his arm around her tiny shoulders.

"You've had no reason to love any world, child! Maybe you'll find a reason here. It's a sad and lonely thing to have no home."

The mutant girl nodded, and two tears shone brightly on her pallid cheeks.

"We must move," Tiorin said practically. "Vix, you'll need to inactivate the ship, fit alarms and booby traps—"

"It's as easy as turning a switch," Vix cut in. "The owners who had my ship before were all suspicious people, and I'll wager when we close her up no one but ourselves will be able to get within arm's length of the hull. In any case, no one comes to this part of the island. No hunting, no fishing worth the name—no reason for visitors."

He patted his chest, making sure he had the concealed sidearm which—apart from good wishes—was about all Tigrid Zen had been able to offer from his resources on Gwo to speed their mission, and led the way down the ladder to the ground.

They picked a route to leave the fewest possible tracks, going first by rocky slopes from which the snow had blown away, then by a road which had been used since the last fall, where there were already plenty of footmarks. It all seemed very straight forward, and Spartak might have relaxed, but for realizing that Eunora was freezing cold; once they got out of the sheltered depression in which they had landed, a wind came off the sea keen as a knife. He had given her his old brown robe from Annanworld, but even kilted up to her tiny size it was still a garment meant for a subtropical climate, and the wind sliced through its wide loose weave.

The chattering of her teeth drummed a menacing accompaniment to the rhythm of his steps.

They had walked the better part of an hour when there was a sharp exclamation from Vix, leading the way because he had visited the island before. The others hurried to see what he had found, and saw that he had halted opposite a form half buried by snow in the meager shelter of a bush.

"He's dead," he said slowly, and the others, shocked, saw what at first their minds had denied. This was indeed a man—very old, for his beard was not white only with frost—who must have sat down to rest here while trudging the road, and never got up again.

Spartak exhaled sharply, his breath wreathing in the icy air. "Well, he has no further use for what little he possessed," he grunted, and began without more ado to strip the clothing from the corpse. Tiorin made to object, and he gave him a glare. "If you're going to be squeamish, perhaps you'd rather strip yourself and lend the clothes to Eunora?"

When he'd finished, she was so grotesque in the miscellaneous rags he had supplied that Vix looked doubtful. "Can we really go into Penwyr with her dressed like that?"

"You're fond of betting," Spartak answered. "I'll bet that most of the people we meet will be worse clad yet."

With a last surge of energy he put the fragile corpse out of sight in a bank of snow beyond the bush where it had rested, and they tramped on.

His estimate of the condition of people in Penwyr was correct. They began to encounter the citizens on the road just before entering the town: this was a day for folk from outlying farms to attend the temple ceremony, that was plain, and they were gathering on foot and in wheezing old groundcars fueled with woodgas generators. None of them offered to speak to Spartak and his companions, which suited them well.

Two things appalled Spartak especially: first, the numbers on foot—for Asconel had been among the few worlds retaining nuclear-powered transport after the withdrawal of Imperial support—and second, the looks of near-ecstasy on all the faces. Even the children, some of whom one would have expected to be sullen and fractious, were uniformly cheerful as they clung to their parents' hands.

In the town, placards depicting Bucyon and Lydis were everywhere, mostly on the fronts of stores long closed for lack of goods to sell. Several people in the now large crowd heading for the temple paused to kiss the pictures.

Wary, eyes taking in every detail around, they let themselves be carried along until they were in sight of the temple itself. Originally it must have been the island's agricultural produce mart, a low-roofed building several hundred feet square. Now it was decked with Bucyon's picture and many crude slogans. The crowd paused as it entered the street on which the temple stood and joined with other streams of people from elsewhere in the town, giving Spartak time to read some of the gaudy exhortations: WE ARE BORN AND WE DIE, BUT BELIZUEK GOES ON FOREVER! BEFORE THE GALAXY BELIZUEK WAS! MANKIND ARE ANIMALS BUT BELIZUEK IS AN IMPENETRABLE MYSTERY!

Spartak tried to keep the grim look of hatred from his face as he shuffled his feet to warm them on the frozen ground. When he felt a nudge, he thought at first it was Eunora huddling close to him for shelter against the cold wind, but it was Tiorin who had pressed up in order to whisper.

"Spartak, you've noticed the—the *joy* with which all these people are going to the temple?"

Spartak nodded.

"It terrifies me," Tiorin breathed. "Spartak, what makes us think that we can resist Belizuek ourselves? How do we know that we're not walking into his jaws by coming to his temple? How do we know we come out we won't be his willing slaves for the rest of our lives?"

XVII

The echo of Tiorin's depressing suggestion made Spartak's head ring like a gong as they were carried willy-nilly forward in the crowd. It was far too late now to change their minds about entering the temple; the people pressed on every side, eager to get out of the cold and into the steamy warmth of the building. He wished achingly that Eunora could speak directly to his mind, telling him what she was picking up from those around, but she could not, and after Tiorin's brief whisper there were too many other people too close for any more private conversation.

Wondering what was going on inside the mutant girl's head, Spartak used the advantage his overaverage height gave to peer around and seek clues—if there were any—to the grip Belizuek exerted on his disciples. None offered themselves. He saw, heard, and smelled a horde of dirty, hungry wretches, who seemed to find their plight perfectly natural and, indeed, enjoyable.

Drug addiction. The concept thrust itself out of a corner of memory, and at once he realized it was apposite. He had only rarely seen victims of an uncontrollable addiction, but they bore the same stamp as the people surrounding him: an expression of single-minded urgency indicating that every other need had been subordinated to the craving for their dope.

He began to make guesses, putting himself into the place of any of millions of people here, who had failed to admit the necessity for starting over from their own resources when the Empire withdrew its economic and military support. To such a person it might easily seem that human vanity had been met with nemesis; after thousands of years of Imperial domination, the idea of Asconel making its own way would be literally inconceivable. And since the Empire was identified with human aspirations, what more logical conclusion than that man was unworthy of the mastership?

From there it was a short enough step to believing that the purpose of the universe was incomprehensible to human beings, and that some higher order of intelligence was entitled to the adulation formerly accorded to the Warden of Asconel and through him to the Imperial court on Argus.

He shook his head. It was only half an explanation. It accounted neatly enough for the existence of a gap in people's world-structure into which Bucyon and Shry were able to fit Belizuek, but it didn't match the traditions of independence and free thought which Asconel had cherished. The story went that as recently as when taxes were imposed to finance the building of temples in all the main towns, the citizens grumbled and at least threatened resistance. Once the temples were built and people went to them, this change followed like a landslide. Ergo, Tiorin was right in his underlying assumption.

They were coming to the door now. Spartak felt his nape tingle as he sought for any instrusion on his mind, any process comparable to conditioning which might turn him too into a loyal disciple of the greedy deity. But it was useless; he could not tell.

Clutching Eunora's tiny hand as fiercely as she ordinarily clung to him, trying to keep within arm's reach of his brothers, he was forced into the temple.

There was nothing remarkable about it, barring three comparatively minor but unexpected discoveries. First, there were no seats; the people were supposed to pack in shoulder to shoulder and stand during the ceremony. Second, the interior walls were decorated with prized personal possessions—paintings, sculptures, tapestries, and objects in precious metal—described on small attached plaques as voluntary donations by adorers of Belizuek. And third, the screen at the far end, behind which Belizuek was allegedly concealed, was not what he had envisaged—some curtain of force akin to the defensive field of a starship—but just a screen of woven metal links on a frame adorned with gems.

More than likely, it would carry a killing charge, but he could not see the point at which it joined the floor to determine if it was insulated from the ground.

He got his first sight of the priests now: wearing robes not unlike those affected by his own order on Annanworld, but in various colors, black, white, green, and gold, they stood watching the congregation assemble. Was there any clue to their origin in their physique? He searched every cranny of his memory, and was driven to the conclusion that they might as easily have been born on Asconel as any other world of the galaxy, so thoroughly had the traffic of the Empire mixed all the existing human stocks.

The eyes of one priest seemed to dwell on him, and he had to repress a start of alarm. Glancing around, he decided that there was nothing to mark them out as unusual—many of the men were taller than himself, many of the children were smaller and younger than Eunora. If the priest was curious, he would only be so because he did not immediately recognize them. It would therefore be wise to slip away from the ceremony, delaying their return to the empty temple until some later hour of the day when perhaps the curious priest would not be around.

The last of the crowd from the street jammed in through the doors; the doors closed; there was an air of expectancy. All at once, a note of music sounded apparently from nowhere, and the assembly broke into a fervent chant of praise for Belizuek.

Equilocal sonar generation, Spartak glossed. He wondered if it was used for any special reason—surely people here would be too sophisticated to be impressed by technical trickery? But he had no time to follow that up at once; he was more concerned with the fact that neither he nor his companions knew this hymn the others were so loudly singing.

Moving his mouth in some sort of imitation of the rest, he saw that nobody near them was likely to notice; all eyes were riveted on the screen behind which was Belizuek.

A possible reason for the unison singing came to him: to inspire a sense of unity, welding the crowd together and making it more susceptible to the priests' appeals. But so far he couldn't detect any more advanced methods of working on the people's minds—no hypnotically rhythmic lighting effects, no airborne drugs. . . . Of course, they might be too subtle for even an aware victim to notice.

The chanting ended. A priest came out before the screen and turned his back on the congregation. There was a pause. He bowed, and everyone bowed with him—Spartak and his companions fractionally late.

Again? No. Once apparently sufficed.

The priest turned, the people hanging on every movement, and began to address them in ringing tones. His theme was exactly the same as what Spartak had heard first from Vix, then from Korisu and most recently from Metchel: that Belizuek was a superior being, that men could have no higher purpose than his service, and that this desire should supersede all personal ambitions.

After a while Spartak let his attention wander. So far, he'd seen and heard nothing to account for the blind obedience of once-rational persons. He was jolted back to awareness with boundless amazement when a yell went up from the body of the hall.

"Proof!" someone shouted. And another voice a woman's: "Proof!"

The priest, unperturbed, continued on his former subject. The voices resumed, now swelling, until the discourse could hardly be made out, and Spartak wondered if he ought to join in himself for fear of exciting notice if he remained silent. He was on the point of doing so when the priest raised a hand.

The shouting stopped as if a switch had been turned.

"Proof you want," the priest intoned. "And proof you shall have!" He turned to face the screen again, and raised his other hand to the same level as the first before bowing more deeply than before.

"Belizuek! We who are less than the dust beseech a revelation of your majesty!"

And Spartak learned the answers to all his questions.

At first, it was merely as though the temple had grown larger, the walls receding into a misty distance and beginning to glow. With a shock, a sense of perspective overtook him. Those walls were the very bounds of the universe, and the faint glow was the light of stars—countless in number, inconceivably far away.

Then there was a pause which had the still quality of eternity. Nothing moved, nothing changed.

Seeping in, then, like water oozing through a porous rock, came a sense of presence. Personality. Consciousness.

And power!

Somewhere in this monstrous emptiness, perhaps as far off as the dim stars, perhaps farther, a being had come into existence to the reach of whose mind the gap between galaxies was no more than a single stride. As though drawn by a magnet, Spartak's dissociated awareness began the aeon-long plunge through nowhere to find it and pay his homage.

Out of the misty blur of stars a form took shape: a lens. The lens of this familiar galaxy. Chance glimpses occurred of well-known features: the Big Dark, which some freak of stellar drift had notched like a saw-cut into the galactic Rim, a hundred light-years wide; the pattern of globular clusters nicknamed the Eyes of Argus for the multitude and brilliance of them. By now, the other galaxies filling the plenum had dwindled to their customary status of bright blobs on the black curtain of infinity.

But the presence knew them. The presence was aware of everything, from the least bacterium to the pattern of those vanishing galaxies; had sounded and plumbed the farthest void, had weighed and measured the nucleons of the atom. It "said" so, and what petty human could contradict such a declaration?

For it knew all human history, and felt contempt—such contempt as made any man wriggle with embarrassment and wish to vanish through the ground—for these squabbling, greedy, half-intelligent creatures which had stolen the techniques and artifacts of their greater predecessors and claimed the conquest of the galaxy. To what end? To the downfall of their vaunted Empire, and the return of the species on tens of thousands of worlds to a state no better than the mud-grubbing life of beasts!

Even when it was over, the vision still filled his head and dazzled his eyes. He was passive among the crowd that forced its way from the temple, letting himself be pushed back onto the street. His questions had been answered, and in a way he had not expected; the shock had dazed him.

Someone tried to claim his attention. He shook his head and went on thinking about what he had learned. The person—Tiorin, possibly—gave up in annoyance and turned to someone else: Eunora. He wasn't interested in what was being said; all that concerned him was in his memory.

It was much later that he realized he was being escorted along a street floored with dirty snow, his companions beside him. He was shivering, having failed to fasten his clothing about him when he left the hot overcrowded temple. Ahead, someone was walking fast with occasional backward glances that suggested anxiety.

"Where are we going?" he forced out.

"You're with us again?" Tiorin came eagerly to his side. "I was afraid you'd been overtaken by the same thing as these unfortunate wretches."

"Hmm? Oh! Oh, yes. I guess I was." The reference drove him back inside himself, his eyes focusing and his feet stumbling occasionally on the unlevel rock-hard snow.

"The man ahead," Tiorin explained, thinking Spartak was still listening. "Vix recognized him from the campaign he fought here—says he was a loyal and brave soldier. And Eunora got close enough to tell that he's still trying to resist Bucyon, only goes to the temple because he'd risk exposure if he didn't. We plan to follow until we get him alone and can approach him openly."

But Spartak was lost again in the depths between the galaxies, playing over in his mind the vision he had had of supernal power, monstrous intelligence, and indescribable conceit.

XVIII

Like most of the towns and all the cities in Asconel's northern hemisphere, Penwyr relied largely on waterborne transport; it was unusual, however, in being built astride a river instead of on the coast. They continued to follow the man whom Vix recognized until he reached the embankment paralleling the river, by which time they were sure he would take the bridge to the other side of the town, a quarter of low-built, rather mean houses.

He was becoming frightened by then, however, and had quickened his pace so much that it looked as if he might break into a run at any moment. People were about on the river's edge, some inspecting boats moored to rings in the stone wall, some working on repairs, some merely leaning over and watching. It was a choice between losing their quarry if he ran, and attracting a good deal of undesirable attention by running themselves.

"Shall I go and speak to him?" Vineta proposed. "He's not likely to be afraid of a girl."

Tiorin hesitated. "That might be the answer, Spartak, what do you think?"

"No use trying to talk to him," Vix grunted. "He's off mooning again."

Tiorin looked dismayed. "Yes, Vineta, see if you can catch up to him and get him talking—Eunora was quite sure he was not a Bucyon man, isn't that right?"

The mutant girl's eyes were on Spartak. She started. "What—? Oh, yes! Yes, he's not one of these miserable dupes, like all the others."

"Go ahead," Tiorin ordered, and Vineta hurried off, leaving them to stroll like any of the other idlers along the quay.

"It's horrible," Vix muttered. "Everything's *stopped*! Even during the worst of the revolution here, we kept the main streets running, and the bridge yonder—" He threw up an angry arm. "It's all going back to the mud now! What's become of the engineers we had, the builders, the craftsmen?"

"Right now I'm more worried about Spartak," Tiorin muttered. "Eunora, can you tell us what's happened to him? I agree, the—the mental show, or whatever it was, that we had at the temple was pretty impressive, but I was on guard against some sort of tampering with my mind, and it's mainly left me with the feeling I'd like to know how it's done."

"Not so impressive," Vix put in. "To people who haven't flown space much, perhaps—especially to people who thought the Empire was all pure magnificence and got some of their illusions dented. But we've seen what it's like nowadays, and made up our minds that's not the best mankind can do."

"If they spread the cult of Belizuek any farther, it's apt to be the only thing we ever did," Tiorin said sourly. "Look, Vineta's beckoning. Spartak, hurry up, will you, instead of dawdling along like a dreamer?"

Tiorin kept one eye on Eunora as they approached Vineta and the man Vix recognized, but she gave no indication of altering her judgment, and it was with some confidence that he addressed the allegedly loyal citizen.

"Your name is Tharl, I understand. You won't know us, but I assure you you'll be very interested in what you hear from us."

Tharl, a nervous man of early middle age, clad in old but carefully patched clothes and with a pinched expression on his face, looked from one to another of the people who had been following him. He said at length, "I took you for a party of Bucyon's men set on my heels by the priests. But I should have known better, seeing the child with you. Well, what do you want with me?"

"We've returned to Asconel from traveling ten long years," Tiorin said. "And—we're horrified."

Tharl let a quick smile come and go on his lips. "Say no more! I can provide you little hospitality—my wife and my son both offered themselves to Belizuek, and my two daughters are married and living away. But I have a home still, and some refreshment; come and join me there!"

"Luck's with us," Vix muttered, and they fell in behind Tharl to cross the bridge over the river. As they had foreseen, its formerly heated and moving surface was immobile beneath a covering of soiled snow, so they had to walk all the way.

Tharl's house was less neglected than those which flanked it; those had snow on their roofs, whereas his was warm enough to melt it away, and the doors and windows still drew power instead of being converted to manual operation. But all he could offer by way of "refreshment" was some stale beer and bread and cheese.

"Ten years!" he murmured as he set out the food and drink. "Why, then I'd have offered you meat and fruit, even in dead winter. . . . Do you know that now they kill all their herds in the fall, salting the meat in sea-brine and keeping only enough stock to breed again in spring? The priests taught them that! I was raised on a farm, and to me it makes no sense."

"You—ah—you said your wife and son both offered themselves to Belizuek," Tiorin ventured. "Since then you've lived on your own."

"That's what's saved me from becoming like all these fools you saw at the temple." Tharl's brows drew together over his nose and he stared into the distance. "I learned to hate just in time. Those who didn't have been duped, and betrayed, and ultimately they won't be human anymore."

He peered curiously at Tiorin; apparently his eyesight was failing. "Tell me, though, how did you know it was safe to address me? If I make myself so obvious the priests will catch me—it's a crime even to think, let alone speak, against Bucyon's rule." Alarm colored his words.

Tiorin hesitated, making a warning gesture to Vix who might have blurted out their true identity. "Ah—we took a chance. My friend here remembers meeting you during the campaign against the rebels hereabout in the time of the old Warden, Hodat's father. You were loyal then, and we felt a man like yourself couldn't have changed so much."

Tharl pursed his lips. "Luck's with you!" he commented, unconsciously echoing Vix's remark of a short while earlier. "You can't have been home long, or you'd know that anyone can be changed and made into a follower of Bucyon. Why, men I fought beside in the old days, Warden's men as they were, have offered themselves to Belizuek since!"

"Does nothing withstand Bucyon, then?" Vix demanded.

It was Tharl's turn for hesitation. Coming to a favorable decision, he leaned forward and spoke in a confidential tone. "There's my old general Tigrid Zen, who's an exile on Gwo. He has forces, and ships—why, occasionally word comes to say there's been a landing in a secret place, and a message is passed as to how those whom the priests are hunting may safely be hidden till a ship can fetch them to Gwo. . . ." He seemed to realize it was thin comfort to his hearers, and the words tailed away.

"You're in touch with a resistance movement here, then?" Vix suggested.

"A movement—well . . ." Tharl sighed. "Put it like this. Over two or three years, I've sounded out those who have a reason to hate Belizuek as I do, and perhaps ten or twelve have proved loyal to the old ways, and of them half have given themselves away, by attacking a priest or profaning the temple, and the rest of us serve to encourage each other. As for rising up against Bucyon, though—which I assume is what you hope to hear news of—I don't see how it can be done."

He pointed at Spartak. "Why, even your friend here has been so deeply affected by what happens in the temple that his mind's adrift in space! First it was a wonder, and the curious talked about it and attracted the reluctant; then suddenly it became the only thing that mattered in the lives of the citizens. I escaped, as I said, because I already had a reason for hate—my wife and boy were the first of all to offer themselves in Penwyr. But that apart, I'd have become as bemused as he is."

Worried, Tiorin nudged Spartak as he sat with pale face and staring eyes on the chair next to him.

"Tharl is wrong," Eunora said timidly. "What's affected him isn't the power of Belizuek, but something else."

"What?" Vix snorted, ready to fall back into his long-time assessment of Spartak as a dreamer and a ninny.

"He— Let him tell you himself," Eunora said, and tugged at Spartak's sleeve.

"Yes?" the bearded man said, coming to the present like a sleeper rousing. "I—I'm sorry. I've been thinking over what I learned down there at the temple."

"That's what we all want to discuss," Tiorin said. "We know what's being done to the people now, and if we can discover how it's being done we can try to counteract it."

"You've missed half the point," Spartak said. "Don't you know what Belizuek is, now you've seen what he can do?"

There was a blank silence. Eunora smiled to herself as though enjoying the secret knowledge she could pick from Spartak's unspoken thoughts.

"Well, go on!" Vix burst out when the suspense had become intolerable.

Spartak shook his head. He seemed bewildered. "Then— well, possibly I'm mistaken, since you haven't reached the same conclusion that I have." He shivered, as if he were still out in the street instead of in the comparative warmth of Tharl's home.

"I must go back and make sure," he added, rising without waiting for objections and on the point of starting for the door.

"Just a second!" Tharl jumped up and strode to stand in front of him. "Back to the temple? What for?"

"I shall have to get a direct look at Belizuek," Spartak explained with the sweet reasonableness of one addressing a child.

"A direct look—!" Tharl was thunderstruck. "How do you propose to manage that? Nobody has ever gone behind the screen they keep around him, except for sacrificial victims and the priests who escort the poor fools. When the temple was new, there were several who tried, and rumor says they were killed by a deadly charge on the metal mesh."

"When the temple was new," Spartak repeated, apparently struck by a new idea. "Tell me, how was it—well—consecrated?"

Tharl curled his lip. "That I know only too well. Some priests came from Gard in a skyboat—Gard, the old royal island, is the site of the chief temple now—bringing some great chest or case affair which was unloaded with much ceremony. It was transported to the market—what's now the temple—and they held the first big sacrifice, with two victims. My wife and my son."

Tiorin, seeing the man was almost overcome, moved to his side to comfort him. He flashed a scowl at Spartak, who remained quite unaffected. Lost in his own thoughts, the other muttered, "It might be the oxygen . . . If only I knew where we found the ships we appropriated! But there's that blank wall of ignorance supposed to be because it was bad for our self-respect to admit the real source of our skills—"

"You're maundering," Vix cut in. "If you have a point to make, make it!"

"Shut up!" Spartak ordered. This was so different from the usual meekness of the younger man's manner that Vix was taken aback; while he was recovering, Spartak rounded on Eunora.

"Do you think I'm right?" he demanded.

The girl blushed. She said, "I can tell you what I felt, if that's any help. . . . Well!" She licked her lips. "I thought there was somebody behind the screen who went—uh—who went an awfully long way. Like very old, but also very big. Sort of connected to other places. Do you see what I mean?"

Tharl's puzzled eyes roamed around the strangers, but he said nothing.

"It fits, doesn't it?" Spartak urged.

"I don't know," Eunora answered helplessly. "You've studied so many things I never even heard about, and it would take ages to track down all the ideas and possibilities which you're considering."

"Then we must go back to the temple," Spartak concluded. "As soon as possible. Tharl, you must have been there at other times than the—the duty services. Presumably you've wanted to appear to be a loyal Bucyon man, to divert suspicion."

Tharl nodded dumbly.

"Then tell me what the routine of the temple is, and how we can get close to Belizuek without the priests driving us away."

XIX

"You can't," Tharl said shortly.

"But we must," Spartak countered, making a movement as if to brush aside all objections. Eunora, however, caught his eye.

"He's probably right," she said. "Let him explain."

More puzzled than ever at the attention they paid to this slip of a girl, Tharl did so. Listening, Spartak came back by degrees to the realities of the problem. Ceaseless supervision, eavesdropping by priests, traps for the unwary—it sounded as though the temple had been prepared to meet just such an intrusion as he had planned.

The solution, however, came from Vix. He gave a shrug. "How about remote detection devices? Won't they do to settle your doubts? I have instruments aboard the ship which could probably be demounted temporarily, and you could probe the back wall of the temple and get some hint of what lies beyond."

"Of course," Spartak muttered. "It must be the depressing effect of coming back to this ruined world, or I'd have thought of that myself. How long will it take us to get the equipment?"

Vix frowned. "We'd best move under cover of dark," he suggested. "It'll be hard to conceal the gear by day."

"That'll be still more difficult," Tharl put in. "There are strict curfew laws now. Even street-lighting has been abandoned—every drop of power and fuel is devoted to Belizuek's cult."

"We'll have advance warning of any patrols we run into," Tiorin said, not offering to give details. "I wish you'd explain more fully, though," he added, turning to Spartak.

But the bearded man was engrossed in some calculations conducted on a memo board from his belt-pouch.

With infinite care and in complete silence they stole back toward the dead-seeming town in the pitch-blackness and icy cold of the winter's night. Half the sky was cloudy, but in the other half the stars burned like the points of white-hot needles.

It had proved necessary to bring from the ship not only the instruments which Vix had mentioned, but means of powering them too—accumulators and a portable generator. When Tharl said all power went for Belizuek's cult, he meant it; there would not be a power source for them to draw on for half a mile in any direction from the temple. Consequently they were all heavily laden, even Eunora, slipping and stumbling along gallantly at Spartak's side.

They had had the greatest possible difficulty in dissuading Tharl from accompanying them, but he was already in possession of a good deal of information about them, and it was judged far better that he should remain at home. Undoubtedly he was both loyal and eager to help, but so—once—had Metchel been.

Reflecting on that traitor, Spartak realized that Tigrid Zen had been deceived even more thoroughly than he knew: he'd been told that the volunteers for sacrifice to Belizuek came forward of their own accord, yet he had accepted Metchel's tale of being a fugitive from a threatened sacrifice.

Or was sacrifice also the fate of the condemned criminal—defining crime in its current sense here, to include activity against Bucyon?

They reached the edge of the town and went between dark walls which afforded a little shelter from the wind. All the windows were shuttered, many with crude hand-carpentered wooden panels instead of the original plastic power-operated ones. Through cracks gleamed an occasional hand-lamp or even a primitive candle.

Once, Eunora gave the faint whistle they had chosen as an alarm signal, and they dodged into an alley between two houses as a woman emerged to empty some foul-smelling garbage into a street drain. It seemed there was no limit to the degree people could regresss under Belizuek's domination, Spartak tolk himself wearily; next they'd be back to open-pit latrines and epidemic diseases.

He ached to find out whether his guess about the nature of this "deity" was accurate.

They had settled on a street behind the temple as the best site of operations; it was usually unfrequented at night, for this had formerly been Penwyr's busy commercial quarter, and all the nearby stores were empty and neglected except one which had been turned into a comfortable residence for the temple staff. The curfew patrols, Tharl had assured them, were negligent in this area, for few people would risk going out under the priests' very noses.

They reached it without trouble, and walked along the far side opposite the temple wall, on which the slogans glared luminously for the benefit of—of whom? Any priest who might glance out, Spartak decided with a curl of his lip.

As nearly as he could tell, he had come to a point opposite the end of the screen inside the temple. He beckoned to his companions to assemble the equipment. Metal stands clinked on the hard-frozen snow as they set down their burdens, and he fumbled with numb fingers to make connections between the power supply and the detectors themselves.

Tiorin headed toward one end of the street, Vix and Vineta toward the other, to keep wary watch. Eunora could do that equally well from where Spartak stood; besides, her tiny hands were deft at the awkward work of organizing the equipment, and she did not have to be given spoken orders.

It was the eeriest task he had ever undertaken. His chief and burning hope was that Belizuek's powers did not extend to the perception of the various probe frequencies he planned to employ.

He coupled in the last device and silently handed the long flex attached to it to Eunora, who dashed across the street and clamped its terminal to the wall of the temple.

That automatically reported the structure-phase of the wall to the other instruments; so guided, they could look through it almost as easily as through glass. Heart pounding, Spartak adjusted the controls and bent to peer at the tiny self-illuminated dials and screens before him.

The range was excessive. He was getting a trace which could only be the nearer side of the concealing screen—irregular metal, probably in mesh or link form. He turned a knob with stiff fingers, and began to get suggestions of something less commonplace.

A mass of complex organics—not quite protoplasmic, but similar. That fitted. He set another knob for the characteristic vibration-modes of oxygen, and read off the data from a quivering needle against an arbitrary scale.

Low oxygen pressure. Very low. But a good deal of carbon dioxide, and nitrogen and a blend of inert gases. *Right*! He began to look for the walls which must enclose this humanly unbreathable atmosphere, and almost at once found the traces which defined it.

Beside him, Eunora was fascinated by the vast amount of information the instruments afforded through a featureless wall; every new conclusion he drew brought a gasp of excitement from her.

"It fits, doesn't it?" he whispered, daring to make the sound which after all was no louder than the chinking and scraping that had accompanied the setting up of their gear.

She gave an enthusiastic nod.

Yes, Spartak thought. *Enclosed in a special atmosphere—organic, but not giving the same traces as a creature from one of our planets—a Thanis bull, say, which would have comparable mass and dimensions. . . . I wonder if I can get any of the internal structure!*

Eunora's teeth threatened to chatter from the cold; she clamped them firmly shut to avoid distracting him.

Two traces came up on the panel—similar, but not identical. An internal reflection, offering a clue to the details he was after? He checked again, and started. No: it was the same trace from two different points in space. In other words, the thing beyond the wall had moved.

I am right! Jubilantly he recognized the final confirmation of his suspicions. Eunora could not repress a chuckle as he hastily continued his examination.

And that was why she failed to give him warning.

The first he knew of their discovery was when lights bloomed like suns all down the front of the building occupied by the temple staff, and a door opened to disgorge about a dozen frantic men. Spartak jerked upright, heart seeming to stop its beating.

The horrified Eunora let out a stifled cry of dismay.

"There they are!" a voice yelled, and feet hammered the icy ground.

The equipment would just have to be abandoned—there was nothing else for it. Spartak snatched Eunora into his arms and fled toward the end of the street at which Vix and Vineta had been standing guard. There was no sign of Tiorin; hand-lamps had been brought out by the emerging priests, and their dazzling glare concealed the far end of the street.

Nonetheless, he also must have been spotted. Two of the new arrivals were dashing in that direction while the rest came on.

"Spartak!" Vix hissed. He had drawn the concealed sidearm Tigrid Zen had provided, and was hiding in an embrasure that had once been the entry to a store. "Go around the corner and turn left—I'll give them something to think about and then we'll make off to the right. Split them up!"

"Where's Vineta?" Spartak gasped.

"Right here!" the girl replied from the shadow behind Vix. "I'm staying with Vix, so don't argue!"

Spartak hadn't thought of arguing. He ignored the remark. "Vix, try to destroy the equipment! Maybe they won't learn just how much I now know!"

"You got what you wanted?" Vix was peering toward the brilliant lights, sighting along the barrel of his gun.

"Practically everything!"

At that instant a bolt seared along the street; why it had been so long delayed, Spartak could only guess—presumably the priests hadn't expected to need weapons when they were alerted. Who had done the alerting was one of the many matters to be left over for later. He ducked reflexively as splinters of stone flew from the spot where the bolt struck.

"See you later at Tharl's!" he whispered, and dived around the corner with Eunora. Behind him, Vix coolly took aim at the abandoned equipment, and fired his first bolt in reply to the priests'.

This district was laid out in conventional grid pattern, so that when Spartak came to the next intersection he could glance back and see clearly the end of the street near the temple. The light there was almost blinding by contrast with the general darkness, but he made out two figures ducking away in the opposite direction from that which he had taken.

Eunora had hidden her face against his chest, satisfied to perceive everything through his eyes.

Vix had obviously kept his promise to give the pursuers something to think about. It was long moments before anyone followed him and Vineta around the corner. The first person to do so was an armed man who fired one random shot; Vix let off another in reply, and provoked a scream, though whether it was of fear or pain Spartak could not tell. Then he ran on again, overtaking Vineta easily, and came to the intersection corresponding to the one at which Spartak himself had paused.

It was foolish, he told himself, not to make himself as scarce as time allowed, but something held him magnet-fashion; later, he decided it was a true premonition.

Vineta stumbled on the icy street. One of the pursuers loosed a bolt at her; it struck within arm's length of her, and she went sprawling. Spartak gasped, and felt Eunora tense against him till she felt like a wooden doll.

From his inadequate cover Vix darted forward, gun in one hand, the other outstretched to seize Vineta and drag her to safety. He fired twice, so that the pursuers held back, and by main force got the girl on her feet, her arm around his shoulder so she could use him as a crutch.

It was a brave thing to do, a good thing to do, but so foolhardy Spartak winced. For with the weight of the injured girl delaying him, they caught up to him at the end of the street and he went down under a mob of yelling priests.

Sick at heart, but driven by cold logic to the decision that he could do nothing more practical than to ensure that he at least got away, whether or not Tiorin did so, he ducked around the corner and made his way unchallenged into dark and empty streets. It was so unfair that he should get away; why not Vix, the brave fool?

"What shall I do?" he whispered to the stars. "On my own, what shall I do?"

And neither the stars nor the sobbing Eunora offered an answer.

XX

For the last half mile of their trip back to Tharl's home Eunora stumbled along beside him. She no longer had difficulty keeping up with the man's longer strides; he had brought himself to the verge of exhaustion.

"Is Tiorin here ahead of us?" he demanded as they came in sight of their goal.

She shook her head. "No one is there but Tharl, and he's in a terrible state of anxiety. He's wondering all the time whether he was right to reveal himself to you."

"But he's dependable?" Spartak insisted.

"I'm not so sure as I was," Eunora muttered. "Fear has been working on him ever since we left."

Spartak glanced at her, and for the first time in their headlong flight noticed that she was clutching something to her with both hands. He didn't have to ask what it was; he recognized it in the same moment that she realized telepathically he was wondering about it. His medical case, which he had brought away from the ship and assumed to have been left on the street with the rest of the abandoned equipment.

"I was holding the handle while you were working," she explained shyly. "And when you picked me up I held on to it."

"Well, it's something." Spartak sighed. "Go and tap on Tharl's window, will you, and get him to let us in?"

It was painfully clear from Tharl's face that fear had indeed been giving him second thoughts since their departure. He hastened to shut the door as they came in, and demanded at once why they were alone.

Spartak told him with crude brevity, and Tharl literally wrung his hands.

"Then you must make off at once!" he exclaimed. "They'll search the whole town, house by house, and if they find you here it'll be all up with me, and you as well. You say you have a ship—you must go back there at once and leave Asconel for somewhere safe—"

"I'm not leaving," Spartak grunted, dropping into a chair. "Not until Tiorin gets here."

"But if he's been taken too—"

"If he's been taken too, there's no chance of my reaching our ship—they'll pry the location of it out of my brothers' minds."

"Your—your brothers?" echoed Tharl uncertainly.

What point in keeping the secret any longer? If Bucyon's men had both Vix and Vineta, and possibly Tiorin as well, no disguise could conceal their identity for long. He said warily, "I'm Spartak, Hodat's half-brother, and the others are Vix and Tiorin."

Tharl's eyes grew round with wonder. "Forgive me!" he babbled. "I didn't know, I didn't guess!"

"You weren't supposed to," Spartak told him curtly, and leaned back, closing his eyes. "Eunora, you can warn us of approaching search parties, can't you?"

"I was supposed to warn you of danger down at the

temple," the girl answered, eyes filling with tears again. "And I failed. I'm—I'm sorry, but I was so fascinated—"

"You're forgiven," Spartak interrupted. "Just don't do it again."

"Excuse my asking," Tharl ventured, "But how can she—?"

"Warn us? She can, I promise you. She's a mutant."

"A mutant!" Millennia of Imperial prejudice sprang up in Tharl's mind, and he looked terrified.

"Stop it," Spartak ordered angrily. "She's of human stock, and that's more than you can say of Belizuek."

Curiosity and alarm struggled in Tharl's mind; the former won. "Did you find out what he is?" he demanded.

"I think so. He's a living creature, presumably capable of being killed; he requires to be housed in an airtight compartment in which the oxygen is far below our normal air; he's very large, and I suspect he's effectively larger than any creature we've ever had to deal with before. And he's intelligent. . . . But he is also insane."

Tharl turned that over and finally shook his head.

"What he is, in fact," Spartak amplified, "is the last survivor—in our galaxy at least—of the race from whom we inherited our starships."

Tharl stiffened. Spartak foresaw the objection he was about to voice, and went on crossly, "Oh, don't give me that nonsense about an insult to human achievement! The idea that we built our own is a piece of Imperial propaganda. I've studied ten years on Annanworld, and I'm satisfied that we went out from our original system—wherever that was—and found a cache of starships left by a previous race. We converted them to our own use and spread through the galaxy, finding more of them wherever we went, but no other trace of their builders. Not that it matters, really, except that it gives us a set of parameters to define Belizuek."

He ticked off points on his fingers. "Low oxygen. We have vague records to indicate that our predecessors were oxygen-breathers, as we are, but that they literally used up the resources of their own planets and went elsewhere before they needed to colonize the ones we eventually took over. Telepathic control of another species. This has been proposed as the ultimate in the domestication of animals. It fits. A view of the galaxy—and that's perhaps the most important thing of all!" He jerked upright in his chair.

"You've seen the picture of the galaxy which accompanies the 'proof' during the temple services? Of course, you have;

it's a key element and must be received by everyone. Didn't you notice that it's an Argian map that it's based on?"

Tharl could only mumble his answer.

"I tell you it is. Because it shows the Big Dark, and the Big Dark is a recent phenomenon; it's anomalous, so it's been carefully studied, and it's only some ten to twelve thousand years old. And at it's present size . . . well, I'm convinced that Belizuek has only seen human representations of the galaxy. That's the clincher for me.

"I said he was insane. Why else would he have been left behind when the rest of his species took off for—for wherever? Why else should he descend to this petty shift of domesticating human beings, to move him from star-system to star-system? I got it direct, down in the temple. Conceit! Illimitable megalomaniac craving for power! And he couldn't get it from his own species, because when he tried he was made an outcast and abandoned on—well, somewhere, presumably on Brinze where Bucyon and the rest came up against him. It's going to be a very interesting story when it's told: how he overcame his first victims, how he plotted to spread through the galaxy again. . . ."

"He?" The word was almost a squeak from Tharl.

"I know what you're trying to say." Spartak nodded. "If there's a living creature in every temple of Belizuek, why not speak of 'they'? This is the final evidence I have for his insanity.

"Equipped with the kind of knowledge and techniques which the Empire enjoyed at the height of its power, it was estimated that a man could breed his kind from his own germ-plasm, artificially, to repopulate an abandoned planet. I have no doubt that Belizuek could do the same if he wished. But he doesn't wish. He's afraid of competition. The part of him which is in the Penwyr temple is a second self, not a bred descendant, an offspring. Ten thousand years ago, before we spread through the galaxy, it was open and empty before him! And it took him that long to make up his mind that he could trust himself on one single other planet besides Brinze! I say he's insane."

"I see!" Eunora breathed. "That's why I had the impression that he was so large in time and space!"

"Exactly. With a vast number of identical selves, he's consequently telepathic between all of them. The Imperial policy of kicking mutants out to the Rim has prevented much study being done on the subject, but it's known that identity of receptor and transmitter is essential."

Eunora blinked, but Spartak shot her some wordless qualifications that satisfied her. Not so Tharl.

"Then how does he communicate with us? We're different!"

"Do you think he eats the sacrifices he's given?" Spartak said with monumental disgust. "Never. He uses them as a biological amplifier till their brains are burned out, to provide a link between himself and his audience."

Tharl felt for a chair and lowered himself into it without looking. "And you worked all this out since you arrived? Within the space of a day?"

"I—" Spartak checked. He stared at Eunora, who was giggling.

"You?" he said incredulously.

"Not really," she countered. "It took your knowledge to solve the problem. But all day since we were in the temple I've been asking questions of your subconscious to find out why I felt as I did during the ceremony, and I guess that sort of—well, brought things to your attention."

Spartak felt sweat prickle on his forehead. "What you're going to be like when you grow up, I just don't know! And if we've been deporting people like you to the Rim ever since the foundation of the Empire, what *can* be going on out there?"

Still, that was irrelevant. He glared at Tharl. "Well, now you know what became of your wife and son; now you know the nature of the beast we're up against. What are you going to do—order me to leave here and hide like a criminal, or help me further?"

"I don't see what I can do!" Tharl said helplessly. "If your brothers have been captured, it'll be known who they are, and—"

Spartak cut him short. "Are you in touch with any centers of resistance on Gard Island? I think you said the main temple, the original one on the planet, was there."

"Yes—yes, that's right, but . . . No, I know of no resistance movement there. It's become Bucyon's private preserve."

"You know the city itself, perhaps?"

"Oh, yes. When your brother Vix celebrated the completion of his campaign, he honored me by including me in a party to stand honor guard and general security duty at the Warden's palace."

"In that case, we should make for Gard," Spartak said. "In

any case we should make for Gard, is what I mean! I can think of nothing else to try except a direct attack on the original Belizuek that was brought to Asconel. A simple breach in the airtight container should be enough."

"So simple?" Tharl breathed. "Why, if I'd known—"

"You'd have gone to the temple here yourself," Spartak finished for him. "But I doubt if that would have helped; the local Belizueks will only be reflections of the original. No, that's the key point." He checked, struck by a sudden thought. "What means would you have used?"

"I'll show you," Tharl said eagerly, and went into the next room. There were scraping sounds.

"Under the floor," Eunora whispered. "A secret cavity."

And Tharl was back, cradling proudly in his arms a shiny energy gun. "The same with which I served your father and brother, sir," he announced. "And charged ready for use."

Spartak pursed his lips. "Here now is your chance to do a far greater service. Will you undertake it?"

Tharl looked extremely unhappy, but he didn't say anything.

"You must hide us here for at least a day, to give Tiorin a chance to rejoin us—this is the only meeting-place we have. During the daytime, however, you must go out and about as usual to avoid suspicion. While you're out, ask what means we can employ to get to Gard—anything, a boat, a skyboat, whatever can still be hired. And as soon as possible, we'll go."

"We, sir?" Tharl ventured.

"I understood your wife and your son—"

"And your brothers, sir." Tharl placed the butt of the gun on the ground and leaned on it, gazing into nowhere. "I don't wish to appear a coward—I'm not, believe me!—but after such a long time, to have a plan of action offered. . . . It takes me aback, you might say."

Seeing his lower lip tremble, Spartak refrained from pushing him any further. He yawned cavernously. "I must sleep," he muttered. "Though I'm not sure I can. Eunora—?"

But she had already closed her eyes.

XXI

"Someone's coming!" Eunora whispered. "Officials!"

Spartak jolted out of uneasy slumber. The long winter night had not yet given way to dawn, but the first thing he saw when he opened his eyes was Tharl, up and dressed and carrying a tray of breakfast: hot broth and bread. His face was pale with alarm.

"Searching for us?" Spartak rapped out.

Eunora, puzzled, shook her head. "Apparently not. There are four of them going from house to house—one's a priest, I think, because he's so arrogant and self-satisfied. . . . But they aren't searching any of the houses, just knocking at the doors and telling the people that . . ."

"Telling them what?" Spartak urged.

The girl bit her lip. "Both Tiorin and Vix were captured, Bucyon's men know who they are. There's going to be a grand ceremony at the chief temple on Gard—is that right?—at which they'll voluntarily give themselves up to Belizuek, and everyone who can is urged to go there and witness this final triumph of Bucyon over those who support Hodat."

Spartak sat rock-still for long moments. Finally he said with ghastly humor, "At least it means we won't be conspicuous if we go there. But do they not know about us?"

"You'd think so, wouldn't you? If they've got an admission of their identity out of them . . ." Eunora knitted her brows. "I think I understand, though. The priest was already aware that there were three brothers, including you, but he's taking it for granted that you'll make a false step and reveal yourself. Then anyone who notices will at once report you."

"That sounds like them, all right," Tharl said sourly. "They know how their dupes behave nowadays. Utter one false word, make one wrong move, and some favor-currying bastard will be off to inform on you."

"They're coming closer," Eunora warned. "Only three or four houses away. We'd better get out of sight."

Tensely, crouched in the concealment of a closet, they strained their ears for auditory confirmation of what she had detected, and when he let them out again Tharl gave it fresh emphasis.

"Just as the little girl says," he muttered. "Everyone who

possibly can is expected to travel to Gard and see your brothers sacrificed, sir. We'd best make haste, hadn't we?"

"Not too fast." Spartak sighed. "Give them a chance to get over the hill, then take some of my money—here—and go book us passage on the fastest available transport." He took some Imperial coins from his belt-pouch.

"As you say, sir," Tharl conceded, and served them the meal he had prepared.

He must have been slightly ahead of the rush; he got them all passage on one of the fastest boats left in the northern hemisphere, an elderly skimmer whose engines wheezed so badly she could barely get up on her foils with the load of passengers that crammed aboard, but which was at any rate better than some of the half-rotten fishing boats in which the latecomers embarked. They must have known, Spartak reflected, that they stood no chance of getting to Gard in time for the ceremony, but either they'd be satisfied to get away from drab poverty-stricken Penwyr for a while, or else the fear of not "showing willing" compelled them to make the gesture and impress the priests. He hoped it was the former, which might indicate they still retained some normal human feelings, but he feared it was more likely the latter.

There was a very bad moment as they approached the dockside toward sunset, shivering in the chill blasts of icy foam that the night wind whipped off the estuary; two priests stood beside the gangway to their skimmer, searching the faces of all those who passed.

"Are they looking for us, Eunora?" Spartak whispered.

"Luckily no," she murmured in reply. "They're turning away people notoriously lax in their temple attendance—this trip is supposed to be a reward for loyal homage. I don't know what they're doing about strangers. So few people travel nowadays, they hadn't considered the problem."

Tharl drew a deep breath. "Leave this to me, sir," he suggested, and as they drew near the priests he pushed his way forward.

"Forgive me, sirs!" he shouted, and their heads turned. "Perhaps you'll remember, sirs, that when Belizuek first came to honor Penwyr with his presence, my wife and my sons were the very first to give him their total service. And I was bitter!" He shook his head in a parody of regret. "I know now it was foolish of me. Why, if the Warden's brothers themselves have returned and agreed to offer themselves up

to Belizuek, what more powerful proof could anyone want
that he is indeed the master of us all and truly superior?"

"Clever!" Spartak whispered. "Is it going to work?"

"Oh, yes," Eunora said with a twisted smile. "They're lap-
ping it up. He'd only better be careful he doesn't overdo it—
one of them is thinking of singling him out for some special
temple duty."

If they had been aware that the long bundle of clothing
and provisions slung over Tharl's shoulder contained the energy gun he had produced last night, they would have been a
good deal less eager. But Belizuek was far away from the
docks, and these were only human dupes.

Tharl came to rejoin them when they were securely
aboard, wiping sweat from his face, and blushing faintly at
Spartak's warm compliments.

"Too early for that, sir," he countered. "We haven't even
cast off yet."

In one way at least he was right. That voyage was among
the most dreadful experiences of Spartak's entire life. To be
with these three or four hundred people who laughed and
sang ribald songs while they passed canteens of precious wine
and the typical Penwyr sour beer as they might on any fes-
tival excursion—then, to remember with a jolt the excuse for
such jollification: the planned sacrifice of his brothers, including Vix whom many of these people had served in the old
days, whom they had cheered as the son of his father, the late
Warden, and brother of Hodat the heir-apparent . . . that was
like living a nightmare. And all the time Eunora was alert for
some keen-eyed person to pierce his disguise.

The chances of his being betrayed receded somewhat when
the word got about that he was a doctor, and a mother whose
child was sensitive to seasickness came begging his help. The
little boy recovered at once when Spartak tended him, and
after that a shy succession of patients surrounded him, asking
help and advice for an incredible range of complaints.

Spartak's fury burned inside him like a coal. When he had
left Asconel for Annanworld, there had been no one hungry,
no one sick except with mild infections which could never be
wholly eliminated, and certainly no one suffering from the
deficiency diseases. Yet time and again when he examined
those who now presented themselves, he saw that their need
was not for drugs, but for soap and water and a proper diet.

Weeping sores. Ulcers. Gums sickly sweet with pus. Children's bones twisted into awkward curves. Eyes matted with a

dirty yellow discharge. So the tale went on. More than once, as he was on the point of bursting out at some silly fool about the true reason for his condition, Eunora caught his eye and gave an almost imperceptible headshake, implying, "Don't! He'll go to the priest at once."

The priest—there was apparently always one aboard any passenger vessel on Asconel nowadays—came to Spartak in the end; that encounter was hardly to be avoided. He put a number of curious questions which Spartak deftly dodged, trying to give the impression that the priest was making himself look ignorant by not knowing the answers already, and in the end the trick worked and the priest made off, embarrassed without being sure why.

It was established beyond a doubt that half the people who had set off from northern islands like Penwyr would never get to Gard in time, when they started to raise the traffic from the nearer ports the next day. The sea seemed to be crawling with passenger vessels; there were even skyboats overhead, the first Spartak had seen since his return. All were converging on Gard for the ceremony. Winter was behind them at this latitude; the sky was blue and the sun mild and warm.

The tremendous strain the influx of visitors—pilgrims, perhaps, would be a closer term, Spartak reflected sourly—put on the resources of Gard city worked in their favor. With boats crowding into the port and disembarkation reduced to a panicky rush down the gangplanks so that room could be made for the next vessel, the guards and priests who supervised the travelers could not hope to keep control. Moreover, here was no poverty-stricken provincial town; Bucyon clearly liked his luxuries as much as anyone, and everything worked, to the wonder of the visiting children. Food was abundant, on quayside stalls and in the city's stores; gaudy posters, banners, and streamers decorated the buildings for the great day tomorrow; and relic hawkers offered—when there were no priests in sight—such precious items as hairs from Bucyon's beard and Lydis's nail-clippings.

Spartak, taken in at first by this deception, was halfminded to buy one of the relics and put it under the microscope to see if Lydis's alleged mind-reading powers were due to a cellular mutation; then he realized these were frauds to trap the credulous.

His heart ached as he beheld his former home. His

knuckles whitened on the handle of the medical case he carried, now much depleted after the voyage.

"If I could only get next to Bucyon!" he whispered.

"Not a chance," Tharl muttered, glancing around to make sure they were not overheard as they trudged, with thousands of others, toward the center of the city. Ahead, the streets were in full operation, and there were delighted squeals from the youngest children who had never seen a molecular-flow street before. "He's always guarded very strictly. And Lydis, who can read thoughts, never leaves his side."

"Where is the temple?" Spartak demanded.

"It used to be the Place of Grand Assembly," Tharl told him. "You know it, of course."

Spartak did indeed. There he had witnessed the seating of Hodat in the Warden's chair, the last day he had stayed on Asconel before his departure, and Vix's and Tiorin's too. It was a vast open horseshoe of seating: the inner rows for dignitaries, the outer for the public.

He came to a decision, arranged a meeting-place with Tharl for later, and sent him off to find them a place to stay. Then he and Eunora went straight to the temple.

It had not been altered much to accommodate its change of function. Behind it loomed the dark shape of the Warden's palace, now Bucyon's home. The Warden's chair had been moved forward to make room for a huge gilded dome. Inside there dwelt Belizuek: the original self of which all the local Belizuek's were only reflections. The size of the dome took him aback. Either this Belizuek was a monster, or there were several layers of armor around him, in which case would even an energy gun . . . ?

He checked himself. Before making any more plans, he needed to get details of the planned ceremony. There was a gang of men at work assembling a high dais close to the Warden's chair; it only required a few friendly words and the flash of a five-circle coin to set one of them to part with the full program.

This dais was to be the place where Vix and Tiorin were displayed to any in the crowd who might doubt their identity, and from which they would state their intention of entering voluntarily into the "full service" of Belizuek. Bucyon and Lydis would present; they would leave the palace in ceremonial procession at such a time, reach the temple at such another time, begin the ritual at such another time. . . .

Spartak seized on the crucial point that they would leave

their groundcar at the far end of the horseshoe. He tipped their informant and returned thither. There were many idle sightseers around, so they attracted no special attention.

"I have it!" he whispered, and snapped his fingers. He shot a glance at Eunora. "Will it work?"

"I—don't know." She was very pale. "Can you get Tharl to the right place with his gun?"

"I'm sure I can. I was raised in the Warden's palace, remember, and that dominates the far end of the Assembly. But am I asking too much of you?"

"I don't think so," Eunora murmured. "Until I meet Lydis face to face I can't be sure. But I had a lot of practice in dissembling back home. I think even to a mind reader I may—may!—be able to tell a lie."

XXII

The following day, the great day when the last traces of the old order would be wiped forever as the late Warden's brothers acknowledged the dominion of Belizuek and entered freely into his full service, dawned mild and sunny, and grew rapidly hot. Long before the scheduled time of the ceremony people were thronging into the streets; those fortunate enough to view it in person crammed the horseshoe seating of the Place of Grand Assembly, where music and songs in honor of Belizuek whiled the time away, and the ordinary populace put on what they had left in the way of presentable clothing and made do with the public watch-screens and amateur tumblers fooling around in the gutters.

The dais was completed. Covered in gaudy banners, it stood waiting for the victims, like an altar readied at the shrine of a bloodthirsty deity.

Punctually on schedule, Bucyon—gorgeous in ceremonial armor that shone chrome-bright and dazzling—entered his groundcar. Beside him, pale, very beautiful, and dressed as always in a floor-long black gown, sat Lydis. The people who gathered to cheer disciplined their minds into adoring patterns, fearing the rumored talent which had brought her to her present eminence.

Everywhere the procession passed, there were yells of delight and applause, and chanting in honor of Belizuek and of Bucyon, who had blessed Asconel by bringing him here. Oc-

casionally a visitor from elsewhere on the planet, who
remembered the old days well enough to have a spark of
envy kindled at the continuing luxury of Gard contrasted
with the poverty at home, shouted less fervently than the rest.
But soon the pressure of anxiety lest he be discovered drove
him to out-bellow his neighbors.

It was a spectacle to dim the most vivid memory of the old
days, anyhow: the guards, the priests in their most brilliant
robes, and at the center the lovely Lydis and the handsome
Bucyon, acknowledging the love of their subjects with an occasional gracious wave.

Certain unscheduled events also took place.

Not long after the honored dignitaries began to fill their
seats in the Assembly, a fat man in the frontmost rank not
reserved for priests—who occupied the first dozen banks of
seating in the official plan, but who had not yet shown up—
clapped his hand to his nape and looked to see if he had
killed a stinging insect. There was nothing on his palm.

Another minute or so, and he began to complain loudly to
his neighbor that it was terribly hot. Sweat ran from his face;
he fought for breath, loosening the neckband of his coat, and
swore at the sun for beating down so fiercely. It was not long
before he closed his eyes and began to breathe in enormous
gasps. Alarmed, those around him sought help, and were relieved at the approach of a fair-bearded man who identified
himself as a doctor.

Instructions were crisply issued to carry the fat man to
shade, rest him, and let him recover his spirits. That attended
to, the fair-bearded man fell talking with those who had appealed for his aid, and it was entirely natural that, as the arrival of Bucyon was signaled he should slip into the place the
fat man had left vacant.

It had not all gone so smoothly. As he tensed to see
Bucyon enter the vast stadiumlike Assembly—he could not
refer to it as a temple, the way everyone else now did—Spartak was vaguely surprised to think that he was here exactly as
arranged. Yesterday afternoon, when he found that Tharl had
been overanxious to please, and provided them with accom-
modation in a place he felt fit for a Warden's son, there had
been a lot of trouble, and ultimately they had had to settle
for the rooms after all—Gard was packed to overflowing
with the pilgrims from overseas. To the Big Dark with fears
of appearing conspicuous, anyway. The short conversation he

had had with those around him here had satisfied him that Bucyon did not rule wholly by the power of Belizuek. Here gathered were men and women who were conscious traitors; they would never be called on for the full service of Belizuek! They were Bucyon's willing accomplices in the business of raping Asconel.

It was only to be expected. Bucyon's own forces—even if, along with the priests, you counted in the crews from a respectably sized spacefleet—wouldn't suffice to administer a population of nine hundred million, no matter how pliant.

But the proof of his suspicions made him feel sick.

At least they hadn't suspected him in their turn. He was acknowledged as a fit companion, a tribute to the glibness of his tongue and his courtly manners. It almost seemed that it was easier to conduct nefarious business in broad daylight than under the cover of night. The trouble they had had sneaking Tharl into the Warden's palace, even though his memory held a clearer picture of it than had ever been given to the old soldier when he was assigned to security duties here in the capital ... ! With Eunora keeping watch for patrols so that they could dodge into shadow every time, they had still spent better than four hours getting Tharl inside.

Spartak's eyes strayed toward the palace. Was the man safe where he was supposed to be?

Tharl twisted himself into a marginally more comfortable position. The hot, clammy air from the discharge pipe of the air circulators coated his skin with dirty moisture. But he had gloves, and his hands would not slip on the switches of his gun. Lovingly he sighted it for the hundredth time on the distant golden dome shielding the alien monster Belizuek.

He felt himself a changed person since the moment he met Spartak and his brothers. He had been given back his sense of purpose in life; he had been offered a chance to avenge the slaughter of his wife and son. He lowered the gun to a resting position and gave a sigh of contentment. Nothing else mattered. He was still bruised from a fall he had taken trying to get up into the interior of this ventilation pipe, still retrospectively anxious about the noise he'd made which might have alarmed a guard—but apparently had gone unheeded—and both hungry and tired in the bargain. To the Big Dark with such complaints! He had the important thing: a job to do.

Once more he lifted the gun and peered through its tele-

scope. His heart quickened. Spartak was in position among
the dignitaries on the steeply banked seating. It couldn't be
much longer now.

If only the little girl played her part—!

The next in the sequence of unscheduled events didn't
come until Bucyon and Lydis were getting down from their
groundcar. The archpriest Shry—a curiously horrible figure,
his back bulging enormously with some soft outgrowth of
tissue—came to greet them, bands played, and the watchers
cheered.

Under the arms of the guards who held back the crowd,
a little girl slipped like an eel, clutching a bunch of flowers.
A cry of alarm went up, and the guards leveled their guns;
then they hesitated, seeing how tiny she was, how well-
scrubbed and attractive in her too-small, faded frock, and
how innocuous the posy was that she now shyly offered to
Bucyon.

The tyrant scowled for a second, wondering who had arranged this "spontaneous" gesture of affection and why he
had not been warned. He glanced at Lydis, who was frowning, but when after some seconds she did not tell him to
desist, he put on a smile and accepted the flowers, afterward
patting the girl's head. She was by now almost overcome by
the strain of her great moment, and when Bucyon had gone
on she slipped out of sight. Under one of the temporary
stands erected to watch the procession she keeled over and
slept for more than half an hour.

The posy had contained the last of Spartak's precious supply of the drug with which he had restored her to sanity.
Handing it to Bucyon, she had triggered an injector that shot
the entire dose into the fleshy ball of his thumb.

And all the time she had slid away from the probing of
Lydis and Shry. To resist them, to lie and deceive them for
about ninety seconds, had cost her every ounce of her energy,
so that when she fell down in a faint she knew neither where
she was nor whether she would ever wake up.

Spartak felt a lurching sensation of relief. Bucyon was
coming up the main aisle of the Assembly holding the posy
he had been given by Eunora. Provided the injector hadn't
misfired, he was going to be extremely tractable. . . .

And that, presumably, was Shry. He shivered as he studied
the gross misshapen form of the archpriest. Yet Lydis found

nothing distasteful in him; she accepted his arm as he helped her to a chair to one side of and behind the Warden's, which Bucyon sank into. Fanfares made the very sky resound, and were themselves scarcely louder than the bellows of applause that issued from the crowd.

Then they brought Vix and Tiorin down the aisle.

Silence fell, for which Spartak was eternally grateful. He ached to see his brothers treated thus. Their disguises had been stripped—their hair restored to its original flaming red—and they were clad in plain white suits, with their feet bare in an age-old penitential gesture.

And there was apparently no sham about Bucyon's claim that they were to sacrifice themselves voluntarily. They were neither bound nor very closely guarded, and as they came down the long aisle they held their heads high and walked like heroes.

The horrifying idea struck him that if they spotted him they would feel it an honor to give him away. He cursed not having found time to change his appearance once again, and made what shift he could to hide his face behind a raised hand.

But they passed on, to take their places on the altarlike dais, and all was in readiness for the great moment.

The only explanation he could think of for their obvious willingness to come to their own funeral was that Belizuek's emanations were already in control of their minds. And indeed, now that he turned his attention to it, Spartak thought he could feel the same awe-inspiring presence which had impressed the Penwyr congregation.

For a moment, indeed, it tempted him to yield, seeming to say, "Fool! Even if Belizuek is in truth a living creature, is he not the last of a line of greater than the human race—those squabbling borrowers of another's power?"

And further: *What can I do to thwart the destiny of this whole planet? I, one man, with a feeble plan that depends on a dozen outrageous coincidences to succeed!*

He hoped Tharl was going to be on time.

People had recognized Vix and Tiorin, and their faces reflected their complete conviction about Bucyon's claims. He really did have them here; they really were about to enter Belizuek's service. Some, especially those near Spartak, had harbored doubts till this very last moment. Now they were men-

tally congratulating themselves on having thrown in their lot
with the winning party.

Shry stepped to the front of the dais and began to address
the crowd in a whining bleat of a voice, describing the event
they all knew they were about to witness. But no one complained; behind the words there slowly grew the sense of Belizuek's presence, the aura of a master of galaxies, the sense of
being in a supernatural creature's power. Spartak sweated and
fidgeted. He had told Tharl to fire arbitrarily five minutes after the commencement of the ceremony. Never had five
minutes been so long! Already the waves of mental control
were battering his defenses; most of the crowd had suc-
cumbed willingly and instantly.

Something must have gone wrong.

Tharl must have been discovered.

The plan was a failure. Asconel was doomed and he with
it.

Shry reached the climax of his introduction, turned his
twisted body, and threw up an arm in a dramatic gesture
toward Tiorin and Vix—

And with impeccable theatrical timing, Tharl loosed the
first of his energy bolts against the golden dome enclosing Belizuek.

XXIII

The second bolt followed, the third, fourth, and fifth, with
the impersonal regularity of a clock's ticking, and on the fifth
the golden dome was broached. A noise like a scream was
heard, half with the ears, half with the mind, and a foul stink
oozed out over the crowd. It reminded Spartak of the stench
from mud exposed by an exceptionally low tide at the mouth
of a river much used for the disposal of sewage.

Paralysis overtook everyone present for the space of long
seconds, except himself. The first shot had brought him to his
feet; before the last had struck, he had fought his way down
the nearest transverse aisle and was clambering over the barrier separating the seats from the longitudinal aisle up which
his brothers had so lately been marched on show.

His head was ringing with both sound and soundless cries:
the yells of dismay that had now broken out among the
crowd, the incoherent jabbering of orders to the guards,

something being shrieked in a high panicky voice by the woman Lydis—all these were commonplace reactions to what had happened. But overlying them, permeating the very air, was a sudden terrible sense of doom, the emanation from Belizuek's mind as his body was exposed to the oxygen-rich air of this planet preferred by men.

Spartak thought of the tens of millennia through which his species had used up the atmospheres of their old worlds, adapting little by little, growing using with every passing generation to a higher concentration of carbon dioxide, a lower percentage of available oxygen, until the contact of this rawer air was like acid poured on naked flesh.

But that was nothing to occupy his mind right now. For the present he had the single advantage of knowing what had happened; it was a slender weapon to offer against Bucyon's armor, but he had to make the most of it.

He glanced at Vix and Tiorin. As he had hoped, they were standing bewildered, blinking at each other and the familiar Place of Grand Assembly, like men newly woken from a bad dream. But it would take Belizuek a while to die, and until he did die, the invisible talons would remain fast on their minds.

Now: action.

Spartak drew himself up to his full height and confronted the man who till this morning had been only a name to him—Bucyon, who had come from space to rape and ruin a beautiful world in the name of an obscene monster. And who now, if he was human, must be open for mastery by the first who seized control of him.

"Bucyon!" Spartak bellowed, hands cupped around his mouth. The name seemed to plow through the oppressive mental aura as the energy bolt had sizzled upward in the rain of Gwo, leaving a visible track of white steam. "Bucyon, *speak to your people!*"

Spartak had spent long on his choice of phrase. That was his ultimate selection: a command both innocuous and deadly.

Shry had gone wailing to see what harm was done to the golden dome; half out of sight from Spartak, he was waving his arms frantically, trying to make guards and other priests come to him and help repair the damage. But the woman Lydis—doubtless aware of the drug now coursing through Bucyon's body—had jerked to her feet and now stood rockstill, her eyes burning Spartak.

The call he had uttered took effect. Hoping for some

guidance from Belizuek's human deputy, the crowd quieted, the guards tensed for anticipated orders, the priests hesitated as they made to obey Shry's beckoning signals.

"Speak to your people, the people of Asconel!" Spartak shouted again. "Tell them—*what is Belizuek?*"

But he was watching Lydis, not Bucyon, and was prepared when she gasped and tried to clutch at the big man's arm, wanting to prevent the betrayal which he could not because the drug compelled him to total honesty.

He jumped forward, hurling himself at the overhang of the dais and rolling onto its boards like a high-jumper clearing a difficult mark. As he moved, he was still calling: "Bucyon, Bucyon, tell them, tell them—the people of Asconel want to hear from you—*tell them about Belizuek!*"

On the last breathless yell he was at Bucyon's side, and his shoulder slammed against Lydis's, heedless of her sex. Fragile as a foam dummy, she staggered back and fell against the chair from which she had risen, and remained dazed for a few precious moments during which Spartak alone had Bucyon's ear.

The drug took over his will, and he spoke helplessly to the attentive audience.

"Belizuek is the last survivor of the species that ruled the galaxy before man."

The oppressive aura of hate and desperation redoubled its intensity, as if a storm cloud had settled over the Assembly. Spartak risked a glance behind him, fearing that Shry might have contrived to effect repairs.

"He's a material creature, isn't he?" he shouted. "Not a mystical spirit, not a supernatural being, but a creature that has to feed and breathe as we do!"

"Yes!" Bucyon agreed, helpless to deny it.

"And that can be killed as we can!"

"Yes!"

Already the impact of this revelation was having its effect among the crowd. Those who had believed otherwise were pale with dismay; the conscious traitors who had never been duped were yet paler, for some of them thought they recognized a familiar countenance behind the new beard on Spartak's face, despite the dyeing of his hair.

"Why is he still with us, when the rest of his kind have gone? Tell them that!"

"They cast him out," Bucyon answered. "They exiled him to the world called Brinze, where men found him."

"Why?"

"They said it was because he was insane, but he isn't."
Spittle was gathering on the corners of Bucyon's mouth and
running down into his beard. His eyes were rimmed white as
he strove and failed to stop his tongue from speaking.

"Ah, but he was supposed to be immortal, wasn't he?"
Spartak thundered. "And he's not! One breath of Asconel's
clean sweet air, and he's dying!"

But so slowly! Was there not another charge in Tharl's
gun, to burn directly into Belizuek's substance? Spartak could
feel the maddened will to survive which the creature was now
broadcasting like raw energy, and so too could everyone else.
In the living brains of those who surrounded him, human and
alien thought were locked into terrible conflict, and—

And it stopped.

Exactly as though the sun had come out, the sense of death
and disaster ceased, and Spartak allowed himself to hope for
victory. He half turned, and was met by a scream from the
cripple Shry.

"Belizuek lives! It's only the servant who's died—burned
out—his brain failed! Bring the captives over here!"

Guards, still blindly obedient to Shry's command, made for
the passively waiting Vix and Tiorin.

"Tell them to stop!" Spartak gasped at Bucyon.

But Lydis was on her feet, thrusting herself between her
overlord and the man who had dared to stand against him.

"No!" she hissed, so close to Spartak that tiny drops flew
from her rage-contorted mouth and struck his cheek. "Belizuek is All, Belizuek is the Master, Belizuek was before the
galaxy was!"

Time froze. The guards were poised to pinion Vix and Tiorin, the people were still too confused to act, and he could
say nothing. Even crippled by the breach in his protective
dome, there was no knowing what Belizuek could do if he
were given a fresh victim to serve as a telepathic link between himself and his slaves.

An idea? A glimmer of hope? Spartak pushed Lydis aside
roughly and addressed Bucyon once more. "Tell the people
what Belizuek does with his servants! Say what becomes of
those who go behind the screen into his presence!"

"He won't answer," Lydis spat out. "Your drug has spent
itself, and I control his mind. Guards! Guards!"

Indeed, Bucyon's face had taken on the vacant look of an

idiot, and he stood swaying and gazing out over the Assembly without seeing it.

A sense of defeat which had nothing to do with Belizuek's emanations overcame Spartak. The guards closed on his brothers, Lydis laughed madly in triumph—

And Tharl let go the last charge from his energy gun.

Like a white-hot steel bar it blazed down toward the rent in the golden dome, and in the final yard of its passage it speared Shry and turned him into a staggering horror wrapped in flame. Beyond him, only half spent on such a petty target, it burned deep, deep into the vitals of Belizuek, and Lydis screamed as though the pain were hers alone.

A unison shock raced through the crowd. The guards about to seize the captives turned, the priests cried out in terror, Spartak in relief.

Then Vix moved.

He shook himself as though rousing from a long sleep, clubbed both fists together, and brought them up into the kidneys of the guard who would have seized him. The man gave a yell of agony and clapped his hands to the seat of the pain. Vix reached past him and took his sidearm and his sword in simultaneous precise movements. The sidearm he thrust into Tiorin's hand as the other man also came to himself, and without a pause jabbed the sword's point home in the exposed neck of the disarmed guard.

He opened his throat in a cry which had not been heard except ceremonially since long before Bucyon usurped the Warden's chair, and it was like turning back the pages of the past.

"For Ascone-e-e-*el*!"

And he was away.

Spartak was giddy with the speed of it. His eyes could not follow the instant blur that his half-brother became, a red-topped living torch of disaster for those who stood in his way. Behind, calmer, Tiorin weighed the gun he had suddenly acquired, then with a thoughtful look raised and aimed it. A bolt scattered the priests from around the golden dome, sending them tumbling off the edge of its raised platform. Another dispersed those muddled guards who thought to come to the rescue of their fellows. Another discouraged a group of conscious traitors who were trying to get out of the far end of the Assembly.

But by then Vix had cleared a path all the way to Spartak's side, and five men lay coughing the same blood which smeared his blade. He clapped Spartak on the arm and yelled at him, "A miracle, brother, a miracle! I love you for it!"

And he was after Bucyon himself, the sword swinging high to split the bemused usurper's skull.

"Stop!" Spartak cried. "He's no more than a booby now—his mind's gone!"

"Let the people see!" Vix answered savagely, and struck.

With that final blow, even before Bucyon toppled headlong, the berserk madness left him. In its place, there was a cold white fury that made Spartak shiver as he looked on it.

Tiorin came forward to stand with his brothers. No one lifted a hand to prevent him.

"I'm Vix of Asconel!" Vix roared at the frightened people. "Here's Tiorin, your rightful Warden! Here's Spartak our brother to whom we owe our deliverance and *yours*!" He pointed with his sword, and the blade dripped red. "There lies a tyrant who had you in his hand—look at yourselves and think, think, *think*! You're underfed, you're dirty, you're lousy, you're like savages and not civilized citizens!"

It began to penetrate. People looked at one another, seeing not so much those present, but the millions of starving and diseased who had appeared on Asconel since Bucyon's arrival.

"And here's the last of those who led you by the nose!" Vix bellowed. "The woman Lydis who betrayed my brother!"

He whirled, and was quick enough to grasp her by the robe as she made to flee. The robe tore, fell away, exposed her maggot-pale body to the pitiless glare of the noontide sun.

There was utter silence. During it, Spartak felt nausea rise to choke his throat.

Lydis was not a human mutant, accidentally gifted with the power to read minds. She was a tool of Belizuek. And instead of breasts on the front of her torso, she had a black pulsating growth that squirmed and leaked a stinking ichor as it followed its alien parent into the doorway of death.

The crowd saw. The crowd rose up, and panicked, and fled, and left the brothers to their solitary triumph.

XXIV

A short eternity later they were together again, in the Warden's suite of the palace: the brothers, and those who had most signally served Asconel during its time of terror, among whom were Tigrid Zen and Eunora. The mutant girl sat a little apart, clutching in both hands a big cup of sweet fruit-juice, while the men relaxed over wine of Asconel's finest vintage. Tharl had taken a place next to her, as a symbol of apology for the way he had first reacted to the news of her talent.

"That's what turned the tide for us," Spartak murmured, thinking of the way Lydis's robe had fluttered to the ground.

"Well, obviously," Tiorin agreed from the head of the table around which they had gathered. "It turned my stomach, I tell you frankly, and I'd already begun to suspect something of the sort."

"But how could Hodat not have known?" Vix snapped. It wasn't the first time they'd had this discussion, but it was the first time they'd been able to relax during it; up till a few days previous, the business of setting to rights the chaos of a whole planet had kept them busy from waking to sleeping.

Tigrid Zen cleared his throat. "I've been making some inquiries. If you'll forgive my admitting that I probed into the private affairs of your family . . . ?"

"Go on," said Spartak. "It's one of the chief penalties of being born into a position like ours that our private affairs are of public interest to a good many people."

"Well put, sir. In fact, what turned up was to your late brother's great credit. There was no foundation for the common gossip about a liaison between him and Lydis. He'd stuck strictly to his original intention of marrying a woman who'd advantage Asconel's future by allying us with some other prosperous world. He was deluded into believing that Lydis's mind reading was—well—at his service, so to speak, and he flattered and bribed her to make her stay on his side."

"Where did the marriage story get started, then?" Tiorin asked.

"Who can say?" Tigrid Zen shrugged. "Perhaps she planted the rumor herself. We'll never know now."

True enough. The death of her alien parasite had killed her within an hour.

"Speaking of things to people's credit," Tiorin murmured, "I don't believe I ever got around to complimenting you, Eunora. I'm sure Spartak and Vix have stood deputy for me, but now that things are less hectic than they were, I must thank you. And ask you something, too."

He paused. Everyone grinned broadly. They had become perfectly accustomed to Eunora's talent, and the last trace of the Empire's anti-mutant policy had faded even from Tharl's mind.

"How I withstood the probing of both Lydis and Shry while I was giving the flowers to Bucyon?" Eunora nodded. "I don't think I shall ever know. All I remember is the sense of shock which I had when I realized the two things I hadn't known beforehand: first, that Lydis was directly in contact with Belizuek, and second, that Shry was also, but far more—more firmly."

"The parasitic growth on his back," Spartak put in, "must have weighed as much as he did."

"And felt like it," Eunora agreed grimly. "All I can say is that when I reacted to the shock, I must have forced myself into the identity I'd taken on. I was just a simpleminded little girl, overawed at being in the great man's presence, scared at my own daring in offering him the flowers. . . . I blanked out until I came to under the stand half an hour later, and then I had to hide to keep out of the way of all the people who were fleeing from this final horror, the exposure of Lydis."

"But that's what turned the tide, as I said," Spartak repeated. "Even with Belizuek dying, and cut off from mental contact with his slaves; even with Bucyon killed in front of them, there were people in that crowd who'd staked their futures on Bucyon, and to the Big Dark with the rest of the citizens—let 'em rot!"

Tiorin's face darkened. "Don't I know it! Most of them came fawning to me directly, saying didn't I want the cooperation of those who had been administering the planet under Bucyon because they knew all the ropes now. . . . Some of them were men I'd known in Father's day, too. And of course, a lot more of them tried to bribe their way off-world. But we caught most of them, I think."

"And got their cooperation," Tigrid Zen rumbled. "If not exactly in the way they hoped. We're going to have the best harvest in years, both by land and sea, thanks to their bare-handed efforts."

"Excuse me, sirs," Tharl put in diffidently. "Something I've been wondering ... How *was* it that killing the—the main Belizuek got rid of all the others so easily?"

"Hmm?" Spartak turned his head. "Oh, yes. I wasn't absolutely right in what I told you back at Penwyr, but nearly so. Remember I told you that Belizuek was insane, and especially afraid of competition, even from his own derived images?"

Tharl nodded, frowning with concentration but making a gallant effort to follow Spartak's exposition.

"For fear that one of his—ah—duplicates should achieve independence and usurp his uniqueness, he'd made sure the mental linkage between them was very tight. It proved too tight. The effect of death on the central organism was reflected in a sort of psychic paralysis of all the others; they could have existed as separate entities, but he'd forbidden them to. They weren't actually dead till they were exposed to the air, but effectively they were in a sort of trance due to the shock of telepathically experiencing death."

He shrugged, and Tharl muttered thanks.

"I'll tell you something, sir," he added after a moment. "You came to me later and congratulated me on the uncanny rightness of the timing for the last bolt I fired, yes?"

"Agreed!" Tiorin said warmly. "It was a real crisis point—"

"Well, sir," Tharl broke in, looking unaccountably depressed, "I'd saved that bolt, for a mixture of all sorts of reasons. First, I was going to save it for myself; then I thought, if I'm discovered, all I need do is jump down this shaft I'm in—a fall of a hundred-odd feet to a rock-hard floor should finish me off. So instead I saved it in case you were wrong about the way to kill Belizuek. I figured I could at least kill Bucyon if he went through with his plan to sacrifice you."

"But you fired again before I struck Bucyon down," Vix objected.

"Yes, sir. I thought and thought, and for a long time I was worried because Spartak was standing so close to Bucyon, I couldn't get a clear shot. Then finally I decided it was taking too long for things to settle down—I couldn't have completed the job—and there was a clear shot at Shry, who was after all Belizuek's chief spokesman and chaplain to Bucyon and all the rest of it. I figured if Belizuek was already dead, he'd be in a really frantic state, and he wasn't—he was calling people up to help him, and peering into the hole my bolts had made, as I could see clearly through the telescope on my gun. ... So I said, 'What's more likely to put a stiff dose of fear in their guts than to see Belizuek's best-beloved shriveled like a leaf in a fire?' And I let the last bolt go."

"To which decision we owe the fact that we're here now," Tiorin said soberly. "Along with some other things, such as that Bucyon wasn't an able man, just a greedy and power-hungry one. And careless! Look at how far we've managed to come in the short time since we took over again! I swear, there's more talent, more know-how, more skill on Asconel than any other world this side of the present Imperial boundary. If he'd made use of the resources under his hand, no one, not even the Empire at its height, could have toppled him."

"That was Belizuek's fault, not his," Spartak contradicted. "Belizuek liked to push his subjects down to the mud. Ignorant, blindly adoring, they'd take anything he offered and come back pleading for more."

"In any case, it's due as much to Spartak as to anyone that we have regained so much lost ground," Vix put in. "For an unpractical person, he's worked miracles of organization and administration."

Tiorin gave a nod of agreement, suddenly looking very tired.

"May I ask a question, Warden?" Tigrid Zen said formally.

"Go ahead."

"Are your brothers going to stay here now? I feel Asconel needs them still."

Tiorin glanced at the other two, inviting them to speak for themselves.

"No," Vix said gruffly, and got to his feet. He paced across to the window and stood with his back to them as he went on. "No, a fighting man is a center of discord on a peaceful world, and that's what Asconel is going to be from now on. I'll away back to my roving. And—and there's something else, too."

He didn't elaborate, but neither of his brothers had to ask what he meant. Vineta had died during the day following their capture by the priests from the injuries sustained when she was shot down. And for the first time in his life, the loss of one of his women had touched his heart. He had said privately that even if it was his home, he could not bear to remain on the world where Vineta had died. . . .

"You, Spartak?" Tiorin said, to distract them from the vaguely embarrassed silence that followed.

"No, I won't stay here either," Spartak said at length. "Oh, I'll not be leaving till I'm sure Asconel is on the proper orbit again, but in a year or so I'll say farewell."

"I shall regret your loss," Tiorin said quietly. "But—as you wish. Back to your studies on Annanworld, then?"

"Annanworld? Oh, no." Spartak gave a smile that made him look briefly like a wild beast.

"Why not?" Vix demanded, surprised. He turned away from the window to face them again. "The way I understood it, your order would take you back if you didn't soil your hands with violence while you were away, and everything you did to help overthrow Bucyon was of the nature of—well—of scheming rather than fighting. Or are they so super-subtle they'd define what you did to him as violence?"

"No, we distinguish force from violence, and force is occasionally unavoidable. . . . But why should I say 'we'?" Spartak leaned back in his chair. "I'm not returning, I'm sure of that."

"No, you see, after much cogitation I've come to a conclusion. My superior, Father Erton, was half right as well as half wrong when he warned me against leaving for Asconel. The rightness lay in his saying that to stand against the— what do they call it?—the onset of the Long Night was beyond any man's powers. What we've done here on Asconel is good, and worth it, but it's not turned the tide of galactic decline, has it? Only built an island around which the tide will flow. Perhaps the clearest warning lies in the fact that one mentally sick survivor of a race which grew weary and departed before we left our original system could bring one of our finest planets into total subjugation.

"I'm going to look for the seeds of the first truly human galactic conquest. I'm going to the Rim, to the worlds where for ten thousand years the Empire shipped its mutants and its misfits, and where rumor says men—yes, men, for they're born of human loins—build their own starships instead of borrowing the leavings of another species. I don't know exactly where to make for, but a good start might be to resume our interrupted journey to Nylock—hmm, Eunora?" He shot a twinkling grin at the mutant girl.

"And when I find someone in a position to do something, I

shall report on the existence of a world called Brinze. For the priests of Belizuek were human too, though they'd sold their birthright and their power of free thought. And before I die I hope to see the people there set at liberty as those of Asconel have already been."

The words died in the silent room. Finally Vix went to Spartak's side and stood gazing down at him.

"You're right," he said. "And if you want a ship and a pilot, say the word." He put out his hand.

THE MAN FROM THE BIG DARK

Prologue

The ship came out of the Big Dark as if every devil in all
the hells of ten thousand planets were after its pilot. The captain of a fat and waddling freighter caught its blip on his
fallible detectors, checked the circuits to see if they really did
show a vessel making so much speed, and just had time to
wish he had not decided to risk cutting direct from Batyra
Dap to the Marches of Klareth instead of following the
patrolled route through Mallimameddy before the pilot of
the streaking ship gave a contemptuous flip to his controls,
and was gone in the vastness of space.

There was only one kind of ship that ever came out of the
Big Dark—the hundred light-year gap which some freak of
stellar drift had cut between the Marches of Klareth and the
outflung arm of the galaxy. A pirate ship.

But this one must be hunting richer prey.

The next vessel to spot the overdriven craft was a naval
patrol boat from Klareth, returning from a rendezvous and
the usual exchange of insults with its opposite number from
Mallimameddy. That was about the hardest kind of work the
patrol had had in the past fifty years.

By that time the pilot from the Big Dark had deliberately
overshot his goal and swung on to a course a hundred and

ten degrees from his original one, which fitted the meek answer he gave to the patrol's challenge about his identity and business.

As soon as the naval craft was off the detector, however, the pilot slammed the power arm back to emergency extreme and doubled toward the world which had been the seat of the Praestans of Klareth when he was only one step below the King of Argus. But that had been a long time ago.

On overloaded and almost worn-out circuits the ship stooped into the air of the planet. The long punishment he had given the vessel did not worry its pilot. It stood up long enough for him to skim through a thunderstorm raging across the trail of a forest fire in Klareth's southern hemisphere and rip apart the placid breezes of the equatorial region before hurling his ship at the largest of the wooded islands girdling the world and setting it without a tremor on the last usable port of the fifty-odd which had once poured Imperial traffic into the star-routes.

He had no papers, but he had Empire currency, of which not much was seen nowadays this far toward the edge of the galaxy. It was still good. The commander of the port fingered the two thousand-circle coins he had exacted as the pilot departed, and then turned his attention to the ship.

It was five days before the complicated locks on the vessel yielded even to his practiced fingers—he had been going out at night and unofficially "inspecting" the port's visitors since he was twenty years old; consequently, at thirty he was nearly rich enough to buy himself out of his regiment and retire.

By the time they discovered the girl's body lying mutilated on the bunk, therefore, the pilot was lost among the people of the islands—and assuredly he would never be so foolish as to come back.

I

The dockside tavern had been patched together out of the fragments of a building destroyed in a rebel raid a few years before. It looked as if one good blow from off the ocean would dismantle it again. But the smell of food which drifted from it appealed to Terak, reminding him that he had an appetite. He climbed the short flight of steps to the doorway and entered.

The only other customers were three men in leather jerkins and breeches exchanging filthy jokes at one of the tables, and a very pale man in jet black who sat alone in a corner, staring into a mug and muttering to himself.

When these people glanced up on hearing Terak's footsteps, they saw a man of medium height with heavy, solid bones, clad in a tattered shirt of Vellian silk which had once cost a lot of money, and thick, rumpled breeches. His hair, in startling contrast to a face as brown as thakrik wood, was curly and stiff and stood up over his scalp like brass wire. He wore a sword in the Leontine style, in a scabbard behind his right shoulder, where he had only to reach up and grasp the hilt to swing it down in a killing blow.

Terak noted the calculating stares and was amused, as much as he could be amused now. He crossed the floor to the counter, moving with unexpected grace for so solidly built a man, and thumped the wood with his fist. A sharp-faced woman in a greasy apron looked out from the kitchens beyond.

"Yes?"

"What food have you? And what liquor?"

"What d'you think on Klareth? Tor-fish stew is on the fire, or d'you want something grilled up specially?"

"Stew will do me. And bread, and a measure of ancinard."

The woman looked as if she would like to spit at him, but seized a mug and filled it with the fuming red liquor. Then she vanished into the kitchen again, to reappear with a wooden platter full of rich-smelling stew and a hunk of coarse black bread. "Fifteen green," she said shortly.

Terak made a roll of circles appear as if by magic between finger and thumb. "What's that in real money? I don't know your local coinage."

The woman's eyes grew large with greed. "Eight circles, forty ring," she said much too quickly. Terak half smiled, and turned to the laughing men around the table nearby.

"Friend, what's a fair rate for an Imperial circle in Klarethly coin?"

The nearest of the strangers gave him a snag-toothed grin. "Four greens to a circle!" he called back. "And don't let her tell you different."

"If she makes trouble, tell her we'll take the place apart for you," added one of his companions.

Carefully, Terak set out the exact sum on the counter; a

red, bony hand closed over it instantly, and this time the woman did spit at him as she turned away.

Shrugging, he picked up his platter and mug and made for a table. The snag-toothed man waved at him. "Come join us, friend!" he invited, and Terak accepted without wanting to. Still, he might learn something from them.

The snag-toothed man hauled a chair across the floor with an outstretched foot and indicated it. Terak sat, and began to eat and drink with restrained ferocity.

"As well you spotted her trying to swindle you, friend," said the snag-toothed man. "She tried it on me once, thinking I was a fool since I was fresh back from space, but I'm as Klarethly as she." He threw back his head and laughed loudly.

Terak waited for him to be quiet, his eyes taking in the way the hair of all three of these men was clipped to fit under a helmet.

"Soldiers?" he said at last.

"That we are. Avrid's my name, and these are Qualf and Torkenwal."

"Terak, I. Where are you serving now?"

"Where any good men should if they can—on our own world."

Terak nodded. "You'll be with General Janlo, then—clearing the southern islands of the rebels. His campaign must be going well indeed, that he is giving furloughs."

"Well enough," allowed Avrid offhandedly. "But how else, since he has all but a handful of the fighting men of Klareth to clear away a measly few camps of rebels?" He burped loudly. "News has been off-world about it?"

Terak dodged the implied question of his origin, said only, "Travelers talk. With their mouths but not their minds, to judge by the way stories grow deformed in a few days' journey." He chewed at something rubbery in his stew.

"That's not the way I heard it," he went on. "I understood that the rebels had it all their own way, and that it was a matter of weeks until a new Praestans stood above the Marches."

The suggestion brought a torrent of indignant denial from all three of them. Qualf, slamming his open palm on the table, declared, "You must come from the other side of the Big Dark to be so out of date in your ideas! That was the way of it three years ago, perhaps, but not since General Janlo took command."

Terak suppressed a smile. He put on an expression of surprised interest and said, "What then has happened?"

"What Janlo saw," said Avrid ponderously, "was that for too long our forces had been scattered over half the face of the world. He judged which of the rebel strongholds were the most dangerous, deployed his maximum resources against them—plus a crowd of mercenaries he got from a-slaver who dropped in thinking to find easy pickings!—and rolled them up one by one instead of attempting to control the lot at once. Of course, some few of the rebel outposts which have been comparatively neglected since his campaign started have grown in size, but they have no way to gain recruits and thus are merely awaiting an attack."

"Like ripe Sirenian plums hanging from a branch for the gatherer," said Torkenwal with relish.

"Ingenious," said Terak admiringly. "You mentioned a slaver, though. I didn't know such people were still working the Marches."

"Mostly, they aren't," said Avrid. "But the patrols, for that reason, have grown slack and lazy." He spoke with all the contempt of a sensible man who liked to fight face to face with his feet on solid ground. "When this one came by, Janlo had no trouble with them at all. If he had not chosen a spot where the Golden Dragon brigade was mopping up an island stronghold, he could probably have got what he was after. But he had a good cargo and they made soldiers for us."

"If he was so well stocked, why did he stop here?"

"Women, my friend. Those slavers are ever short of women."

Terak nodded understandingly. "This campaign had been going on long before Janlo took over?"

Avrid snorted, and Qualf supplied the answer. "All of twelve years—since the death of the last Praestans. Y'see, we choose our Praestans in the old tradition—by a call of the islands. When Lukander—may he rest easy—joined his company, the choice lay between Farigol and Abreet, his uncle and his stepson. Now Abreet was much liked by the younger sort, but he was no metal for ruling, believe me. So the call was for Farigol, though he was already an old man. But the call was near level—a hundred and six islands, was it, to ninety-nine?"

"Hundred and eight," said Torkenwal shortly.

"So Abreet, displeased, raised his banner in the south on the island which had stood most strongly for him, and in a while he had a rebel army near as good as the Praestans's. It stayed near as good till Janlo came along."

"And where *did* he come from?"

"So they tell me, he was a fisher and trader in his youth, who won honors fighting the occasional pirates who used to raid the ships. Most of 'em have gone with the rebels."

Avrid staged an elaborate yawn. "Getting so this planet is too dull to live on," he complained. "No pirates, no rebels—just fisher-folk, traders, and woodsmen. I can see this is our last chance to serve on Klareth, friends!"

Qualf and Torkenwal looked appropriately glum.

Terak put out one further question which was on his mind. "It's safe, then, to ship among the nearer islands now?"

"Safe?" Avrid laughed. "Only danger is from the crew you pick to sail with! Ask at the docks if you seek a boat—there are enough junks, ketches, and wherries making up for the trade lost during the revolt to suit you easily."

"Thanks," said Terak. He emptied his mug of ancinard, clasped hands with each of his newfound friends, and took his leave. He noted without more than passing interest as he did so that the pale man in black was gone from his corner chair.

II

Fillenkep was the largest island on the planet; it had the only decently sized city, the only spaceport still open, and the seat of government. In consequence, the docks were large and busy, and Terak walked for a long time through them. The sun was dropping toward the skyline. He judged he had two hours to sunset—time enough, so far, but he had not had *too much* time for a long while, not since he began his journey. The journey had begun with blood, and, fate willing, it would also end with blood. Not Terak's.

He picked his way through the confusion of the port. Stacks of goods in bales and cartons and wooden packing cases were ranged alongside the unpaved way, guarded by savage Sirian apes on iron chains. The animals never seemed to learn that their bonds could not be deceived, but would wait as patiently as their brutish minds would let them and then rush out in a single instant to the limit of their stretch, hoping that one day the restraining metal would be caught unawares. Terak gave them a wide berth, as did the sailors fresh off the junks plying between the islands who came singing up from the shore, bottles in their hands and women of easy virtue on their arms.

He came at last to a jetty, where the slow heaving of the sea had eaten the once-level stonework into subsidence, and the going was slippery and dangerous. Surefooted, he passed among the dockers, the idlers, and the beggars, looking down at the moored boats. The first two he passed were fishing smacks: one back with a haul of vivid green fish, one stretching nets for a night voyage. Beyond them were three traders—junks—but since they had plainly docked together in convoy they were of no use to him.

Beyond them again was what he sought: a broad-beamed wherry sitting low in the water, her decks scrubbed clean and a scarlet sailing pennant flying to advertise imminent departure.

There was a man checking goods on the quay nearby; taking him for the wherry's tallymaster, Terak hailed him. "When does she sail?" he called, jerking his thumb down.

"The *Aaooa*?" The tallymaster spat; he had a scar twisting the side of his face which drew up his mouth and made his expectoration messy. "How should I know?"

He went back to his counting. Terak shrugged and leaned over the side of the jetty. "*Aaooa* ahoy!" he called; the vessel had been named for the sighing wind which blew around Klareth's equator, and called for a high moaning when saying her name. There was no answer; the only sign of life down there was someone clearing kelp from the stern reactor pipe with an iron hook.

Terak looked around his feet and found a rotting fish of the weight of a katalabs hoof. He aimed carefully and let it fall so that it struck the bent back of the kelp clearer and burst asunder with a squelch. He had barely five seconds to get over his amazement before his target was out of the water and swarming dripping up the iron staples which served as a ladder on the jetty, hook wildly swinging.

Terak caught it an inch before it cracked his skull and wrenched it free. Then he waited a while to enjoy what he saw before speaking. The attacker was a girl—taller than himself, with fire-red hair and eyes as green as Klareth's oceans. Her fine-boned face was tautened by rage into a white mask. Her body was equally beautiful, without question, for she wore the ideal costume for her watery task. She was as naked as a newborn babe.

But the urgency in his mind drove his enjoyment away.

"Answer my call next time and I won't have to do that again," he said shortly. She took half a step forward and punched—not slapped—his jaw. The blow jolted him, but he gave with it, reached up and caught her wrist, forcing her to complete the half-step, put his free hand behind her and kissed her hard on the mouth.

For a second she struggled, then yielded pleasantly. He felt her left hand steal around his waist. Releasing her, he stepped back and shook his head.

"Use your eyes," he said in mock scorn. "When did you see a man who carries his sword as I do wear a knife at his *right*?"

"Was it for *that* you wanted me to come up?" she said in a steely voice. "There are women aplenty in the port who will give you what you could only take from me at the risk of your life."

"I'm going to insult you. It was not for that. I want to buy passage on the *Aaooa*. Take me to your captain."

The girl jerked her thumb at her perfectly molded breast. "You're looking at the captain. Well?"

Terak's surprise melted in a moment. A spitfire like this could captain any vessel he had ever heard of, he was sure. He said in a level tone, "My apologies for not recognizing you in your present costume. Does your next voyage take you toward the fighting in the south?"

The girl seemed to be hesitating between answering and turning away contemptuously. She settled for answering. "It does. Our main cargo is supplies for General Janlo's forces. But we do not take passengers, stranger. *Aaooa* is a fast freighter, and this trip I have a military contract to fill."

"Have you signed your crew for the trip yet? If not, I'll ship on your complement."

"You know the sea? You look more like a spaceman to me."

"Ships at sea and ships in space I know, both."

"My first mate is out in the town now getting us men," said the girl shortly. "He'll be bringing back men who are all sailor, no spaceman. Sorry, stranger." Her eyes were mocking.

"I will pay for the privilege of shipping in your crew," Terak pressed. He made a thousand-circle coin appear between his fingers and held it out. The girl swung her hand casually and knocked it ringing to the stones of the jetty. Terak did not look to see where it fell.

"That much I care for your money," she snapped. Then— "Are you not going to pick it up?"

"What for?" Terak shrugged. "It is no use offering it to you again, and if money cannot get me passage, what good is it?"

The girl studied him for a moment. "Stranger, here comes my first mate. If he has not filled all the places on my roll, you can ship with us. A bargain?"

"Agreed," said Terak instantly, and turned to see a group of hard-bitten men approaching, each carrying his bundle of belongings on one shoulder. They were a motley bunch, but they had one thing in common—the hint of a roll in their walk which indicates a man is feeling for the shift of a deck even with solid earth under his feet.

At their head was a fat man with a broken nose and one foot chopped off short an inch behind the toes. This man the girl hailed.

"Bozhdal! Have you filled the roll?"

"All save two," the fat man answered. "We're short a deck-hand and a galley-boy."

Behind him the assembled recruits to the *Aaooa* stared and shifted from foot to foot at the sight of their new captain. She seemed completely unconscious of their gaze.

Glancing at Terak, she let a hint of amusement show in her eyes. This was her chance to level with him for that rotten fish, Terak thought.

"You're big enough to do duty for both of them," she said. "What's your name?"

Terak told her. "Very well, Terak! Join your shipmates. Where's your duffle?"

"I'm wearing it."

"All right. You're my man." She swept a glare across the entire group facing her. "So are you all! My name's Kareth Var. To you I'm *Captain* Var! I own the *Aaooa* and I've run her seven times around this planet, and I know what I'm doing. Anyone who thinks different can have it out with my first mate!"

Bozhdal crossed his arms and drummed with his fingers on his very solid biceps. No one said anything.

"All right. Get below and stow your duffle. You, Terak!"

"Yes?"

"Yes, *Captain!*" said Bozhdal, stepping forward.

Terak echoed him. "That's better," said Kareth. "Since you have no duffle to stow, get over the jetty and put that hook you're holding to some purpose. I'll be down to see the job's done properly in an hour. I want to sail at sunset, so you'd better be thorough. Jump to it!"

Terak gave her a broad grin, and went over the side of the jetty before she could utter the comment that boiled up inside her.

The water came up to his waist, but it was warm, and he fell to work vigorously. The hook seemed pretty useless at first, until he got the knack of twisting it half a dozen times in the matted weed. Then a single sharp pull removed the clinging stuff by the pound. There was worse in the pipe than weed, though; some sort of blue-shelled animals had crusted around the end of the pipe, and he shuddered to think what their massed bodies would do to the jet. He hammered, chipped, and levered at them with violence.

He was so engrossed that he almost failed to notice Kareth coming down to him. Wiping his brow, he stepped back in the water and looked up at her hanging on the staples in the jetty wall. She had put on a green tunic that matched her eyes, which came barely halfway down her thighs; it was the same costume that most of the sailors wore. Her waist was girdled with a belt of woven bark in which a knife was thrust.

"Good," she said grudgingly after inspecting his work. "Get aboard and help the cook dish up the night meal. And I don't want your soaking clothes to mess up my decks, or you'll have to scrub them before you sleep!"

He obeyed. After wringing out his breeches and rubbing down, he carried the fish stew in the inevitable wooden platters—since Klareth was so heavily wooded, maximum use was made of the material—into the fo'c'sle for Bozhdal and the crew. Kareth herself ate on deck, sitting on the gunwale and studying charts.

Directly afterward, they sailed. Just before the anchor was weighed, Bozhdal went ashore and came back with a Sirian ape which had been guarding the cargo during loading. He kept it at bay on the end of its chain with a sharp metal goad, skillfully driving it toward the stern. Wielding the goad with one hand, he fastened the chain to a staple in the bulkhead of the after cabin with the other. Then he placed the goad just out of the ape's reach.

Terak wondered why that particular place had been chosen for the ape's abode, instead of the usual cage on deck. He got his answer when he was swilling down a couple of hours later before going to his berth. He heard someone else splashing and gurgling over the side, and looked down. The light from the navigation lamps was just bright enough for him to make out Kareth rubbing herself over one-handed in the sea, clinging with the other hand to a rope. Shortly she came nimbly back up the line, wearing the same costume—or rather lack of one—as when he had first seen her.

"Good night, Captain," he ventured, and was rewarded with a curt echo as she strode toward the stern cabin. Seizing the goad, she drove back the aroused Sirian ape far enough to let her get into her cabin and slam the door. The ape dashed forward and kicked against the tough wood until it grew bored and returned to its task of trying to outwit its chain.

So that was how Kareth looked after herself among a shipload of men! Terak could think of no more effective means.

The voyage was fast, as he had been promised. They beat down toward and across the equator, mostly under power, but taking advantage when they could of the aaooa wind for which their craft was named. They put in at a couple of island ports for fresh water and fruit, but most of the time they maintained a steady southward heading.

He found the work hard, but that was good, for it kept the ache in his mind down to a bearable level. He got on well enough with the rest of the crew, including Bozhdal, although he was a stranger and an off-worlder, once they had decided he was capable of doing his job. Bozhdal ran him hard when Kareth was around, but it was largely staged for the captain's benefit—she took quiet delight in extending her revenge for that one stolen kiss.

Shipping under a woman seemed not to worry the sailors; Terak judged it was because they lived from voyage to voyage, and by the time they were broke enough after their shore-leave between trips they were temporarily sick of the kind of cheating female they met in port. So long as Bozhdal—a man they respected—gave the actual orders, they could not have cared less who the owner of the *Aaooa* was.

They passed comparatively few other vessels—mostly traders like their own craft—until twenty days after they set out.

On the morning of the twentieth day a fast two-reactor patrol boat raised them and ordered them to halt for searching, and Terak knew the end of his journey was at hand.

III

"Cut the engine!" bawled Bozhdal. "Stand by to receive boarding party!"

The crew scampered to their posts, and Kareth mounted the stern castle beside the wheelman to study the oncoming boat. She hove alongside the *Aaooa,* and a group of hard-bitten sailors together with an officer in the brilliant uniform of Janlo's forces leaped one by one onto the slightly lower deck of the wherry and pressed forward.

"Where's your captain?" demanded the officer, and then caught sight of Kareth aft. "Ohé, Captain Var!" he called. "What's your cargo and destination?"

Kareth came down to meet him, and they clasped hands. Signaling Bozhdal to bring the manifest and the copy of the contract, she said, "Supplies out of Fillenkep for your army, Major! We're a day ahead of schedule as yet—I hope you aren't going to make us waste it while you search us."

"Faugh!" exploded the officer. "You know me better than to think I'd search *you* for contraband, Captain Var! No, if that had been all I'd have hailed you only to be sure it was your ship and no impostor."

The crew stood around listening with ears wide. Bozhdal took notice of the fact at this point and bawled them back to their stations. "You, Terak!" he snapped. "Get below to the galley! You can stop being a deckhand for the moment."

The galley, fortunately for Terak's curiosity, had a port almost directly over the place on deck where Kareth and the officer stood. As he seized a tor-fish and began to gut it, he caught the thread of their talk again.

"—no description of him," the officer was saying. "Of course, there's practically no chance of finding him again, unless he attempts to leave the planet and the guards at the spaceport recognize him. But five days had elapsed between his arrival and the discovery of the crime."

"What *was* the crime?" asked Kareth in a cool voice.

"Rape and murder," said the officer, seeming a trifle embarrassed.

When Kareth did not comment, he went on. "While you were in Fillenkep, did you run across anyone—an off-worlder—who could have been the man?"

Terak's heart stood still, and he set the tor-fish down with exaggerated care. The sword he had been wearing when he came aboard was out of reach in the crew's quarters, but the gutting knife he held would make a dangerous weapon.

"I didn't go farther ashore in Fillenkep than the jetty," Kareth answered calmly, "Bozhdal did, though, to pick up new crew. Bozhdal, did you see anyone like that *while you were in the town?*"

The stress she gave to the last few words was fortunately lost on the officer, but the first mate picked up the implication swiftly. "Not that I can remember," he rumbled.

"Well," the officer said after a pause, "you can't help us, anyway. Sorry to have delayed you, Captain Var, but you are still ahead of schedule."

To the sound of the sailors accompanying their officer back to the patrol boat, Terak, his mind whirling, picked up the half-cleaned fish and methodically continued his job.

Several times between then and the time they put into the port of their destination, he caught Kareth looking at him quizzically, and his puzzlement grew. It was obvious that he could well have been the man the officer was referring to, and he had expected her to turn him over almost with relish. Why hadn't she?

They docked late the following evening to the accompaniment of the sounds of battle drifting over the still ocean. The port was on a small island which Terak knew could be no farther now than twenty miles from the thickest fighting, yet life in its one town seemed to be going on much as it was in Fillenkep, far away to the north. On the waterfront, there were even gangs of workmen busy repairing the damage caused by Janlo's siege and reduction of a rebel stronghold here a few months before. The sight shook Terak. He had not known—not really known, in his bones—that Janlo had such a command of the situation. His heart sank. Time was running very short, and he had so much to do. . . .

All the time he was busy with the unloading, he itched to be up and away, but he forced himself to sweat over the heavy bales until the job was over. It was an hour past full dark when Bozhdal judged that the work was done, and called for the hands who wanted to be paid off here instead of making the return trip to Fillenkep.

Only four of the crew made the choice, and naturally Terak was among them. Kareth brought her coffer onto the deck and set it on a small table. As soon as they had received their pay, the sailors ran to collect their stacked duffles and made off along the dockside in the hope of seeing something of the town's night life—if there was any—before it went to sleep.

"Well?" said Kareth finally, looking at Terak. She signed to Bozhdal, who shut the coffer and carried it away. "What are you doing here?"

"I promised to pay you for the privilege of my passage," said Terak. "What's your price?"

Kareth threw back her head, and for the first time since they met, laughed aloud. She had a lovely laugh, which ran and trilled like music. Then she stretched, which made her shapely body tauten the thin fabric of her tunic. Rising to her feet, she strolled across the deck and leaned with her elbows on the gunwale, facing Terak.

"You can forget about that," she said. "You've worked hard and honestly, and I'd ship with you again any time you cared to sign."

Terak knew that the urgency of his task demanded he should waste no time standing here and listening. Yet somehow he could not tear himself away.

"You've seen a lot more of our world in a few days than most off-planet visitors," she said abruptly. "Tell me, what do you think of it?"

"I think it is a very good world," said Terak, and he meant it. The many islands in the tideless sea, crowned with their forests, and the small but busy towns on them, appealed to him. His unwilling liking for the planet, in fact, stimulated him to his task.

"Yes," said Kareth softly. "I'm glad you said that, Terak, because I know you mean it. You know, I love this world. I haven't seen many others, but I've been around the Marches, and I've been to Mallimameddy and Batyra Dap. My father was a trader in space, and my elder brothers still are, but he loved Khreth and came home to die here. He came clear from Argus originally—then he found this world and knew it was for him. He married a Klarethly girl, and gave his children names based on the word Klareth. My brothers are called Lareth and Areth."

Terak stood perfectly still, wondering what all this was driving at.

"That's why I was so sick at heart when civil war began to tear the world apart," the girl went on, almost to herself. "And so happy when a strong man was found to put the rebels down."

Terak hardly caught the last few words, for she turned and stared out across the dimly glowing sea. There was little noise; the sound of fighting had stopped, and the town was far enough from the dockside to disturb the air scarcely at all.

Therefore he stepped lightly across the deck and came to the gunwale beside her, waiting to hear what she would say next.

After a while she turned her head and looked at him. "Terak, what do you do on Klareth? And why did you have to come here with such urgency? And why do you seem to have forgotten your purpose now?"

Terak started to answer, and then the real impact of her first question hit him. It left him as it were standing back from himself and marveling that he had had the sublime self-confidence to imagine for a moment he could carry it out. The trouble was, probably, that he had never realized just what a whole planet was.

Resolution hardened inside him. It was idiocy to think of carrying out his plan single-handed any longer. Given more time, perhaps—but time was short and here at hand was an ally he could count on.

Before he could speak, a cold gust blew up off the sea, and Kareth shivered in her thin tunic. Bozhdal, who had been making sure everything was shipshape, called out to her to ask if she wanted him for anything further. She told him no, and he picked up the goad to lead the Sirian ape ashore and set it to guard their goods piled on the quay.

"Captain Var," said Terak steadily, "I think I'm going to answer your questions, and I think that because you love Klareth you will be very in interested in the answers. But I warn you that the story I have to tell will sound fantastic, and you will probably have Bozhdal kick me over the side."

She stared at him thoughtfully for a few moments. Then she turned away. "Come with me," she said quietly and strode across the deck toward her cabin. Opening the door, she held it for him. He hesitated, but she nodded him in impatiently.

The room beyond the door was low-ceilinged and lit by a flaring lamp filled with fish-oil. There was a narrow bunk with a rich green coverlet, a chair fastened to the deck in a sliding groove, and—almost the only feminine touch—a large, handsomely framed mirror. The bulkheads were faced with cupboard doors.

"Sit down," she said, indicating the chair, and went to one of the cupboards. She took from it a large can of ancinard and two mugs. One of them she dusted with a cloth—it was obvious it had not been used for a long time.

Then she poured drinks for them both and sat down on the edge of the bunk facing Terak. They drank, and she said reflectively as she lowered the mug, "You know, you are the only man who has ever set foot in this cabin. Even Bozhdal has never been past that door. . . ."

She became brisk. "All right. What's your story?"

"You already know," said Terak, choosing his words with care, "that I am the man from the Big Dark that officer was looking for."

"You're from the Big Dark?" Kareth tensed and looked unbelieving. Terak nodded.

"What do you know about that part of space?"

"Only what—what everyone knows. That it's the home of pirates and slavers. The same kind of thing in space that islands such as Petoronkep used to be here on Klareth." She eyed him carefully. "Are you of that stock?"

"I was," admitted Terak without a tremor.

"You know something else about it, too, though you may not realize it," he went on after a pause. "Think back—no further than your own childhood. Did you not hear tales of the ravages the pirates, and especially the slavers, caused on the worlds around here—on Klareth, and on Mallimameddy and Batyra Dap and the rest of them? Yet it was only a few hours after I landed that I heard the patrols had grown lazy through having nothing to do. What do you imagine caused that falling off in the pirates' attacks?"

She took another draft of the ancinard, not removing her gaze from his face. "I think I follow you," she said. "All right. Explain how that affects Klareth, as I presume you mean it does. I can only say that it seems very satisfactory for us."

"*No!*" said Terak explosively, and began to tell her why. When he had finished, she was sitting as still as a statue, with her face drawn and serious. But her first comment was characteristically womanish.

"Poor girl! You loved her—very much?"

"I did," agreed Terak, and the admission still brought a pang of sorrow.

"I have never heard the name of Aldur," was Kareth's next remark. "And I thought that the names of many of the leaders among the pirates were well known. How is it that his is not, if he is as completely in command of them as you maintain?"

"Aldur is a very sensible man," said Terak. "He knows as few others of his breed have known, that foolish pride has been the downfall of many before him. He does not seek a reputation which will cause children to cry at night. He desires real, absolute power—and he is going the right way about it."

And that, his mind added somberly, *is the man I have to destroy before he can destroy me.*

He gulped at his ancinard. Kareth said abruptly, "I believe every word you say. It is amazing. It's completely opposed to all I've thought for the last three years—since Janlo took command against the rebels—but it fits. By the winds of Klareth, it fits too well!"

"You're with me? You will aid me?"

"In every way I can," she promised, and Terak knew he had made no mistake in his choice of ally.

She got up and fetched more ancinard. While she was pouring it, he uttered the question which had been burning his mind for more than a day.

"Kareth"—he used her name awkwardly—"when that officer inquired for me, why did you deny that you had seen anyone who could be the man?"

She gave him his answer with utter frankness. "Because," she said, "I did not think you, of all the men I know, would ever have to resort to rape!"

IV

He remembered Celly at the beginning, of course. He remembered her as he had last seen her when he took a final glance around the cabin of his ship. In seven days the fuse would have worn away and the inside of the vessel would have been purged with clean fire. But they had solved the tricky locks in less than that time, and other people had seen her as she lay broken on the hard, untidy bunk.

Anger burned in him, that they should know her only as she was in death and not as she was in life—alive with a vitality that shone through her eyes like sunlight.

Next he remembered her as she was then, the way Aldur had seen her and desired her, and taken her when he, Terak, was out of the way. It was known that anyone who did more than look at Celly (for everyone looked at her!) would have a furious Terak to answer to, though it be Aldur himself— and men who had to answer to Terak usually did so with their life's blood gushing from their mouth.

So Aldur had done it—and what had it gained him? Nothing. But it would, swore Terak, cost him the empire for which he gambled.

This was Aldur: a man of cruelty who saw through shams, who had seen when he was young clear through the sham maintained in the lawless colonies of ship-born men and women yonder in the Big Dark; had seen that the degeneration was not halted, only slowed down, by the increasingly rare additions to their numbers gained by slave-raids and the occasional outlaws who came running to them and satisfied the powers that were of their genuine desire to join.

So Aldur had plotted, and because Terak had also seen that the only life he knew was doomed, he had aided him.

They had played one pirate lord against another, one slaver grown fat with indolence against another, until Aldur stood unchallenged at the head of his savage bands.

And then he had launched his plan for empire.

Too long they had lived on the memory of past glories; too long they had fed, and bred, and done nothing. Aldur said, "The dissolution of the old Empire is complete. No strong king flies his banner over Argus, the Praestans of nearby Klareth has been challenged in civil war. . . . The power that harried us out into the Big Dark has vanished. But we remain, *and we are going back!*"

The realization of the plan would be slow. Chafing and fretting, Aldur's subjects groaned at the fact, and Aldur too grew bored waiting. In the end, he signed the warrant of his own destruction—and took Celly.

Terak's mind filled with the sweet-sad memory of their first embrace, the first time she had lain yieldingly within his arms, and he remembered also his purpose.

And yet ... His arms held someone else, and something else as well. He had seen, on occasional raids, what it was like to live under open sky and breathe natural air. He had seen the people he had always regarded as fatted cattle awaiting the butchery of the pirates. And he had realized that there was a better reason than mere revenge for destroying Aldur.

At last, as if a clean wind had swept the smell of death out of his memory, he looked directly at Kareth.

He could tell without asking that she knew what she had done for him.

He fell asleep peacefully for the first time in weeks.

Kareth brought him his breakfast of grilled tor-fish with her own hands. He imagined it was the first time she had done such a thing. Thanking her, he ate ravenously, and studied her as he ate. He did not understand her, because he did not really understand the way of life of planetary folk, but at least he knew they were both worth understanding.

"I suppose your plan was originally to kill Janlo and take the army away from him?" suggested Kareth when they had been silent a long time.

Terak nodded. "Don't think I'm stupid," he told her wryly. "But in the terms to which I'm used, it could be done. There are no more than three or four hundred thousand people yonder in the Big Dark—counting women, children and, slaves. One man can—and does!—rule them. Here, there must be many millions."

"So now ... ?"

"At least go to the battlefront and find out the situation before we make our decision. I fear the time is very close for Janlo to signal Aldur. Then, with all the defenses on the other side of the planet, and a horde of pretended 'freed slaves' to destroy them from within, Aldur can descend on the planet and take it for his own." He spoke with bitterness, and regretted that the words brought sadness to Kareth's eyes.

Oh, but it was a simple plan! And a masterly one!

"Then we must find some excuse for going thither." Kareth frowned. "The water between here and Janlo's army will be thick with patrols out to stop both escaping rebels and intruders carrying news or supplies to the remaining strongholds. My government contract was only to bring supplies this far. I had intended to return with either a cargo of timber—which is plentiful here, for the rebels have built little in three years—or soldiers on furlough."

"We will find something," declared Terak.

Long cogitation, though, found nothing, and when they went on deck later there was no sign of life except from the Sirian ape on the quay, which was chattering fretfully to itself and passing the links of its chain stupidly from paw to paw. The metal made a chinking noise.

"Where are the crew?" asked Terak, puzzled.

"Bozhdal will be ashore seeking new hands for the return voyage, to replace the three we lost. The rest are below asleep."

"Then who—?"

"Cooked your breakfast? Why, I did."

Terak did not have a chance to utter his surprised comment, for Bozhdal came striding down the quay at that moment. With him was a tall, very thin man in jet black who struck a chord of recognition in Terak's memory, although he could not place where they had met.

"Captain Var!" said Bozhdal loudly. "This here is Ser Perarnith, wishing to speak to you about a proposal which sounds interesting."

Kareth nodded. "The best of mornings to you, Ser Perarnith, and come aboard!"

The man in black descended awkwardly, as if infirm, to the deck, and Terak saw that his face was old and lined.

"And to you, Captain Var," he rejoined, his sharp gray eyes on Kareth's face. "I understand you're at liberty."

"At the moment," agreed Kareth. "You wish to charter my vessel?"

"Yes," Perarnith said. He reached into his black garment and fumbled in a pouch; his fingers trembled a little. Terak tried to decide whether he was truly old, or simply very ill.

But the movement with which he flung open the scroll he brought out was practiced and deft. Kareth read it, and then touched the heavy seal at the bottom.

"Why, if this scroll is genuine, can you not command any naval vessel on Klareth?" she demanded.

"I wish to discover how efficiently the patrols operate—whether they are as good as General Janlo claims. I have no doubt, truly, that they are, but I wish to be *certain*. Rather than proceed to the battlefront in a naval craft, therefore, I intend to charter a private one and see how well it is challenged."

Neither Terak nor Kareth, by some superhuman effort, betrayed the sudden tense eagerness they both felt. This was a gift from the gods!

Kareth kept her voice businesslike, and said, "Your fee, Ser Perarnith? I have only my vessel and its cargo to live by."

"Your man here"—he indicated Bozhdal—"has told me what you make on a cargo of timber over such a journey as this. I will pay double for your time in returning empty."

"Done," said Kareth, and bared her breast over her heart for Perarnith to touch it as a token of a bargain sealed. He hesitated a moment, as if he were unused to a woman performing a man's gesture, and then his thin, withered fingers rested there for an instant as lightly as the bird's claws they so much resembled.

"I am moderately well-known among the fleet," Perarnith said after a pause. "I shall therefore not appear on deck at the time you are challenged. To the captain of the patrol vessel you will show this—" He flicked open a second scroll, smaller than the first.

Kareth took it, bewildered, and said in amazement, "It bears the signature of the Praestans himself, not?"

"It does," said Perarnith, and smiled as if with secret amusement. "When can you be ready to sail?"

"We are short three hands," said Kareth, and was about to direct Bozhdal to return on shore and round up substitutes for the men who had been paid off, when Perarnith forestalled her.

"I have a personal retinue," he said. "Three men and a girl. They are acquainted with matters of the sea."

Bozhdal was on the point of protesting when he realized as Terak and Kareth had at once that Perarnith had spoken in the voice of a man who was not disobeyed.

"Then we can sail as soon as they ship with us," Kareth said bluntly. "Bozhdal, go bawl out the sleeping hands!"

The reorganization was difficult. The three male slaves who came with Perarnith—big, silent men with fast reflexes and thoughtful eyes which belied their brawniness—where settled easily enough among the crew, but Perarnith could not go into a deckhand's bunk. Kareth gave up her cabin to him, therefore, and with a twinkle in his eyes Perarnith decreed that she need not worry about the girl slave—she attended him night and day and would not be in danger from the crew. That left Kareth out in the cold—literally, for here they were beyond the even warmth of the tropics.

It almost made Bozhdal weep to see the *Aaooa* sail with a tent on her afterdeck, but it served the purpose. . . .

Perarnith showed himself not at all except occasionally after dark when he came above to walk, deep in thought, on deck. His meals were brought to the cabin door by Terak, who—to outward appearances—was still acting as the galley-boy and deckhand of the earlier leg of the voyage. The girl slave took the dishes in and returned them later, often with the meal scarcely touched.

Terak tried to sound Perarnith's male retinue on their master's behavior, but beyond repeated assertions about his seniority in the government of Klareth, he got only a grin and a shake of the head.

The scroll signed by the Praestans worked wonders when the challenges came up, as they did with monotonous regularity. They had only to show as a dot on the horizon to a patrol craft, and inside the hour they were under the nose of an arbalest loaded with enough liquid fire to soak them in flame from stem to stern, while fierce-voiced officers demanded their excuse for using this stretch of ocean.

And Kareth would flash the scroll, and they would blink, step back, salute respectfully, and let the *Aaooa* continue her voyage.

After two days, they saw signs of the fighting. Men on deck with nothing to do would take their revenge on glob-fish migrating north to the equator for the southern winter with partly digested human limbs still projecting from their external stomachs like extra pseudopods. One in particular among the sailors—Kareth explained he belonged to a cult which held that a man's body had to be buried or at any rate prayed over for him to achieve resurrection—was violent in his attacks on the bloated carrion-feeders.

After three days many of the naval craft that challenged them were heading north with burn-scars and ram-holes to be repaired at a refitting station. Twice they passed prize convoys, patrol vessels slowly towing battered rebel hulks whose decks were lined with prisoners in chains.

And on the fourth day Perarnith appeared without warning on deck and told them where Janlo's headquarters was—a secret guarded jealously. It was a bare three hours away, and Kareth immediately put about for it.

As soon as they docked, harbor guards came down to challenge them. Perarnith showed his scroll, and they became obsequious. They posted a guard alongside the *Aaooa* to prevent further inquiries.

Perarnith thanked his temporary hostess, paid the fee agreed, and climbed carefully and with much assistance up to the jetty. His three male slaves followed, nodding to the friends they had made among the crew, and last came the girl slave whom they had hardly seen. Escorted by a squad of soldiers, Perarnith vanished from their ken.

This was a town which had only lately been taken from the rebels. It was searred with the fire which was the most potent possible weapon in Klarethly timber-built cities. Tents sheltered the many soldiers and sailors who were temporarily here, though there were a few intact houses which seemed to be full of officers. It was satisfyingly small, and Terak informed Kareth that he stood an excellent chance of tracking down Janlo at once.

"How about going ashore, though?" Kareth demanded. "Will you not be challenged immediately?"

"Probably. If the worse comes to the worst, I'll have to appeal to Perarnith, but I should think I could talk myself out of most kinds of trouble."

Hopefully, he strapped his sword into place on his shoulder and scrambled ashore.

He kept both eyes and ears open as he went along, finding that life was proceeding in a nearly normal manner. Small traders had improvised stalls out of burned timber, drinking houses were open, the ladies of easy virtue who had survived the siege were plying their trade again among the new occupying forces, and he was astonished to see that at least one school had reopened. At any rate, twenty ill-washed urchins sat in a ring on the ground listening to a teacher without benefit of books.

He had been walking for almost an hour, occasionally paying his respects to an officer as if he were a mercenary on Janlo's payroll, and had gained a very clear idea of the layout of the town, when there was a sudden cry from behind.

"Stop, you, *Terak!*"

V

Terak whirled, and was astonished to see a soldier facing him, looking like thunder. It was Avrid, whom he had met in the dockside tavern back on Fillenkep.

Avrid pulled out a whistle and gave three shrill blasts on it before striding swiftly toward Terak and sharply grasping his arm. Terak wrenched free. "What are you playing at, Avrid?" he demanded.

"You remember me, eh?" The soldier set his hands on his hips and met his gaze with a steely glare. Men were coming at a run in answer to the whistle-blasts, among them an officer resplendent in black and red.

"What's the meaning of this, soldier?" the latter asked. Avrid took a step back and saluted him.

"This here is an off-worlder called Terak, sir," he informed the officer. "Few weeks back they found a murdered woman in a ship newly landed at Fillenkep. I saw this man on the dockside that very day the ship had landed!"

"Off-worlder, hey?" The officer rubbed his plump jowls. "And what's *your* story, Terak?"

"I know nothing of what this man tells you," Terak lied stonily. "When we met, I'd been five days on Klareth."

"And in those five days you'd learned nothing of Klarethly coin!" said Avrid. He explained the episode of the exchange rate to the officer, while Terak's heart sank.

"Jail him," said the officer briefly to the other soldiers who had arrived. "He can have a hearing tonight if there's time at the court."

Avrid's hand swept up like a snake striking, and the slight hiss of metal on leather as well as a small jerk told Terak that his sword had gone from its sheath. Then brawny hands closed on his arms and he was being frog-marched through the streets.

He was taken to one of the intact buildings now being used as administrative offices and handed over to a dour, dark jailer who took brief details of the accusation against him. He was allowed to keep everything he had except his weapons and the means of making fire. The reason for the last precaution he recognized soon enough—the cell into which he was then thrown, like almost everything else Klarethly, was made of wood. But it was wood as hard as stone and many inches thick.

Having explored the possibility of escape and decided that it was nonexistent, Terak sat down sickly on the one piece of furniture—a rough bunk with a mattress stuffed with leaves—and wondered what would happen to him now.

Part of his answer came an hour later. The dour jailer, escorted by two armed soldiers, entered his cell and gave him a slow, searching stare. Finally he spoke.

"You're due for a hearing tonight. Before your case is heard, you're allowed to call anyone you can here in town in your favor. If you don't satisfy the general you'll be shipped back to Fillenkep to stand trial there. All right?"

"I came here as one of the crew of a vessel bringing a high government official," said Terak eagerly. "She's called the *Aaooa*, and you'll find her captain at the docks. A woman called Kareth Var. She'll speak for me."

He broke off. The jailer was pointedly not listening, but gazing at the ceiling and absently whistling to himself. He caught on fast enough, and pushed a hundred-circle coin into the man's palm. Obviously this was more than the jailer had expected, for he almost beamed after he had made sure it was genuine.

"Anyone else you'd like to call? We can get anyone you know here."

"Are slaves allowed to give evidence?" asked Terak doubtfully. To Perarnith himself he was just another of the crew, but he had grown quite friendly with one of his male retinue.

The jailer shook his head regretfully. "Slaves will do anything for the price of their freedom," he said. "So we cannot trust them. Still, I'll get hold of this woman for you."

When the visitors had left, Terak paced savagely up and down his cell for more than another hour. Then the door of the cell slid back again, and he was escorted down a number of corridors into a room where a semblance of a court had been set up. Janlo's banner hung on the wall behind a high-backed chair, which faced a small dock guarded by swordsmen. A few curious idlers and passersby filled rows of chairs at the back of the room.

Terak searched madly for signs of flame-red hair. He saw none. Where was Kareth, then?

His attention was distracted as a herald shouted for silence, and a door at the side of the room opened to admit the presiding judge. Terak's heart pounded for a moment, and then he knew that he was defeated.

It was Janlo himself.

With a sword at his back, Terak was forced into the dock, and it was as Janlo settled in his chair that he first saw and recognized the prisoner. Blank astonishment swept across his face, to be replaced with a smile of quiet satisfaction as he surveyed the situation.

The proceedings were brief. "Accused is a sailor," the dour jailer announced. "Off-worlder called Terak. Charge is rape and murder." He gave details of the discovery of the crime, which he read from what looked like an official "wanted" notice.

"Grounds for accusing this man?" questioned Janlo in a soft, purring voice.

Avrid stood up in the well of the court and recounted his first meeting with Terak. After him came Qualf, and after him Torkenwal, his companions of that day.

"Good enough." Janlo nodded. "Prisoner, have you anything to say?"

"I asked for a witness on my own behalf who has not been brought here," Terak said sourly.

"True," agreed the jailer under Janlo's questioning gaze, and described Kareth's connection with the case. "But maybe she has something to fear herself. She didn't come."

"Prisoner committed to trial at the place nearest the offense," said Janlo briefly. "Arrange for him to be sent to Fillenkep tomorrow morning."

Head whirling, Terak was hustled from the dock and returned to his cell. He felt wildly angry at the triumph now coursing through Janlo's mind. Doubtless Aldur must have warned his puppet-general of Terak's escape, and to have him arrive a prisoner in court was a gift from the gods. There could have been no doubt in Janlo's mind who was before him—they had sat opposite each other at council table with Aldur often enough three years ago.

It was worse to picture the way Aldur himself would laugh when he heard the news. . . .

He was sitting on the bunk with his head in his hands when the door opened to admit Janlo himself, together with a gigantic Leontine slave whose mouth worked in a way that indicated his tongue had been cut out. "Well, Terak?" said Janlo with a hint of a chuckle. "What brings you here?"

"You know well enough," said Terak bitingly. Janlo nodded.

"I gather Aldur took a fancy to that attractive girl of yours. What was her name? Celly, was it?" Janlo's gaze was mocking. "Terak, Terak, I never suspected you of being a fool!"

Terak spat in the man's face, and the Leontine slave hit him open-palmed across the mouth. He was flung against the wall as if by the butt of a Thanis bull, and lay groggy on the bunk.

"Yes, your spittle is the only weapon you have left," said Janlo with equanimity, wiping away the wetness with a finely embroidered kerchief. "So you set out to conquer a world out of sheer pique, with no more powerful tool than spittle. Amazing. It shows weakness of mind—it puzzles me why Aldur trusted you so long."

He threw back his handsome head and laughed aloud. "A prince of fools!" he exclaimed. "It suits you well to be fighting on the side of these other fools who inhabit Klareth, doesn't it? So sure that they are right, they are sensible! It never occurs to them to question whether a simple fisher could truly conquer half a planet. . . . I must congratulate you, by the way, Terak. Remember those plans for reducing an island stronghold which we worked out with Aldur when we were first preparing to take Klareth? They work wonderfully well, and your contribution to them is not the least important."

Terak forced himself up on his elbows and looked straight into the pretender's eyes. "You talk finely now, Janlo! You have ruled for a long time. I wonder if you will talk so gallantly when Aldur comes to claim for himself what you have sweated for three long years to win!"

The taunt struck home. Janlo's face went abruptly dark, like the piled clouds of a thunderstorm, and he swung on his heel and swept from the cell. The Leontine slave, with a lingering glance at Terak, followed him.

Terak lay still for a long while, cursing himself for a fool. If he had not let his anger run away with him, make him spit in Janlo's face, he would not have been struck stupid by the slave, and might have managed to sink his teeth in Janlo's throat before being dragged off.

Sleep crawled over him like a horde of Loudor slugs, but he could not fight it past a certain stage. He was awakened abruptly long after full dark by the sound of the door opening.

"Out, you!" said the dour jailer in a whisper, and Terak obeyed before his sleep-drugged mind could question whether this was a dream. But it was not. In the dim light of a flaring torch beyond the cell, he made out—

Kareth!

"Why—why did you not come this afternoon?" he demanded.

"I was bringing you something better," she said. She held up a scroll. "I went in search of Perarnith, and from him I have a free pardon signed by the Praestans!"

"But—how?"

"He says he brought some with him for the freeing of prisoners known to have been tortured into aiding the rebels. Come now, though—quickly."

Terak hesitated, glancing at the jailer behind him. "Does Janlo know of this?" he said in low tones.

"No, he's feasting." Kareth could not understand why he delayed.

"Here's your belongings," said the jailer in a flat voice. He gave back the sword, knife, and means of making fire which he had taken earlier. Terak gave him twenty circles and told him to get lost. Inside a few minutes he and Kareth were safely on the streets and running toward the maze of narrow streets near the dock.

In a dark alley they halted, and she flung herself into his arms. "I was so afraid when I heard they had taken you!" she whispered against his cheek. He felt unexpected wetness well from the corners of her eyes.

"How did you get the pardon?" Terak inquired gently, and Kareth stepped back from him.

"Terak, I had to tell Perarnith, of course. I had to tell him everything!"

VI

It took Terak a long time to comprehend the words. He managed to speak finally. "But you were crazy! Suppose he had laughed you down and sent the report to Janlo? You would have been dead from a sword in the dark within a day!"

"Terak, could I risk less for Klareth?" the girl demanded, and he relaxed slowly, almost with a feeling of guilt.

"No," he said softly. "There was nothing else to do. But—well, the gamble came off. Or did it?"

"Yes," insisted Kareth. "Come now, and judge for yourself. We are going to Perarnith now. He told me to bring you to him as soon as you were free."

At this, Terak hesitated anew. "This is not to my liking," he said. "Could it not be a trap? Could an official of Klareth willingly render aid to a man from the Big Dark?"

"You will see why," said Kareth determinedly, and Terak yielded.

She led him to a small house on the waterfront, from which light seeped past the edges of curtains. A guard before the main entrance studied them as they stepped into the pool of radiance cast by a resinous torch. He recognized Kareth and saluted her, and rapped in a coded pattern on the door.

One of Perarnith's own male slaves opened to them, and when they entered the low-ceilinged room beyond, they found the man himself stretched out on a bed spread with katalabs hide, his thin body naked except for a loincloth. The silent girl slave was massaging him with oil.

Sharp, intelligent, his eyes transfixed them. "I see my scroll worked wonders," he said dryly. "Slave, bring these people chairs and a jug of wine," he added, and the girl rose obediently.

"We must cover this escape of yours," Perarnith went on, sitting up. "How fast can your *Aaooa* run, Captain Var?"

"No more than a freighter is expected to," Kareth said.

"A shame. Still, it will have to be tried." He paused as the girl poured and handed over the wine she had found, and then continued musingly.

"Your man Bozhdal knows your handwriting? Good. Write directions to him on a scroll—you will find ink yonder. Balaz!"

The male slave at the door came forward.

"Balaz, you are much of a height with this Terak here. I want you to take his outer clothing and put on your sword as he wears his. You will take the scroll Captain Var gives you and go down to the *Aaooa* at the dockside. Go aboard. Give the scroll to Bozhdal. Tell him to leave port with little noise but with enough to attract attention, and make sure it is clearly seen that you are on board in the guise of Terak. By the time Janlo hears of your departure, it should be accepted that Terak has left the island by that means. Understood?"

Balaz nodded. Slowly Terak stripped off his outer clothing and exchanged it for black garments of Perarnith's which Balaz brought. Meantime Kareth wrote busily at a small desk behind Perarnith's couch, folded the message, and gave it to Balaz.

When the slave had gone into the night, Terak rose from his chair and looked down at the thin, bare body of his protector.

"Why," he demanded, "are you, a trusted official, aiding a refugee and a pirate?"

"Be seated again, Terak," directed Perarnith with equanimity. "In reality, it is quite simple. First, why do you think I have come down here to the battle-front to spy on Janlo's doings? Think, man! Is it in truth likely that a fisher should rise to conquer half a planet?"

Terak remembered how Janlo's own words, earlier that day, had presaged the remark, and began to understand.

"The Praestans, as you know," Perarnith continued, "is old and now infirm. Soon—how soon we do not know—the question of the succession will arise. Abreet, the nearest of kin of the old line, forfeited his rights and those of his descendants when he raised the banner of revolt against Farigol—who had gained the choice lawfully in a call of the islands, remember.

"Now it sometimes happens that a strong man, a conqueror, who has won his actual battles, looks around him for fresh victories. Do you not think that if it was called around the islands that a new Praestans must be chosen, Janlo would offer himself, and probably gain the day?"

Perarnith spoke with fierce intensity. Terak wondered how so bright a flame of life could burn in such a withered carcass.

"Now it happens also that a general who commands well in war does not rule wisely in peace. Something which does not happen, on the other hand, is that a man with no skill in strategy save in defending fishing fleets against the love-pat raids of our Klarethly pirates becomes a great Praestans. Much of Janlo's career has given us at Fillenkep food for thought. In fact, it worried us so much that nothing else would serve except that I myself should come hither and evaluate the situation. What your Captain Var had to tell me is so perfect an explanation of what has happened and will happen that I could not but accept it."

Musingly, Perarnith added, "It is of interest that no one questioned Janlo's origin until after he had led his first great raid and laid waste the island of Osterkep, towns, forests, and all, with fire. Only then, when he had destroyed all possible traces, did he claim to have been born and bred on that island."

Kareth drew in her breath sharply. Terak knew why; it was inconceivable to her, as to any Klarethly person, that someone should destroy all that he had known as a child.

"Moreover," Perarnith pursued relentlessly, "it was a matter of surprise to us that the shipload of slaves he 'rescued' from their captors when they made their seemingly ill-judged raid here a while ago should have included so many first-class fighting men and military captains. Men of that caliber make poor slaves!

"It becomes clear as crystal now. At his orders, these supposed 'freed slaves' will resume their true identity and turn on their comrades. Meantime, while Klareth is licking its wounds and all its best fighting men are torn apart by internecine struggle half the world away, Janlo will signal Aldur and the hosts from the Big Dark will descend on Fillenkep and the islands of the northern hemisphere. . . . It makes my blood run cold, Terak. Tell me, have I understood the plan aright?"

Terak nodded. "But how can you trust me, who"—he forced himself to admit it—"who had a hand in the preparing of that plan?"

"Because I believe, with Captain Var, that you are a man who will fight for the best cause he can find. Until you came to Klareth, the best cause you knew was that of your own lawless people. Now you have found a better."

"It is true," said Terak.

"Janlo, I take it, knows who you are?" Perarnith went on after a short silence. "And will report your presence to Aldur?"

"Yes, I imagine so."

"Will he report your escape so readily?"

"Not until he's forced to, I shouldn't think. Otherwise his head may roll on Aldur's arrival—and he is very conscious of his danger from Aldur."

"Then," said Perarnith with a smile of pure joy, "we will just wait here quietly until he is firmly convinced that you are on the high seas—I think until about noon tomorrow, when he will have sent ships in pursuit of the *Aaooa* and will not yet have heard that you cannot be found aboard her. My slaves will see you to suitable quarters. Good night to you."

And with the calmness of a man perfectly in command of the situation, he rolled over and told the girl slave to continue her massage.

Waiting was the most irritating and hard-to-bear part of the plan, though with Kareth for company it was easier. The first sign that they had of their scheme's fruition was shortly past dawn the next morning. Sounds of high, arguing voices came to them in the room adjacent to the entrance hall, where they had spent the night.

Terak slipped from the bed and pressed his eye to a crack in the jamb by the door. A uniformed senior officer was arguing with one of Perarnith's slaves, demanding to be taken to his master's presence.

The altercation was cut short by the materialization of Perarnith himself, wearing a night-robe. The girl slave pushed him into the hall on a four-wheeled chair with a hood that almost obscured his face. Steam issued in wisps from the hood.

"Your pardon, Colonel, for appearing before you in this undignified posture," said Perarnith thickly. "My physicians, however, have enjoined an hour of this for me daily, to purge my lungs of the night's rheum, and I apprehend that your business is urgent."

Terak, from the time Perarnith had spent aboard the *Aaooa,* knew that this was a subterfuge. Its purpose he could not guess.

"A prisoner committed for trial at Fillenkep was released from jail last night on a forged pardon, Ser Perarnith," the officer stated. "General Janlo ordered me to inform you immediately."

"Really," said Perarnith in faintly bored tones. "An important prisoner of war, I take it? A senior rebel?"

"No," said the officer. "An off-worlder, charged with rape and murder."

"What precautions has General Janlo taken?"

"He has ordered out all available naval patrol craft to search for a freighter believed to have taken the escaped prisoner from the docks last night."

"Really!" said Perarnith again with slightly more emphasis. "Tell General Janlo I should very much like to know why he is wasting my time and that of these patrol vessels looking for one insignificant off-worlder who will in an any case be apprehended soon enough, when there is a civil war raging." He put sting into the words, and the officer blushed as red as the facings of his uniform. "Tell him also that I am not concerned with minor matters of this kind, and in any case they reflect discreditably on his adminstration of the civil affairs of this town. Get out."

"Good man," whispered Terak to the air.

"But," he remarked as he was relaying what he had heard to Kareth a few moments later, "I should dearly love to know who this man Perarnith is!"

They passed the morning pleasantly enough in talk with Perarnith, who discussed Klareth and its affairs with a knowledgeable air. To Terak, accustomed to the rule by sheer power which was all he had known out in the Big Dark, it came as a revelation to understand that the Praestans himself, here on Klareth, being chosen by popular vote, might walk the streets unmolested and ruled with no trappings of office or authority. Almost, he did not quite believe it, until Perarnith gave him a sardonically humorous glance and said, "This applies to all officials of the government. Do you not recall, Terak, a certain dockside tavern in Fillenkep where you sat eating in the company of three soldiers from Janlo's army?"

"You were the man sitting by himself in the corner!" said Terak, thunderstruck.

"And no one knew me," agreed Perarnith. "It is not customary, you see, for any of the officials of the government to be known by sight to any except their colleagues. Every man in the army knows General Janlo, but as far as casual passerby is concerned, a man entering the government building at Fillenkep could be the steward of the household—or the Praestans himself."

"Yet you are well enough known here."

Perarnith shook his head. "Not I, but the documents I bear."

He pulled himself together, and ordered the girl slave to bring him a cloak. "It is time, I think," he said, "to take advantage of the panic Janlo will by now be in. It is his habit to hold a levee at noon each day, followed by a staff conference at which his officers report. I believe I should like to arrive at the opening of the levee, when some thousands of soliders are paraded. I am invited to attend the staff conference anyway."

"But suppose I am recognized and taken?" said Terak.

"Hood yourself. To be in my company will be sufficient guarantee until we confront Janlo himself."

VII

And so it turned out. It was raining gently as they left their quarters, which suited Perarnith excellently, for, as he explained, the levee would now be held in an indoor hall and not in the main square of the town. They took about twenty minutes to reach the place.

The soldiery grew thicker as they approached, but Perarnith's slaves cleared a way for them, and occasionally an officer glanced at Perarnith, looked startled, and gave him a smart salute. Terak queried this, and Perarnith told him, "Officers visit the Praestantial court when they are given their commissions, you see. Naturally they know me."

Obsequious aides ushered the party into the headquarters building, down passages and then out onto a balcony overlooking a hall perhaps two hundred feet long. Sergeants were shouting squads of men into a three-sided hollow square below the balcony, and bored-looking officers, many obviously fresh from the front, stood about talking.

At length a group of Janlo's personal aides joined them on the balcony, and one them barked a command which immediately stilled the babble of talk from below. Janlo marched forward toward the front of the balcony from the door, and as soon as he came in view, the parade saluted.

Then there was a sudden mutter of amazement, and a roar!

Bewildered, Terak saw only that Perarnith, holding himself stiffly erect, had walked to the front of the balcony and was standing alongside Janlo, who turned with a face of thunder to see the old man gazing at him with a hint of amusement.

"*They* know me," said Perarnith. "Is it not amazing, Janlo, that you—senior officer of our army—are the only officer not to recognize the Praestans of Klareth?"

"You—*what*?" said Janlo, comprehending belatedly.

"I am Farigol," said the man who had called himself Perarnith. "And the reason, Janlo, that these people know me and you do not, is that they, though not you, are Klarethly!"

In that instant Janlo went mad. He must have pictured his

entire plan lying open and naked to the enemy. First he swung to face the parade again and screamed for Aldur's men to turn on their comrades. White-faced, a few of the officers, though none of the rank and file, drew their swords and stood irresolute. Knowing only that this was wrong, their companions swiftly disarmed them.

Seeing that his appeal had gone for nothing, Janlo curled his lips back from his teeth in a snarl like an animal and unsheathed his knife to bury it in Perarnith-Farigol's belly. Before the blade could reach its goal, Terak's right arm had gone up—and down again—and there was Janlo's hand lying, still grasping the knife, on the floor. So swift was the blow that no red marred the shining metal of Terak's sword.

The puppet-general gazed stupidly at his forearm, spurting blood, for a long instant. Then the tremendous shock overcame him, and he collapsed weeping to the floor, trying to staunch the flow with his remaining hand. Terak bent over so that Janlo could recognize him.

"You!" said Janlo vehemently. "You! But I've beaten you, Terak, though you escaped me once. I've beaten the whole of this craven, planet-bound horde! I signaled Aldur last night, as soon as I knew you were safely jailed and could not raise an army against mine!"

He barely uttered the last few words, and then his head slumped forward. The last of his life leaked out with the stream of blood.

Terak glanced up to find that the Praestans had also heard the last sentence. Shocked, worried, the officers who had trusted Janlo were demanding orders, and the men below the balcony were humming like swarming bees.

"How long does it take to get from deep in the Big Dark to the Marches of Klareth?" the Praestans demanded, and Terak shook his head.

"Depends whether the fleet has already moved in. But although Aldur may have mounted the invasion at once and already be on the move, I, in the fastest ship I could steal, and traveling on emergency extreme, which he will *not* be, took eleven days."

"Eleven days! It takes a fast patrol craft nine to get from here to Fillenkep! Let alone a heavy-laden trooper." The Praestans bit his lip. "Where is the invasion due to strike first?"

"Unless Janlo and Aldur altered the plans when I left, first at Fillenkep and then at various important islands all over the northern hemisphere. They relied on the time news takes to travel south, and the traitors planted among Janlo's army, to prevent the defenses from interfering until they were well established."

"Then our first task is to weed out the traitors," said the Praestans. "The second—to move north like wildfire!"

It was not until, three days later aboard on of the fastest patrol vessels in the Klarethly fleet, they tore past an island whose wooded head was crowned with flame and smoke, that Terak realized how exactly apt the comparison was. There must have been many among the fleet who looked on that island as home, who felt sorrow at seeing wildfire strip it to barrenness, but there was danger of a worse kind of fire laying waste the whole of Klareth.

Red-eyed, the Praestans sat with his officers on the deck of the patrol vessel listening to Terak expound what he remembered of the pirates' plan. Again and again, an officer would exclaim, "But you can't reduce"—such an island—"in *that* space of time!" only to find Terak wearily recounting just how he, Janlo, and Aldur had proved you *could* do so.

"But this bears the signs of master strategy!" the Praestans said at one point, and Terak gave him a sour grin.

"It took three of us to work it out! The real test is whether one of us—me!—can spot the weak points in it within the next few days."

But he did, and as he commanded and deployed and stationed the Klarethly forces, the Praestans eyed him thoughtfully.

The strain was telling on the old man, but he insisted that the welfare of his people came before his own. To know that their ruler was planning with the generals, he declared, was worth another regiment or flotilla to the defenders. Yet his girl slave had to attend him more frequently, and the healing steam treatment was no longer a subterfuge but a dire necessity.

His weariness and illness, though, seemed not to hinder his judgment or the shrewdness of his suggestions. Many a time Terak was grateful for his intimate knowledge of Klarethly affairs.

"The defense plan must depend on the landing actually taking place," Terak hammered home again and again in his planning conferences. "If the pirates suspect anything, they will attack before they actually land, and we have no way of dealing with spaceborne weapons. An invasion we can counter—but not bombardment."

"How about the naval patrols?" or "How about the rebel army?" someone would snap, and Terak would wipe his brow and repeat with dogged insistence that the patrols must *not* be alerted, but go about their ordinary routine, and the rebels must be contained with a minimum force under instructions to behave as much as possible like the entire Klarethly army and navy.

Conscious of the way time was slipping by, Terak begrudged even the short while their racing craft had to lie to so that the officers from the other vessels who had come aboard from the conference could return. On the fourth day the Praestans found him impatiently pacing the deck and murmuring against just such a delay as he watched the other ships bump up against their own in succession and take back their passengers.

"What worries you, Terak?" Farigol inquired, and broke into a cough on the last word.

"Time!" said Terak bitterly. "Four days gone of our precious eleven, and even when we reach Fillenkep we still have to alert the population and dispose our forces."

"It will be done," said Farigol peaceably. There was a pause; then, "Terak, why are you so eager to save my world from your kinfolk's ravages?"

Terak shrugged. "I suppose—because this is a better way to live . . . ?"

Farigol's eyes fixed him. "You have noticed, perhaps, that our names here are full of sounds which are short, and abrupt. Where did your ancestors come from, Terak—do you know?"

Terak shook his head. "Few people yonder in the Big Dark take much account of ancestry."

"Terak," said the Praestans musingly. "Terak—Klareth. Has it not occurred to you that you may have found your true kinfolk here?"

Terak turned the idea over in his mind, wondering, and the other signaled his ever-present girl attendant and made his way below, throwing a cheery good night over his shoulder and beginning to cough again as he went.

Interest in Farigol's suggestion mingled in Terak's mind with thoughts of the rapid failing of the Praestans's health. He hoped that the strain of the next few days would not prove too much for the old man.

Nine days from Aldur's fatal signal! And the fleet hove in sight of the island of Fillenkep. By now the plan was smooth, concerted. It needed only putting into action.

First the officers went ashore with the message. Criers raced through the streets, commanding the people to attend a public meeting forthwith, and they came, alarmed, to hear the terrifying news.

"As you love Klareth!" they were told. "Wait until the pirates are confident. Act as you would if you were afraid of being enslaved. But *don't* be afraid, for we are only lying in wait until the right moment comes."

The people listened in grim silence, and then dispersed to their homes, to talk quietly, watch, and await the invasion.

Meantime, Terak busied himself with the concealment of the better part of Klareth's forces among the wooded fringes of the islands. Their last two days passed in a frantic testing of their organization; it worked without a hitch.

After that, there was nothing they dared do but wait. The stragglers, the slow freighters who had not made it to the latitude of Fillenkep by the eleventh day, were perforce held back and likewise driven into concealment. It irked Terak almost beyond bearing that still another full day passed without event.

"If I'd known!" he fretted as he and Kareth walked together on the deck of the command ship, overhung by vast, wide-leaved trees which securely hid them from above. "We could have moved up six thousand more men and forty, fifty more ships!"

"But we didn't dare!" Kareth reminded him. "There must be no chance of the pirates realizing their plans were forestalled."

"No, I guess not," said Terak wearily, acknowledging the force of his own argument, and dashed up on the stern castle to thrust aside the overhanging branches and stare yet again into the enigmatic sky.

VIII

And then, at last, it came.

Terak had been out on occasional slave raids, though nowadays the pirates could seldom organize enough effort to launch one. He had sometimes wondered what it was like to stand helpless and see the sleek giants descending on your homeland, arrowlike, prepared to trade as many as two of their crew for every ten of your friends they stole away as slaves: bloody, violent fighters, brilliant, persistent, well-nigh invincible.

But this was more than a slave raid, more than a brief occupation, a few hours under an iron heel while suitable slave material was kidnapped and dragged aboard ship. Instead of the usual three or four ships, there were ninety-odd, and this was only the first wave.

He wondered where Aldur was.

The ships dropped swiftly; their hulls were still glowing red from friction when they hit land. They went down anywhere, on beaches, in open spaces in the towns, and often among the woods, which they set blazing from the heat of their hulls.

But even trees on fire did not hinder the outgush of men from the locks. Almost before the vessels had settled, it seemed, they were swarming forth, descending on the "unsuspecting" towns and villages.

Reassured already by the obvious lack of preparation by the patrols out in space, they gave no more than a passing thought to the defenses. As far as they could tell, Klareth's fleet and its army were half the world away, far beyond hope of interfering until the invasion was well established—and torn apart by the pretended slaves who had been planted earlier, into the bargain.

The populace reacted magnificently. Terak had arranged that a few officers should be placed at strategic points, to direct halfhearted "counterattacks" carefully designed to dissolve in confusion with a minimum of loss of life. Except for those isolated conflicts, the inhabitants ran around like a disturbed nest of ants, strikingly, but to no purpose.

By nightfall the pirates had been on Klareth ten hours; they were in apparent control of every major island in the northern hemisphere from Fillenkep on down.

Almost biting their nails with anxiety, Terak, Kareth, and the Praestans with his staff waited aboard the command ship. At intervals couriers had slipped away to apprise them of the situation, but at sunset it was long since a message had reached them. All the news they had was the negative knowledge that the pirates had not been forced into a major battle anywhere, for that would instantly have been reported to them.

But with night fully on them, they saw a trail in the

ocean—a wake of phosphorescence which might have been left by the fin of a tor-fish. No tor-fish, however, would have ventured so close to shore, and the lookout identified it well before details could be distinguished.

Followed by the hobbling Praestans, Terak hastened down to the stern and was among those who lent willing hands to hoist the man aboard. It was one of Farigol's personal slaves, who had been sent into Fillenkep as a spy.

He gave his master a flashing grin as he wiped water off his face and thrust back his soaking wet forelock. Terak pressed him urgently for information on their work.

"Gone perfectly, Terak!" said the slave with enthusiasm. "Those pirates seem determined to find out everything a planet-bound life has to offer in their first night here." His face darkened. "They tend to take what they want when they want it, and I've seen some nasty sights. . . ."

Terak remembered that Aldur had done just that, and his stomach seemed to fill with the quintessence of anticipation. "What of Aldur?" he questioned fiercely.

"There was something afoot around the government building early this evening," the slave stated. "A further ship came down to join the first wave. Someone of importance went from it to the government building, like I say. Could well have been Aldur, don't you guess?"

Terak nodded grimly. "It would fit well with Aldur's ambitious ways to sleep in the capital of his newly conquered world," he answered. "Do you think the time is ripe?"

"As a Sirenian plum," said the courier with relish, and the entire group about him tensed. Terak half turned to address the man with the signal lamp at the stern, and then relaxed, sighing.

"No, not even yet," he decided. "How long would you say the people will be patient?" he demanded of the courier.

The man shrugged. "Past midnight—perhaps. But already those who knew who I was were asking when the moment to strike would come, before I left. Once an incautious word reaches the ears of an invader—"

"One hour more," said Terak, drawing a deep breath. "One hour and an eternity."

And, though it cost him dear to try to remain calm, not until that whole hour had slipped into the past did he look up at the man on the stern castle with the signal lamp and raise his right hand.

Instantly the signaler unshielded the flame of the lamp; the next ship astern repeated the sign and relayed it, and so on around the island. The last in line flashed it across the few short miles of ocean to the neighboring islands. Inside thirty minutes, they knew from tests, that signal would reach every island held by the invader, every island where the defenders waited their chance to hit back.

Men leaped to power the reactor of the command ship; the helmsman used the very first kick to swing her bows and begin the short journey to the beach where they would land. Now the whole fleet of Klareth was on the move, and lightless and almost soundless they stole over the sea.

The first target, of course, was the pirate fleet. Up from the shore moved silent men, creeping along paths they had known since childhood; the lax sentries posted by the invaders had no time to do more than gurgle before they were strangled at their posts.

Soon, each ship from the Big Dark was ringed by a circle of invisible foes, attending the panicky rout which they knew would bring the pirates running to a massacre in the darkness. The often haphazard choice of landing places they had made suited the Klarethly purpose to perfection.

Runners came back from each detachment of the landing party as soon as the encirclement of the spaceships on Fillenkep was complete. Terak heard the news with grim satisfaction. The ship which had landed last and presumably had brought Aldur was plainly visible from most parts of the island, including the government building. If Aldur were to look out at it, he would not guess that there was anything to hinder him from returning to if and when he wished.

Terak chuckled mirthlessly at the thought. "We can move in, then," he said softly, and turned to the Praestans, who waited on deck behind him. "I hope in an hour or two to give you back your planet intact, Ser Farigol," he declared. "And I hope to gain—*my* planet in the doing of it."

"You may be more right than you think," said the old man cryptically. "Good luck go with you, Terak!" He turned aside and leaned on his girl slave for support; the sound of his breathing was almost raucous in the silence.

"Good luck, Terak!" said Kareth, stepping forward. "I wish I could be there beside you, fighting for my world!"

"You will be, in spirit," said Terak steadily, and took her in his arms for one brief moment before he signaled his men onward with a sweep of his arm, and clambered lightly over the side of the vessel into the shallow water.

Ahead of the army went stealthy messengers, who knocked at doors and whispered to those who answered, *"Now!"* The word almost at once outstripped the messengers, and the city closed on its invaders like the clawed talon of a bird of prey, like a hand crushing a ripe fruit, like an executioner's noose on the neck of a condemned man.

Men who had been lying hidden for two days rose, stretched their cramped limbs, emerged with weapons from their secret places and went hunting. In the drinking shops, the bartenders chuckled as they added drops of poison to the latest orders; in the eating-houses, waiters picked up the carving knives and carved throats instead of the waiting roast katalabs meat; in the streets, drunken pirates walked around corners into welcomes of steel.

Before Aldur could learn what was happening, the back of the invasion was broken.

The ladies of easy virtue crept from their beds without pity and regretted only that the blood of their victims would stain the bedding before they put away their knives. Householders on whom pirates had been forcibly billeted stole into the street with their families and seized the night's issue of torches from the sconces on the wall and set them to the timber. There was no hesitation, for there were enemies inside.

Some of the pirates were nearly lucky. They were the ones who were sober or wary enough to guess what was happening, overcame their attackers, and rushed into the roads crying a warning to their fellows. But by that time Terak's men were already within the city, and though they banded together and fought desperately, soon they were put to flight.

Striking down the enemy one after another with the blood of Klarethly victims still wet on their sword-blades, Terak knew it was worth all he had been through to see their faces as they recognized him and died trying to utter his name.

To see Aldur do the same . . . !

"Where's Aldur?" he demanded of them one by one, and received sobbed assertions that they did not know. He'd believed them; a man in fear of a bloody and imminent death can seldom lie convincingly.

"Ask them where Aldur is!" he yelled, turning to his men, and the order was passed from mouth to mouth, each man flinging the question as he brought up his blade to the throat of a pirate.

"In—in the big building at the center of the town," finally

choked one of those of whom Terak sought the knowledge. "Spare me! Have mercy!"

"Your life I will spare," said Terak thickly. "For your kind assistance! But I will not have you running to warn your fellows when we are gone by. *Thus* I spare you!"

His sword flashed, and the man screamed and fell groveling with his right wrist slashed. "Hold it tight!" Terak advised him. "That way you will not bleed to death."

He turned and called his men to him. "Aldur is in the government building!" he informed them. "Get there as quickly and as silently as you know how."

He himself began to eat up the distance at a run.

Amazingly, the huge bulk of the building was still in comparative quiet. Apparently no one had passed the Klarethly soldiers in the nearby streets to warn Aldur and his staff within.

The building, though large, was not fortified, but men who were acquainted with its interior told him that it would be hard to take.

"Set fire to it!" suggested one of Terak's soldiers, panting and near berserk.

"No!" snapped one of his companions. "I have it from a pirate whose throat I cut a moment gone that there are many Klarethly prisoners there, and many women Aldur had taken in for the amusement of his officers."

Terak's head swam for an instant; he knew what that term *amusement* implied.

Celly! Oh, Celly, my dead beloved!

He forced the memory into the back of his mind, and snapped swift orders. His men split up to seek a vulnerable entrance to the building, and one came back in a moment with report of an unguarded doorway.

"Aldur!" murmured Terak under his breath as he approached the entrance. "Make the most of your little triumph! You have not long now. . . ."

He threw himself bodily at the door; his left shoulder felt pain for a moment, and then he was sprawling on the floor of a passage beyond, his hand still grasping the jamb which he had seized as he fell and which had come clean away with the violence of his charge.

He leaped to his feet and hastened down the passage, the sound of footsteps behind him enough to let him know he was being followed. But at the moment he felt he could make

his way to Aldur single-handed, against the entire might of
the pirates here in the government building.

A startled man caught sight of him in the dim glow of a
resinous torch; before he could cry out, Terak was on him,
sword poised.

"One yell, and you're dead," he whispered. "Where is Aldur?"

The man had a pasty yellow face; it turned near white as
he recognized Terak, and his mouth went so slack that drool
spilled over his chin. "In—in an apartment which belonged to
the Praestans," he gulped, and Terak corrected him with a
sardonic smile.

"Which still *belongs* to the Praestans!" he said. "I go to
restore it to its owner. *Which way?*"

The man gestured, too overcome to speak; Terak knocked
him unconscious and raced in the indicated direction. His
men followed, but he outdistanced them, and only a handful
were behind him when he stormed into the Praestantial apartments. The remainder were flinging open doors and surprising
Aldur's officers asleep, drinking, wenching, making plans to
exploit their imagined victory. . . .

Astonished guards within the apartment leaped to their
feet. Terak paid them exactly no attention, and as they recovered and started to go after him, the Klarethly soldiers who
were following him also took them from behind. They died
with the gurgle of blood in their mouths.

And—yes! Terak had judged all right: to sleep in the
Praestantial bed was much to Aldur's taste. Here, now, at
last, he was face to face with his enemy, and the leader of
the invaders was starting awake alongside the woman of his
taste of the moment, who cowered frightened between the
covers.

Face like thunder, Terak stood over the bed and made his
sword whistle in the air. He spat contemptuously at Aldur's
companion, thinking of the vast gulf between this com-
plaisant chit and Celly, who was dead. The picture of Aldur
holding Celly in his embrace made him coldly, completely angry.

"Terak!" said Aldur, and his voice was pleading, as though
he prayed to some unknown deity that this should be a
dream.

"That same. You took away from me what I most loved
and most desired, and made me look on it as you left it—ruined. You love nothing and no one so much as naked power.

Therefore I have taken that from you, and you too shall look on the ruins of what you have loved." He stepped back. "Go to yonder window, from which you can see your spaceship."

Aldur made no move to obey, and with one furious motion Terak stripped away the covers and seized his arm. "If you won't go, I will take you," he said between clenched teeth, and with more strength than he knew he had remaining in his body he dragged Aldur forcibly across the floor.

Beyond the window, beyond the city, was the ship which had brought the pirate lord out of the Big Dark. It was ringed with liquid fire, and very faintly on the air came the screams of men dying by the light of the flames.

Aldur went quite limp in Terak's grasp at the sight.

"Now you have seen, as I had to see," Terak said savagely. "Now I have a debt to settle, and so have you." He rounded on the soldiers who had followed him into the bedroom. "Give this undead carrion a sword!"

They obeyed; three hilts were at once offered. But Aldur grasped none of them. Instead, he put his hands giddily to his head, sagged slowly at the knees, and slumped to the floor.

Terak's disappointment lasted only a moment. He had thought to take personal revenge, but vengeance had long ago ceased to be the mainspring of his actions on Klareth, and in that moment he ceased to desire it. He sheathed his bloody sword with none of Aldur's gore on it, and grew conscious of an infinite weariness.

He stood gazing at Aldur's prostrate form for perhaps minutes on end, until a sudden familiar voice made him start alert again. *Kareth's* voice!

She was shouting, "Terak! Is Terak here? Have you seen Terak?" And suddenly she appeared in the doorway.

"Kareth! You're mad to come here now," Terak declared, starting forward. "You could have been killed in the streets!"

The girl's manner had changed the instant she saw him. She shook her fiery head. "Not now, Terak," she said. "Klareth is yours!"

And she bowed to him, deeply, ritually, so that her hair nearly swept his feet.

"What is the meaning of this?" Terak demanded, bewildered.

She straightened. "Klareth is yours, Terak! I wanted to be the first of your subjects to do you honor. Farigol is dead. The strain was too much for him and he passed away when

the news was brought that we had won back Fillenkep. But
with his dying breath he named you for Praestans."

"How could he do that?" Terak's head whirled.

"When the vote is called among the islands, since there is
no near member of the line to be chosen, the voice of the
dead Praestans will ensure your right to succeed." She spoke
clearly, somehow *hopefully*.

"Will you take Klareth, Terak? Will you learn to rule what
you have saved?"

The soldiers in the room, recovering from their amazement, had started to bow clumsily to the Praestans-elect. Ignoring them, Terak closed his eyes momentarily and heard
Farigol's voice in memory—a voice he would never hear
again.

"You may have found your true kinfolk here!"

And Terak knew it was so, and that this was the way it
had to be.

"I will have Klareth," he said, opening his eyes again, "if I
can have Kareth, too."

And for a moment it was as if the oceans of the planet
were telling him yes, but it was the sea-green eyes of a girl.

THE WANTON
OF ARGUS

I

It was a wild night. The wind shouted in the bending trees like a giant's child, shrieking its glee at the black, cloud-racing sky, and the rain poured and spattered on the earth, churning even the tough thin Argus grass from its place, dancing like a cloud of devils across the hard bare roads, whipping the faces of travelers like a myriad of icy needles, soaking and resoaking the Imperial banners over the castle of the kings till they were too heavy to stand out from the staffs at the bidding of the wind, too heavy to reveal that they hung upside down to signify the passing of a king.

Outside the black castle, people waited, watching. They were gray people, common people, men with the coarse hands of farmers and mechanics, women with lined, careworn faces and eyes like dying coals.

A bell was tolling.

The same storm whipped at the windows of a lone helicopter but a few miles distant in the night. It had not the look of something made with human hands, for it came from one of the mutant worlds beyond the bounds of the Empire, whither the unhuman children of men had been harried by the lash of hatred, and where they had built themselves a culture that still retained knowledge lost to the Empire in the Long Night that had swamped the stars ten thousand years before.

The man at the controls handled them with delicacy, for she was bucking like a live thing, and half an impatient move might tear the blades from the screaming rotors and toss them a mile to the barren lands below. He had a high bald forehead and sensitive lips, but the nose and eyes of an eagle, and his hands were pale and long, his voice, when he spoke, low and pleasant.

He glanced for a second over his shoulder and said conversationally, "Nice weather, eh, Sharla?"

There were two other people in the cockpit behind him, uncomfortable on seats built for not-men bigger than mere humans. The girl on the left shuddered, and drew her cloak tighter around her, and tried to force herself closer into the corner where she sat. She said, "Landor, is there much further to go?"

Landor risked a quick glance from the wildness outside to the position marker glowing like a firefly in the corner of the control panel. He said, "Not far. Perhaps another ten minutes' flying time will get us there."

The third passenger grunted expressively. He said, "This is the ride of the furies, Ser Landor, and no mistake!"

Landor laughed shortly, without taking his eyes from the storm or shifting hands or body an infinitesimal fraction. He said, "You have the makings of a poet, Ordovic."

"A poet? Not I!" Ordovic retorted, his eyes straying from the windows to the pale, set face of Sharla across the seat beside him.

"I'm nothing but a common fighting man, more at home with a spear than a pen and happier with a sword than either."

He dropped his hand to the hilt of his own blade, and the steel rang very softly in its scabbard, and at the noise his dark eyes filled with something that belied his self-deprecation.

He added, putting his hand to the clasp at his neck, "You're cold, my lady. Will you take my cloak?"

Sharla stopped him with a gesture. "Not now, Ordovic. We have but ten minutes' flying to do, and I have no wish to freeze you for that space of time. There will be warmth at the castle."

Landor said pointedly, "There may be a warm reception for us in more ways than one, Sharla.... Ordovic, I'm no fighting man—my swordsmanship departed with my youth— and I place our safety in your hands."

Ordovic squared his shoulders and under the coarse brown cloak there was a glint of metal. "But twenty-eight years, Ser Landor," he boasted, "and as strong as a Thanis bull."

Sharla glanced at him very swiftly, and away. Her lovely face was troubled.

The crowd before the castle thinned slowly. Many of them had watched since sundown last evening, and had seen the banners dip and vanish and rise again inverted in the dim red glow of the winter sun, and had raised the Passing Cry for Andalvar of Argus, and watched in the wet chill of the storm in honor of their ruler.

On a bare slab of rock beside the road waited a boy of seven and a crone of sixty, bent and worn, for old age came quickly on this harsh bare world. The boy yawned and huddled against the old woman, trying to share the impact of the blast. Nearby, men stamped and shifted and blew on their hands, and their leather coats dripped wet.

Suddenly the old woman closed her eyes, folded her cold hands together, and whispered, "Ronail?"

"Here, Granny," the boy said, putting his arm around her wasted shoulders.

"Ronail, I see bad days," the old woman whispered, her voice like the rustle of dry leaves in the wind. "Ronail, I see evil days ahead of Argus, and I pity you."

One of the men nearby turned suddenly, his beard spangled with drops of rain like tiny jewels. He bent low and said urgently to the boy, "What was that?"

The boy said casually, with the inconsequentiality of youth, " 'Tis only Granny. She's a seeress."

The man's eyes lit, and he bent closer to hear the faint words as they fell from her stiff, withered lips. Other men stepped near.

"Ronail—Ronail, where are you?"

"Here, Granny," said the boy comfortingly. He pressed up against her.

"Ronail—I see bad times for Argus soon. I see the black witch scheming to oppress us and forget the Empire—the people groaning and the soldiers bought—the Empire become dust."

"Ay!" whispered the bearded man. "The black witch. Andra! This is an evil day for Argus."

"Ssh!" said a man behind him. "There may be more."

"The purging of the fire and the chastening of the whip,"

recited the old hag in her mumbling tones. "The sores and the wrath of the lords. . . ."

The bearded man signed himself, and the boy, after gazing in wonder for an instant, followed suit.

"Ay, the dark of the Long Night is near to be seen, and ere the black witch be forgotten there are black days for Argus!"

There was another sound than the storm, faintly, in the distance, like the buzzing of a monstrous fly, and the crone opened her eyes and stared unseeing at the castle.

The noise grew. Even the deaf could feel it now, a great steady drone that made the ears ring and the heart falter. They stood, searching the bare black sky.

Then there was a light that shone more brightly than all the moons of Argus—called after the many-eyed god for its nine bright satellites—which flared out of nothing in the sky and grew steadily as the noise grew. Above it there became visible a shimmer like the wings of an insect.

"A devil!" shouted someone, and they threatened to break and run, but the bearded one said scornfully, "What devil would venture near the castle of the kings? No, 'tis a machine, a flying machine. I have seen such in my travels, but I never thought to see one in the air of Argus."

They passed the explanation from mouth to mouth, and they signed themselves and stood fast. Slowly, the light settled, tossed by the wind but driving gently down into the bare space that the first drawing-aside had left. The noise was like the drumming of a demon.

It touched the wet ground before the castle, and the light vanished and the noise ceased.

The door of the thing opened and three figures came out, the first two dropping lightly to the ground and turning to aid the third.

Together the newcomers passed through the crowd, who drew back at the air of authority worn by the leader of the three. He was a tall man with a shining helmet and a cloak that stood out behind him like great wings, and he strode through the gale-strong gusts as if the storm had not existed.

Before the mighty iron doors of the castle he paused. Then with sword reversed he hammered on the door till it rang and rang again, and he threw back his head and roared in a bull voice that shook the castle and drowned the storm.

"Open! Open in the name of Andalvar's daughter, the Princess Sharla of Argus!"

Senchan Var raised the drape from the narrow slit in the wall, and glanced through it at the black night outside. He said, "There are quite a few of them left, my lady."

"But naturally, Senchan," said Andra lazily, and there was half a laugh hidden in her voice. "Did you expect less from a people loyal to its kings?"

He dropped the curtain again and turned to lean against the wall beside it, his face thoughtful. "Things have happened, my lady—sooner than we expected. Perhaps too soon. I counted on a month more."

Andra reclined on the yellow silk pillows of her divan like a well-fed cat. She had cat's eyes too—yellow, with heavy lids—and her black hair hung around her shoulders as the night hung around the castle.

"What makes you say that, Senchan?" she said casually, picking grapes from a bowl before her and splitting them with her perfect teeth. "Why should our plans not go through as well now as later?" She tossed one of the fruit to the black Sirian ape chained to the opposite wall of the room, and laughed when he caught and rejected it. His kind were no vegetarians.

Senchan Var followed the movement with his eyes and shuddered. He confessed frankly, "It is not that our plan is not working, my lady. It is working too well. All's going too smoothly. I cannot rid myself of the fear that there will be a flaw."

"Is it the thought of Sharla that makes you afraid, Senchan? A child—forgotten, lost? She hasn't been seen or heard of for seven years, Senchan."

Senchan Var elbowed himself away from the wall and paced restlessly up and down, his bare feet brown and thin on the snow-white fleece of the carpet. He said, "No, my lady. Sharla's the least likely untoward factor to crop up. If she's not dead, she still will not hear of your father's death for long after you're established regent."

"Is it Penda, then, that worries you? Where is he, by the way?"

"Asleep, my lady. He displayed deep feeling earlier—wept, and fell asleep weeping."

"He would," said Andra. " 'Tis natural for a child."

"Natural!" said Senchan Var scornfully. "Your pardon, my lady, but to weep like a girl at his age is shameful. If my son did that, being as he is much of an age with Prince Penda—

King Penda, I should say, I suppose—I'd rise from my deathbed and strike him!"

Andra curved her full red lips into a smile, and picked a bloody bone from the floor beside her. At the movement the ape across the room bounded out to the full length of his silver chain and dropped to his knees, his thick lips drawn back from teeth like chisels. She laughed again, very softly.

"That's a loyal sentiment, Senchan," she said. "Which reminds me—he brought his hound into the dining hall again today, against his father's commands. Have Dolichek brought, will you? And the whip-master."

Senchan Var's grizzled face turned to meet her gaze in astonishment. He said, "My lady, if you ask me, Dolichek is half the reason Penda is so insolent. If you'll allow me the suggestion, Dolichek should be dismissed now, and this practice discontinued."

Andra's fingers folded like a steel trap closing on the bone she held, and the blood from the meat on it welled red between her fingers. She said in a sort of sibilant whisper, "No, Senchan! Think! Spoiled he may be—spoiled he *is*. But as such he is most suited to our purpose. Fetch Dolichek."

Senchan shrugged, mute rebellion smoldering in his eyes. He said, "Very well, my lady; but it makes my heart ache to see the fruit of a fine stock go rotten."

Andra relaxed, and the ape whined tentatively, extending black hairless paws toward the bone. Impatiently she flung it at him. He seized it out of the air and curled up contentedly to gnaw it on the floor.

Very faintly above the muted roar of the storm, dulled by six feet of stone, there was a buzzing sound like a gigantic fly. Senchan Var noted it and frowned, but since Andra did not comment on it he said nothing, and tugged at the gold-woven bell-rope beside the window. A small brassy bell rang somewhere outside.

A slave with the hot brown skin of a Marzon and the twitching eyes of a man born under a variable star entered silently and stood waiting for orders.

Andra picked more fruit from the silver bowl and said, around a soft Sirenian plum, "Bring Dolichek and the whip-master, Samsar."

The slave bowed and vanished again, and she said a little peevishly to Senchan Var, "Senchan, what's that row?"

"I don't know, my lady," Senchan Var reported. He was

straining his eyes into the blackness beyond the window. "It's dark as a wolf's throat out there."

"Then drop the curtain," Andra commanded. "It's cold enough in here as it is, in all conscience. And it may be this way for days. You know these storms."

The slave stood again, silently, at the far end of the room, three paces from the black ape, grunting over his bone. He said, "My lady, Dolichek and the whip-master wait."

"Bring them in," said Andra, inclining her head. Senchan Var snorted and strode over to the window again, stood with his back to the entrance as the slave ushered in Dolichek and the wielder of the whip.

Dolichek was a boy of perhaps fifteen, with a thin peaked face and a body more bone than flesh and little of that. He brushed back his straggling blond hair, matted with dirt, and essayed a bow to Andra, who smiled slowly and took another fruit.

She said, "Dolichek, Prince Penda—King Penda, now— brought his hound into the dining hall again today, against his father's command." She took a tiny malicious delight in saying it.

Dolichek sighed so slightly that one had to look hard to notice it, and said, "Very well, my lady. That was three strokes last time."

"This time four, then," said Andra casually. "Slave, four lashes!"

The wielder of the whip was black, and seven feet tall. He hailed from Leontis, where under the first king of Argus his ancestors had sweated to mine platinum on a world scant millions of miles from its primary. When he nodded at Andra's bidding, the muscles of his neck rippled down his chest and shoulders like waves in oily water. He spat on his hands and wetted the thong of his silver-mounted whip, flexed it, raised his arm—

Andra stopped him with a gesture. "Listen!" she said. "Senchan, that noise has stopped. Look outside."

Senchan Var needed only take a pace to lift the yellow drape from the window. He peered out into the night, shook his head.

"Too dark after the light in here," he reported. "There seems to be some sort of cart or carriage outside on the road before the castle—"

From somewhere below came the crash-crash-crash of a smitten iron, and Andra froze as if struck to stone by an enchanter's wand. In utter silence, save for the slobbering of the ape over his bone, they heard a man's voice from below shout, "*Open!*

"Open in the name of Andalvar's daughter, the Princess Sharla of Argus!"

II

Kelab the conjurer looked both ways along the Street of the Morning, surveying the wet gray stones of the cracked paving and the pools of water in the blocked gutter.

A few yards down the road from him an aged crone, one of the many beggars who sat along the Street of the Morning, huddled on a doorstep. He looked her over, from her closed eyes to her stiff hands and bare feet, and noted the mouth, slackly open like that of an idiot. She was dead.

He signed himself, as any vagrant would, and tossed a few coins into the tin cup at her feet. No sweeper would touch those coins, for they were burying money and as such tainted. She would have her funeral.

He sniffed the air. It had a part-clean smell, made of the newly washed streets and the unwashed thousands of the Low City, and he inhaled it gratefully, his eyes running along the ill-matched roofs of the houses till they fell on the flagstaff over the fortress on the Hill of Kings a mile away.

The banner on it was upside down, the proud golden sun hanging sadly in the bottom quarter instead of the top, the black-lettered motto of the House of Argus inverted above it. Kelab's lips formed the words slowly.

"Be strong; be just; be faithful."

Without taking his eyes from the banner he fumbled in his pouch and pulled a watch from it—a watch that had never come from any forge within the Empire. He looked at it, and his eyes filled with satisfaction and his lips took on the shadow of a smile.

Under a swinging rain-worn sign that had once said *The House of the Bubbling Spring,* he paused and rubbed his clean-shaven chin. He seemed to come to a quick decision, descended the few steps below the sign and pushed open the ill-fitting door.

Beyond it, the air was thick, twice-breathed; it was laden with the stench of sweat, stale liquor, and smoking drugs. At

one table a party of thin, shifty-eyed spacemen sat around
five empty bottles of tsinamo, playing the endless game called
shen fu, and their soft-spoken bids and the click of chips
were the only noises in the muggy-hot room.

There was a long bar on the left, littered with empty drink
cartons and stained with spilled liquor, and behind it a fat
man with thinning sandy hair sat, his back to the room, playing a color-sonata on a Mimosan chromograph.

He didn't turn as Kelab came up to the bar and hitched
himself onto a reasonably clean seat, said only, "What's
yours?"

Kelab said, "Water, Finzey. Water from the Bubbling
Spring."

Finzey shut off the chromograph and whirled, his fat face
splitting in a lavish grin. He said explosively, *"Kelab!* How
long have you been on-world?"

"Since about midnight—and a rough coming I had of it,
too. There wasn't so much as a mile of clear weather between
here and the Silent Mountains."

"It was pretty bad," said Finzey sagely, reaching below the
counter for a bottle and a mug. "But you know what they
say—weather bad, trade good."

"Trade looks to have been good," agreed Kelab, glancing
around the littered room. He took the mug Finzey filled with
the heady potent fuming liquor he laughingly called the water
of the Bubbling Spring, sniffed it, and drank a few mouthfuls.

Finzey eased his bulk onto a stool opposite and said eagerly, "Where've you been lately, Kelab—hey? You haven't
touched Argus since—must be two years back."

"And two months." Kelab nodded. "I've been out of the
Empire, around the fringe. Picking up new tricks among the
mutant worlds till I was broke, and then working my way
back toward the big money. But I see the banner's inverted
over the fortress yonder."

He jerked his head eastward.

Finzey plucked his lower lip with pudgy fingers. "Ay," he
agreed. "We had a man in around midnight with the news
that Andalvar had passed."

"You have the burying money?" Kelab asked, and Finzey
pushed a white pottery bowl toward him. It was more than
half full of coins, Imperial and Outland currencies. Kelab
shook it reflectively, added another coin to it, pushed it away.

Finzey's eyes widened, and he touched the coin with his

finger to make sure it was real. He said incredulously, "You said you were broke, Kelab!"

The conjurer shrugged. "I *was* broke. Money given in a good cause, they say, is money gained, and I can earn that again in three days. The poor have need of the burying money of the kings.

"There is another outside who will need burying," he added, picking up his drink.

Finzey nodded. "I have been told so. She will stay till noon—the burying money is more, so. I will charge myself with her funeral. But, Kelab, you haven't heard?"

"Heard what, fat one?"

"The sight of the banner was the first news you had of Andalvar's passing?"

Kelab nodded, and Finzey rushed on, bubbling like his own liquor with excitement. "Then no one has told you how, around three this morning, a flying machine such as none ever saw on Argus came to earth before the castle of the kings where Andalvar lies, bearing, they tell me, a soldier, a counselor, and the Princess Sharla!"

Kelab's hand faltered only for the slightest fraction of a second as he took the mug away from his mouth, and his voice was quite steady when he said, "Sharla, fat one? You speak in riddles. Andalvar's daughter is called Andra."

"No, you do not understand." Finzey struggled to explain. "Princess Sharla is the lost princess, the one who was thought dead."

Thoughtful, Kelab drained his mug, set it down. He said, "I recall stories—but remember, Finzey, I am no Argian, and so much goes on in the Empire that I cannot know all the news. Tell me."

"Well, as you doubtless know, Andalvar was married late in life, some twenty-odd years ago, and his wife Lora first bore him a daughter, who was named Sharla. Since he was king, he hoped for a son to take his place on the throne in after years, but his wife bore him next another daughter, Andra—her whom they call the black witch, though she's a beauty and no mistake."

Kelab's smoky eyes stared fixedly at the black screen of the chromograph. He said, "Go on."

"Then, five years later, she bore him a son at last—Penda, who's now officially king—and died in childbed. And Andalvar, fearing lest his time be short, made certain of having a good regent for the time before his son came of age by sending Sharla—then some twelve years old, much Penda's age now, in fact—to study at a school far away from here, where some of the arts of the Golden Age live on, I'm told.

"After two years she disappeared, and none could be found to trace her. They tore the empire apart—I'm surprised you heard nothing of it."

Mechanically Kelab reached for the bottle and refilled his mug, said, "Seven years ago I was out of the Empire. I heard only rumors."

"I'm amazed, even so. However, she was gone, and 'tis credibly reported that the loss drove Andalver a little crazy. In his ruling he was just, as ever, and in his bargaining as shrewd; but he would not tolerate that the others of his children should come to the slightest harm. For instance he would not let Andra be trained for the regency as Sharla was to be, nor would he suffer his son to be beaten or punished for his transgressions. He kept a slave's son—one Dolichek—as whipping-post for him, in accordance with a very ancient custom lapsed previously these four hundred years. And they tell me, shorn of the discipline which made Andalvar a firm ruler, Andra has grown spoiled and capricious and self-seeking, and there is no sign in Penda of the quality that will make a good king."

"I see," said Kelab reflectively. "Tell me more. Who are considered to be the powers at court?"

Finzey was growing expansive. The spacemen behind Kelab went on making their whispered bets, and the curious blue chips changed hands with a soft click-clack. Finzey said, "Why, Andra herself, of course, and Senchan Var, a man they call the Lord Great Chamberlain. They say he has the Council of Six in his pocket—that's the council of the rulers of the vassal worlds, you know?"

Kelab nodded. There were six worlds in the Empire that had nominally equal rights with Argus in ruling the straggling remnants of a union which had once spanned half a galaxy, but they were powerless singly whereas Argus was not, and their wealth, in these days when wealth was measured in ships and fighting men, only balanced Argus's when they stood together. Apart, they were negligible.

"What kind of man is this Senchan Var?"

"Noble," said Finzey. "Of good descent. And honest too—but, if I'm any judge, in love with the black witch. He holds, they say, that Andalvar was more than just in his dealings with his subjects—generous, rather—and would sooner the iron-harsh rule our ancestors knew, saying openly that leniency courts revolution. But he is admired for his feats in war when young. His swordsmanship was all but legendary. The people would follow him, *I* think."

"Why add that, fat one?" Kelab demanded.

Finzey shrugged elephantine shoulders. "No reason, but that you asked me who were the powers at court. He is the greatest after Andra—except perhaps for Sabura Mona. No one knows much of her."

"And who is Sabura Mona?"

"That's one I can't answer. She is a woman, fat—fatter than I by far, which is no mean size. There are rumors—but rumors only. They say she has a spoon in every stew cooked in the Empire, that Andalvar trusted her implicitly, that she advised him. But she is very seldom seen in public, she does not appear at palace functions, and if she is served by the castle servants or indeed any servants at all, they do not speak of her."

"Enigmatic," commented Kelab.

"In very truth," agreed Finzey emphatically. "And I know no more about her than I've told you, so you don't need to sit there looking as if anquar wouldn't fizz in your mouth."

Kelab grinned like a boy, flashing white teeth in his dusky face, and swept a lean brown hand through his black sleek hair, knotted behind with a gaudy cloth. There was a tiny gold disk in his left earlobe that caught the light from the lamps beyond. He said, "All right, Finzey, but you're the first man I've spoken to on Argus since two years ago, and things change in two years. And the voice of the people—what's it saying now?"

Finzey said shrewdly, "Do you mean the big voice or the small voice?"

"The small voice," said Kelab. He swirled the liquor around the bottom of his mug. "The voice that matters."

Finzey glanced past him at the group of spacemen. Nothing seemed to have changed at first glance, but there was suddenly an abstracted look in their eyes, and they made their bids in a whisper, and the chips shuffled from hand to hand instead of click-clacking as before. He got down from the stool noisily and began busily swabbing the bar.

Kelab smiled very faintly, and a blue shimmer drifted like smoke between the bar and the spacemen at their game. It curled and writhed like a live thing, and remained, a curtain hanging on nothing, a web stirred by intangible winds—and a barrier that no sound would pass. He said, "Finzey, what does the small voice say?"

Cautiously the fat bartender leaned across the bar and nodded at the blue veil. "I'd forgotten that one," he said. "They don't call you the Conjurer for nothing. But you cannot tell these days who is not seeking money as an informer—"

"Speak," said Kelab impatiently.

"They say there have been prophecies. At times of doom there are always prophecies. When Sharla disappeared and again last night the voice of the seers was heard. Last night, they say, the word was spoken before the castle of the kings itself. Black days for Argus, my friend, and the Empire dust and forgotten—and the black witch is the cause. Princess Andra. There are those who say her regency could itself end the Empire."

Kelab nodded. His eyes glowed somber-bright, like a lantern behind a horn shade. "From what you say of her I can well believe it. And the small voice—does it say 'Ay'?"

"It roars like a caged lion," said Finzey flatly.

"Of the coming of Sharla it says—what?"

"As yet, nothing. But there are high hopes. . . ."

"I see," said Kelab slowly. "And the burying of Andalvar will be—when and where?"

"On the third day after the passing, as the custom is, at the castle of the kings. The chieftains and the lords attending will be here tomorrow or the next day and will be received by the Princess Sharla, I assume—if she *is* in truth Sharla."

Kelab halted his mug halfway to his lips and said slowly, "Of course. I hadn't thought of that."

"Decision rests with the Council of Six as to the regency, of course, but traditionally the eldest daughter of a dead king is chosen regent if one is needful. But it could be otherwise, in theory."

Kelab tossed down the rest of his drink and said, "How much do I owe you?"

Caught by surprise, Finzey blinked. He said, "So soon? But why? I wanted to hear of your marvelous travels since last we met. Why must you go?"

Kelab grinned, jerked a thumb at the thousand-circle coin he had left in the burying money bowl, while with the other hand he rolled up the blue veil and squeezed it into nothing. "I have to earn my bread. How much?"

"A gift, Kelab," said Finzey, spreading his fat hands. "Call it my share in that coin. But pickings for entertainers will be small until the mourning days are over."

"I'll take that risk," said Kelab the Conjurer.

He went out of the bar, away from the drunken girls and the spacemen playing shen fu and the smell of stale liquor, and he walked for many hours in the Low City, his heels clicking on the paving and his head bent in thought.

Senchan Var said furiously, "This is the sort of thing that should not happen!"

Andra seemed quite composed about it all. She sat blandly picking fruit from the silver bowl, as undisturbed as the black ape curled up and snoring very softly against the wall, one paw still clutching the stripped bone. The noon sun shone yellow through the slit windows. Inconsequentially she said, "This is the sort of thing that the common people will take as an omen, I feel—the storm clearing at her arrival, I mean. There is, I take it, small doubt that she is indeed my sister Sharla?"

Senchan Var said bitterly, "None, my lady. You would not know it, my lady, but she looks as did your mother at her age down to the finest detail. And if she is as tender as she looks outside we may say good-bye to the Empire."

Andra laughed. "My dear faithful Senchan, she may prove to be the very leader the Empire needs to hold it together. What does Sabura Mona think?"

Senchan Var whirled on her and said, "My lady, where is Sabura Mona? She came to the bedside of your father but she did not stay and watch with us."

"No more did I, Senchan. It is a woman's weakness."

Senchan Var snorted. "In *you* I am prepared to forgive it, for you are young, my lady, but that Sabura Mona is tougher than a thousand men I could name. She has the heart of a Thanis bull—"

"But the looks of a demon," supplied Andra quietly. "And does it matter *who* saves the Empire?"

"By the winds of Argus, *yes!*" said Senchan, driving fist into palm with an explosive slap. "One thing can save the Empire from the downhill path, and one only. A firm hand at the controls! What can this upstart Sharla do? She's been away from the Empire nine years, while you've been here at the heart of affairs. What is to be done must be done now! But the common people already know she is here, and their voice says *she* is the one to save Argus!"

Andra shrugged. "What care I for the common people? What do they know of statecraft? We have the support of the people who matter, Senchan—the rich men and the nobles. How do we stand on the Council of Six?"

"They may vote together or they may split three and three. Lorgis, Draco, and Bunagar have little love for you, being from the poor pastoral worlds, and may be willing to stake all on a new deal; but Heena, Dolon, and Mesa should stay true."

"They better had," said Andra ominously. "I made them all three, and what I made I can break. But, Senchan, there is one point you have disregarded."

Senchan Var frowned doubtfully. He said, "That the union with Mercator could rescue the Empire? But you forget, my lady—a royal union is effective only when the woman is a ruler in her own right, else she must swear allegiance to her husband and deny her own people. As regent you would have secured a valid union—though really a back marriage would have been required to cement it when Penda came of age."

Andra said lazily, "No, I didn't mean that. Think, Senchan. You and I know that is the best course for the Empire—new strength grafted on the old stock. There is an easy test of whether Sharla does too. Think over the wording of that contract we made."

Puzzled, Senchan began to recite it under his breath, from memory. After a while he understood.

Slowly, he began to smile.

III

"That's the dangerous one," whispered Landor.

Sharla, regent since twenty hours ago on a split vote of the Council of Six, tradition having the deciding say, nodded imperceptibly. She sat, black-robed and veiled, on a black-draped throne at the end of the Hall of State, waiting to receive the lords and chieftains who had come to honor her father at his burying, Landor beside her where Senchan Var had stood to her father in the office of Lord Great Chamberlain, Ordovic stiffly uncomfortable in formal uniform as captain of the royal bodyguard. Andra was not present. Ostensibly, she wished to attend to the ordering of her father's affairs in the city, but in effect she had ceded her rooms in the castle to Sharla and snubbed her by walking out, and Sharla was much distressed at her attitude.

But it worried Landor not at all.

Immediately after the Council of Six had split their votes three and three, and the precedent of other occasions had decided the course to be followed, Senchan Var had tendered his resignation, and Sharla had promptly appointed Landor in his place, for Landor seemed to have the notables and the history of Argus at his fingers' ends. And certain people were muttering, displeased.

Far down the hall a black-clad trumpeter made the rafters ring behind a man framed in the vast open doorway of the hall, a tall, insolent-faced man with black hair and fiery eyes, polished helm under his left arm, its plume nodding as he turned casually from side to side surveying the rows of courtiers lining the hall, his right hand on his sword-hilt. He wore the brass and leather of a fighting man.

The trumpeter put down his silver horn, and the nomenclator announced, "Barkasch of Mercator, come to pay tribute to Andalvar of Argus!"

The tall man ceased his survey of the hall and began to walk up it with an easy, swinging stride, his sandals padding on the carpeted floor and his accouterments making the ghost of a jingling rhythm as he went.

In silence he paused before the throne and faced the black-veiled regent.

Finally he bowed, and in a voice that the shouting of orders had made like a brazen gong said, "Greeting, my lady of Argus."

Ordovic signaled to the company of the bodyguard without taking his eyes from Barkasch, and they stood easy, their shields crashing in unison between their shoulder blades. He was glad that there was still precision and efficiency here, among the soldiers.

"Greeting, my lord of Mercator," said Sharla, and her voice was firm and musical, but she shaped strangely the words of a tongue she had not spoken save with an Outland accent for seven years.

Barkasch straightened from his bow slowly, and his eyes rested for a moment on the veil before her face. He said, "My lady, I know not that voice! Yet I know well the voice of my lady Andra. Ho! Trickery!" He flung back his head and his voice went rolling among the rafters, while Sharla looked up in dismay. Of course—to be here so soon he must have left Mercator before more than the first news of Andalvar's passing had gone out.

"Let me handle this," whispered Landor, and she nodded.

Stepping forward, he rapped the ground with his staff of office. The courtiers along the hall had shifted like waves breaking when Barkasch had shouted, and a small murmur of resentment had gone up. Now it rose again at Landor's movement, for there were those present who held that Senchan Var had been unjustly displaced, more who had coveted his post for themselves, and some even who held Sharla as all but an impostor.

Now Barkasch, hand on hilt of sword, drew his blade to half its length from the scabbard and let it drop back, ringing. He said with a hint of contempt, "And who may you be?"

"I am Landor, Lord Great Chamberlain of Argus, and this is no trickery."

"No trickery?" Barkasch's eyes searched Landor's unlined face suspiciously. "Yet I know that voice is not the voice of my lady Andra."

"Indeed it is not," said Landor composedly. " 'Tis that of my lady Sharla."

"Sharla, Ser Landor?" said Barkasch incredulously. "The lost daughter of Andalvar? What tale is this?"

His hand shot out like a striking snake, and Sharla gave a tiny cry of fear as he ripped the black veil from her face. For a long instant he stood there, the shred of cloth held in his strong fingers as in a trap, while he stared at Sharla.

Eventually he relaxed the sternness of his face and began, very slowly, to smile.

"Your pardon, my lady of Argus, but I am a direct man. I trust no one's word who is not known to me of old, and that you should be here to stand in your father's place is too strange to take unchecked." His eyes ran over the delicate loveliness of her face, the hairlike spun gold that shone beneath her black hood, the curves of her body beneath the mourning robe.

He said, "Indeed, my lady, it is as if your mother were alive again."

Sharla nodded slowly. "Ay, my lord. I have been told I do resemble her."

The courtiers rustled and craned to see past Barkasch, and there was a low murmur of surprise. Since custom decreed that the king's daughters should wear veils in public till the dead ruler was buried, this was the first opportunity many of them had had to see her face, and those who remembered the last queen of Argus saw the similarity and marveled.

"And," said the lord of Mercator after an interval, "I beg to present the bond for honoring three days hence."

Someone of Andra's retinue among the watchers sniggered very briefly as Sharla looked up in amazement. "Bond, my lord?" she said questioningly. "What bond?"

"This bond," said Barkasch, sliding a roll of parchment from one of the pouches at his waist. He held it out. "A marriage bond!"

He stepped back with something that on a less regal face would have been a self-satisfied grin, and Landor whipped open the scroll and began to read. A rustle of amazement and wonder ran among the courtiers, and the member of Andra's retinue who had sniggered, laughed aloud. Ordovic turned toward him and half drew his sword, his face like thunder. The laughter stopped short.

Sharla, without taking her eyes from Barkasch's face, laid one hand on the arm of the throne, and Landor covered it with his own, still scanning the rough, much abbreviated uncial script of the document in his hand. Hastily Sharla rapped out, in the Outland finger-code of the bandits of Hin, "Isn't it in Andra's name?"

Landor rapped back, "Andra's not mentioned by name, though she must have made it."

"What does it say?"

"I'll read it," offered Landor. He nodded to Barkasch, said aloud, "With your permission, I'll read this out, my lord."

Barkasch showed assent, and Landor began to speak in a firm controlled voice, his accent flawless. Sharla had wondered often in the past days how he, who swore he had never been on Argus in his life, had gained that and his intimate knowledge of Argian affairs.

He read, "Bond of marriage between the lord of Mercator and the regent of Argus, to be confirmed upon the death of Andalvar and the accession of his daughter as regent in the stead of Prince Penda, being under the age of ruling, which marriage to be a royal union between the thrones and crowns of Argus and Mercator, Mercator to have its place on the Council of Six instead of Lorgis of Phaidona—"

A roar of rage went up from among the courtiers, and Lorgis himself, a bull of a man from one of the pastoral worlds, one of the three who had voted in favor of Sharla's election, bounded to his feet. He shouted, "Let them but *try* to take Phaidona's place and they shall pay dearly!"

Landor, who had raised his eyes and waited patiently when Lorgis leaped up, remained silent till he had subsided, muttering threats into his beard, while Barkasch of Mercator looked at him without interest. Then Landor resumed.

"... And the lordship of the Empire, in the event of Penda's decease before attaining the age of ruling, or of his death without children, to descend by the joint line of Argus and Mercator."

Amid dead silence, he rolled the parchment up again, finished baldly, "It is sealed with the royal seals of Argus and Mercator."

Barkasch said, "And so, my lady, after your lamented father's burying, we shall talk again of this." He bowed ironically, turned to go.

A voice said, "Wait."

The single word was spoken no louder than one would speak across a table, yet everyone in the hall heard it and turned to see who had said it, and saw, in the arch of the door through which twenty fighting men might pass abreast, a small slender man with dark sleek hair and dusky skin, wearing a tattered suit of brown homespun, high boots, a gaudy silk cloth on his head.

Ordovic's sword leaped into his hand, and in three steps the men of the bodyguard had turned to face the doorway, their halberds at the ready. Barkasch of Mercator straightened up and raised his eyebrows quizzically as the slender man walked lightly down the hall.

He made a strange contrast to Barkasch, who last had done that, for he was small and wiry where Barkasch was broad and muscular, and he wore drab civilian clothes while Barkasch had the outfit of a soldier, and while Barkasch had borne helmet, sword, and knife, he had only a battered brown hat and no weapon at all.

He came up between the leveled halberds of the bodyguard to before the throne and bowed to Sharla with a flourish before he turned to Barkasch and said, "My lord of Mercator!"

Casually Barkasch looked down his nose at the smaller man. He said, "What is it, impudent one?"

"My lord, did you not remark upon a mistake that Ser Landor made in the reading of the marriage bond?"

Sharla felt Landor's hand tighten over hers on the arm of the throne.

Barkasch said, his forehead creasing in puzzlement, "Mistake, impudent one? I heard him read it distinctly, as it is written."

"Who is this man?" tapped Sharla, and felt Landor reply, "I do not know."

"Yes, a mistake," the stranger insisted. "An omission. Ser Landor." Then, turning, "If it please you, let my lord of Mercator read it out aloud."

Numbly, Landor passed the scroll. Barkasch snatched it angrily and spread it with a crackle. He began to read in a voice that burned with impatience.

"Bond of marriage between Barkasch, lord of Mercator, and Andra, regent of Argus, to be conformed upon—"

He broke off, his face showing most undignified astonishment. He began to scrutinize the writing, while Sharla, who had gasped in amazement when he had read out her sister's name, exchanged glances with Landor, who looked as completely taken aback as she was, and as relieved.

"Indeed, you see, my lord," said the small man, "there was a mistake, an omission. Ser Landor did not read the names of the parties. And since it is specified in the contract that the marriage is between yourself and the Princess Andra, and since the Princess Andra is *not* regent of Argus, it is in effect void."

Barkasch struggled to speak for a long time, his hands quivering on the scroll. When he finally succeeded, his voice was almost choking with rage. He crumpled the offending parchment into a ball and threw it on the ground, and raised his hand as if to strike the small man, who stepped adroitly out of range.

Finally he turned to Sharla and forced out, "Your pardon, my lady. It seems I was indeed mistaken. But by the wind that blows over Mercator"—his voice rose to a shout—"Argus has not heard the last of me!"

He turned on his heel and strode out, and everyone seemed to relax at his going. The herald shouted that there were no more chieftains in attendance, and with a wave of her hand Sharla dismissed the watchers and they filed out.

But when she looked for the slender man he was nowhere to be seen.

The bodyguard came to attention as she descended the steps from the throne, but before she hurried out with Landor she said, "Ordovic!"

"My lady?"

"Find that man and bring him to my rooms!"

"My lady," said Ordovic, clicking his heels.

He turned to the guards, shot out his arm. "Dismiss, and go find the man who was here just now. Report to me with him outside my lady's quarters. At the double!"

They broke ranks, piled their halberds against the wall, and left the hall at a trot.

Most of the courtiers were already at the far end of the hall, and only a few slaves remained nearby, straightening disarrayed hangings after holding them aside for Sharla, but a movement at the corner of his eye caught Ordovic's attention. He remained perfectly still, as if watching the departing courtiers.

Someone bending over. Picking up something, he could see by straining his eyes to one side. Now he was standing up—

Ordovic whirled. It was a slave with hot brown skin and twitching eyes, and he was trying to stuff something hastily into a pouch. Ordovic knocked him flying with a blow from a fist that had killed men twice the size of this, stepped up to him as he writhed on the carpet. With ungentle fingers he opened the fist that held whatever he had picked up.

Eyes narrowing, he scrutinized it. He spoke Argian badly and read it worse, but he knew this could be only one thing—the marriage contract between Andra and Barkasch. What would a slave want with it?

He said in atrocious Argian, "What's your name, slave?"

"Samsar," said the slave sullenly.

"Why did you pick this up for?" Ordovic continued, shaking the parchment before Samsar's face.

"It is my duty," said the slave, still rubbing his jaw. "It is my duty not to leave litter to make the castle untidy."

"That was not why you tried to *hide* this," insisted Ordovic. He picked up Samsar as if he had been a child, put him on his feet and held him there by one shoulder. "A document bearing seals is not litter!" He shook Samsar till his teeth rattled, and lapsing thankfully into thieves' argot which he spoke far better than Argian—and which, if he was any judge of slaves, this man would also understand—he added a phrase descriptive of a very elaborate and uncomfortable form of torture that few people who did not frequent the Low City and talk with thieves would know. Samsar, however, must have understood, for he blanched under his brownness, tore himself away, and ran unsteadily from the hall.

IV

When Ordovic reached Sharla's apartments the guard on duty outside saluted him casually, and his eyes flashed fire. "Do that again," he ordered crisply, his Argian accent even worse than usual.

The guard did it again, more smartly.

Ordovic looked him over. "That's better. Have any of my lady's bodyguard who were on duty in the Hall of State come here yet?"

"No, sir," said the guard.

"If one of them does, send him in."

"Yes, sir," said the guard. Ordovic nodded, rapped on the door with bunched knuckles.

After an instant, a slender girl slave opened it, and at the same time he heard Sharla's voice from within inquire faintly, "Who is it?"

The slave spoke over her shoulder through a red velvet drape. "The captain of the bodyguard, my lady."

"Let him in," Sharla commanded, and the slave stepped aside, bowing.

Ordovic thrust the hangings apart, took one step through them, and stopped. He tilted his helmet back as he gazed around the room, and finally whistled in amazement as he took in the lavish fittings.

Landor, leaning against the wall opposite the door, laughed briefly. "My lady Andra has sophisticated tastes, has she not?"

"Indeed yes," said Ordovic feelingly. His eyes took in the red and yellow velvet drapes, the yellow silk couches and cushions, and the silver bowls—some of them containing fruit, some cakes; the candelabra in carved crystal, worth a king's ransom; the white fleeces on the floor, the tapestries and paintings on the wall.

Finally he stepped across to the couch where Andra had sat the previous evening, sat down, and helped himself to some fruit. Landor elbowed himself away from the wall and jerked a thumb at a heavy iron staple across the room. "See that? I'm told Andra keeps a Sirian ape—as a pet!"

"Wildcat," grunted Ordovic. He reached into his pouch for

the folded parchment he had put there. "Where's my lady, Ser Landor?"

"Her attendants are readying her for dinner," Landor answered. "There is a ceremonial meal, I believe." He came over and took a Sirenian plum from the bowl in front of the couch.

Ordovic held out the parchment between two fingers, said, "Here's the bond of marriage or whatever. I caught little of the drift of that scene, but I guessed most of it, so when I spotted a slave named Samsar trying to sneak it away, I knocked him flying and threatened him with—"

Again the phrase descriptive of a certain protracted torture. He grinned like a boy.

Landor chuckled without mirth, examined the scroll carefully. After a pause he said, "Ordovic, I don't understand. When I read this the first time it was as I read it and named no names—yet here they stand both, the names of Andra and Barkasch, clear as day."

Ordovic stopped another fruit on the way to his lips and said incredulously, "It's magic, Ser Landor."

"It looks like it." Landor nodded.

"Who was the man who came in?" demanded Ordovic, and Landor shrugged.

"Whoever he was, he worked a miracle and saved much trouble. Why? If we knew who he was, we might guess his motive for aiding us."

The slender slave girl pushed aside the curtains, and Landor said, "What is it, Valley?"

Valley said, "There is a guard outside who would speak with Ser Captain Ordovic."

Ordovic rose to his feet, swallowing his fruit in haste. He said, "That'll be one of my men, Ser Landor. I sent the bodyguard after the stranger on my lady's orders, and I expect one of them is reporting."

He strode to the curtains and disappeared through them.

A moment later Sharla came from an inner room, her hair fluffy and shining, her face freshly made up, and wearing a blue robe which had certainly not been in her exiguous baggage when she arrived.

Landor looked her over, said finally, "Sharla, I never saw you look lovelier. Where did you get the robe?"

She sat down on one of the couches, frowning. "Thank you, Landor. I'm told it belonged to my mother. But there's a certain amount of business to see to. Did I not hear Ordo-vic?"

"One of the men he sent after the stranger is reporting. He'll be back in a moment. How did your interview with Penda go? What do you make of him?"

"Of course, he's completely changed since last I saw him. He's no child now, but a youth, and he'd have a tremendous physique if he were less soft. But soft he is, and he made little impression on me. He'll need schooling to be a king, Landor."

Landor nodded soberly. He said, "As I expected. Where is he?"

"In his own apartments. The death of our father has hit him hard, and he said he would not be out till the time of burying."

Landor nodded again, held out the scroll he held in his hand. "Here's the bond Barkasch threw down," he said. "Ordovic caught a slave by the name of Samsar trying to sneak it away; he doesn't know why. And the amazing part of it is—but read it for yourself, remembering how I read it at first."

Sharla ran her eyes down it, studying it for signs of an alteration. Finally she folded it and laid it on her lap, stared fixedly ahead, shivering.

"It's magic," she said finally. "How else could that man have changed it?"

Before Landor could reply, Ordovic pushed through the drapes and halted on seeing Sharla. He bowed, came on.

Landor said, "Well? What did your man report? Who was it?"

"They call him Kelab the Conjurer," said Ordovic. "The sergeant of the guard came to me with a wild tale of him. 'Tis reported, they say, that there is a man whom no bars will hold, who comes and goes where he will, and who has strange powers that surpass the human."

"The last I believe," said Landor grimly. "No human agency changed these words on the parchment."

"I inquired what sort of man he is, and learned that he is an entertainer—a conjurer for display as well as for such strange purposes as the changing of the marriage bond, but the sergeant of the guard insisted with such vehemence that no ordinary hunt would find him that I resolved to let him wander."

Sharla said suddenly, "By the winds of Argus, I recall him now. I have heard of a man named Kelab, and I saw him once perform, doing things that a human never could. He was held in repute as a mutant, and feared, even in the Outlands, which was where I saw him."

At the mention of the Outlands Ordovic's eyes lifted to her face for an instant and as quickly looked away. Landor said musingly, "But you know of no reason for this action?"

"Not any at all," said Sharla.

"And you never met face to face?"

"Never. But if half the stories current are true, no ordinary spies will trap him, and he will come only if it suits him."

Ordovic said, "By the winds of Argus, my lady!"

Sharla motioned him silent. She said, "Let that wait. There are two matters that concern us more—Penda, my brother, and Sabura Mona."

"Sabura Mona! Sabura Mona!" said Ordovic fiercely. "Am I never to hear more of Sabura Mona than her name? Who is she or what is she? Does no one know?"

"Sit down, Ordovic," invited Sharla. She indicated a place beside her, and Ordovic, after a moment's hesitation, took it.

"Sabura Mona was my father's chief adviser and confidant," said Sharla softly. "He used to say of her, I'm told, that she knew everything from the smallest whisper of the beggars on the Street of the Morning to the cry of the mutants beyond the Empire, and that she was never wrong save once, when she advised him to send me away to learn the craft of ruling, and it seems now that she was less wrong than he believed. 'Tis said she planned his dealings with the Outlands and the mutants more than he did himself."

"But you have not met her?" Landor said.

"I recall her vaguely when I was a child," Sharla answered.

The heavy curtains over the door parted with a swish and Valley stood in the gap, her hands folded demurely, her delicate face expressionless save for her big brown eyes. She said, "My lady, there is word from Sabura Mona."

Landor and Sharla exchanged glances, and Landor said, "Speak, Valley."

"She desires that my lady shall come to her apartment tonight at the hour of ten, preferably alone, her messenger says."

Ordovic half rose, said, "Is this Sabura Mona such that she may order the regent?"

Valley remained in the doorway, not understanding him, for he had spoken in his own dialect and she in Argian, and Landor said to Ordovic, "She has ordered kings."

He subsided, and Sharla raised her voice, "Tell the messenger I will attend her."

Valley nodded and disappeared silently, while Ordovic said, "You are going then, my lady?"

Sharla nodded. "Not quite alone. With Landor, I think. My excuse can be that my command of Argian is dimmed with seven years' disuse. . . . Now, Landor. About my brother. Strength is his lack. There shall be no more of the whipping-post. He shall be taught statecraft. He will not like it, but you I trust to undertake the task."

A shadow of a smile of pride touched Landor's lips. "I am flattered, Sharla, that you have confidence in me."

"The name of his scapegoat is Dolichek, I believe. He is a slave's son. Find him. And find his father too, if he lives."

Landor nodded and went out, the curtains swaying behind him. Ordovic sat silently staring at nothing. After a while Sharla said gently, "Ordovic."

"My lady?"

"Call me not *my lady*. We are three strangers together here on Argus, even though I was born here. This coldness is unbecoming." She laid her hand gently on his knee and looked at his hard profile.

He said woodenly, "The fact remains, my lady, that you are regent of Argus and daughter of a king, and I am but one of your subjects."

"You are an Outlander, and no subject of mine!"

"Your subject by adoption," said Ordovic firmly.

"You called me Sharla before, Ordovic."

His face went rigid and he rose abruptly to his feet, began to pace the room with long light strides. He said, "Must you taunt me, my lady, with the memory that I took you for a woman of the streets? I can never forgive myself."

"I *was* a woman of the streets, Ordovic! And would have remained so, for who would credit the tale I had to tell? Slavered from the peaceful world where I was schooled, sold into a brothel—who believed I was a princess, of royal birth?"

"Landor did," said Ordovic harshly. "He gave you back your heritage—all this." He gestured at the lavish fittings of the apartment. "He gave you back your honor and your rightful station!"

He whirled and stood before her, towering over her, and his eyes were like chips of granite. "There was only one thing I could give you—my service. . . . If you have no further orders for me tonight, my lady, I shall withdraw."

Sharla looked up with parted lips, shaking her head slowly. At last she sighed and said composedly, "Very well, Ordovic, if that is the way you wish it. But I have one further task for you tonight."

"At your orders, my lady."

"Find Kelab the Conjurer and bring him to me. If you can, buy him—if you must, drag him."

Ordovic saluted without expression and turned and walked out, not looking back.

For a long time Sharla sat gazing into vacancy, her face set and white.

Then the curtains stirred again and Valley stood there, hands folded as before, her eyes big and limpid. Sharla thought, not for the first time, that her younger sister had picked her slaves well for quick obedience and silent service.

She roused herself, said, "And what is it, Valley?"

"Dolichek attends my lady's pleasure," said Valley. "The Ser Landor sent him, so he affirms."

"Let him enter," Sharla commanded and, as Valley withdrew, arranged her robe and patted straight the cushions of the couch. Then she looked up and saw Dolichek.

He stood there pale and silent, his bony body white with cold, and bowed a little hesitantly toward her. She thought, *There is a queer pride in him, somehow—though he is only whipping-post to a prince, there is pride there.*

Behind him the whip-master, who had come assuming the usual purpose for the summons, waited patiently like a basalt statue.

She said, "Come here, Dolichek," and there was no resemblance to the way Andra would have said it in the tender voice she used. He looked puzzled, but obeyed, walking forward with a trace of a limp. There were blue bruises and long weals on his bare legs. In front of her he paused, his eyes asking a mute question.

She looked past him to the whip-master, "Slave!"

"My lady?" said the giant, his voice a deep rumble.

"Are you of my father's slaves, or a purchase of my sister's?"

"I was of the lady Andra's following, my lady."

"Break your whip and go to her," said Sharla casually. "I have no further use for you."

The giant looked at the whip in his hand, snapped its silver-mounted stock without effort, tossed it away, and walked out.

In still amazement Dolichek watched him go, and then turned to Sharla, his lip trembling.

Suddenly he was on his knees, his head buried in her lap, sobbing, "My lady! My lady!" while she stroked his matted yellow hair mechnically and stared at nothing.

Ordovic left Sharla's rooms with his mind in a turmoil and his face set grimly. The passage was dimly lit by high windows, and torches flared at the intersections. Under one of these torches, in the shadow of its sconce, a man stood waiting.

"Who stands yonder?" he challenged.

The man moved from the shadow into the light of the torch and said, "It is I, Captain—Tampore, sergeant of the guard."

Ordovic laughed shortly. "Have you come with more fairy tales of Kelab to tell?"

"No, Captain. I have a word or two of advice." Tampore spoke in thieves' argot, the crisp, guttural form of Argian salted with slang which Ordovic comprehended better than the formal tongue.

"Speak on," he invited, his eyes searching Tampore's face.

"It is a good thing for Argus that you and Ser Landor and my lady Sharla came, for you are a soldier, and we understand soldiers well on Argus, and Ser Landor is a statesman of power and the lady is well thought of by the common people from the sheer mention of her name, though few have seen her, and she is reputed tender. The lady Andra is not called the black witch for her kindness."

Ordovic, watching his face, nodded.

"*But* you are strangers. We admire soldiers, ay—but Ser Senchan Var, too, is a soldier, and famous within the Empire, which you are *not*. The lady Andra has filled the high places with her own men. It would seem to us of the guard, who hear the whispers from those same high places, that had she retained the regency and had her marriage to Barkasch of Mercator gone through, she would have broken the last shackle holding her—the even splitting of the Council of Six for and against her. But she sprang that marriage bond upon your mistress unawares. Beware of other hidden pitfalls. And beware of a knife in the dark lest the lady grow impatient."

Ordovic did not move his steady gaze. He said, "What manner of man is Barkasch of Mercator? And what purpose is served by the proposed alliance?"

"Barkasch is a fighter and a brave man, and he rules an independent kingdom of three harsh worlds whose soldiers are the fiercest in the galaxy. A royal union that united the worlds of Mercator and the Empire *could* be the first step to a newly glorious Empire. It could also be a weapon of unbounded power to further the designs of a ruthless woman."

"The designs being . . . ?"

Tampore shrugged. "They are not blown kisses, but who save a wizard can know the heart of a witch?"

Ordovic permitted himself the shadow of a smile. Landor had some inkling of those designs. He said, "While we speak of wizards, where may I find Kelab the Conjurer tonight?"

Tampore plucked his beard, said, "I said he was not to be found if he did not wish it. He could make you forget you found him—they say he can make a man blind to him a foot away, yet still see all but Kelab. But if he chooses to be found he may be found in the Low City when not busy entertaining some noble or rich merchant."

Ordovic said, "What is the Low City?"

"That part of Oppidum west of the fortress on the Hill of Kings where Lady Andra is resident. Oppidum is the greatest city of the planet, and city imperial for ten generations.

"East of the fortress lies the spaceport and the wealthy quarter and the markets. They have a saying at the port— passengers go east, spacemen go west."

Ordovic nodded. He said, "I thank you for your advice, Tampore. I'll follow it."

"Good luck, Captain Ordovic. And here is one last piece of advice worth all the rest." He pressed something hard and cold into Ordovic's hand, turned with a swish of leather sandals, and was gone in the darkness. Ordovic fingered what he had been given and laughed with a strangely bitter sound when he found what it was.

The oldest remedy of all. Cold steel.

He tucked the knife in his belt and went on down the passage, thinking of the past few minutes. Landor . . . Sharla . . .

The memory of their first meeting was as angry as an old wound broken open.

V

Ordovic was feeling very pleased with himself. He pushed open the swinging gate by the hand-lettered sign that read *Pirbrite's Gardens,* and walked in with the rolling gait of one just in from a long trip in free fall. He had two thousand circles to spend—good solid Empire currency—and all the time he wanted. And he intended to dispose of both to his own pleasure.

He paused with one hand on the gate, surveying the garden. There were little tables here and there among the bushes, and there was soft lighting, part artificial, part the glow from the two-foot globes of white and pink luminescence on the birbrak trees that made any night on Loudor glorious. There was a mixed scent of clean fragrant foliage and rich liquors from a dozen worlds, and many men and women sat under the outstretched branches, talking, drinking, and making love. And of course the inevitable party of spacemen playing shen fu. They said there was not a city on any world where you could not find one game in which to lose your money.

As he looked around, a small stout man in pink and green like one of his own birbrak trees came up to him and said, "The best of evenings to you, Ser soldier, and your request?"

Ordovic looked down and smiled slowly. "You are Ser Pirbrite?"

"I am."

"Excellent. I wish to get drunk, by degrees—loudly and noisily drunk."

Pirbrite looked anxious, and Ordovic laughed. "Not all here, my friend. I doubt if all the liquor in this place could make me drunk. I shall merely lay the foundations of it. Have me brought a measure of ancinard and a plate of strine, and if there is music I would like it."

Pirbrite nodded and moved away. Ordovic picked a nearby table in the bay of a birbrak tree, where he could see the stars in a great thick band across the moonless sky. A pleasant place, and of higher class than most that he frequented. And—his eye swept appreciatively along a line of girls standing close to the little covered hut that served for bar and kitchen—it had a neater line in hostesses.

The girl at the end of the line took a laden tray from the serving hatch and came over to him. He studied her with interest, and began to consider revising his plans for the evening. Blond hair, delicate face, a figure which was in no need of support. . . .

She set down the tray and waited, looking him over with a brassily insolent stare while he took the brimming mug of fuming red liquor and drank, and after it sent one of the tough balls of strine meat that were so useful for prolonging the process of getting drunk.

He looked up and grinned, and spun a fifty-circle coin with a flip of his thumb. She caught it expertly and turned to go, but his hand closed on her wrist like a steel trap and he said, "Since when has a measure of ancinard and a plate of strine made fifty circles?"

She sat down beside him on the bench, smiling like a child caught stealing sweetmeats, and said, "I like you, soldier. What's your name?"

"Ordovic," he answered. "And yours—thief?"

"Sharla," she said smoothly. "Are you going to spend all your money on yourself, then?"

"Oh, take it, subtle one," said Ordovic in mock disgust. "But I'll have my change in kind!"

"A kiss for it," offered Sharla, half rising, the coin clutched triumphantly in her hand, and she leaned forward to press her lips on his. But a right arm as strong as a steel bar went around her body, and she did not move away.

Ordovic was revising his plans for the evening.

Again the swinging gates beside the hand-painted sign parted, and a thin man with a balding head and a nose like an eagle's beak stood on the threshold, keen eyes surveying the garden. The glow of the birbrak trees and the dark green of their foliage made the scene like paradise, but there was no appreciation in his cold, unsmiling face. He wore a patrician gown like a well-to-do merchant, but there was a short sword belted to his waist.

As usual, Pirbrite himself came bustling over to him and wished him the best of evenings.

"Evening," said the man curtly. "You are the proprietor?"

"At your service," agreed Pirbrite, his eyes anxiously searching the other's face. "You wish, Ser—merchant?"

"I am no merchant," said the newcomer briefly. "You have here a girl by the name of Sharla—Empire-born?"

Pirbrite's brow cleared. If that was all . . . He said doubtfully, "I fear she is engaged with a customer just now, but we have many others just as charming—"

The newcomer seemed on the edge of losing his patience. He said with an effort, "You misunderstand me. What is the history of this girl?"

"Really, I hardly know," admitted Pirbrite. "I purchased her at auction three quarter-years since, and she has proved accomplished and attractive in her task as hostess."

The stranger raised his eyes to the sky as if praying for self-control. He said, "And her previous owner?"

"Heneage, master of the Mooncave out of town to the east. He had her from the slaver who picked her from some school on Annanworld, fringeward in the Empire yonder." He jerked a thumb indiscriminately at the galaxy overhead.

"That sounds like the one," muttered the stranger. "Where is she?"

"In shadow of that tree yonder," said Pirbrite, pointing. He cupped his hands around his mouth and gave forth the deep-throated boom of a Loudor moth. Instantly the nearer trees glowed brighter to attract the insect, and the dark bay he had indicated was flooded with a soft pink radiance.

"Ay," said the stranger after a pause. "Her price?"

"Her *price*?" echoed Pirbrite, taken aback. "Well, really—I had never thought of selling her—I mean . . ." He gasped.

"Come now, man!" the other rapped out impatiently. "Delay not! Name it!"

Pirbrite took a deep breath and shut his eyes. "Three thousand circles," he said flatly. It was more than double her worth.

Then he felt something hard and cold pressed into his chubby hand, and he opened his eyes again to see the stranger striding down into the garden with his hand on his sword, and in his own hand . . .

His eyes grew as round as the coins with wonder, and he picked up one of them and turned it over.

A thousand circles! Thrice!

The newcomer surveyed the soldier coolly. A fighting man plainly. A mercenary who would fulfill his contract or die.

He transferred his attention to Sharla and said, "You are the Princess Sharla Andalvarson of Argus?"

Ordovic said huskily, "Man, you are crazed!"

The stranger said, "I think not. Is it not truth, Sharla?"

She nodded, very slowly, with parted lips, but otherwise made no move.

Ordovic rose slowly to his feet, his face bearing an expression of mingled doubt and amazement. He said, "What sad jest is this?"

"No jest, soldier, but the sober truth. This lady is indeed Sharla of Argus, and elder daughter of King Andalvar. As I read the story she was slavered from a school on Annanworld seven years back and sold into a house of shame on Louder here, Mooncave by name. In due course she was resold here—a princess of the Imperial blood, but who would believe the tale?"

Sharla's eyes were dim and far away, but she said huskily, "Ay. They took it for the tale of a child half crazed when I tried to tell them first, and the slavers never realized they held the Empire's wealth at the swordpoint.

"My father would have bought me, or laid waste the world on which my blood was spilled if I had been slain. And then I learned to shut my mouth, and have kept it shut these seven years, for most of the old courtesans spin such tales—I met one who claimed to have been my father's mistress scant ten years before, but she knew nothing of the court of Argus. She was a liar like all the rest, and what was I?"

She sat there hardly moving her lips, telling her tale of shame in a low but tearless voice.

"I had almost forgotten," she concluded.

Ordovic looked bewilderedly from one to the other. He had thought he knew every trick of the trade when it came to parting money and its owner, but this was a new one. There were ways of testing its validity—

He said fiercely, "By the winds of Loudor, stranger, this is no common tale. Who are you that you spin so wild a story?"

"No one that you would know, soldier. And none that you would know either, Sharla. My name is Landor, and I am neither of Loudor nor of Argus, but of Penalpar, half the galaxy away."

"Well, Landor of Penalpar as you call yourself, what if this tale of yours be true? What is it you want?"

Landor ignored him and bent his brilliant eyes on Sharla. He said, "Sharla, your father is sick and approaching death. These two months I have sought you, beginning on Annanworld and tracing you hither to Loudor to bring you back."

Sharla seemed to come to life again slowly. "My father sick?" she echoed. Landor nodded.

She sat up, pulling her costume together, her eyes fixed on nothing. She said, "We must go to him then—at once, quickly."

Landor said, "Ay, Sharla. You must go to him. It was to that end that I sought you out, for in you stands the future of the Empire. Your sister Andra—"

Sharla blanched and looked at him fiercely. "Andra! My sister! What of her? And what of my brother Penda—a child of three when last I saw him?"

"Well, both of them, but Penda spoiled and Andra known by the name of the black witch—and she it is who will be regent in your father's place till Penda comes of age. This must not be!"

Ordovic looked from one to the other in puzzlement. He said, "Ser Landor, I do not understand."

Impatiently, without looking at him: "Soldier, no one cares whether you understand or not. Get you gone in peace and seek another trull—the Princess Sharla must come back to Argus with me. Here, take this purse." He held out a small leather bag which jingled and hung heavy from his fingers.

Ordovic's face went slowly white. He said, "My lady! Forgive me for what I would have done!"

Sharla's voice was metallic and emotionless. She said, "I forgive you, Ordovic. Take your money and go."

He said, "You wish me to take your money, Ser Landor?"

Landor shook it at him in annoyance. "Take it!"

Ordovic snatched it from him and tossed it in his hand. A strange set smile played on his lips. "Right, Ser Landor!" he said. "Whether you like it or not, you have bought you a fighting man. I take no pay without service."

Landor looked at him with astonishment and then chuckled reluctantly. He said, "Soldier, you are a man of mettle. You are right. The road is grim from here to Argus as I know to my cost—"

"How great a cost?" said Ordovic.

"Some seven thousand circles," said Landor, his eyebrows rising.

"My price is a fraction of that," said Ordovic. He set his helmet on his head and waited.

Sharla said, "Ser Landor, there is the matter of my price—"

"I bought you, Sharla. You are free—and when should you

have been otherwise? Come, put my cloak around you and let us go."

She moved like one in a dream.

Three months, it took. They came by way of Tellantrum, Forbit, and Poowadya, and wasted three precious days at the frontier world of Delcadoré because Sharla was without papers and needed an Outland visa to enter the Empire. Ordovic rattled his sword under the nose of a frightened bureaucrat, and they obtained clearance in three days instead of three weeks. Then they came to Anfagan and Neranigh, and mercifully found a friend of Landor's whose private ship was heading for Penalpar by way of Mercator, and brought them within hailing distance of Argus. And then by one last of the big slow traders that were now the only ships on the star-routes save the fleet and wicked vessels of the pirates and the navies of the autarkic worlds, to Oppidum on Argus, and by helicopter to the castle of the kings.

But they had come too late.

And then the knowledge that Sharla was indeed heiress to the regency of the Empire—and a burning shame was in him at what he had done, not to be quenched till he had given her back what he and his breed had taken from her: honor, dignity, rank, and the right to hold up her head in the company of kings.

He slapped his hilt thoughtfully.

After a short while he went to his quarters and was met by three silent slaves who offered to take his harness off and bathe him. He dismissed them angrily.

"Am I a woman, then, that I should need aid in undressing? Out, slaves! Fetch me a meal, and get gone!"

They vanished in a flurry, and he stripped and slid luxuriously into the steaming tub before the log fire that spat and crackled on the hearth. He had learned long ago that sorrows are best forgotten as soon as recalled, and what Sharla had said had faded from his mind.

He was toweling himself lustily when the slaves reappeared with trays of food and drink, and he paused to look at it. He poked the food suspiciously and said, "What is this?"

"The brains of katalabs and the hearts of nugasha fried in pebab oil," said the first slave proudly. "This is honey cake with Thanis garlic, and this frozen breast of quail."

"Faugh! You call that a meal? Fetch me the roast thigh of the katalabs whose brains you would have done better to lend

to your own, and three measures of ancinard, and as much
fruit as one of you puny children can carry. I wish to *eat*—
not peck!"

A quarter hour later he obtained what he wanted, and he
chased the slaves away and, with caution born of long experience, searched the room thoroughly from floor to ceiling for
spy-holes. He found three, and after pushing his sword down
each to discourage eavesdroppers, he plugged them with
strips tore from a curtain until he could obtain mortar and
fill them permanently.

Lastly he called for a swift horse and rode into Oppidum.

The Street of the Morning had seemingly been so named
because it was never so alive as at night. There were harsh
yellow lights at the eaves of its buildings, and it was thronged
with people of all colors and shapes. The beggars clustered in
droves around the cheap infrared lamps at the intersections,
claiming a few ring from the passersby. Occasionally a spaceman or a soldier on a spree was foolish enough to toss one of
them a full circle or even more, and they flocked after the
one who was so lavish like bees after honey.

There were the women of easy virtue, too, but most of them
were in the cafés and drinking-shops, for the night was far
spent already when Kelab the Conjurer again came down the
Street. There were stars thick in the sky, and six of Argus's
nine moons hung over this hemisphere, but there were also
yellow torches on the battlements of the fortress on the Hill
of Kings, and he listened to the talking of the wind and not
the noise of the crowds.

He descended the steps and pushed his way into the House
of the Bubbling Spring. It was bright and hot and noisy; a
good deal of extravagant lovemaking was going on; there was
a three-piece orchestra playing curious Outland instruments,
one with strings to be bowed, one blown, and one struck with
little yellow mallets; there was the same party of spacemen
playing shen fu, and their low-voiced bids and the click of
chips went on unnoticed.

The lid was over the Mimosan chromograph behind the
bar, and four attendants moved among the tables. Finzey sat
in front of his rows of bottles, grinning like a fat idol. At the
sight of Kelab he let go a joyous shout and reached for a
bottle of the conjurer's choice.

Kelab nodded and leaned on the counter while it was being

poured out, his head cocked to one side, the gold disk in his left ear gleaming in the garish light.

Finzey set the mug before him, said, "So you're back, Kelab! What have you done today? Earned your thousand circles yet?"

The conjurer smiled faintly and nodded. "I think I have earned them again. Your burying money rises well?"

"Seven thousand and ninety circles and a few odd ring at sundown last," said Finzey proudly. "There has not been such a bowlful before in Oppidum, even at the burying of a king."

Kelab nodded. He said, "The poor will feast well if all the cities on Argus give so freely."

Finzey's expression suddenly became drawn and worried. He said, "Kelab, while we speak of burying money, there was one who needed burying above on the Street—remember?"

Kelab said, "I recall her. Well?"

"At noon there was but three ring in that cup."

The conjurer looked up. "I put a circle there myself, fat one."

"As I surmised. Will you divine the thief? Here is her cup." He pushed a little tin mug across the bar, and Kelab picked it up and handled it, his face going strained and his eyes unfocused in the effort to recall.

His hands, if any had watched them, would have seemed to flow like water on and in the mug, as though hands and mug were one, and there was a curious flicker of blue fire when at length he relinquished it. He said, "It is hard to see, for the theft was the act of a moment and the thief thought little of the cup. Where are the three ring he left?"

Finzey picked three tiny coins from a shelf behind him, and passed them to Kelab, who felt them one by one. He said finally, "Two of them were placed there after the theft, but the third remembers. The thief thought very hard about the money."

"His name?" said Finzey eagerly.

"Arcta the Wolf. You will see to it?"

Finzey nodded. The conjurer said, "It wearies me, that divination. I need rest." He picked up his mug of liquor and walked into the deep shadowed bay at the far end of the room among the loving couples, and chose an empty alcove and a bare table. He sat down, and became a shadow among shadows.

Later, Ordovic too came into the Street of the Morning. He had walked the Low City since close on sundown, asking for a dusky man, a conjurer named Kelab, and since his Argian was scanty and his thieves' argot scarcely better, his temper had frayed thin.

But one of them had mentioned Finzey, at the sign of the Bubbling Spring, and he had come here, hoping.

Also he wanted a drink.

Finzey approached him, his face expressionless.

"Ancinard," said Ordovic. "A big measure, fat one. And some strine."

Without more expression than a statue Finzey slashed three strips from a side of strine under the bar and folded each into a ball and laid them on a plate. He filled a measure with fuming red ancinard, and pushed both across the counter.

"Seven circles," he said.

Ordovic dropped the coins tinkling on the bar, took the measure and the plate, and turned away to seek a table. His eyes swept the room.

And suddenly, as he looked into the darkness at the far end, shadowed with consummate artistry for the lovers using it, the loud noise and the bright lights vanished and there were three birbrak trees, and a sky above powdered with stars rare except where the galaxy lay in a monstrous wheel. There was a shadowed pool of darkness facing him—a bay in one of the trees.

Someone, somewhere, gave forth the drone of a Loudor moth.

He took a few steps forward like a man in a dream as the trees brightened. Sharla? *Sharla?*

Then there was a puff of smoke and a great crashing wind. . . .

And nothing before him except a slender man with a dusky face, staring into a mug of liquor cupped between his hands.

"You?" said Ordovic hoarsely. "*You?* How did you know?"

Kelab swirled the liquor in the mug and a stream of bubbles fled up from the bottom like a flock of birds rising into clear air. He said, "Be seated, Ordovic."

Ordovic lowered himself by touch onto the seat opposite him in the alcove, his eyes fixed on Kelab's face. He found the forgotten drink and the strine in his hands, and pushed them to one side of the table. There was some kind of blue curtain drawn across the mouth of the alcove, which pulsed as if it were alive and glowed with a quiet light.

Kelab said finally, "It was blazed like a beacon on the surface of your mind, Ordovic. You have met Sharla and you can never be the same again."

"That is truth," said Ordovic. His hand stole out and he took the ancinard and sipped it. The fumes did something to his head, and when he looked at Kelab again it was with a new clarity.

He said, "I have been seeking you since sundown, here in the Low City."

Kelab nodded, still gazing into his mug as if it were a divining-bowl. He said, "I knew."

"You knew? And yet you let me tramp on, hunting for you?"

The conjurer nodded again, with the suspicion of a smile. "I am not found unless I choose to be found, Ordovic. There are few men so completely master of their fate as I."

"My lady Sharla sent me to bring you to her," Ordovic said slowly.

"Her words were, to be exact, 'If you can, buy him—if you must, drag him,'" agreed Kelab.

Ordovic's mouth fell open and he said, "Can you know *everything* that passes in my mind, wizard?"

"Only that which is close to the surface. But, in answer, tell her I am not to be bought and that the man is not born who could drag me. Besides, she already owes me a thousand circles."

"What for?" demanded Ordovic, aghast.

"For the regulation of the matter of the marriage bond. If she chooses to pay me, I shall be at my ship on the spaceport tomorrow, about the hour of ten. If not, not; but I shall not choose to see you again."

Ordovic bounded to his feet. "Of all the insolence!" he shouted, his hand closing on the hilt of his sword.

Kelab's hand moved like a ripple on water and the sword stuck fast in its sheath. He said, "Sit, Ordovic."

"Coward!" accused Ordovic bitterly. "You dare not fight with a man's weapons!"

"For that," said Kelab evenly, "I am entitled by your standards to kill you. You would kill a man who called you a coward. I, whose powers are immeasurably greater than yours, dare not be so casual. I hold this world in the hollow of my hand, Ordovic. Remember that when you call me a coward. . . . You will come tomorrow morning."

He stood up and crumpled the blue curtain over the mouth

of the alcove and shook it into nothing. Ordovic said, "Suppose I do not choose to?"

"You will come," said Kelab, and walked away into the brightness beyond.

Ordovic followed him with his eyes, his hand automatically seeking the hilt of his sword. It moved easily in its scabbard again, but now that he had the chance of drawing it he left it, and sat slowly down again behind the table, his hand pulling his ancinard toward him.

VI

Ten o'clock. Six moons over the castle of the kings, a few flying clouds, a chill wind that rustled the crowns of the trees. In the castle—near silence, for there was no carousing tonight. Andalvar of Argus lay dead in the castle, and tomorrow was the day of burying.

Sharla had eaten at the table of her guests, and there was a blank space left for Barkasch of Mercator. But rumor said Barkasch and his company of fighting men had lifted at sundown from Oppidum and were bent for Mercator again, Barkasch in a towering rage.

She had eaten in somber silence, bowing to the guests as they arrived and departed, and took the first opportunity of returning to her apartment with Landor. When she did so, Valley and the other quick, quiet maids bathed her in scented water and combed her hair.

Landor sat in the antechamber, thoughtfully sampling the fruit that packed the silver bowls and considering the impending visit to Sabura Mona. An enigma, that one: all-powerful over Andalvar, seeking perhaps to establish the same control over Sharla.

Suddenly a smile touched his lips. A worthy antagonist, perhaps: for Landor held that the man—or woman—who could match him in the game of statecraft was not yet born.

Sharla came through from the inner room, her hair golden and shining around her face, wearing a plain white kirtle without sleeves that reached to her knees. She was barefoot.

Landor surveyed her appreciatively. He said, "Sharla, I don't despair of you. It seems that your childhood schooling in the arts of deception is not entirely lost to you."

Sharla nodded seriously. She said, "The innocent Outland girl without much experience—is my disguise."

He nodded back. "If you will put on your least subtle expression, I think it is near the hour."

Sharla turned to the trio of waiting slaves, said, "Valley, Lena, Mershil, I shall not need you again tonight. Call me at the same hour tomorrow. You may go."

They curtsied silently and withdrew.

Then Sharla and Landor called the guard from the door and requested escort to the chambers of Sabura Mona.

The guard led them down echoing stone passages lit only by flickering torches. They passed slaves on errands who failed to recognize Sharla in her unregal attire and went by with a scuffle of bare feet. The passages grew colder and the torches more and more infrequent.

Sharla said in a low voice to Landor, "She doesn't live in state, does she?"

"That's an understatement," said Landor softly. "This is a part of the castle reserved to the slaves, as I recall, apart solely from Sabura Mona's apartment. I do not understand. A woman of power and influence—"

The guard stopped before a plain wooden door set in the stone wall. There was no mat before it and no curtain, no guard stationed outside. Just the plain door.

"This is it," said the guard.

"Strike the door and say the Princess Sharla awaits," commanded Landor, and the guard pounded twice at it with his fist.

A soft voice from within questioned, "Who stands there?"

"The Princess Sharla awaits, Sabura Mona," answered the guard.

There was no sound of bars being withdraw or bolts shooting into place, but the door began to open gently and the guard turned and strode wordlessly away.

Sharla looked questioningly at Landor, and he nodded. She went in.

The room beyond was bare—quite bare. The walls were unadorned stone and the floor was uncarpeted. There was no fire in the hearth, two flaring torches were the only lights. There was a rough bed with a coarse cloth spread, a table with half a dozen pens and ink and sheets of paper, some wooden chairs. . . .

On one of the chairs sat Sabura Mona.

She wore a homespun robe of brown which did no more

than cover her fat body, nothing to decorate it. She was the fattest woman Sharla had ever seen. Her arms were like tree branches and her legs like tree trunks, but soft. Yet she was not absurd.

No. She was not *fat*. She was big. She was imposing. There was no shadow of the ludicrous in her monstrous bulk. And Sharla wondered why.

It was her eyes, she thought. They were big and dark and there was the sorrow of a world in their depths, as if the wisdom of all the ages hid behind that mask of soft pendulous flesh.

Her voice too was as beautiful and as melancholy as her eyes.

She said, "Welcome, my lady. I fear I cannot offer you the hospitality to which you are accustomed, but I live, as you see, in humble circumstances."

Sharla said, a little uncertainly, "It is of no consequence, Sabura Mona."

The other extended a fat hand and indicated one of the wooden chairs. "Be seated, my lady. And—this is Ser Landor?"

Landor nodded, said smoothly, "My lady Sharla asked me to accompany her, since her Argian is worn with long disuse and I speak it to perfection."

"Really?" Sabura Mona's eyebrows rose on her forehead. "And in which of the Outland dialects are you most at home?"

"It is of no consequence," stammered Sharla. "We cannot impose upon you—"

"I speak them all," said Sabura Mona, and there was a finality in her voice that defied further argument. She spoke next in the dialect of Loudor.

"So you see, Ser Landor, your presence as interpreter is really not required."

Landor could not avoid the pointed hint, but there was a flicker of unreality about the way he turned and withdrew, leaving Sharla very alone and helpless, as if he had been fighting very hard to control himself, doing consciously what he should have done naturally.

As soon as the door shut behind him, Sabura Mona turned her eyes from following him and looked at Sharla with a curious abstracted expression. Sharla noticed that her sole ornament was a tiny gold ear-clip, and strove to remember where she had last seen one like it.

Sabura Mona said, "I called you hither, my lady, in this way, for two reasons. The ostensible one is that here we cannot be overheard or spied upon. The more pressing is that I am growing old, and am anyway a fat and clumsy woman, and I cannot do much walking or attendance at ceremonies."

Sharla said, "But, Sabura Mona, you should have more exalted quarters than this. If you do prefer to live here, at least let me order you better furnishings—"

"I do not choose to have them," said Sabura Mona.

"But you have no slaves, no attendants . . . ?"

"I do not choose to have them," repeated Sabura Mona firmly. "And therefore let us talk no more about them. My comfort or discomfort is a small thing compared to that of the Empire.

"I called you hither to speak of two things: Barkasch of Mercator, and the people of Argus. First—of Barkasch. You would do well to beware of him. He cannot fight the Empire alone, though he would dearly like to, for he is a scheming and ambitious man whom fate has chosen to set at the head of a trio of the wildest worlds in the galaxy—wild not in terrain but in people.

"His are the fiercest warriors of all. His are the ambitions of a merchant prince magnified a millionfold. It seemed that his alliance with Andra and his seat on the Council of Six would give him the power he sought, but far from that he was made to look a fool before many people, and when his temper cools he will ally himself with Andra's cause and will not rest until she is in your place. Beware of him. He is crafty. Have your adviser Landor see to it.

"And the second thing. The people of Argus. They are fickle. They believe like all the peoples of the Empire in prophecy, and though they welcome you now, someone will one day soon realize that no prophecy is current proclaiming you beneficient and just ruler of the Empire, though many run the crowds with the word that the black witch shall bring about the Empire's ruin. It would be the work of a day, no more, for Andra, your sister, and Barkasch of Mercator to have the crowd howling for your blood on no stronger grounds, than that it is not you but your sister who is to ride the Empire to oblivion."

Sharla said after a long silence, "That is all, Sabura Mona?"

"That is all. There will be more. I have spies, my lady, and I ordered them to warn me of such rumors as might cause your overthrow. I, who planned so much for your father, have no plan now—yet. What is to come remains inscrutable. But rest assured: I have small love for your sister or for Barkasch of Mercator, and shall guide you—with the assistance, doubtless, of your Lord Great Chamberlain, Landor"—this with the air of an afterthought—"as I did your father. . . . I shall see you at the burying tomorrow, my lady. Farewell."

Feeling a little foolish and disappointed, Sharla rose. She said, "Is there a guard nearby that I may summon to escort me to my apartment?"

"No need, my lady. Walk and be assured."

Sharla gazed at the immense bulk of the woman before her for a while. Eventually she turned and went away.

Though the passages were dark and bare and cold, somehow she felt no apprehension at walking along them alone after Sabura Mona's words.

When she reentered her own rooms, Landor was waiting. He greeted her and said, "First, with regard to what you said earlier—Dolichek's father is dead."

Sharla brushed it aside, and suddenly weary, sat down on the couch beside him. She said, "I have talked to Sabura Mona."

Landor nodded. He said, "She is a strange woman, is she not? I am intrigued to have met her. She impressed me with an air of power." He shifted to face her. "Tell me, what did she say?"

Sharla told him, in outline. When she came to the part about the prophecies, he snorted. "Faugh! I have no faith in prophecies. The bad guesswork of a few old women, and they follow it because they think it is a prophecy, and point to it when they have followed it as true foresight. Go on."

She finished her tale, and he said, "All? It seems little enough, in faith, to insist on conveying in private."

Sharla said, yawning, "Landor, yours is the statesman's brain, not mine. I am weary and would sleep. In the morning, if Ordovic has found this conjurer, we will see him, and find out more from him. Till then, Landor."

Landor rose without more speaking and withdrew.

Senchan Var looked gloomily from the narrow slitted window without benefit of a drape, westward over the Low City. He could see the lights along the Street of the Morning and hear the clamor of the city at play.

He said, "Andalvar of Argus dead at the sundown before last, and they still drink and sing in the Low City. A rootless stock—craven and unworthy of Argus."

"While the burying money grows, Senchan," said Andra.

Senchan Var turned angrily on her. "Burying money or no, my lady, it is an insult to the memory of your father Andalvar, and I am all but ashamed for you, my lady, that you do not take it seriously."

Andra's composure was fraying visibly. She sat on a couch covered with badly cured katalabs pelts, and the floor was hard and cold and the walls bare, for the fortress on the Hill of Kings was a fortress first and a palace after, and though it was the focus of Imperial government and state-owned trading it was still a soldiers' barracks rather than a home.

Across the room her ape whined and chattered fretfully.

She snapped, "Senchan, there is no need to lose your temper with me simply because my minx of a sister dismissed Dolichek from whipping-post and told the whip-master to break his whip and come to me again, and you happen to agree with her. She did it out of sentiment and not anxiety for the strength of Penda's moral fiber. Further, she is a weakling and neither she nor the fool whom she put in your place is acquainted with the veriest elements of intrigue."

"No?" said Senchan Var. "It seems to me, my lady, that she is strong and self-possessed, as witness the way she disposed of Barkasch of Mercator and the marriage bond."

Andra spat. "According to Samsar's story? Not at all. Only this conjurer and his fantastic trick saved her. And there is one thing more—"

A soldier of the fortress company entered and saluted. He said in harshly accented Argian, "A slave below, my lady, demands entrance. Female slave called Valley."

Andra shot a triumphant glance at Senchan Var and said, "Fetch her to me, and also the slave Samsar, the wizard Kteunophimi, and the black Leontine slave who came hither from the castle of the kings this evening."

The soldier saluted again and went out. Andra said, "See, Senchan? Can anyone be skilled in intrigue who does not have wit enough to chase away spying slaves? She took them all from me, trustingly, and her idiot of an adviser, Landor, knew too little to warn her. I tell you, Senchan, a week and we shall have torn this sister of mine to shreds. Ay, and scattered the shreds to the eight winds of Argus."

The door opened again, and the same soldier ushered in

Valley, swathed in a thick cloak from head to ankles, but her dusty feet bare, the great black slave who had been whip-master to Dolichek, Samsar of the hot brown skin and twitching eyes, and a small, nervous man with a withered face like an old apple and a mirthless grin that displayed toothless gums. The soldier himself turned to go out again, but Andra stopped him with a gesture.

"Stay, soldier," she commanded. "There may be need of you."

He closed the door obediently and stood with his back to it.

"Now," said Andra, a gleam in her cat's eyes, leaning forward on the pile of skins that formed her resting-place. "You, Samsar!"

Samsar stepped forward sullenly.

"Your tale again, Samsar. Not that part about the entry of Kelab nor the departure of Barkasch, but that about the fate of the bond itself."

"Why—why, my lady, did I not make it clear?" stammered Samsar, his jaw working stiffly, for there was a vast black bruise all across his cheek where Ordovic had hit him. "I would have recovered it for you and preserved it, but Ordovic, the captain of the royal bodyguard, picked it up while it would still have been but foolish to attempt to steal it under the eyes of the courtiers."

"Enough!" said Andra, holding up her hand. "Step back! Kteunophimi!"

The withered man came forward, mumbling.

"Work the miracle of full memory on the slave Valley," she commanded. Mumbling from the aged wizard.

"Do not waste time in vain attempts to speak!" said Andra. "But a few simple movements are all you need, Kteunophimi."

The wizard turned to face Valley, who stood very straight with her big eyes bright and limpid and the hood of her cloak thrown back on her shoulders, and began to move his hands in a complicated pattern. After a few seconds he stepped hastily aside, and Valley, her eyes wide open but unseeing, walked unhurriedly forward to face Andra.

"Well, Valley? You have heard all that passed in the apartment my sister took from me?"

The slender slave nodded.

"Tell me of what was said concerning Barkasch and the

marriage bond," Andra commanded, and sat back on her pile of skins.

Valley began to speak as a machine would speak. In flatly unimaginative terms she described the reactions of Sharla and Landor, and the entry of Ordovic. Senchan Var listened, a frown on his face, marveling at the way Valley copied the very accents of the speakers. Landor and Sharla had talked in Argian, but with the arrival of Ordovic switched to their Outland tongue, and since Valley did not herself understand the meaning of what she had heard, but could only repeat it parrotwise, Andra called for an interpreter and heard the talk with interest. Samsar stood in the background, a faint beading of sweat on his brow.

When Valley repeated Ordovic's version of Samsar's clumsy attempt to steal the marriage bond, Andra raised an imperious hand, "Enough!" she said. "Samsar, step foward."

Samsar did not budge.

"Soldier—" said Andra, and the soldier before the door caught Samsar's arms and frog-marched him in front of the couch.

There was a gleam in Andra's yellow eyes that was not all due to the torches. She said softly, caressingly, "Samsar, you lied to me."

"My lady!" stammered the slave, his eyes twitching. "I did my utmost—"

"Utmost or not," cut in Senchan Var, "you lied to my lady Andra! I should rip your false tongue from your throat!"

Andra was regaining her self-confidence and poise. She said, "Hold, Senchan. I have it how this may turn to our advantage even now. What was the meaning of the threat Ordovic used to this man, interpreter?"

Samsar's eyes filled with abject terror, and his mouth trembled, but he could not speak. The interpreter shook his head.

"I know not, my lady. 'Tis not of their dialect, nor of Argian."

With a casual glance at the wretched Samsar, Andra turned. "Senchan, explain its meaning."

The old man blanched. He said, "It is—it is ..." Then he turned his back sharply and said with an air of finality, "It is not seemly for you to know, my lady."

"Fool, Senchan! Will none of you tell me? Then I demand it of a common soldier. You before the door! Explain!"

Woodenly, his eyes focused on empty air, the soldier explained.

When he finished, Andra nodded, her lips drawn back from her teeth like a cat's. She said slowly, bright-eyed, "Slave!"

The Leontine giant stepped forward.

"Take this Samsar and do to him as you have heard—and stop him wailing!"

A broad hand clapped across Samsar's mouth and he fell to moaning faintly. "Then go into the Low City and spread it abroad that Ordovic threatened this. Let Samsar be found on the streets later—about dawn?"

The giant said, "I hear and obey," and picked up Samsar casually under one arm and went out. Senchan Var turned to Andra with an expression of despair on his face and would have spoken, but Andra cut him short.

"Senchan, we cannot afford to be squeamish. We are playing for the glory of an Empire, and one man—or ten thousand—cannot be permitted to stand in the way of it. You're a soldier, Sechan, not a ninny! Kteunophimi, take that soldier and make him forget what he has seen, believing it to be Ordovic's work."

The aged hypnotist nodded and led the soldier into a far corner. After a while the latter departed like a walking doll, and Andra turned to Valley, still standing motionless before the couch.

"Continue," she commanded.

They listened in jubilant silence when she came to the scene between Ordovic and Sharla, and Andra said, "So my precious sister was a women of the streets in her long absence. How much capital could we make of that, Senchan?"

All the old man's puritanically moral upbringing rose in revolt at that. He said, "That a woman without honor should come to stain the throne of Argus! 'Tis the most shameful thing I ever heard!"

"Agreed," said Andra. "It will be common knowledge three days from now. Continue, Valley."

When she finished her recital, he said, "She is visiting Sabura Mona; that is dangerous, my lady. Sabura Mona is unpredictable and very, very shrewd."

Andra frowned. "Indeed, I do not know whether she will stand to our side or to Sharla's."

"Is there a way to spy on *her*?"

"None. The walls of her room are stone as thick as you are

tall, and she has no slaves to be bribed and never leaves the castle of the kings."

"Then she is too dangerous to be allowed to live."

"True. Kteunophimi!"

The wizard came forward.

"Take away your pupil Valley, send her again to attend to my sister. You will then send up my black Leontine slave when he has dealt with Samsar, the liar."

The old man bowed and left the room unsteadily, leaning on Valley's arm. After a while Senchan Var said, "Word from Barkasch?"

"None. He went off-world in a huff at sundown. I expect his messenger some time. He will not accept being made a fool of lightly."

The door opened. Another soldier stood there, saluted.

He said, "There is a man craving audience who will give no name but is come in connection with the marriage bond of Barkasch of Mercator—my lady," he added hastily.

Andra and Senchan Var exchanged glances.

Andra raised her eyebrows as if to say, "What did I tell you?" and ordered the soldier, "Let him enter."

The soldier stepped aside and a man came from behind him, and both Andra and Senchan Var tensed and began to flush with rage.

Kelab the Conjurer.

VII

"Ser Landor! Ser Landor!" A patter of feet, panting, shouting in high feminine voices. Landor struggled from sleep and found a gray rain-washed sky shedding dull light through the windows. His door burst open and Valley came in, her face tearstained.

"Ser Landor! My lady Sharla has disappeared!"

Instantly Landor tossed the covers off and reached for his clothes. He said, "How? When?"

Valley said, "It must have been early today, Ser Landor. When she went to see Sabura Mona, as you know, she dismissed us and I for my part went into Oppidum. This morning, when we went to awaken her, she was gone from her bed, and there were signs of struggle."

Landor buckled his sword-belt and forced his feet into sandals. He said, "Call out the guard! Find Captain Ordovic! Let him see that none leaves the castle!"

Valley bowed and vanished, and Landor, his face like thunder, went striding down the passage to Sharla's rooms. Here he found Mershil and Lena, her other personal slaves, weeping and wringing their hands. The door to the bedroom was open, and the bed visible beyond was disarranged, as if by a struggle. He ordered harshly, "Peace, you! No one is blaming you—you were dismissed and all is in order. Let me pass!"

He pushed between them and went into the bedroom. They followed, howling, and he rounded on them. "Has anyone touched this bed since it was found so?"

"None," Lena assured him eagerly through her tears.

"Then keep silence. I have a little skill in divination." He turned to the bed, while the slaves ceased their sobbing and watched with interest. He laid his hands caressingly on the covers, his eyes blurring and his fingers seeming to melt and run into the fabric as Kelab's had on the beggar's cup.

At last he shook his head and turned away, as there came a clatter of feet and a jingle of metal, and Ordovic burst into the room, closely followed by Tampore.

He said, "The slave Valley came with a wild tale of Sharla vanishing."

"True enough," said Landor. "You have put guards at the entries of the castle?"

"Ah, though it's by way of locking the ship after the air has blown. When did she go? Did she return from her meeting with Sabura Mona?"

"We spoke together after she came back. But her slaves were dismissed, and there was none to see or hear."

Ordovic cursed. "Tampore! Was there no guard before the door?"

"There was one. Where is he?"

"Bought?" suggested Landor, and Tampore flared, "The man who can be bought does not enter the bodyguard. He is dead for certain."

"Who was it?"

"One Elvir."

"By the winds of Argus!" said Ordovic, and stormed into the passage. There was a squad of guards there. His eyes switched over them, and he shot out a brawny arm and said, "Elvir!"

A big man in the second rank stepped out and came up to

him. Behind, he heard a furious growl of astonishment from Tampore.

He said in clipped thieves' argot, "Elvir, were you not on guard at the royal apartment—here—last night?"

"I was. I came at midnight and changed places at dawn with my relief."

Landor came out behind Ordovic, bidding Tampore be quiet. He listened. Ordovic said, "Who was your relief?"

"Darbo, Captain."

One of the other guards spoke up. "That's so, Captain. I went in search of the sergeant when the slave came with news of the disappearance."

"Elvir, did you let anyone in—anyone at all—last night after you came on duty?"

"As is customary, I let pass Dolichek, the prince's whipping-post, and the whip-master—the black giant."

Ordovic cursed. "And they came out again?" Landor demanded, striding forward.

"Of a truth, yes!"

"But did you not know that Dolichek is no longer the prince's whipping-post? That my lady told the giant to break his whip and go serve the Princess Andra?"

Elvir's face went ashen. He said, "No, Ser Landor, I swear it. I heard nothing of that. I did merely as usual in letting Dolichek pass to bear the burden of the prince's misdemeanors."

Landor said suddenly, "There is something wrong. I can sense it. Guards, into the inner rooms!"

They filed inside and fell in again in order. Landor said, "With your permission, Sergeant?"

Tampore nodded, and he continued, "Search this apartment! Shift everything. Something is wrong. Elvir, you are not to be blamed. With the others—to it."

They left no fraction of an inch of all the rooms in the suite unsearched, but found nothing to justify Landor's misgivings. At length the latter sat down on the bed with his head in his hands and said, "Still there is something wrong. It is as if there was unreality.... Which of you searched beneath the bed?"

Three of the guards signified assent, Elvir among them, and Elvir said, "Ser Landor, I felt strange on doing so, for though there was nothing there I felt there should be. I felt that way too, now I recall, when Dolichek came last night with the whip-master—worse when they went away again."

"Lift the bed," commanded Landor harshly, and six brawny guards bent to it and tugged and carried it half across the room. The space where it had stood was curiously shifting, as if it were seen through water, and he walked up to it and bent and searched the floor with his fingers, his face drawn and strained.

After a while it changed to a smile of triumph, and he heaved and lifted out of nothing a still, doll-like figure with matted yellow hair.

"Sharla!" Ordovic said, but Landor shook his head and stepped out of the shifting unreality.

"Dolichek," he said. "That is how it was done."

He laid the boy on the bed. It was amazing how closely in repose his young-old face resembled Sharla's.

"He lives?" questioned Ordovic.

"Assuredly. But he sleeps."

"How was he hidden?"

"Magic, Ordovic."

"This is the black witch's doing," said Tampore, stepping forward and glowering. "Did I not warn you, Captain Ordovic?"

But Landor shook his head. "I know few wizards and not one witch whose powers are capable of that. Kelab is one of them, of course. Wait, Ordovic," holding up his hand as Ordovic was about to speak. "*But* it was a strange thing to save us from the marriage bond and then to steal Sharla."

Ordovic said fiercely, "Would he take her for himself?"

"He would not dare," Landor said confidently.

Tampore said, "I do not see how it could be done. Anyone could mistake my lady Sharla for Dolichek if her hair were dirtied, her face bruised and if she wore a similar garment, but one could not take Kelab for the Leontine giant."

"He is a magician, remember," Ordovic insisted. "Landor, I think he is likely. When I met him in the Low City this morning, he demanded a thousand circles for his regulation of the marriage bond and said he would be at his ship today at ten."

"If he had just stolen Sharla from the castle of the kings, he would not have faced you in the Low City."

Ordovic said, "With his insolence he would dare anything!'"

Tampora coughed, put in, "Ser Landor, the lady Andra is in the fortress on the Hill of Kings in Oppidum."

"What of it?"

"I have friends among the guards there. We could find out if Kelab has been to see the lady Andra."

Ordovic said hotly, "You deny that this is the black witch's work, yet can you name any other who would do it? Save Barkasch of Mercator, who is off-world?"

Landor wasn't listening. He said, "Tampore, what were your guards doing to let them leave the castle?"

"The black giant is well enough known to my men, but it is strange that they should have let out Dolichek."

"Then perhaps they did *not* leave the castle. Tampore, organize searches of every room and hole in and under the castle, and ask all the guards who were on watch last night whom they let pass—without exception."

Tampore nodded and signaled to his men, but Landor stopped Darbo, let the rest go. He said to Ordovic, "Does Sabura Mona know of this?"

"Not that I know of."

"Darbo!" said Landor, turning to him. "Go down and inform her, and beg her to come to us if she will. In either case, return at once yourself."

The soldier saluted and withdrew.

They waited in silence, Ordovic pacing the room like a caged lion, his face grim and set, Landor struggling to preserve his outward calm. Almost a quarter of an hour passed.

Eventually Ordovic said, "Darbo is slow in returning. It irks me to wait and do nothing. I'll go seek him." He left the room and followed the passage, inquiring at stages where he could find Sabura Mona, and came eventually into the right corridor. He glanced down it. There indeed was the door to which he had been directed.

And something more.

His heart leaped and his hand closed on the hilt of his sword, and he padded silently up to the embrasure of the door. Darbo lay in it. There was fresh blood all over his face, and his pulse had ceased to beat.

Ordovic rolled him over and his face showed his amazement, for the tough metal of the soldier's helmet had been crushed and driven into his skull with a blow like the butt of a Thanis bull.

He flung the body aside, ripped his sword from his scabbard, and forced open the door.

The room was dim, but he could make out two figures, two

monstrous figures, locked together in the center of the room, struggling; one vast and ebony—the Leontine giant, seven feet tall—the other also huge, but shorter and fatter. A woman. Sabura Mona.

He gaped in amazement at what he saw.

For Sabura Mona had the measure of the giant. He had one enormous hand sunk in the softness of her throat, but she did not appear to notice it. With the other, he was seeking vainly to force her arms from their grip on his waist, constricting the vulnerable organs of his belly as surely as a steel band.

And she laughed. The incredible woman laughed, soundlessly, and instead of letting his arm drive back her head and snap her spine as the giant intended, she was forcing it forward—forward—

He snatched his arm away while he still had room to bend it, just an instant before joint and muscle and tendons would have torn apart, bent backward at the elbow, and her head snapped forward, came up under his chin.

Then in one huge astounding heave compounded of legs and arms and body and head, in that one instant when he had no grip on her, she flung him bodily at the ceiling.

He went up like a lifting ship and fell like a mountain, his skull split on the hard stone twelve feet above, and Sabura Mona, without a glance at the corpse, turned to dip her hands in a bowl of water, while Ordovic, sword limply in his hand, gaped speechless with disbelief.

The incredible woman wiped her hands and turned to him. "You are Ordovic?" she demanded, and he stared at her.

"You are Sabura Mona?"

"Yes. Your messenger told me you wished me to come. My lady Sharla, it seems, has disappeared."

Ordovic nodded. He gestured at the body of the giant. "With him, supposedly—if *he* was whip-master to Dolichek."

"He was."

"But if he is still in the castle, Sharla—uh—my lady Sharla cannot be far either."

"Possibly." Sabura Mona nodded. "Let us go, then. But first, one small matter. Tell no one about my killing *him*." She nodded at the dead man with a quivering of four chins. "Say you slew him, if you like, but tell no one I did. Understood?"

Her eyes were strangely luminous, and he nodded dumbly, followed her up the bare passages. As they approached

Sharla's rooms, he noticed she began to wheeze as if she were exhausted.

Landor met them, demanding, "What kept Darbo?"

"Struck down by the Leontine giant, Ser Landor, and if Ser Ordovic had not saved me, that would have been my fate too," said Sabura Mona. She glanced commandingly at Ordovic, who nodded weakly.

"By the winds of Argus, then!" exploded Landor. "If he was still here, perhaps Sharla—"

A soldier came stumbling down the passage, breathing in great sobbing gasps as if he had run too far too fast. He said, "Ser Landor!" and saluted with difficulty. "Ser Landor, your flying-machine—the one in which you came to the castle of the kings—it's gone!"

"Gone!" said Landor, electrified.

"Yes, gone! And what is more, Sergeant Tampore sent a messenger on a fast horse to the fortress in Oppidum where the lady Andra is, and he has signaled by sun and mirror that Kelab the Conjurer visited her last night close on midnight, and stayed half an hour, and departed."

Landor said, "A fast horse—he could have done it in time to be here with the whip-master by a quarter before one, and left, taking the helicopter and Sharla. . . . By the winds of Argus, soldier! Have horses prepared for us! There is but one wizard on all Argus who could blanket the sound of a helicopter taking off, and that one is Kelab."

The soldier saluted and went back down the passage at a lope. Sabura Mona said, "Is this the doing of my lady Andra?"

Landor said, "Hers and the conjurer Kelab's, I fancy. The Leontine giant took her out under the eyes of the guard, in guise of Dolichek, and doubtless also with some charm against discovery provided by Kelab."

Sabura Mona shook her head sadly, with a vast trembling of chins and pendulous cheeks. Ordovic could not believe her the same woman who had tossed the giant like a Thanis bull. She said, "Ser Landor, I have certain spies—"

"Among my lady Andra's slaves?"

"Assuredly!" said Sabura Mona, her eyebrows rising in surprise. "All places."

"I shall need your counsel, then. At this moment the most important thing is to find Sharla, which means going in search of Kelab the Conjurer at once. If we still had the helicopter—"

Sabura Mona shrugged her elephantine shoulders.

"I can do no more than sit here in the castle of the kings and weave plots as a red liana weaves its beast-traps. But I shall do what little I can, Ser Landor. Be assured of my aid at all times."

Landor said with an attempt at graciousness, "I am grateful, Sabura Mona, and am sure you will serve Sharla as you served her father. If you will pardon us ... Come, Ordovic. Our horses should be ready by now."

There was a gray sky over Oppidum. Toward dawn it had rained, but now it had ceased, though the streets were still deserted in the Low City. The night's gaiety had passed.

Two bodies lay on the Street of the Morning. One was that of a hungry-looking man with a face like a wolf. His throat was slit in tribute to Kelab's skill in divination, and there was a cross carved on his face to show he was accursed and no burying money should be left for him. The other was Samsar's, but that one was barely recognizable as human.

There was a chill wind, too, but Kelab the Conjurer sat on the balcony of his ship, sixty feet above the brown concrete of the spaceport, and sipped a hot brew from Thanis.

Opposite him sat Sharla, her face strangely composed and quite relaxed, and she also was drinking the heart-warming beverage.

Every now and again the conjurer cocked his head on one side as if he were listening, and Sharla's eyes rested on him and saw the glint of gold in his left earlobe, and remembered that this was the clip of which Sabura Mona's had reminded her. She thought for the first time not how small and slender he was, but that he was vaster than he seemed, like a volcano filled with smoldering fires, as if he were the strongest man in the world and also the most gentle.

He for his part sometimes looked across at her and smiled faintly, and thought how very beautiful she was in her white kirtle, with her pale lovely face and her golden hair.

But he did not need to look. He knew her, directly, as he knew everything near him; and certain things farther away, much farther away.

They had sat out on the balcony in silence for some time, no words being needed, when he glanced at the watch that had come from nowhere in the Empire, and said, "I think they are approaching, dear. Go to the place I showed you."

She rose with a quick smile and went into the ship, and he

cleared away the tray from which they had eaten breakfast and checked that all was in readiness.

Then he sat down to wait.

VIII

At the entry to the spaceport hostlers came out from the stables, and Ordovic and Landor dropped from their mounts, sweating and panting.

Curtly, Landor tossed the men their pay and demanded, "Where is the ship of Kelab the Conjurer?"

One of the hostlers, a big fair man with a red scar from eyebrow to chin, shifted the stick he was chewing to the side of his mouth and said, "She stands most east'ard on the port, Ser Landor. 'Tis Ser Landor, ain' it?"

Landor nodded curtly and turned to Tampore and the squad of soldiers who had clattered into the yard with them.

He said, "Out of sight till called for, men! There's little you can do against this magician, but perhaps we'll need you to bring away his body."

Tampore saluted, and they reined in under the eaves of the gallery around the yard. Ordovic and Landor, swords swinging, stalked out of the yard onto the damp brown concrete of the port beyond.

There was only one ship that could have been Kelab's—a lean black vessel, her sides shiny with wet, that reminded Ordovic uncomfortably of certain fleet pirate craft he had tangled with in the Outlands. He glanced at Landor, but Landor had suddenly withdrawn into himself, and there was a tiny bluing of the air around him. Ordovic looked away quickly. There was a new smell in the air—a smell of powers beyond the human.

They walked across to the lean ship and stopped twenty feet from the nearest fin. Above them, on a balcony built out from the side of the ship, they could see Kelab leaning back in a chair, drinking.

Landor shouted, "Conjurer!"

He put down his mug and glanced at them, and his dark face split in a smile of welcome. He raised a hand in salute.

"The best of mornings to you, Ordovic and Landor! You are early in bringing me those thousand circles."

"We bring no money, traitor," said Tandor harshly. "What have you done with the Princess Sharla?"

Kelab raised his eyebrows. "I? I have done nothing with any princesses to my knowledge."

"Liar!" accused Ordovic fiercely. "Who else but you could have stolen her from the castle of the kings?"

"Come down, Conjurer!" called Landor. "Come down from that ship!"

Uneasily for the first time, Kelab said with a hint of peevishness, "I will not."

"Come down!" ordered Landor with a bellow, and the bluing of the air around him became stronger. Kelab puckered his brows and staggered; then he turned obediently and went into the ship. Ordovic looked at Landor with new respect, and fresh hope sprang up in him. It had seemed hopeless to walk out and face the conjurer like this, but maybe Landor had known what he was doing after all.

He was an enigma, Landor. From obscurity to Lord Great Chamberlain of the Empire at a step: guide to Sharla, yet unknown; a man who—as far as he and Sharla, and even the Empire, were concerned—walked out of nowhere on Loudor three months and a few days ago, after, as he claimed, a two-month search for Sharla.

And now he was in a position to wield the powers of the Empire, via Sharla, as Sabura Mona had done with Andalvar. There should be a battle royal between those two.

Save, of course, that it was now Kelab who held the ring. . . .

The lower door of the ship before them opened, and a flight of steps grew from the side of the nearest fin. Kelab the Conjurer came out the door and began to descend the steps, and behind him—

"Sharla!" said Landor. "This liar said he had not seen you."

He stopped suddenly, because Sharla was gazing at him from the topmost step with something that was almost contempt and yet was mixed with pity. Kelab continued to come down undisturbed.

She said, "I am not Sharla of Argus."

Ordovic's mouth fell open and he gazed in blank astonishment, but Landor rounded on Kelab and said furiously, "This is of your doing, Kelab!"

Kelab nodded quite calmly. He said, "Indeed it is."

Ordovic's sword flew from its scabbard and he made it

whistle in the air an inch from the conjurer's chin. He said, "As you value your life, restore her senses!"

Kelab made a tiny movement, and the sword blued, flared, and melted into nothing. He said, "I did already, Ordovic. This girl is *not* Sharla of Argus."

"Not . . . ? Conjurer, you lie!" Ordovic tossed aside the useless sword hilt and made as if to smash Kelab's face with his bunched fist.

"I tell the truth," Kelab insisted, with a glance at Landor. His face was strained, and around him, too, the air was beginning to glow blue. Landor was scowling anxiously, and his eyes burned with an inner light. "This girl is no princess, but a puppet, a dupe, a slave."

"Of whom?" demanded Ordovic.

Kelab's face twisted into a snarl like a tiger's, but he forced out, "Why, who else but Landor, Ordovic?"

Landor said furiously, "Conjurer, you are mad!"

Kelab relaxed, shrugged easily. He said, "Answer me this question. When did Andalvar fall ill? Five months ago without warning?"

Landor nodded, puzzled.

"Yet," said Kelab devastatingly, "it is a three-month journey from here to Loudor, longer by way of Annanworld, and when you found Sharla you claimed to have been engaged in searching for her two months already. *Three months* before Andalvar fell ill you went in search of Sharla. Why then?"

"There was a—a prophecy," began Landor, reddening, but Kelab cut him short.

"You do not believe in prophecies, Landor. You have said so often. Only last night you said so again. *Why then?*"

There was a sudden crash of thunder, and darkness came, blacker than the depths of space.

For an instant Ordovic feared he had been struck blind. He could feel nothing, hear nothing but the echoes of that tremendous thunderclap, and—

And there was nothing beneath his feet, no concrete, rain-wet, and no cold breeze on his face.

Death?

Then there was a great ripping of the blackness like frozen lightning, and solidity returned to his body. He gulped air and stared around.

No ship. No concrete landing-ground. No low buildings around the port. No city of Oppidum beyond them. But a lavender sky and a cruel red sun, and a hot blast that tore at his eyes, and bare hard rock beneath his feet. He was alone.

He cried out in terror. There was no fear in him of human weapons, of sword or spear or even the mutants! thing-that-kills-at-a-distance, but this was magic, and it was more than human.

The cry went echoing among the rocks around him, and echoed and echoed again, and seemed to grow with distance instead of fading. Twenty miles ahead he saw a mountain like a bleeding finger in the harsh red light split and fountain into the sky without sound save the echo of his cry.

The splitting of the mountain made the earth shudder like a pool of water. He saw the frontal wave of an earthquake flow across the flat bare plain toward the rocks where he hid, parting it into chasms a mile deep and folding it like waves breaking.

Then it reached him, and the ground shook with terrifying silence, and he fell, blinded and nauseated, into a vast crevasse.

Down . . . down . . . down . . . .

Then the blackness split again and there was a cool green bower among drooping trees that were not birbrak trees but enough like them to awaken a stir of longing. There was green lush grass before it and a clear still pool with a few pebbles on the bottom. He looked, entranced, into the bower, and saw Sharla.

She sat there on a bank of the cool grass, naked, and stretched out her arms toward him with a glad cry. He made to run forward, embrace her—

And a voice—*her* voice—said in his memory, "I am not Sharla of Argus."

Sharla—not Sharla—real or imaginary . . . ?

He hesitated, and she called again. Her voice?

Or the voice of Landor, whose puppet she was?

He stopped, planting his feet firmly on the ground, and looked away. She began to weep. He steeled himself not to move.

Then there was a touch on his shoulder, and he half relented, turned to face her.

But it was not Sharla. The green and shading trees had put out their branches like tentacles, to constrict. . . .

Again he screamed, and began to run. On the water's edge he tripped and fell into the pool. It parted before him, and he fell without breaking the surface.

Down . . . down . . . down. . . .

Then searing heat, blistering heat. He stood among rocks that glowed red, and before a pool of molten metal that bubbled like water, white-hot. Flames flickered and spat around him, and there was a high thin singing in the air, which stank of sulfur and had the hot, unsatisfying flatness of a furnace-room.

He looked up. There was no sky but a veil of hot, smoky vapors that whirled and scudded and sometimes tore to show, straight overhead, an unbearable white flame that was a sun. And not only straight overhead—eastward another, dimmer, and southward another, blue instead of white. Three blazing suns and rocks that were ready to flow down as lava.

The pool before him boiled furiously, bubbling and spitting. One of the red bubbles did not burst, but grew larger. He drew back, but the rock behind him was red-hot. He froze, staring with horrified eyes at the surface of the monstrous bubble. Higher it grew. Taller than himself, its base all but touching his feet. Higher—

He fell forward and it burst, leaving a hollow roundness into which he fell.

Down . . . down . . . down . . .

He crashed into the branches of a thick tree, its leaves blue-green and shiny. The heat here was wet, muggy; the air smelled of decayed vegetation and fetid swamps. There was a monstrous roaring noise in the distance.

All around was the tree, obscuring the sky except for the gap straight overhead caused by his fall—a real, physical fall, which had bruised him and torn his clothes and stunned his mind.

He shifted in the crotch where he lay, and something slender and black rustled away, hissing. A serpent!

He stared around wildly in the green-dark shade, and saw more of them, coiled on the branches or sliding without noise up or down the trunk. One of them disturbed a creature which flapped away on many leathern wings, uttering a curious harsh scream.

Then the roaring was nearer, and he saw *things* coming toward him through the jungle. They were all mouth and great sagging belly, with many shifting eyes and long whiplike tentacles.

One of them came up to the tree where he was, and a thin long tentacle wrapped around his body and tore him from his perch, held him for an instant above that horrible black maw. The stench of rotten meat from it made him vomit.

Then he was falling again, down. . . .

A bare expanse of snow and a bitter, cutting wind. He lay in the snow for a while, panting, weak in body and mind. Delicious coldness—he could lie here forever and sleep. . . .

He forced himself to stagger to his feet and wrapped his torn garment around his cold body. At once snow drove into his face and a blizzard shut down around him like a wall.

What now? Was this the end? Was his fall from world to world to finish here? Was this even real? His frantic mind beat at the numbed confines of his comprehension, seeking an answer which he could not give.

Someone was coming toward him through the snow. A big figure, larger than life. The Leontine giant?

No, he was dead. He himself had done the killing.

And yet not. . . . That was Sabura Mona's hypnotic conditioning. *She* had done the killing. And here she was. Walking out of the blizzard.

He turned and stumbled away, fell and lay still in the snow till she came and picked him up as if he had been a child, and walked with him into the whirling whiteness.

Sometimes, as he looked at her, she seemed not to be Sabura Mona, but Kelab, and she spoke with Kelab's voice, soothing him to sleep, and he drowsed, warm in her arms, as if she radiated warmth in this sub-zero world. It seemed to last a long time. . . .

The air blued for a moment, and he was suddenly fully awake again, blinking in bright yellow light. Sabura Mona set him down upon a soft couch before a leaping fire, which Kelab was tending. Then she went aside to the wall and stood motionless.

Ordovic sat up and stared at Kelab. The little conjurer was cut and bleeding. His gaudy headscarf was muddy and his brown clothes were torn. But there was a kind of strange contentment on his face.

Ordovic thought, minutes—or years—ago, *I hated this man more than I hated anyone in the galaxy. But I cannot hate him any longer because I know now who did to me what has been done, and beside the hatred I feel for that man I can have no other.*

Without looking up, the conjurer said, "I owe you an explanation."

Ordovic looked around him. He saw a square room with this couch where he lay, a stool beside the fire for Kelab, the walls bare and featureless. He said grimly, "A small debt beside what Landor owes me."

"You got it pretty badly, no?" said Kelab sympathetically. "I did what I could for you, but Landor is powerful in his way, and it wasn't a lot." He shifted a log, and the flames spat and crackled.

"Explain then," said Ordovic, rising and coming over to spread his hands at the fire. "Where are we?"

"We are no place in any physical sense, Ordovic, since this and all the other places you have been swept through are countries of the mind—those, visions from the sick mind of Landor, but this is a creation of mine."

Ordovic shook his head to clear it. He said, "I owe you my life. Or Sabura Mona. Somehow I have a strange impression that you are the same person. Who *is* Sabura Mona?"

"You already have an inkling of the truth," said Kelab. "She is not human. She lives alone, without comforts and without one slave—yet she guides an empire. *The* Empire. She is a robot, a mechanical woman."

Ordovic nodded slowly. He had known, really, since he saw her kill the Leontine giant. He looked at her again, standing with inhuman stillness against the wall, and this time he did not shudder, for she was only a machine.

He said, "But how is she here? Is she too an illusion?"

Kelab shook his head. "Things of the mind are real here, and so she is real. She is as much a thinking being as you or I. She is here in her own right. Also she is my only advantage over Landor."

"And you? You are no mere man. Are you a robot?"

Kelab shook his head.

"A mutant, then? From one of the Outland worlds?"

"I'm not Outlander."

"Then you must be an emissary from the Golden Age."

"Not what you mean by the Golden Age—the time of the greatness of the Empire—but from a better age than this nonetheless. I'm from your future."

He accepted it without disbelief. The skepticism was washed out of him. "But Sharla?" he said. "The girl who is not a princess after all?"

Kelab glanced at his watch. He said, "We have a short time before Landor can strike again. I stunned him, with a lucky blow you might say, but it was no physical weapon I used. Next time or never, I'm afraid. . . . But your explanation!

"Landor too is from the future, and it is in the creation of that future that I am engaged now, and that's why I was so anxious to secure Andra in the Regency. I'm going to have a devil of a time putting things to rights even if I do beat Landor.

"The history of my time depends on Andra marrying Barkasch and bringing Mercator into the Council of Six. The prophecies about the ruin of the Empire, which Landor sealed his doom by affecting to despise, will come to pass, and revolt and rebellion will tear it apart. There will be another Long Night, in which most of the histories and most of the knowledge will be lost. Yet out of that will evolve the first human society to approach perfection.

"Somewhere in the Long Night a mutation will occur which will give—from my point of view, *gave*—to men for the first time unbounded power *and* a standard by which to control their using of it. The power—well, I said I held the planet of Argus in my hand. I did and do. I could crush it like a soft fruit with no other tool than my mind. And all— or nearly all—the men and women of my time have that power. The standard by which they control it is telepathy. That was the key. It gave men a sense of unity, of belonging to a union rather than fighting for themselves alone.

"The result—peace between man and man. The end of your breed, Ordovic, and of all fighters, but the fine fruit of this tangled tree of humanity.

"But not quite the full fruit. The mutation had not yet bred to perfection in my time and one or two individuals lacked the sense of common ground and still craved the feeling of power over their fellow men. Such atavisms must be shunned by us, for their insanity is in part contagious, so we segregate them and watch them.

"Once, one of them vanished. I do not mean died, or went away. Our sense of unity is not dulled by distance, and death is a slow fading after tens of thousands of years to one who controls his environment as completely as do I, for instance. He—whom you know as Landor—had taken himself and his pretensions to power to a time and place where he could indulge them.

"What time? That was the question we had to answer.

"We guessed that the by then almost legendary Empire would have attracted him. We studied the few flimsy records we had for any spot at which he might try to interfere, and posted scouts to watch them, of whom I was one. I knew as soon as I was told of the coming of Sharla that something was wrong—and behold: Landor. Ambitious to wield real power over people—imperial power.

"He knew who I was, of course, as soon as I changed the marriage bond. My motive in that was not what you thought, but to prevent Barkasch from being unable to marry Andra later. That was the first move—in the nature of a challenge.

"The girl you know as Sharla is not Sharla. She is much as the real Sharla might have been, but her name is Leueen and she is of middle-class birth and no princess. Landor slipped in between her sale by Heneage at Mooncave on Loudor and her purchase by Pirbrite, took her out of time long enough to give her some resemblance to the real Sharla and construct a complete and detailed hypnotic personality for her. Then he shifted to the time of Andalvar's death, and planned to use her as a puppet, to front for his ruling of the Empire.

"But there were holes—vast lacunae—in his story, if anyone had looked for them. Did you truly believe that anyone shrewd enough to be a slaver would not have investigated the claims of a child to be Sharla Andalvarson? He could have named his own price to her father—half the galaxy! No, the real Sharla died when one of the holds of the slaver blew into space during takeoff. I've met the slaver—he didn't know even then whom he'd kidnapped. And his pretensions to statecraft! You're no skilled hand at intrigue, but you knew enough to walk warily and plug the spy-holes in your room. He? He did not even expel Andra's slaves from Sharla's quarters.

"He played badly, considering they were the highest stakes he could name."

"Or I," said Ordovic. "Imperial dominion—it could have made the Empire great again."

Kelab laughed shortly. He said, "You owe the Empire no allegiance. You're Outland born. Besides, I can name a higher."

"Name it."

"Peace between men."

Ordovic considered it soberly for a while. Then he said, "I lack the sense of unity you say you have. And all my life I've lived by violence. But I can understand, I think. Maybe it is a higher stake."

"Landor has not yet lost," said Kelab. "Ordovic, our time's shortening. Listen to this.

"Remember that what happens to you is illusion as far as you're concerned. If you fall into the trap of believing, you're lost. I cannot protect you always, for Landor has the strength of the insane and I—I say it in all humility—I am more important to the safety of the human race than you. Landor has hidden Sharla as I hid Dolichek when the Leontine giant kidnapped Sharla for me, but his is no mere illusion of warped light as mine was, but a twisting of the mind, of space, even of time. If you want to find her, remember for all you are worth that all is illusion save the spaceport at Oppidum. When we return there, the battle's over."

Ordovic said, "Kelab, once I called you a coward, afraid to fight with a man's weapons. I am ashamed. The weapons you fight with are not a man's. They are the weapons of gods."

"Hush!" said Kelab, his dark face suddenly alert. He shot out one hand, and the robot that was called Sabura Mona came to life—

And there was blackness.

IX

He was aware in a strange extrasensory way of the presence of Kelab and Sabura Mona, casting their minds here and there, searching, and of an atmosphere of struggle beyond ordinary human striving. In the midst of the darkness he clung with all his powers of mind to one bubble of brightness. It framed Kelab's face, set and serious, saying, "If you fall into the trap of believing, you are lost."

This is illusion!

The pounding of his heart was like a trip-hammer, and the rush of blood in his ears like a mighty tide. He felt neither heat nor cold, only an overpowering sense of evil, wrongness, insanity.

That wasn't illusion.

Then the darkness began to drift away, like a curtain falling in low gravity, revealing a blank landscape with a ghastly sun setting behind black mountains ahead of him. Stars shone down with the unwinking glare of empty space. There was a bare orange plain before him and around him, and he felt sand soft and dusty between his toes.

This is illusion!

But things of the mind had reality here, even as he was real, and as conscious as if he were physically present. What twisted creation of Landor's warped brain might not also be real here? Sabura Mona was real, though she was a robot.

In panic, he crouched, stared all around, hardly daring to look from one spot to another lest what he feared should slip his eye. Nothing. Upward, nothing. Blackness.

It dropped from above like a wet pall, softly, coldly slimy, and folded over him from head to foot, a constricting nothingness. He screamed, kicked, fought—

And still it clung to him, like an engulfing kiss, a wet kiss from a demon, till there was nothing but *it*.

And a bubble which showed Kelab's face, lean, cut and bruised, but oddly content, saying, "If you fall into the trap of believing, you're lost."

He had almost believed!

With a shout he stretched out his arms and tore the illusion apart. The blackness divided with a sigh and beyond he saw a familiar scene. A ship—a lean black ship, her sides shiny wet. Brown concrete underfoot, a gray sky above. The spaceport at Oppidum!

This was reality, Kelab had said. Then they had won?

Kelab, his face tired but jubilant, nodded. His headscarf was gone and his clothes ripped, but he stood by the fin of his ship and smiled. And beside him, alive and well, Sharla! He cried out in joy and strode forward to take her in his arms. The greatest prize of all. . . .

And then he heard Kelab's voice say again, "If you fall into the trap of believing—"

Landor was quick, but Ordovic was quicker. He whirled, and saw that there were no low buildings at the port edge, no city of Oppidum beyond. The concrete ended at his feet.

This is illusion!

He laughed, and at his laughter the illusion cracked and fell in a thousand shards and there was more blackness.

Even the blackness was not real blackness, for he could sense—more than see—the figure of the conjurer on his left, lean and serious, and behind him the soft cheeks and pendulous jowl of Sabura Mona. They overshadowed the galaxy, and the Nebula In Andromeda floated behind Kelab and was dwarfed by him. He himself was as a shadow beside him.

He knew the reason. This was the true Kelab, who held worlds in the hollow of his hand.

And it was as if he could hear mighty footfalls in the distance, a vastly slow and measured and inevitable tread. Kelab and Sabura Mona looked up expectantly, waiting.

At last Landor was coming face to face with his antagonists, and for the scene of the last battle he had chosen the deeps between the stars.

He came almost casually up to Sabura Mona and Kelab, looked at them, and made as if to pass them by.

Sabura Mona blocked his way.

He flickered like a blue flame, and there was no Sabura Mona, only a vague impression that was nothing more than a change in the outline of empty space. She was there still, Ordovic knew. But she was powerless.

Landor said, in a voice that was more than any mere speech could be, "Kelab, this is between us two."

Kelab nodded, his bright smoky eyes on Landor's face. He was watching, waiting . . . ?

Then Ordovic understood. The fight was on already, a battle of wills without physical reality. And as soon as he realized that, he saw the weapons they used.

He saw Landor facing a flame from which—impossibly—Kelab looked out. He saw the lightnings that flared and flamed and heard the soundless clash of mind on mind. They matched illusions—hot worlds, cold worlds, pseudo-realities scuttered like rabbits through the circle of their minds. Sometimes Ordovic recognized one of the ingredients that made up the worlds he had visited. More often they were greater, more terrifying: some there were almost too big for the mind to hold, that distended the powers of imagination to unveil things from the darkest corners of the brain, that made him want to scream aloud in pain.

Kelab engulfed them in bright clean flame and whirled them to nothing.

Then came a formless universe of horror that made him rock and stagger, and Landor was after his advantage like lightning. Kelab recovered and came back, a splendid figure dripping flame at his fingertips, hurling bolts of silent lightning, but Landor seemed like a mountain, untouched by fire. He had made Kelab falter once. He was bent on doing it again.

He did. The flames on Kelab's body died for a moment

and he staggered. Landor made one step forward and his right hand swept down like a sword, bearing horror and fear and shapeless insanity.

And Kelab poised for a moment and tumbled headlong into an endless black gulf.

Landor stood for a moment, vast and inscrutable, and then his icy composure shattered and fell apart, and he passed his hand across his forehead wearily, while Ordovic stared in sheer horror. He had not for one second believed that Landor would win. What would become of him now?

Then, as Landor turned slowly, an expression of savage triumph on his face, he felt something in his mind that chilled him with awe. He heard Kelab's voice say quietly, "This is reality, Ordovic."

And suddenly he was not only Ordovic. He was part of a great shining organism among the stars that was the human race, and he towered over the galaxies and over Landor, who froze with his face set in a mask of terror.

Then he was striding after him, and Landor was a tiny black figure running desperately, more afraid than he had ever been, a deformity, a blot on the shining beauty of the human race.

And he was lost in a bottomless gulf, turning over and over, while the walls of the past fled by him and he fell beyond space and beyond time into the formless not-being before the universe was, where he would never do harm again.

Then the horizons of the universe closed in around Ordovic, and he suddenly had weight again. There was a lean ship before him, her sides rain-wet and glistening, and brown concrete beneath his feet.

"This too is reality," said a quiet voice. He turned and saw Kelab standing where he had stood before, unmarked save for the contentment on his face. He found that he himself was also unhurt. But there was a monstrous tiredness in his mind, and a fading memory of a temporary glory that was beyond imagining.

And—his eyes lifted and met hers—Sharla, too, on the top step of the flight leading to the lock. But of Landor not one sign. He said, "So we won."

Kelab nodded. "He is gone now, and I must be about the setting to rights of the Empire. You, of course, must leave Argus, and Leueen whom you know as Sharla, and Andra must be installed as regent."

Ordovic said, "But the people had high hopes of Sharla. Will they stand for it?"

"A long time ago," said Kelab, "a poet you would not have heard of said something about making us rather bear those ills we have than fly to others that we know not of. There you have the people of Argus. Besides, there are rumors that their hopes were unfounded—Andra, whom I visited last night, and I have seen to that. For instance, yesterday you made rather a brutal threat to a slave, one Samsar. Today at dawn that slave was found, mutilated according to your threats, on the Street of the Morning. Andra's doing—not mine. And it is now common knowledge that Leueen-Sharla was a woman of easy virtue, which is itself a bar to the regency. They may regret your passing, but there are still the prophecies, so they will sigh and say it was foreordained."

"Is it not strange that a conjurer should regulate the destiny of worlds? Why a conjurer, Kelab?"

Kelab's face grew soft. He said, "To put aside my powers would be to me as cutting off your hands would be to you. As a conjurer I can use them, for show 'tis true, but you cannot hide a sun under a dish-cover. Thus I use them without exciting comment. Even so"—his smoky eyes showed somber regret—"I miss the sense of being part of the human race."

Ordovic was about to speak, recalling that brief moment of splendor when Kelab stepped into his mind, but the conjurer made a tiny gesture with one hand and he had a sensation as of something tremendous that instant forgotten. He shook his head to clear it.

Kelab continued, "I can buy you passage on a ship whose captain will ask no questions. You are an Outlander, Ordovic—and so is she."

Ordovic's eyes went up to the blond girl whom he had called Sharla.

"She is very beautiful even if she is not the regent of an empire," said Kelab. "And I think she is in love with you."

She came down the steps to Ordovic, and put her arm around his waist, smiling. They looked at each other for a long time. Then she turned to Kelab.

"Which is this ship you spoke of?" she said.

"Yonder," said Kelab the Conjurer.